Orwell in Context

Orwell in Context
Communities, Myths, Values

Ben Clarke

First published 2007 by
PALGRAVE MACMILLAN
Houndmills, Basingstoke, Hampshire RG21 6XS and
175 Fifth Avenue, New York, N.Y. 10010
Companies and representatives throughout the world

PALGRAVE MACMILLAN is the global academic imprint of the Palgrave Macmillan division of St. Martin's Press, LLC and of Palgrave Macmillan Ltd. Macmillan® is a registered trademark in the United States, United Kingdom and other countries. Palgrave is a registered trademark in the European Union and other countries.

ISBN-13: 978–0–230–51769–1 hardback
ISBN-10: 0–230–51769–2 hardback

This book is printed on paper suitable for recycling and made from fully managed and sustained forest sources. Logging, pulping and manufacturing processes are expected to conform to the environmental regulations of the country of origin.

A catalogue record for this book is available from the British Library.

Library of Congress Cataloging-in-Publication Data
Clarke, Benjamin James, 1977–
    Orwell in context:communities, myths, values / by Ben Clarke.
        p.   cm.
    Originally presented as the author's thesis (Ph.D.-Oxford).
    Includes bibliographical references and index.
    ISBN-13: 978–0–230–51769–1 (cloth)
    ISBN-10: 0–230–51769–2 (cloth)
    1. Orwell, George, 1903–1950—Criticism and interpretation.
    2. Orwell, George, 1903–1950—Political and social views.   3. Politics
    and literature—Great Britain—History—20th century.   4. Social classes
    in literature.   5. Sex role in literature.   6. Nationalism in
    literature.   7. National characteristics, English, in literature.
    8. Political fiction, English—History and criticism.   I. Title.
    PR6029.R8Z619 2007
    828'.91209—dc22   2007060027

10   9   8   7   6   5   4   3   2   1
16   15   14   13   12   11   10   09   08   07

Printed and bound in Great Britain by
Antony Rowe Ltd, Chippenham and Eastbourne

For Lyn and Carl

Contents

Acknowledgements

This book began as a doctoral thesis, which I wrote at Oxford under the supervision of John Carey and, following his retirement, David Bradshaw. I am grateful to both for their help and guidance. I am also indebted to the A.H.R.B., Exeter College, and to all those in Oxford who offered advice and support, love and friendship. My final year was a particular pleasure, and I imagine few people have found writing up so enjoyable.

James Howarth has been involved with this project since its inception almost ten years ago and has helped at every stage. Robert Eaglestone gave me invaluable advice on turning my thesis into a book and patiently worked through the various versions of my proposal, whilst the reader for Palgrave provided guidance on restructuring the text. I am grateful to Helena Feder for many things, including her help and support whilst I was rewriting the book in its final form. Paula Kennedy, Christabel Scaife and Geetha Naren have been kind and efficient in guiding me through the publication process.

Chapter 4 was first published as 'Orwell and Englishness' in the *Review of English Studies*, volume 57, number 228, pp. 83–105. I am grateful to the editors for permission to republish it here. Quotations from Orwell's *Collected Works* are used by permission of Bill Hamilton as the Literary Executor of the Estate of the Late Sonia Brownell Orwell and Secker & Warburg Ltd. Excerpts from *The Collected Essays, Journalism and Letters of George Orwell, Volumes I–IV*, copyright © 1968 by Sonia Brownell Orwell and renewed 1996 by Mark Hamilton, are reprinted by permission of Harcourt, Inc.

Note on Text

All references to Orwell letters, journalism and essays in this book are taken from Peter Davison's edition, *The Complete Works of George Orwell* (London: Secker & Warburg, 1997–8). In contrast to references to other works, these are given in brackets in the text, rather than in endnotes. The format used for the first reference to a particular entry is:

(Volume Number:Page Range:Page Reference)

A reference to the first page of the article 'Charles Dickens', for example, reprinted on pages 20 to 57 of the twelfth volume, *A Patriot After All*, would thus be given as (12:20–57:20). In future references the page range is omitted, although the volume number is repeated where it is felt this would help the reader in locating the article. For obvious reasons, no page range is given where an article occupies only a single page. References to Orwell's novels and documentary studies, published in the first nine volumes of *The Complete Works*, are given in endnotes.

Introduction

I

In his introduction to *Twentieth Century Interpretations of 1984*, Samuel Hynes argues that Orwell's texts construct 'a Myth of the Proletariat' and a 'Myth of the English People'.[1] This book explores these myths, and, in addition, what might be described as his 'Myth of Masculinity'. These areas have been selected because they are the most prominent bases of community and, indeed, value in his work. Idealised images of the working class, the English and masculinity form the basis of many of his political ideas. These three categories, however, do not have an inherent significance, or indeed coherence, but potentially cover a multitude of distinct or even competing myths. 'Masculinity', for example, encompasses a variety of very different archetypes, from the 'gentleman' to the 'worker' or 'breadwinner'. Orwell's development of 'positive' myths, therefore, is not only a simple repetition of defined formations, but also an active process involving the selection, adaptation and deployment of a multitude of popular narratives and stereotypes. The idealised portrait of working-class men in *The Road to Wigan Pier*, for example, relies upon a network of established images that associate them with solidarity, courage, responsibility and, indeed, virile heterosexuality. It also, however, excludes other, more negative associations. It reinforces the notion that working-class men are characterised by physical courage, for example, but dismisses the equally widespread ideas that they are violent or stupid.[2] His texts both interpret and produce myths, defining the communities they ostensibly describe.

The book explores this selective use of myth by locating Orwell's work within its conditions of production. These include both its historical context (the social, economic and political structures within which the texts were written) and its 'literary' context (the generic or narrative models that the texts use). As Pierre Macherey argues, a 'work never "arrives unaccompanied"; it is always determined by the existence of other works',[3] which determine its meaning and significance. The statement emphasises the importance of interpreting literary texts, not as isolated, self-contained artefacts, but as inseparable from other works which precede them or with which they are co-existent. The present study consequently figures Orwell's work and political ideas as interventions in a variety of contemporary debates rather than as the isolated product of an individual consciousness or 'genius'. It analyses his reinterpretation of myth within the context of the images and concepts which his society made available to him, whether through 'literature' or other forms of representation. The aim is to trace the distinctive, even idiosyncratic character of Orwell's writing, and the relation of his ideas to those of his contemporaries. As Kristin Bluemel argues, although he is often represented as 'a uniquely autonomous writer',[4] only a contextual reading of this kind can 'do justice to the complexities of Orwell's literature'.[5]

This interpretation of his work is divided into three main parts. The first of these focuses on class and, in particular, the working class. It explores Orwell's two major works on poverty, *Down and Out in Paris and London* and *The Road to Wigan Pier* within their historical and 'literary' context. This means it analyses not only the political debates that frame his texts, but the genre of 'social exploration' they both inhabit and challenge. The chapter traces the evolution of this genre from the mid-nineteenth century to the 1930s, and examines, for example, changes in techniques of research and representation. In particular, it focuses on the differences between Orwell's texts, the developments in his political thought they reveal, and the 'Myth of the Proletariat' he constructed. The second part of the text, concerned with his ideas of gender, explores the largely uncritical use Orwell makes of images of active, heterosexual, working-class masculinity to sustain his notions of value, and, indeed, community. The third and final section, on the nation, is divided in three. The first analyses Orwell's theories of national identity within the context of other theoretical models, concentrating on the distinction he draws between 'patriotism' and 'nationalism'. The second is concerned specifically with his representation of England, whilst the third explores his ideas of totalitarianism. This final section focuses upon the idea that totalitarianism attempts to eradicate all independent communities, and, therefore, identities, replacing them with a single, oppressive structure that distinguishes only between member and non-member, the elect and the damned.

Throughout his work, Orwell suggests that individual identity is structured by a variety of different but co-existent formations such as class, gender and nationality. In this respect, his position parallels that of Anthony Easthope, who argues that 'each of us performs a number of identities' and that these 'extend in overlapping circles into work and leisure, ethnic and sub-cultural identities as well as local and regional ones, and, above the national register, continental and potentially international identities'.[6] These identities, which may reinforce or undermine one another, enable individuation and personal validation, but they can also involve the commitment to established hierarchies or structures of power. The idea of 'Englishness', for example, provides a cultural identity founded in shared traditions, but the dominant model of 'Englishness' in the 1930s incorporated a commitment to class hierarchies and imperialism that enabled the reproduction of the established order. As George Schöpflin argues, the 'question of who is able to control the myths of collectivity is an important one'.[7] For Orwell, the attempt to reinterpret collective identities and remove their associations with the dominant order is part of a process of social reconstruction. It is therefore an integral element of his socialism. He both critiques and uses popular myths, attempting to reconstruct their meaning rather than reveal them as illusions. As outlined above, however, this process can only be studied by locating his work within its literary and historical context, and by considering it as a response to specific problems and possibilities. There can, as Raymond Williams argues, be 'very little "pure" study of Orwell',[8] study that limits itself to the discipline of 'literary criticism' or isolates itself from 'politics'. By focusing upon Orwell's representation of class, gender and nationality, this book analyses the complex relation of his work to its period, and reveals in the process both its achievements and limitations. It is founded upon the premise, as expressed by Williams, that 'the contradictions, the paradox of Orwell, must be seen as paramount', and that no 'simple explanation of them will do justice to so complex a man'.[9] These contradictions are nowhere more visible or more complex than in his representation of communities.

II

In 'Notes on the Way', published in *Time and Tide* in 1940, Orwell argues that

People sacrifice themselves for the sake of fragmentary communities – nation, race, creed, class – and only become aware that they are not individuals in the very moment when they are facing bullets. A very slight increase of consciousness, and their sense of loyalty could be transferred to humanity itself, which is not an abstraction. (12:121–7:126)

The statement illustrates a number of related concepts central to the representation of communities in his work. First, it emphasises the commitment of individuals to entities such as nations, 'races' or classes which are 'abstract' insofar as they are not founded upon personal contact. As Benedict Anderson observes, an American, for example, identifies with America despite the fact he 'will never meet, or even know the names of more than a handful of his 240,000,000-odd fellow-Americans'.[10] America is instead an example of what he describes as 'imagined communities', networks established by the identification and solidarity of their members. As David Miller argues, 'national communities are constituted by belief'.[11] The attachment to these communities, however, as Orwell illustrates, is not weakened by their 'abstraction', as people are willing to 'sacrifice themselves' on their behalf. The passage therefore undermines what Easthope describes as the 'nostalgic and sentimental desire to believe that face-to-face contact is real, free from interference by signs, language, "writing", while opposed to this the larger, more impersonal groupings constructed by modernity are imaginary, false, unreal'.[12] The 'fragmentary communities' are 'real' insofar as they determine action, and indeed in 'Our Opportunity', Orwell condemns the idea that patriotism, for example, which 'makes men willing to die in battle', is 'a sham' (12:343–50:347). The 'imagined communities' Orwell describes are not 'false' or 'unreal', but active constituents of individual existence.

Despite their importance in structuring individual consciousness, however, Orwell suggests that these forms of identification remain largely 'unconscious', characteristics of which people 'only become aware' in moments of crisis or, implicitly, in analysis such as he himself undertakes. Perhaps it is because the 'sense of loyalty' to nationality or class is internalised and determines experience that he suggests its redeployment rather than its future 'dissolution'. Indeed, the idea of such a reinterpretation permeates his work, and, as a consequence, this book. In the passage quoted above, Orwell calls for a transposition of loyalties in which the attachment to 'abstractions' such as the nation would be transferred to 'humanity itself'. In other instances, however, he emphasises the potential for a radical reinterpretation of these identities, and the possibility of their integration within 'democratic Socialism'. Throughout his work, he develops the image of a form of socialism founded, in part, upon established identities. The basis of this is the interpretation of communities, including modern 'imagined communities', as essential components of individual identity, social value and political activism. The commitment to these can of course, as he acknowledges, also be destructive, as in the case of nationalism, which he describes in 'Notes on Nationalism' as the practice of 'identifying oneself with a single nation or other unit, placing it beyond good and evil and recognizing no other duty than that of advancing its interests' (17:141–57:141). The process of identification is a necessary focus of political dispute, however, because it is also 'positive' or at least 'productive'. Collective identities not only establish solidarity and a basis for mutual support, but provide the space within which personal identities develop. 'Englishness', for example, shapes the identities of individual English men and women, though in a wide variety of ways. It is not an 'addition' to their 'real' character, but an integral part of it, even when it simply provides a model to rebel against. The redefinition of class, nationality and gender, the attempt to establish their basis and significance, is consequently integral to Orwell's work. Louis Althusser argues that 'Marxist–Leninist philosophy can only complete its abstract, rigorous, and systematic theoretical work on condition that it fights both about very "scholarly" words (concept, theory, dialectic, alienation, etc.) and about very simple words (man, masses, people, class struggle).'[13] The considerably less 'abstract' and 'systematic' attempt to establish a model of 'democratic Socialism' in Orwell's work relies on a parallel struggle about 'very simple' words such as 'working class', 'man' and 'English'. The terms of this struggle are defined by a number of basic ideas about the relation between the individual, society and 'reality'. The theoretical exploration of these ideas involves a temporary diversion from the work of Orwell himself, but it constructs a critical framework for the more detailed analyses of his writing undertaken in subsequent chapters.

The notion that collective identities shape individual consciousness and actions relies upon the broader idea that the personal is a product of the social. This is elaborated by, amongst others, Karl Marx, who argues in the *Grundrisse* that 'Man is in the most literal sense a *zoön politikon*, not only a social animal, but an animal which can individuate itself only in society.'[14] The individual, in this account, establishes his or her personal identity in their interaction with society, which is itself, of course, not autonomous or pre-existent, but the 'abstract' product of all such interaction. As Marx insists in his *Paris Notebooks*,

> *just as* society itself produces *man* as *man*, so too he *produces* it. Man's
> activity and enjoyment, in their content and their modes of existence,
> are *social* activity and *social* enjoyment.[15]

The social, in this as other instances, is not only defined in terms
of direct interaction, but also, amongst other things, the internalised
network of shared values, practices and beliefs that connect individuals
to one another. It is, therefore, not dependent upon immediate contact
between individuals, a point Marx emphasises when he writes that

> even in my *scientific* activity, and in others like that, which I can
> seldom perform in immediate community with others, I am also
> *socially* active, because I am active as a *man*. Not only is the material
> of my activity – in the case of thinker, the very language in which
> he expresses himself – given to me as a social product, but my *own*
> experience *is* social activity; and so what I make of myself, I make
> of myself for society and with consciousness of myself as a social
> being.[16]

The 'social', therefore, permeates even the apparently private realm,
which it not only frames, but indeed determines. The individual is not
isolated or autonomous, but a 'social animal' defined by his or her
position within broader social networks.

Interpellation within such networks enables individuals to interact
with one another upon the basis of their shared access to particular
codes, the most prominent of which is, of course, language itself. Indeed,
Marx insists in *The German Ideology* that language 'is as old as consciousness – language is real, practical consciousness, existing for other men
as well as for me, and language, like consciousness, first arises from
the need, from the necessity of commerce with other men'.[17] It is,
according to this account, an essential basis of socialisation, an interpretation reinforced by Jürgen Habermas, who argues that 'Linguistically
and behaviourally competent subjects are constituted as individuals by
growing into an intersubjectively shared lifeworld, and the lifeworld of
a language community is reproduced in turn through the communicative actions of its members.'[18] This 'lifeworld', however, encodes certain
values determined ultimately, for Marx, by material conditions in the
historical period in which it operates.[19] Language and, more broadly,
networks of representations and symbols, are consequently integral to
the reproduction of the dominant values within a given society. As
Schöpflin states, language, 'in the broad sense, including both symbolic

and grammatical codes, exposes a community to a particular experience, to particular ways of constructing the world'.[20] The means of representation, therefore, are pivotal to 'ideology', the formations that determine the construction of the 'real'. Indeed, Althusser insists that ideology itself is 'a system (with its own logic and vigour) of representations (images, myths, ideas or concepts, depending on the case) endowed with a historical existence and role within a given society'.[21] This position is reinforced in his definition elsewhere of ideology as 'the system of the ideas and representations which dominate the mind of man or a social group'.[22] This 'system' establishes the categories within which 'reality' is interpreted, and is therefore a determinant of experience itself. Indeed, Althusser argues that when 'we speak of ideology we should know that ideology slides into all human activity, that it is identical with the "lived" experience of human existence itself'.[23]

Ideology, in this account, reproduces and legitimises established social structures, including, of course, divisions of power founded, ultimately, upon material relations. Althusser observes that

> As Marx said, every child knows that a social formation which did not reproduce the conditions of production at the same time as it produced would not last a year. The ultimate condition of production is therefore the reproduction of the conditions of production.[24]

Ideology enables this process of reproduction, as it justifies the 'conditions of production' from which it emerges. As it is internalised, or 'unconscious', the values it encodes within the dominant modes of representation moreover appear to be 'natural'. As Rastko Močnik argues, 'Only so far as "it goes without saying" does an ideology have interpellative force.'[25] The reproduction of existing material and social relations, therefore, relies upon the narratives and representations that legitimise and indeed 'naturalise' them. Modern capitalism, for example, is founded upon an ideology which Fredric Jameson argues 'assures us that human beings make a mess of it when they try to control their destinies ("socialism is impossible") and that we are fortunate in possessing an interpersonal mechanism – the market – which can substitute for hubris and planning and replace human decisions altogether'.[26] Indeed, he insists that, for this reason, ' "The market is in human nature" is the proposition that cannot be allowed to stand unchallenged; in my opinion, it is the most crucial terrain of ideological struggle in our time.'[27] His arguments emphasise both the central role of ideologies in maintaining established social systems, and their consequent position as the site of attempts to redefine these systems.

This model of ideology, as an internalised system of representations that determines interpretation and reproduces social structures, provides a basis upon which to analyse the 'abstract' or 'imagined' communities Orwell describes. The ideas of 'nation, race, creed, class', which produce solidarity and commitment, can be interpreted as 'ideological' formations. The precise nature of the relations between these ideas and the structures of advanced capitalism are, of course, extremely complex, and as such beyond the scope of a book concerned primarily with a particular literary figure. However, the argument that these identities are interwoven with the existing structure of modern societies, and indeed enable its reproduction, is extremely relevant to Orwell's work. The dominant forms of the identities he focuses upon encode the commitment to a particular structures of power and varieties of social organisation. The most prevalent idea of 'America', or perhaps more accurately of 'being American', for example, incorporates the commitment to capitalism, limited central government and individualism encoded in the 'American way of life'. The reinterpretation of the term 'America', therefore, undermines, not only a particular system of representations, but the institutions and practices this legitimises. It is consequently a political act.

The 'struggle' to define terms such as 'English', 'working class' and 'man' is a persistent element of Orwell's work. His emphasis upon such identities is founded upon the idea that the narratives that determine such communities are, to use Althusser's phrase, 'identical with the "lived" experience of human existence itself'. The position is illustrated in his 1940 review of *The English Revolution*, edited by Christopher Hill. Orwell argues that in a particular 'cocksure paragraph' from this text,

> one can see the main weakness of Marxism, its failure to interpret human motives. Religion, morality, patriotism and so forth are invariably written off as 'superstructure,' a sort of hypocritical cover-up for the pursuit of economic interests. If that were so, one might well ask why it is that this 'superstructure' has to exist. If no man is ever motivated by anything except class interests, why does every man constantly pretend that he is motivated by something else? Apparently because human beings can only put forth their full powers when they believe that they are *not* acting for economic ends. But this in itself is enough to suggest that 'superstructural' motives should be taken seriously. (12:244–5:244)[28]

The idea that 'superstructural' motives, or those determined by ideology, 'should be taken seriously' is, in fact, integral to numerous Marxist texts.[29] Indeed, Engels himself argued that the 'various elements of the superstructure [...] exercise their influence upon the course of historical struggles and in many cases determine their *form* in particular'.[30] Nevertheless, the passage illustrates the importance of such motives to Orwell's political theories, and his perception that they form the basis of identity, activism, and indeed, to a considerable extent, value. He therefore does not suggest that such forms of identification should be abandoned, but that they should be reinterpreted within the terms of a 'democratic Socialism'. This is not, of course, an alternative to material reform, but co-existent with it, an attempt to retain the 'positive' elements of traditional identities within a future socialist society, with its more egalitarian economic system.

The actual process of reinterpretation can be analysed using the idea of 'myth' developed by Roland Barthes in 'Myth Today'. Barthes describes myth as a *'second-order semiological system'*[31] that 'transforms history into nature'.[32] It is, he argues, a form of representation through which ideology operates, and which it uses to 'naturalise' certain ideas, values and principles of interpretation. Myth effaces both the historicity and complexity of that which it represents, figuring the values of, for example, a particular nation or class, operating in a particular period, as possessing an inherent legitimacy. Barthes uses as an example an occasion when

> I am at the barber's, and a copy of *Paris-Match* is offered to me. On the cover, a young Negro in a French uniform is saluting, with his eyes uplifted, probably fixed on a fold of the tricolour. All this is the *meaning* of the picture. But, whether naively or not, I see very well what it signifies to me: that France is a great Empire, that all her sons, without any colour discrimination, faithfully serve under her flag, and that there is no better answer to the detractors of an alleged colonialism than the zeal shown by this Negro in serving his so-called oppressors.[33]

The *'secondary'* signification of the picture is, of course, its mythic 'content'. The image reinforces the French Empire, but obscures its complexity, its history, the oppression it produces, with the result that the value of French imperialism 'goes without saying'. The picture therefore illustrates the operation of myth, which Barthes insists,

> does not deny things, on the contrary, its function is to talk about them; simply, it purifies them, it makes them innocent, it gives them

a natural and eternal justification, it gives them a clarity which is not that of an explanation but of a statement of fact. If I *state the fact* of French imperiality without explaining it, I am very near to finding that it is natural and *goes without saying*: I am reassured. In passing from history to nature, myth acts economically: it abolishes the complexity of human acts, it gives them the simplicity of essences, it does away with all dialectics, with any going back beyond what is immediately visible, it organizes a world which is without contradictions because it is without depth, a world wide open and wallowing in the evident, it establishes a blissful clarity: things appear to mean something by themselves.[34]

The concept of 'myth', therefore, describes the operation, rather than the theoretical function of ideology, the process by which it attaches values to particular images. Myth enables values to be inculcated in those who uncritically consume these representations, and indeed Barthes argues that it 'has in fact a double function: it points out and it notifies, it makes us understand something and it imposes it on us'.[35]

The example of the picture of a 'young Negro in a French uniform' in *Paris-Match* illustrates a method of tracing a dominant ideology, in this instance French imperialism, through its 'minor' manifestation in a popular magazine. It emphasises, therefore, the diffusion of such discourses, their permeation of all aspects and levels of society. The ideology of the French bourgeoisie, for instance, to use Barthes' example, is located and reproduced, not only in what he terms its 'inventive core', but in a broader national culture founded upon the notion that the values of this section of society are 'universal', or, indeed, 'human'. For Barthes, the

whole of France is steeped in this anonymous ideology: our press, our films, our theatre, our pulp literature, our rituals, our Justice, our diplomacy, our conversations, our remarks about the weather, a murder trial, a touching wedding, the cooking we dream of, the garments we wear, everything, in everyday life, is dependent on the representation which the bourgeoisie *has and makes us have* of the relations between men and the world.[36]

The insistence that seemingly neutral, or indeed 'trivial' elements of popular culture encode certain values, in particular those of the dominant intellectual class, has an obvious relevance to Orwell's work, much of which attempts to expose such values. In 'Boys'

Weeklies', for example, he insists that all 'fiction from the novels in the mushroom libraries downwards is censored in the interests of the ruling class', and focuses upon the extent to which 'boys' fiction [...] is sodden in the worst illusions of 1910' (12:57–79:76). In 'Raffles and Miss Blandish', he similarly illustrates the function of such 'secondary' signification in popular fiction, arguing that James Hadley Chase's *No Orchids for Miss Blandish* is a 'daydream appropriate to the totalitarian age', which has 'the same relation to Fascism as, say, Trollope's novels have to nineteenth-century capitalism' (16:345–58:355). These examples, however, are part of a broader pattern, in which dominant discourses are traced through their manifestations in culture, rather than located solely in their most prominent institutions. The idea of 'Englishness', for example, is explored, not only in terms of the Houses of Parliament or government foreign policy, but using images of what he describes in *The Lion and the Unicorn* as a 'truly native' culture, which 'centres round things which even when they are communal are not official – the pub, the football match, the back garden, the fireside and the "nice cup of tea"' (12:391–434:394).

This detailed analysis of specific aspects of culture enables Orwell to trace the 'anonymous ideology' that operates in, for example, boys' stories, popular novels or picture postcards. The concept of myth, however, can also be used to explore his writing on communities, which rely on precisely such processes of representation to establish their values, interpretations and coherence. It can, moreover, be used to detail and assess his attempts to use myths in his model of socialism. For Barthes, revolutionary practice is in fact characterised by the 'absence of myth'.[37] He recognises, however, that this absence is problematic insofar as it results in an inevitable loss of value. As he argues, 'when a myth reaches the entire community, it is from the latter than the mythologist must become estranged if he wants to liberate the myth', and so to 'decipher the Tour de France or the "good French Wine" is to cut oneself off from those who are entertained or warmed up by them'.[38] It is, in other words, to dissolve the positive values that the 'myth' of 'good French wine', for example, produces. The model of revolution Orwell constructs is, in contrast, defined by an attempt to retain elements of such value, to reassess the dominant myths, and indeed as a consequence, ideologies, that shape ' "lived" experience'. It is, therefore, a socialism that explicitly operates within ideology, that uses the categories and practices established in prior or existing societies. Indeed, Bernard Crick argues, Orwell 'held (rightly or wrongly) that a good and decent way of life already existed in tradition'.[39] This past, however, is mythic, a selective interpretation of history and culture that is inevitably always more ambiguous and contradictory than the image of a coherent 'tradition' allows. This book explores how Orwell drew upon a variety of histories, cultures and traditions to construct myths of a 'good and decent life' that could provide the foundation for a socialist future.

1
Class

The Road to Wigan Pier both continues and transforms a literary genre. There is a long history of reports on the 'condition of England', dating back at least to Defoe's *A Tour Through the Whole Island of Great Britain*, which describe personal journeys through the diverse, sometimes conflicting, communities that make up the nation. These texts, which explore both economic conditions and social difference, inform mid-nineteenth-century accounts of urban deprivation such as Henry Mayhew's *London Labour and the London Poor* and Friedrich Engels' *The Condition of the Working Class in England*. All the narratives incorporate personal observations that both supplement and modify research. Indeed, Engels insisted, in a preface addressed 'To the Working Class of Great Britain', that

> I have studied the various official and non-official documents as far as I was able to get hold of them – I have not been satisfied with this, I wanted more than a mere *abstract* knowledge of my subject, I wanted to see you in your own homes, to observe you in your every-day life, to chat with you on your condition and grievances, to witness your struggles against the social and political power of your oppressors. I have done so: I forsook the company and the dinner-parties, the port-wine and champagne of the middle classes, and devoted my leisure-hours almost exclusively to the intercourse with plain working men; I am both glad and proud to have done so.[1]

The passage represents both narrative and narrator as witnesses to poverty, a position that enables them to trace forms of suffering absent from statistical reports. In the second half of the nineteenth century, the genre was extended further still by the publication of texts such as James Greenwood's 'A Night in the Workhouse', which focused not merely upon the observation of poverty but the experience of it, however temporary. These various methods of research together defined the modern form of what Peter Keating describes as 'social exploration', a 'distinctive branch of modern literature in which a representative of one class consciously sets out to explore, analyse and report upon, the life of another class lower on the social scale than his own'.[2] The genre developed rapidly and, as Crowther argues, by 'the time Jack London arrived in England to gather material for *People of the Abyss* (1903), his actions were part of a well-established formula'.[3] Although, as Valentine Cunningham observes, '*The Road to Wigan Pier* is sometimes wrongly taken as a wonderfully unique achievement',[4] it redefines rather than invents a tradition. In so doing, it questions the techniques and ideas Orwell used in his first work of social exploration, *Down and Out in Paris and London*.

Generic conventions provide one context within which to interpret *The Road to Wigan Pier*. However, the text also intervenes in an intellectual culture shaped by particular economic and political conditions. In this sense too it is not 'unique'. The increased interest in social exploration during this period forms part of a broader concern with what Marx and Engels described as the 'class that holds the future in its hands'.[5] As George Woodcock argued, 'Books of reportage were in vogue during the 1930s; they fitted in with the prevalent atmosphere of Mass Observation and fashionable bolshevism.'[6] Accounts of poverty and descriptions of working-class life were conspicuous amongst this 'reportage'. Some, of course, were produced by working-class writers, but many were by middle-class radicals, writers, intellectuals and activists keen to gain first-hand knowledge of what Cecil Day Lewis described as the 'temper of the people'.[7] Indeed, in James Hanley's *Grey Children*, an account of conditions in the South Wales coalfields, John Jones insisted that 'all the people down here, have grown very, very sensitive about the enormous number of people who come down here from London and Oxford and Cambridge, making inquiries, inspecting places, descending underground, questioning women about their cooking, asking men strings of questions about this, that and the other'.[8] Many used their observations to support their political ideas, though they also frequently tried simply to explain poverty and unemployment to an audience, socialist or otherwise, who, as Ralph Glasser observed, did not know 'what it was like to starve or go wet-shod in the rain'.[9] *The Road to Wigan Pier* therefore both reinterpreted an established genre and contributed to the political and cultural debates of the 1930s. It used a variety of contemporary forms, images and ideas to produce a distinctive myth of the working class that provided a foundation for Orwell's evolving socialism.

These interwoven textual and historical narratives are the 'conditions' of *The Road to Wigan Pier*, to use Macherey's term, the 'real diversity of elements' from which it is 'composed'.[10] By analysing them and the text's construction, this chapter does not deny that Orwell's book is 'original', but merely recognises that 'novelty and originality, in literature as in other fields, are always defined by relationships'.[11] It first outlines the development of social exploration from the late nineteenth century to the 1930s. As part of this, it traces the shifting values that underpinned such a development. It examines, for example, the transition from the interpretation of the impoverished as 'savages' or a 'mob', albeit one many writers argued could be 'civilised', to the notion of distinct, positive working-class values and communities. This provides a basis for the detailed analysis of Orwell's own work. His first book of social exploration, *Down and Out in Paris and London*, is a picaresque account of the narrator's personal experience of poverty in the tradition of texts like 'A Night in the Workhouse' and *The People of the Abyss*. It promotes particular reforms rather than broad social change, and focuses on individual, often idiosyncratic characters, rather than on communities or classes. There are numerous continuities between *Down and Out in Paris and London* and *The Road to Wigan Pier*. The many differences, however, demonstrate how Orwell reinterpreted the concepts, imagery and ideas he had used in his first book. The later text combines personal observation with an attempt at a more systematic analysis of poverty, and focuses upon the working class, conceived as a distinct strata of society, rather than isolated individuals. It also explores the conventions of the genre itself, exposing and analysing the position of the middle-class observer. A variety of factors inform these changes in technique and perspective, including economic conditions in the period and the influence of theories such as Marxism. This emphasis upon context further undermines the notion that Orwell's works of social exploration are a 'wonderfully unique achievement'. It demonstrates, however, the distinctive contribution he made to the genre he inherited, and the importance of these works of reportage to the evolution of his political thought.

Literature of social exploration is, by definition, founded upon the ignorance of the prosperous concerning their impoverished fellow citizens. It traces the experiences of a narrator to whom poverty is initially alien, and who explains the causes, forms and implications of deprivation to a reader who is presumed to be equally ill-informed. The texts therefore examine, amongst other things, the distinction between the dominant images of poverty and its 'reality'. The explorer attempts to establish, as Charles Booth wrote, whether the dominant images and myths of the poor are accurate, or whether 'they bear to the facts a relation similar to that which the pictures outside a booth at some country fair bear to the performance or show within'.[12] This involves considering not only the economic position of the impoverished, but also their behaviour, communities and values. Culture as well as money divides the investigator from those he or she observes. Virginia Woolf emphasises this dual foundation of class barriers when she argues that because

> the baker calls and we pay our bills with cheques, and our clothes are washed for us and we do not know the liver from the lights we are condemned to remain forever shut up in the confines of the middle classes, wearing tail coats and silk stockings, and called Sir and Madam as the case may be, when we are all, in truth, simply Johns and Susans.[13]

She describes a division that is established by both economic inequalities and consequent distinctions in, for example, education, accent, language usage, mannerisms and codes of behaviour. The 'tail coats and silk stockings' indicate greater prosperity, but also different assumptions and values. Because, as Woolf argued 'all imagination is largely the child of the flesh',[14] material differences produce divisions not only of experience, but of perception and values. As a result, she insisted, the boundaries between classes were 'impassable'[15] whilst these conditions persisted.

Orwell also emphasises the cultural differences between classes in *The Road to Wigan Pier*. He argues that

> All my notions – notions of good and evil, of pleasant and unpleasant, of funny and serious, of ugly and beautiful – are essentially *middle-class* notions; my taste in books and food and clothes, my sense of honour, my table manners, my turns of speech, my accent, even the characteristic movements of my body, are the products of a special kind of upbringing and a special niche about half-way up the social hierarchy.[16]

Indeed, these distinctions sustain the boundaries between individuals even in the absence of economic differences. Orwell argued that the divisions between the working class and 'the private schoolmaster, the half-starved free-lance journalist, the colonel's spinster daughter with £75 a year, the jobless Cambridge graduate, the ship's officer without a ship, the clerk, the commercial travellers and the thrice-bankrupt grocers in country-towns'[17] are not financial but the product of social distinctions, such as that between 'those who pronounce their aitches and those who don't'.[18] The emphasis upon these codes illustrates the fact that identities are realised in social as well as material differences, though the two categories are, of course, densely interwoven. Social exploration consequently involves not only an encounter with deprivation, but with a different culture. This idea of culture becomes increasingly important as the genre evolves, and is informed by developments in fields such as anthropology and sociology. Orwell's own understanding of the implications of class difference increased with his broader political consciousness. Whilst *The Road to Wigan Pier* constructs a complex if idiosyncratic model of class structure, *Down and Out in Paris and London* relies upon the image of impoverished areas as a foreign country.

The image of social exploration as an encounter with a foreign country was established by the pioneering writers of the nineteenth century, who represented their studies of domestic poverty as analogous to those of anthropologists or travellers in 'exotic' societies. James Greenwood, for example, described the inhabitants of a London workhouse as drinking the water provided for them 'just as the brutes do in those books of African travel',[19] and George Sims promised 'to record the result of a journey into a region which lies at our own doors – into a dark continent that is within easy walking distance of the General Post Office'.[20] William Booth similarly insisted that the explorer might 'discover within a stone's throw of our cathedrals and palaces similar horrors to those which Stanley has found existing in the great Equatorial forest'.[21] Numerous novels concerned with the working classes also used this method of comparison. As Keating writes,

> The image of the working-class novelist as an explorer is common in both the industrial and urban traditions. Drawing upon the reader's familiarity with the literature of foreign travel popular throughout the period, the novelist presents himself, or one of his central characters, as someone who undertakes a dangerous voyage of discovery into an uncharted working-class world, from which he eventually returns with a fully documented report of his adventures.[22]

The model of travel writing emphasises the direct individual experience of poverty and reaction to it. Indeed, this distinguishes a work of social exploration from, for example, a statistical analysis of poverty, such as a government report. Such texts represent their more limited, personal perspective as a guarantee of their authenticity and value. As the explorer is by definition an 'outsider' in the communities he or she visits, the structure also exposes social divisions. Figuring impoverished areas as alien territories emphasises the level of 'ignorance about working class life', and is used 'ironically to rebuke the reader for his lack of knowledge or concern – while he may not be able to visit Tahiti or India, there is no good reason why he should not know what conditions are like in Manchester or Drury Lane'.[23] Many writers and commentators on poverty used similar images. Engels, for example, quotes Mr G. Alston, a preacher at St Philip's in Bethnal Green, who stated that 'I believe that before the Bishop of London called attention to this most poverty-stricken parish, people at the West End knew as little of it as of the savages of Australia or the South Sea Isles.'[24] Indeed, even sensationalist writers employed the technique. In *From the Abyss*, first published anonymously, C. F. G. Masterman wrote that novelists 'jaded with battues [*sic*] of blacks in unknown lands, select as heroes the denizens of lands still more unknown at their very doors; relate of their travels into our dangerous and desolate regions, of the life and manners and habits of aborigines'.[25] The image of travel was one method of making visible the inequalities suppressed by the idea of the homogeneous nation. Orwell's statement, at the end of *Down and Out in Paris and London*, that 'I can only hope that it has been interesting in the same way that a travel diary is interesting'[26] illustrates his debt to this tradition.

This does not, of course, mean that the image of exploration has the same significance for Orwell as it did for his predecessors. Indeed, he both uses and challenges the images and ideas he inherited. The prevalent nineteenth-century use of the image of the 'dark continent' relies upon the idea that civilisation is hierarchical and the poor are equivalent to the 'savages' whom Dickens hoped would 'be civilised off the face of the earth'.[27] Indeed, Joseph McLaughlin argues that 'analogies between savages and the urban poor are seemingly ubiquitous in nineteenth-century writing about the poor'.[28] These images illustrate the widespread middle-class fear of the 'barbarians already within the gates',[29] but were also used to support the demand that 'higher' forms of civilisation be extended to the destitute. This parallels the ostensible project of imperialism, and indeed numerous texts demanded the diversion of resources from efforts to 'improve' colonial subjects to the domestic poor. Sims, for example, complained that 'We organize great military expeditions, we pour out blood and money *ad libitum* in order to raise the social condition of black men and brown; the woes of an Egyptian, or a Bulgarian, or a Zulu send a thrill of indignation through honest John Bull's veins; and yet at his very door there is a race so oppressed, so hampered, and so utterly neglected, that its condition has become a national scandal.'[30] Henry Mayhew similarly argued 'that we should willingly share what we enjoy with our brethren at the Antipodes, and yet leave those who are nearer and who, therefore, should be dearer to us, to want even the commonest moral necessaries is a paradox that gives to the zeal of our Christianity a strong savour of the chicanery of Cant'.[31] These passages use the image of imperialism as a process of enforced 'civilisation' to emphasise deprivation within Britain. They consequently suggest that the central problem is one of social integration rather than of social structure. Reform, in other words, should extend the values of the prosperous classes to the nation as a whole. Those values themselves are not, in the main, in doubt.

In these texts, the desire to 'civilise' the poor is, however, inseparable from the fear of the 'masses'. The 'mass', as John Carey argued, is a 'metaphor for the unknowable and invisible', as it does not indicate a specific set of people but 'the crowd in its metaphysical aspect'. It consequently 'turns other people into a conglomerate' and 'denies them the individuality which we ascribe to ourselves and to people we know',[32] obscuring the 'intricacy and fecundity of each human life'.[33] The term suggests a uniform section of the population defined primarily in terms of its size. This image is central to *From the Abyss*, for example, in which Masterman describes the 'dense black masses' who 'have been turned up in incredible numbers through tubes sunk in the bowels of the earth, emerging like rats from a drain, blinking in the sunshine'.[34] The 'first thing to note' of these 'masses', he insists, is 'not our virtues or vices, beauty, apathy or knowledge, but our overwhelming inconceivable number',[35] which is such that 'it seems incredible that each individual should count for anything at all in the sight of man or God'.[36] The image figures individuals only as parts of a homogeneous whole, denying their difference and, indeed, significance.

Masterman argues that, despite its size, however, the 'mass' is not creative or capable of improving its own condition. It has, for example, 'no leaders, no interpreters, no recognised channels of expression'.[37] It cannot even articulate its experience, with the result that 'no voice will pass from the million-peopled ghetto of London',[38] and no 'future historical novelist will be able to reconstitute from contemporary documents the inner life of Pentonville and Camberwell'.[39] His very capacity to describe conditions in the 'Abyss' consequently divides Masterman from the inarticulate 'black masses', undermining the claim, in its sub-title, that *From the Abyss* was produced 'by One of them'. José Ortega y Gasset reinforces this idea that the 'masses' as passive and anonymous. He argues that in 'a right ordering of public affairs, the mass is that part which does not act of itself',[40] but has instead 'come into the world in order to be directed, influenced, represented, organised'.[41] This absence of individuality is the defining quality of the mass and

> In the presence of one individual we can decide whether he is 'mass' or not. The mass is all that which sets no value on itself – good or ill – based on specific grounds, but which feels itself 'just like everybody else,' and nevertheless is not concerned about it; is, in fact, quite happy to feel itself as one with everybody else.[42]

This interpretation posits a division between the 'noble life', which is 'ever set on excelling itself', and the 'common or inert life, which reclines statically upon itself'.[43] Hannah Arendt also claims that the 'term masses applies only where we deal with people who either because of sheer numbers, or indifference, or a combination of both, cannot be integrated into any organization based on common interest, into political parties or municipal governments or professional organizations or trade unions'.[44] The focus here is upon the absence of political commitment, but the statement reinforces the image of the 'mass' as inert and inarticulate.

These ideas of the 'mass' parallel those held by the dominant class in both *Nineteen Eighty-Four* and *Animal Farm*. O'Brien, for example, insists the 'proles' 'will never revolt, not in a thousand years or a million',[45] and describes them as 'helpless, like the animals'.[46] Syme similarly claims they 'are not human beings'.[47] The Party itself, Winston observes, 'taught that the proles were natural inferiors who must be kept in subjection, like animals'.[48] This figures them as a passive 'mass' that can be 'lashed into [...] periodic frenzies of patriotism',[49] but which does 'not act of itself'. The image of an inert populace manipulated by an elite evokes *Animal Farm*, in which Pilkington insists upon the common interests of 'pigs and humans', and compares the 'lower animals' with the 'lower classes'.[50] The 'lower animals' are undifferentiated save in their economic functions. Indeed, a proportion of these animals, in particular the sheep, even behave as a 'mass'. Their views are redefined to suit the needs of the elite, and their insistent repetition of official slogans stifles protest, putting 'an end to any chance of discussion',[51] for example, when Napoleon abolishes the weekly meetings. Both texts, however, associate the idea of the 'mass' with oppressive states that produce and exploit inertia. The division between the 'masses' and their leaders does not represent 'a right ordering of public affairs', but injustice and oppression.

The images of the 'mass' Orwell satirises in these texts originate in the fear of a shift in power from traditional elites to popular parties or communities produced by developments such as the extension of the franchise, industrialisation and mass communication. The term also, however, encodes the connected fear that cultural value is eroded by popular participation. As David Bradshaw argues, at the turn of the century, factors such as the 'intelligentsia's aversion to the spread of mass literacy and the looming threat of American materialism' led to a 'resurgence of interest in cultural elitism'.[52] This is illustrated in the work of George Gissing. As Keating observed, Gissing maintained a 'persistent belief in the natural superiority of one code of behaviour above another', which meant, for example, that a 'man who possessed a highly developed aesthetic sensibility, immaculate table manners and a standard English accent, was inevitably "better" than other men'.[53] In his novels, the successful manipulation of privileged social codes by a character is an important signifier of their value. However, he insists that the masses undermined this value, as they did not maintain such manners or standards. The narrator of the *Nether World*, for example, claims that at the popular Bank Holiday celebrations 'nowhere could be found any amusement appealing to the mere mind, or calculated to effeminate by encouraging a love of beauty'.[54] Gissing figures the individuals who make up such crowds as incapable of mastering 'high' culture or 'correct' etiquette. In *New Grub Street*, he states that a 'London work-girl is rarely capable of raising herself, or being raised, to a place in life above that to which she was born; she cannot learn how to stand and sit and move like a woman bred to refinement, any more than she can fashion her tongue to graceful speech'.[55] Indeed, even when a worker has adopted 'graceful speech', the achievement is precarious. In *Demos*, for example, the accent of Richard Mutimer 'deteriorated' during arguments with his wife Adela, when 'he spoke like any London mechanic, with defect and excess of aspirates, with neglect of g's at the end of words, and so on'.[56] His failure to maintain standard pronunciation demonstrates his inability to master 'civilised' manners. As Williams wrote, Gissing's work illustrates

the desire of the outcast from another class, who in material circum-
stances is not to be distinguished from the amorphous ignoble poor,
to emphasize all the differences that are possible, and to insist that
they are real and important – the attitude to working-class speech (a
thing in itself not at all uniform) is characteristic of this.[57]

For Gissing, cultural codes are important, even pre-eminent, signifiers
of value.

The threat posed by the 'masses' to established 'civilisation' is, of
course, always also material. In Gissing's *The Unclassed*, Maud Enderby
writes, in a letter to Osmond Waymark, that 'you marvel that these
wretched people you visited do not, in a wild burst of insurrection, over-
throw all social order, and seize for themselves a fair share of the world's
goods'.[58] The statement emphasises the exclusion of those in the slums
Waymark visits as a rent-collector from the overall national prosperity.
Jack London also emphasised this co-existence of wealth and poverty
in Britain when he described, for example, how in London, '*the heart of
the greatest, and most powerful empire the world has ever seen*', two tramps
ate '*stray crumbs of bread the size of peas, apple cores so black and dirty
one would not take them to be apple cores*'.[59] Even those in employment
were often impoverished, and indeed in *The Nether World* the narrator
argued that many worked 'without prospect or hope of reward save the
permission to eat and sleep and bring into the world other creatures
to strive with them for bread'.[60] In order to 'humanise the multitude',
an 'entire change of economic conditions'[61] was therefore necessary.
As David Grylls argues, Gissing 'despised the mob as a physical entity
for its violence, its coarseness, its hysterical emotion',[62] but his work
nevertheless describes conditions in which 'venial fault putrefies into
crime'.[63] It also exposes the extent to which 'culture' and prosperity
are interwoven. For Waymark, 'cash' is the 'fruitful soil' upon which
'luxuriate art, letters, science' and without which 'they drop like with-
ering leaves'.[64] Those deprived of 'art, letters, science', however, Gissing
implies, threaten the 'civilisation' that excludes them.

It is these images of the 'mass' to which Orwell refers when he
describes, in *Down and Out in Paris and London*, the 'fear of the mob',[65]
founded on the middle-class belief that the poor are 'a horde of submen,
wanting only a day's liberty to loot his house, burn his books, and set
him to work minding a machine or sweeping out a lavatory'.[66] The text
attempts to counteract such stereotypes, and insists that there is, in fact,
'no difference between the mass of rich and poor' and 'no question of
setting the mob loose'.[67] It directly opposes the myth of an anonymous

'mass' that needs to be civilised so it will not destroy the established order. Instead, Orwell focused upon the individual and specific, undermine the tendency to treat the urban poor as a 'conglomerate'. The text nevertheless retains a number of features of the 'well-established' tradition he inherited. In the first place, it represents itself as a 'travel diary', analogous to accounts of 'exotic' exploration. The inclusion of a list of London slang and swear words, for example, along with glosses and speculation about their possible derivations, figures the text as the record of an 'alien' culture. In addition, it continues the tradition of the narrator who temporarily 'becomes' one of the impoverished, established by writers like James Greenwood, Jack London and Mrs Cecil Chesterton. The object of reform also remains central, and the insistence on the need for specific measures, such as 'adequate bedclothes and better mattresses'[68] in cheap lodging-houses, implies that the present social and economic structure requires improvement rather than fundamental change. The text, in other words, operates within an established tradition, despite challenging the images of the 'mob' or 'masses' that pervade the work of earlier writers such as Gissing or Masterman, and contemporaries such as Gasset. Detailed analysis of *Down and Out in Paris and London* reveals its constant interaction with inherited conventions, which it both questions and reproduces.

II

In 'A Night in a Workhouse', James Greenwood pioneered the use of what McLaughlin describes as 'epistemological privilege of the participant-observer'[69] to research and represent the urban poor. As its title suggests, his narrative relies upon his direct though temporary experience of poverty. The technique derives from anthropology and the belief that, as R. R. Marett later wrote, 'the student of wild-folk' must have 'become as one of themselves' to be 'qualified to act as their spokesman, putting into words as we can understand the felt needs and aspirations of a less self-conscious type of humanity'.[70] The investigator who immerses him or herself in the society of 'wild-folk', whether the 'head-hunting aboriginal tribes in the mountains of Formosa'[71] or the London working class, is in the privileged position of being able to both speak for a 'primitive' people and exercise an analytical detachment. Later social explorers extended this method. As McLaughlin observes, Jack London, for example, employed a variety of 'ethnographic methods' in *The People of the Abyss*, including 'an account of his trip to the field site, participant-observation, the use of a "safe house," and photography – to get firsthand, face-to-face knowledge about the inhabitants of an urban locale in the heart of empire'.[72] These texts, and particularly the latter, provided a model for *Down and Out in Paris and London*. Like them, the book insists it is not a detached analysis of poverty, but a record of Orwell's personal observations and experience. However, in contrast to most earlier explorers, he insists his poverty was involuntary, and his participation therefore more 'genuine'. This idea of authenticity has shaped, or even dominated, critical responses to the text.[73] Orwell writes that he found himself destitute in Paris after an Italian stole money from his room, leaving him 'just forty seven francs – that is, seven and tenpence',[74] which had been in his pockets. In London, his poverty resulted from a delay in starting a job looking after a 'congenital imbecile',[75] for which he had returned from France. This left him 'a month to wait' and 'exactly nineteen and sixpence in hand'.[76] The text represents his enforced hardship as a guarantee of its own value. Many critics have accepted this reading. An unsigned review in *Nation*, for example, stated that 'No writer submitting himself for the nonce to a horrible existence, for the sake of material, could possibly convey so powerful a sense of destitution and hopelessness as has Mr Orwell, on whom these sensations were, apparently, forced.'[77] W. H. Davies supported this view, and wrote that Orwell's account was 'all true to life, from beginning to end'.[78] Even more recent criticism retains this emphasis on his personal experience of poverty. In the introduction to the 1989 Penguin edition, for example, Dervla Murphy argues that

> Most writers who share for a time in the lives of the poor are not genuinely down and out, though they may choose to appear so to their new neighbours. What gives the Paris chapters of *Down and Out* such pungent immediacy is the fact that Orwell was not then 'playing a game'.[79]

Dan Jacobson also distinguishes Orwell from the 'slummer', whom he describes as 'one who makes day-trips into the lower depths, and then hastens back, positively refreshed by what he has seen, into the security and comfort of the middle classes',[80] whilst Malcolm Bradbury insists that Orwell 'had known poverty and pain'.[81] These interpretations distinguish the text from the work of other social explorers who simply 'appear' to be poor.

There are several problems with this reading. *Down and Out in Paris and London* is not, of course, a simple transcription of Orwell's experience but instead a literary representation of it. It is neither 'innocent' nor unmediated. Indeed, it illustrates Janet Montefiore's argument that the 'brilliant rhetoric of authenticity' used by thirties works of 'Eyewitness history' is often, if not invariably, 'the product of deliberate and skilful construction'.[82] Even the identification of the narrator with Orwell himself is problematic as it obscures the text's rhetorical strategies. As George Woodcock argued, the

> 'I' in *Down and Out in Paris and London* and *The Road to Wigan Pier* is no more and no less George Orwell than the Marcel of *A la recherche du temps perdu* is Marcel Proust, and the autobiographical form of his works can be deceptive, if it is taken too literally, for Orwell rarely tells of his own experiences except to make a point illustrating some general argument, usually of a political or social nature.[83]

Orwell himself emphasises the artifice of his work in his preface to the French edition, in which he writes that

> As for the truth of my story, I think I can say that I have exaggerated nothing except in so far as all writers exaggerate by selecting. I did not feel I had to describe events in the exact order in which they happened, but everything I have described did take place at one time or another. At the same time I have refrained, as far as possible, from drawing individual portraits of particular people. All the characters I have described in both parts of the book are intended more as representative types of the Parisian or Londoner of the class to which they belong than as individuals. (10:353–4:353–4)

His later observation that 'nearly all the incidents described there actually happened, though they have been rearranged'[84] reinforces this point. In both instances, he emphasises a process of literary production. He maintains that the text is 'truthful', that the events described 'actually happened' and are faithfully represented. However, he also describes, for example, the transformation of individuals into 'representative types'. His account of the process of selection and construction undermines those who take his autobiographical writing 'too literally'.

The text is also, of course, indebted to generic conventions. Like earlier works of social exploration, it traces the experience of a 'participant-observer' and describes poverty to an audience to whom it is unfamiliar. The statement 'You have thought so much about poverty – it is the thing you have feared all your life, the thing you knew would happen to you sooner or later',[85] for example, implies that the reader has not experienced deprivation. The phrase 'we have been taught that tramps are blackguards',[86] suggests that the reader and narrator even share a background that encourages a hostility towards the destitute. As John Newsinger argues, 'Orwell, the middle-class writer, shows his readers the painfully debilitating effect that hunger has on a middle-class person, not on the poor, but on someone like themselves.'[87] His meticulous descriptions of the 'peculiar *lowness* of poverty'[88] and of 'what it is like to be hungry'[89] also illustrate this process. The text therefore uses forms established by writers such as James Greenwood. Despite its emphasis on involuntary poverty, it describes a middle-class observer who temporarily lives amongst the poor and describes the experience to their more prosperous fellow citizens. It also continues to employ the framework of the travelogue, and indeed the model of imperial travel. For Newsinger, there is 'inevitably a "colonial" dimension to the exercise: Orwell was exploring darkest England (and Paris), and then returning to civilisation with exotic tales to tell about the lives of the poor'.[90] Woodcock also insists that 'Orwell continued to view society according to the imperialist model he had observed in Burma' and therefore interpreted Britain as 'a world of master race and subject race',[91] and even Orwell himself later observed that in this period he had thought of the 'English working class' as the 'symbolic victims of injustice, playing the same part in England as the Burmese played in Burma'.[92] Indeed, he compares the position of the Parisian *plongeur* to that of exploited workers in the colonies, though he argues that even an impoverished European is 'a king compared with a rickshaw puller or a gharry pony'.[93] In *The Road to Wigan Pier*, he recognised differences as well as parallels in exploitation in London and Burma. However, his initial use of a colonial model to represent divisions between rich and poor demonstrates the persistence of nineteenth-century conventions, as well as his own background in the imperial police.

Orwell nonetheless rejects the idea that there is any essential or even cultural division between the prosperous and impoverished. He challenges the images and ideas of the 'masses' that dominated much nineteenth-century social exploration, arguing that

> Fear of the mob is a superstitious fear. It is based on the idea that there is some mysterious, fundamental difference between rich and poor, as though they were two different races, like negroes and white men. But in reality there is no such difference. The mass of rich and poor are differentiated by their incomes and nothing else, and the average millionaire is only the average dishwasher dressed in a new suit.[94]

In his later work, he contradicts this statement and insists that class boundaries are difficult to cross. Here, however, Orwell suggests the dividing lines between social groups are fluid, or at least permeable, and that the status of an individual is a straightforward reflection of their material position. He illustrates this idea using the example of clothing, a visible signifier of wealth. In *Down and Out in Paris and London*, the narrator exchanges his 'second-best suit'[95] for a shilling and a set of old clothes with a 'patina of antique filth'.[96] These

> put me instantly into a new world. Everyone's demeanour seemed to have changed abruptly. I helped a hawker pick up a barrow that he had upset. 'Thanks, mate,' he said with a grin. No one had called me mate before in my life – it was the clothes had done it.[97]

This recalls Jack London's insistence that, following a similar exchange of clothes,

> in the twinkling of an eye, so to say, I had become one of them. My frayed and out-at-elbows jacket was the badge and advertisement of my class, which was their class.[98]

As Crick observes, the 'borrowing is obvious'.[99] The implication in both instances is that there is no essential difference between the prosperous and destitute, but only a series of signifiers and practices that can be altered. A 'new suit' can transform a dishwasher, just as one ingrained with 'antique filth' can, temporarily, transform an old Etonian.

This transformation enacted by a change of clothes is, of course, only effective if nothing else reveals the deception. Orwell insists that whilst he anticipated he would experience problems when tramping, few actually materialised. For example, he claims that although in London he initially 'dared not speak to anyone, imagining that they must notice a disparity between my accent and my clothes [...] I discovered that this never happened'.[100] In *The Road to Wigan Pier*, he argues this is because a tramp is

> used to hearing all kinds of accents among his mates, some of them so strange to him that he can hardly understand them, and a man from, say, Cardiff or Durham or Dublin does not necessarily know which of the south English accents is an 'educated one'. In any case men with 'educated' accents, though rare among tramps, are not unknown.[101]

This observation relates specifically to the destitute. However, he insists that even in northern working-class communities 'your "educated" accent stamps you rather as a foreigner than as a chunk of the petty gentry'.[102] Tom Harrisson supports this suggestion that the working class were ignorant of the social connotations of accents. He insists that whilst researching in 'Worktown' (Bolton), the

> fact that I had a so-called Oxford accent in no way led to suspicion that I was a spy. It was necessary only to claim to have come from another dialect area a few miles away.[103]

These comments do not, of course, prove that the poor were in practice unable to recognise an 'educated' accent. Indeed, in his diary entry for 5 March 1936, Orwell recorded that James Brown, a politically committed unemployed man he had met, '*remarked on my "public school twang"*' (10:447–51:448). This does not appear to have caused problems, despite Brown's declared hatred of the bourgeoisie. However, other writers with 'educated' accents did find it difficult to interact with members of the working class. McKibbin records that Nancy Mitford, for example, 'was asked to leave her London firewatching unit in 1940 because her fellow-watchers found her accent intolerable'.[104] Even Harrisson appears, in practice, to have worried that his 'Oxford accent' would hinder his research, as Peter Gurney claims he 'attempted to mimic a northern working-class accent during his sojourn in Bolton and Blackpool'.[105] Orwell and Harrisson's comments nonetheless illustrate their belief, however ill-founded, that their accents did not exclude them from working-class communities. They suggest that social codes such as clothing, accent and mannerisms can be adopted or abandoned, and that class boundaries can therefore be crossed by an act of will. This belief is implicit in any text founded upon the idea that a middle-class explorer can temporarily 'become' one of the destitute and thereby function as a 'participant-observer'.

Orwell insists that his 'lower-upper-middle class'[106] background did not significantly effect the way others behaved towards him whilst he was tramping. Indeed, the only occasion he records on which it led to better treatment was when he gave his trade as 'journalist' during registration at a spike, and was asked by the 'Tramp Major' whether he was therefore 'a gentleman'. When he admitted he was, the official informed him 'that's bloody bad luck guv'nor', and afterwards behaved towards him 'with unfair favouritism, and even deference'.[107] However, he concedes that his integration was possible due to the particular sections of the poor he mixed with in both England and France. In Paris, he worked and socialised in an amorphous, largely immigrant community. The 'hotel' he lived in had a 'floating population, largely foreigners'.[108] His workplace, the 'Hôtel X.', was similarly diverse, though fragmented, as

> Different jobs were done by different races. The office employees and the cooks and sewing-women were French, the waiters Italian and German (there is hardly such a thing as a French waiter in Paris), the *plongeurs* of every race in Europe, besides Arabs and negroes.[109]

The employees also had different social and educational backgrounds. Orwell insists that one of the waiters, for example, had previously held 'a well-paid job in a business office', before catching a 'venereal disease'[110] and losing his position, and that 'there are men with university degrees scrubbing dishes in Paris for ten or fifteen hours a day'.[111] The hotel moreover had its own 'elaborate caste system',[112] with the manager at the top and *cafetiers* at the bottom, based upon the job rather than background of those employed. This diversity enabled the integration of new employees, regardless of their origins. However, it also meant that the staff were not an integrated community but a series of individuals connected only by their work. Even the 'caste system' operated only within the hotel, as it was the 'etiquette in hotel life that between hours everyone is equal'.[113] The hierarchies and social structures Orwell described were, therefore, explicitly limited. He does not, for example, suggest there is any fundamental division between the employees, or attempt to describe a French working class.

The tramps Orwell encountered in England were similarly diverse. Paddy had been a worker in a 'metal polish factory'[114] before losing his job, but the narrator also meets an 'old Etonian'[115] in a 'lodging-house in a back alley near the Strand',[116] and speculates that the 'first woman tramp I had ever seen', a 'fattish, battered, very dirty woman of sixty', is 'a respectable widow woman, become a tramp through some grotesque accident'.[117] These characters are connected by their poverty and share only the characteristics this imposes. In *The Road to Wigan Pier*, he argues that, to be regarded by tramps as one of themselves 'all that matters is that you, like themselves, are "on the bum"'. As a result, once 'you are in that world and seemingly *of* it, it hardly matters what you have been in the past'. The emphasis upon economic position is important to both sections of the book because it implies that the social explorer can temporarily 'become' a *plongeur* or tramp. All that is necessary is to adopt the role by wearing the appropriate clothes and performing the appropriate labour, whether washing dishes or walking between spikes. The destitute do not, Orwell suggests, have a distinct culture. Indeed, one can 'become a tramp simply by putting on the right clothes and going to the nearest casual ward'.[118] By focusing on these sections of the population, as opposed to communities defined by codes which cannot be readily adopted, he reinforces the notion that he was able to become a 'participant-observer' and that his book is a direct, authentic account of poverty.

The emphasis on diverse characters in *Down and Out in Paris and London* reinforces what Alex Zwerdling describes as its 'extreme loose-ness of structure'.[119] The text lacks a coherent analytical method or model of social structure, and is instead a picaresque account of individual experience. It opens with a description of some of the 'eccentric characters' living in his hotel, people Orwell insists had 'given up trying to be normal or decent',[120] and unfolds as a series of anecdotes and commentaries. It focuses upon idiosyncratic characters, examples of which include Boris, a Russian waiter who had been a 'captain in the Second Siberian Rifles',[121] Jules, a Communist who 'could prove to you by figures it was wrong to work',[122] and Bozo, a London pavement artist who is also an amateur astronomer with 'two letters from the Astronomer Royal thanking me for writing about meteors'.[123] It incorporates, moreover, numerous digressions, asides, authorial commentaries and self-contained tales. The first section, for example, includes Valenti's account of praying to the picture of 'some famous prostitute'[124] under the misapprehension it was 'Sainte Éloïse, who was the patron saint of the quarter',[125] and concludes with what Crick describes as the 'stock, rather nasty, indeed positively anti-Semitic'[126] story of Roucollo, a miser who is swindled when he is sold face-powder rather than cocaine by a young Jew. The second section incorporates a chapter on 'London slang and swearing',[127] one of 'general remarks about tramps',[128] and another concerned with 'the sleeping accommodation open to a home-less person in London'.[129] These are largely independent of one another, a series of interrelated studies of particular, frequently unusual, examples of deprivation.

As Hammond argues, 'Apart from one section (Chapter 36) in which Orwell sets down some general reflections on tramps and recommend-ations for the amelioration of their lot, the book is remarkably free of sociological comment.'[130] It does not outline a coherent model of poverty, and those described in the text do not form communities, bound by cultural, political or religious ties, but instead are connected only by work or poverty. Their experiences are particular, rather than indicative of broader patterns. Bozo, for example, who is 'half starved throughout the winter', but nevertheless insists that if 'you set yourself to it, you can live the same life, rich or poor',[131] is too idiosyncratic to be representative of a class. As Zwerdling argues, 'What is absent is an authoritative sense of the nature of poverty and destitution, some theoretical base that would make the "I" less of an aimless observer and more of a reliable (or even misguided) interpreter.'[132] Instead, the text focuses on those whom poverty had liberated from 'ordinary standards of behaviour',[133] whether in the Parisian slums, the Hôtel X., or the English casual wards. It is moreover, as Rai insists, a work defined by Orwell's 'schizoid affiliation – to literati and to tramps',[134] his simultaneous concern with his subject matter, poverty, and commitment to a literary tradition that emphasises the individual and eccentric.

Down and Out in Paris and London is not, and does not represent itself as, an examination of economic conditions in Britain or France. Indeed, as Newsinger writes,

> When *Down and Out* was published in 1933, there were over three million registered unemployed men and women in Britain and yet the book shows no awareness of the scale of the problem. Indeed, in many ways it seems to be rooted in an earlier age before the onset of the Great Depression.[135]

Orwell returned from Paris 'in time for Christmas 1929',[136] and submitted a short version of the Parisian material, entitled 'A Scullion's Diary', to Jonathan Cape as early as 1930,[137] though the book was not accepted by Gollancz until 1932. He therefore wrote and revised it during a period of economic crisis. Unemployment amongst insured workers rose from 1,334,000 in December 1929 to 2,850,000 in January 1932 and 2,950,000 by January 1933.[138] As Richard Croucher observes, the 'real' figure was almost certainly much higher, as such statistics excluded many without work, from those who were not covered by insurance policies to those 'for whom, like many married women, there was no financial benefit in signing on but who would have welcomed work'.[139] However, although Orwell recognised that unemployment was 'one of the realities of postwar English life' (10:122–8:122), *Down and Out in Paris and London* does not analyse, or even represent, national or international economic conditions. Its limited scope is illustrated in the reforms it proposes for the amelioration of the poor. Orwell suggests, for example, that tramps should not be limited to one night in each casual ward per month, and that every 'workhouse could run a small farm, or at least a kitchen garden, and every able-bodied tramp who presented himself could be made to do a sound day's work'.[140] In the chapter detailing his 'opinions about the life of a Paris *plongeur*',[141] he makes no concrete proposals, but simply suggests that the 'instinct to perpetuate useless work is, at bottom, simply fear of the mob'.[142] The text neither attempts an economic analysis nor suggests political solutions. Instead, it concentrates on measures to improve the particular conditions it has described. Its conclusion, that 'I shall never again think that all tramps are drunken scoundrels, nor expect a beggar to be grateful when I give him a penny, nor be surprised if men out of work lack energy, nor subscribe to the Salvation Army, nor pawn my clothes, nor refuse a handbill, nor enjoy a meal at a smart restaurant',[143] illustrates its limited ambitions. In this, it parallels earlier, liberal works of social exploration, proposing the reform of the established system rather than fundamental change.

III

Down and Out in Paris and London is, of course, not the only work of social exploration written in the 1930s to employ the images, forms and structures established in the nineteenth century. Numerous other texts of the period focus on the individual experience of poverty, and use the model of anthropological studies or travel writing to emphasise the distance between the classes. Hugh Massingham, for example, wrote that 'I could not get out of my head the astonishing fact that the East End is as unknown to us as the Trobriand Islands, that the unexplored regions of the world are just round the corner.'[144] Tom Harrisson used a similar image to explain his investigation into life in Britain, arguing that 'We barely know the elementary facts of intercourse or conception in Bolton or Bournemouth; we know more, as a matter of fact, about Borneo or New Guinea.'[145] Mass-Observation, which Harrisson helped found, illustrates the attempt to produce what he and Charles Madge described as 'the anthropology of ourselves',[146] or, as Cunningham writes, 'to treat Britain as though it were no different in kind from any other *Savage Civilisation* [...] in which intriguing kinship systems obtained, and strange rituals and odd instances of religious faith occurred, and where a lot of dancing went on'.[147] For Angus Calder, the organisation was 'part of the broad movement' attempting to 'meet and understand the working-class',[148] and for Gary Cross it was similarly part of a 'populist trend' to 'discover [...] that "race apart" – the working-class of the industrial North'.[149] It explored the culture of working-class communities, producing detailed reports on, for example, public houses, the Lambeth walk, the football pools and holidays in Blackpool.

Many nineteenth-century texts also employ the idea of a cultural or even 'racial' division between the working and middle classes. However, as illustrated above, these images of difference frequently rely upon the same hierarchical models of human society that sustained imperialist ideologies. They represent the poor as 'savages', though often savages capable of 'civilisation'. There are, however, exceptions to this pattern, texts that provided precedents or even sources for works of social exploration and reportage produced in the 1930s. Engels, for example, argued that

> the working class has gradually become a race wholly apart from the English bourgeoisie. The bourgeoisie has more in common with every other nation of the earth than with the workers in whose midst it lives. The workers speak other dialects, have other thoughts and ideals, other customs and moral principles, a different religion and other politics than those of the bourgeoisie. Thus they are two radically dissimilar nations, as unlike as difference of race could make them, of whom we on the Continent have known but one, the bourgeoisie. Yet it is precisely the other, the people, the proletariat, which is by far the most important for the future of England.[150]

The passage reproduces the notion that the nation contains two distinct 'cultures' or 'races'. However, it undermines the dominant hierarchy, insisting that it is the 'proletariat' rather than the 'bourgeoisie' that is more 'important'. It therefore both legitimises the study of working-class life and attaches an importance to it. This pattern is repeated throughout the 1930s. However, the representation of class difference as analogous to those cultural divisions revealed by foreign travel nonetheless persists in these later texts. Massingham, for example, describes how in London 'two communities were living side by side, each with its own peculiar customs, superstitions, culture, sex life and to some extent even language, and that each was ignorant of the other'.[151] Many texts produced in the period reinforce the idea that the deprived areas were a 'foreign country', alien to middle-class investigators and readers. Their emphasis upon a distinctive working-class culture, however, figures these differences as a source of value. Harrison's decision to shift his attention from the 'jungles' to 'the wilds of Lancashire and East Anglia',[152] for example, reproduces the images of exploration and anthropological analysis established in earlier texts, and thereby the image of an observer able to analyse and classify a distinct group of people. However, he also exposes the complexity of working-class life in Britain, and thereby undermines simple, hierarchical ideas of 'civilisation'.

Images of the 'masses' also recurred in texts produced in the 1930s. Indeed, Cunningham described the decade as an 'age of mass-production, mass-demonstrations, mass-meetings, mass sporting occasions, mass-communications, mass-armies, a time in which things would be done in, and to, and for crowds'.[153] Both Left and Right used 'mass' action, and totalitarian movements in particular conspicuously exploited the potential of large, regimented meetings. Adolf Hitler, for example, argued in *Mein Kampf* that the

> man who is exposed to grave tribulations, as the first advocate of a new doctrine in his factory or workshop, absolutely needs that strengthening which lies in the conviction of being a member and fighting in a great comprehensive body. And he obtains an impression of this body for the first time in the mass demonstrations. When from his little workshop or big factory, in which he feels very small, he steps for the first time into a mass meeting, and has thousands and thousands of people of the same opinions around him, when, as a seeker, he is swept away by three or four thousand others into the mighty effect of suggestive intoxication and enthusiasm, when the visible success and agreement of thousands confirm to him the rightness of the new doctrine and for the first time arouse doubt in the truth of his previous conviction – then he himself has succumbed to the magic influence of what we designate as 'mass suggestion'. The will, the longing, and also the power of thousands are accumulated in every individual.[154]

In this instance, individual action is structured by a central 'doctrine' or source of authority. However, collective politics obviously does not necessarily suggest such a centre of power. Many politically conscious writers of the 1930s, particularly on the Left, argued that 'mass' action emancipated individuals, who realised themselves in the shared response to common problems. In Blumenfeld's *Jew Boy*, for example, Alec, when attempting to organise a strike, thinks of

> Young people and older people; scattered, animated by different problems. Heterogeneous, diffused. The job was to weld them all into one, to get them to think and feel together; to unite, and agree on a common course of action.[155]

The crowd is not a threat or an anonymous instrument but a demonstration of working-class solidarity. In *I Was One of the Unemployed*, Max Cohen described the 'vast elemental roar'[156] of demonstrators, and the 'tramp of thousands of feet' which 'seemed to make the very roadway tremble and vibrate'.[157] Collective action paradoxically restores a sense of individual value and agency eroded by unemployment. In Gibbon's *A Scots Quair*, an unnamed protestor similarly considers that with 'all your mates about you, marching as one, you forgot all the chave and trauchle of things, the sting of your feet, nothing could stop you'.[158] These examples represent unity as a condition of emancipation. Nineteenth-century texts frequently represent the 'masses' as responsible for the dilution or destruction of cultural values. In the 1930s they are figured as the potential basis of social renewal. For left-wing writers, who produced the majority of accounts of the working class in this period, the fact that the poor might 'seize for themselves a fair share of the world's goods' was not a threat to be resisted, but essential to the development of a more equitable society in which, as Marx and Engels wrote, 'the free development of each is the condition for the free development of all'.[159]

Radical political theories such as Marxism transformed the connotations of the 'mass'. In *Jew Boy*, Alec perceives his political commitments as integrating him in a 'world-wide fellowship', as part of 'the new life force, the new blood stream', and this provides him with 'something to live for, even here'.[160] In *We Live*, during a protest march by the miners, a 'mighty demonstration of their own power', Len initially 'felt himself as a weak straw drifting in and out with the surge of bodies'. The 'power' of the crowd asserts itself, however, when 'something powerful swept through his being as the mass soaked its strength into him, and he realised that the strength of them all was the measure of his own, that his existence and power as an individual was buried in that of the mass now pregnant with motion behind him'.[161] Here, the term 'mass' is a positive one, suggesting mutual support and political unity. The 'movement of masses', Rex Warner insisted, was also the 'beginning of good'.[162]

This revaluation was, of course, not universal. J. B. Priestley, for example, demanded, after describing a group of Communists singing the 'International',

Why is it always 'the masses'? Who cares about masses? I wouldn't raise a finger for 'the masses.' Men, women and children – but not masses.[163]

However, many on the Left used the term positively. In part at least, the shift in its connotations illustrates the prevalence of the radical political ideas in the period. Indeed, there were numerous direct references to these in descriptions of the working class. In George Garrett's 'The First Hunger March', for example, the marchers initiate a discussion whilst resting overnight in a workhouse, in the course of which,

> interested groups ringed around talkative enthusiasts were urgently advised to read this book, that book, and the other book to help understand the implications of warships and workshops, workless and workhouses, and the reason for the unemployed march to London. The names of Dietzkin, Lenin, and Marx cropped up, also the usual interruptions on the correct interpretation of a paragraph from *Das Kapital*.

The discussion leaves the workhouse inmates 'bewildered' at the 'continuous rush of strange phrases',[164] but illustrates the widespread circulation of such ideas. Their influence on left-wing literary circles, in particular, initiated a shift in the perception of the working-class crowd and 'mass-demonstration'.

The conventions of social exploration were also reinterpreted within this political context, although numerous writers and commentators nonetheless continued to use images and ideas drawn from anthropology, much as their nineteenth-century predecessors had done. Mass-Observation, for example, compared the 'Lambeth tradition' of 'dancing and song', for example, to 'primitive dancing',[165] the 'Keaw-yed' festival in Westhoughten to the 'totemism' of 'primitive peoples',[166] and dancing at Blackpool tower to the 'ancient ritual' of 'Bacchic dance'.[167] A retired Major, quoted in *Britain by Mass-Observation*, represented the scenes in 'a public dance hall' as similar to those at 'a "deluka" (native festival) in the Southern Sudan, where anything from 40 upwards of naked young men and women get in a circle and jump up and down, giving ecstatic groans, sweating and stinking, to the beat of a darabuka, in the flickering light of a fire'.[168] The equation of social exploration with the investigation of 'exotic' countries recurs throughout the period. Orwell himself describes the 'industrial North' as a 'strange country', and argues that the 'Southerner goes north, at any rate for the first time, with the vague inferiority-complex of a civilised man venturing among savages'.[169] Massingham even claims that it would 'have been far easier had I decided to explore remotest Africa' than the East End, and that if 'I had decided upon the interior of the Congo, I should at least have had a fairly general idea of the difficulties that lay ahead of me'.[170] Despite the continued equation of the poor with 'primitive peoples', however, these texts describe a distinct, positive working-class culture.

The notion of distinct working-class cultures and values also lead to a reinterpretation of the idea of the reform. As observed above, many works of social exploration, including *Down and Out in Paris and London*, promote specific changes intended to correct 'errors' or 'inconsistencies' in the treatment of the poor. Implicit in this is the idea that 'civilisation' is a known, though evolving, quality that needs to be extended from a minority to society at large. According to this view, the poverty of the working classes prevents their attaining the values or culture of the more prosperous. Virginia Woolf used this argument in her 'Introductory Letter to Margaret Llewelyn Davies', which was published as a preface to *Life as We Have Known It*, a collection of writing by members of the Women's Co-operative Guild. She argued that the material hardship experienced by working-class women activists had inevitably focused their attention on 'baths and ovens and education and seventeen shillings instead of sixteen, and freedom and air'.[171] Their conversation was therefore concerned with 'matters of fact', unlike that of the more prosperous, 'whose minds, such as they are, fly free at the end of a short length of capital'.[172] Woolf recognised that the women she encountered possessed valuable qualities, but nonetheless insisted that the middle classes could 'give' the poor 'wit and detachment, learning and poetry, and all those good gifts which those who have never answered bells or minded machines enjoy by right'.[173] The statement does not posit inherent differences between the classes, as the working class are capable of receiving these 'good gifts', but it insists that positive qualities such as 'wit' are the product of prosperity. The essay argues that the poor are capable of cultural achievement but have been denied opportunities to develop. Nevertheless, although she noted that essays produced by members of the Guild had 'some qualities even as literature that the literate and instructed might envy',[174] she argued in 'The Leaning Tower' that if one were to take 'away all that the working class has given to English literature [...] that literature would scarcely suffer'.[175] Like women, who she insisted 'have not had a dog's chance of writing poetry',[176] the working class had been prevented by their poverty from contributing to 'learning and poetry'. This materialist reading of the relationship between poverty and 'culture' recognises the extent to which economic deprivation constrains individuals. However, it also naturalises the values of the prosperous, and represents them as possessing a 'wit' and 'learning' the working class have not attained.

For Woolf, poverty excluded individuals from particularly valuable spheres of cultural production, preventing women and the working class, for example, from producing poetry or achieving 'detachment'. Other writers argued that the effects of deprivation extended further and severely retarded the physical and mental development of the poor. Jack London, for example, insisted that once 'workers are segregated in the Ghetto, they cannot escape the consequent degradation',[177] with those at the 'bottom of the Abyss' becoming 'feeble, besotted, and imbecile'.[178] The 'men of the spike, the peg, and the street' are, he argues, 'of no good or use to any one, nor to themselves' and are 'better out of the way'.[179] He describes a complete, irreversible 'degradation' that extends even to subsequent generations, as the children of the very poor 'grow up into rotten adults, without virility or stamina, a weak-kneed, narrow-chested, listless breed'.[180] Most writers were, of course, more sympathetic to the impoverished, but many emphasised the debilitating effects of poverty and the extent to which it excluded individuals from social and intellectual life. Mrs Cecil Chesterton, for example, wrote that 'outcasts often appear stupid, stolid, almost mentally deficient', and 'know nothing of the affairs of the political or the literary world', but insisted this was because the 'avenues of interest open to the well-fed are closed to them, they are haunted always by the spectres, hunger and sleeplessness'.[181] Despite their diversity, all these examples represent poverty as limiting development, an idea also illustrated in Gissing's description, in *The Nether World*, of Stephen Candy as a 'a very tolerable human being, had he had fair-play'.[182]

The passages above focus attention on the fact that poverty restricts access not only to material goods, but also, for example, to leisure time, healthcare, education and social or cultural opportunities. This idea recurred in descriptions of working-class life produced in the 1930s, including those by working-class writers. Many emphasised the ways in which both poverty and work itself prevented individuals from pursuing education or an interest in the arts. In Walter Brierley's *Sandwichman*, for instance, Arthur Gardner initially believes that study, rather than 'pit life', fulfils his 'real self'.[183] However, his surroundings and the demands of work prevent him from realising his potential, and he eventually concludes that studying 'does you no good'.[184] In Greenwood's *Love on the Dole*, Larry is tormented by the thought of the 'Books, music, brief holidays'[185] he cannot afford. Even when working-class scholars successfully pursued their education, they met further problems. James Hanley, for example, describes the case of a 'young miner' who had 'won a scholarship and reached the University', as 'a tragedy', because it 'was nothing but struggle for the parents, they simply couldn't afford to give their son what they saw other students having with the greatest of ease'.[186] Jack Common similarly describes a 'clever young miner [...] taken up a well-meaning folk and coached to win a scholarship at Ruskin College' who is '*daunted*' by the 'many-rooted prestige of Oxford' because 'he didn't go there with a brick in his hand, as a substitute for the bankbook other blokes have'.[187] As Ralph Glasser observed, 'for a Gorbals man to come up to Oxford was as unthinkable as to meet a raw bushman in a St James's club',[188] and he describes his own struggles to adjust to an environment in which there 'were no common points of reference' and 'words themselves were deficient'.[189] In fact, working-class scholars at all levels suffered from isolation, and a lack of time, resources and advice.

Poverty did not simply limit access to education, but restricted or distorted development in a variety of spheres. Indeed, it even shaped the bodies of the working class. Texts from the 1930s are full of images of ill-health, much of which began in childhood. Wal Hannington, for example, observes that

> Dr. Spence, the Newcastle Medical Officer, in 1933 made an enquiry in his area into the effects of poverty on children between one and five years of age. An examination was made of 125 children of the poorer classes whose parents were unemployed and an equal number of children of the well-to-do professional and commercial classes. It was found that there was a very conspicuous difference of height and weight. Nearly one half of the poorer children were anæmic, one-eighth of them seriously so.[190]

Deprivation had a very immediate effect, limiting physical growth and development. The impact of ill-health continued into adulthood. Numerous writers argued that excessive work and poor food led to illness and premature ageing not least amongst women working in the home. In *Hungry England*, for example, A. Fenner Brockway describes a woman who is 'still young', insisting that

> If her life had been different, she would have been good looking; black hair, dark eyes, good features, good figure. But she doesn't worry much about her appearance now. Her hair falls over her face, the brightness has gone out of her eyes, there are hollows in her cheeks and her skin is colourless.[191]

In *The Road to Wigan Pier*, Orwell similarly refers to 'the usual exhausted face of the slum girl who is twenty-five and looks forty, thanks to miscarriages and drudgery'.[192] The figure of Katie in *Coming Up for Air* reinforces this image, as following her marriage to a tinker, she looks like a 'wrinkled-up hag of a woman [...] at least fifty-years old', despite being only 'twenty-seven'.[193] Maud Pember Reeves also comments that in working-class areas 'women who look to be in the dull middle of middle age are young',[194] Dame Janet Campbell that it is 'heartbreaking to see how rapidly a pretty attractive girl grows old and drab after a few years of marriage',[195] and B. L. Coombes that miners' wives 'become old when they should be mature and still attractive'.[196] Robert Roberts also describes 'many women broken and aged with childbearing well before their own youth was done'.[197] These images are problematic insofar as they interpret women's experience of poverty in terms of their attractiveness. Nonetheless, they emphasise the ways in which poverty distorts even physical development and trace the 'stealthy and sinister deterioration of the woman's health and happiness'[198] due to childbearing, overwork, poor food and inadequate living conditions.

The representation of poverty as a constraint upon individuals supports a complex model of deprivation that recognises that the poor lack not only material goods, but leisure, security, and access to a wide variety of educational, cultural and political resources. In addition, it undermines the notion that there is an essential difference between rich and poor, and that the latter are incapable of mastering 'civilised' values or 'high' culture. It therefore challenges what Orwell described as the tendency, prevalent in the nineteenth century, to 'write off a whole stratum of the population as irredeemable savages' (16:12–17:14). However, it also tends to replicate the notion of a cultural hierarchy, in that the attainments from which the poor are excluded are, implicitly, those of the more prosperous. Reform continues to be conceived as a process in which the prosperous will extend to the poor, for example, the 'good gifts' of 'wit and detachment, learning and poetry'. The model figures the wealthier classes as possessors of a way of life which the poor desire. Insofar as this life is represented in terms of material resources, access to education or leisure, this is not problematic, as the examples above illustrate. However, much of the literature of the 1930s rejects the idea that the working class aspire to the values of middle class, are 'primitive peoples' who desire 'civilisation'. In *Sandwichman*, for example, Arthur is 'content to know', despite his educational ambitions, that 'however far he reached from the practical atmosphere of his class, he would still be one of them, no better than the miner conscious of life' and that he 'didn't want to be, either'.[199]

Writers on the Left in particular, therefore, attempted to recognise the complexity and value of working-class culture as well as the restrictions upon it, its achievements as well as its limitations. This did not, of course, mean abandoning established ideas of 'civilisation'. Although Alec Brown argued in *Left Review* that 'LITERARY ENGLISH FROM CAXTON TO US IS AN ARTIFICIAL JARGON OF THE RULING CLASS; WRITTEN ENGLISH BEGINS WITH US',[200] most attempted to construct a model of culture that encompassed both the achievements of the past and at least some previously excluded groups. Indeed, Lenin himself argued that

> Marxism has won its historic significance as the ideology of the revolutionary proletariat because, far from rejecting the most valuable achievements of the bourgeois epoch, it has, on the contrary, assimilated and refashioned everything of value in the more than 2000 years of the development of human thought and culture.[201]

The statement is, of course, problematic, as it implicitly identifies a well-established narrative of European development with 'human thought and culture' as such. However, it also recognises that the 'valuable achievements of the bourgeois epoch' are simply an inheritance to be used with discrimination. It is one example of an attempt, particularly on the Left, to undermine the identification of 'civilisation' with 'bourgeois' culture and values. This was complemented by a simultaneous effort to explore the culture, values and achievements of the working class. *The Road to Wigan Pier* is, in part, an example of the latter. Orwell insisted that he had 'seen just enough of the working class to avoid idealising them',[202] but nevertheless praised, for example, their 'plain-spokenness',[203] 'kindness',[204] 'extraordinary courtesy and good nature',[205] and solidarity. In *Nineteen Eighty-Four* it is the 'proles' alone who have 'stayed human'.[206] Despite Woodcock's description of *The Road to Wigan Pier* as 'Orwell's account of his further expeditions among English primitive',[207] the text emphasises the distinct values of working-class communities, rather than figuring them as evolving towards middle-class ideals.

The shared codes and values that produce a cohesive working class also, however, produce the 'plate-glass' barrier of 'class-difference' which excludes him from such communities. In contrast to *Down and Out in Paris and London*, Orwell emphasises in *The Road to Wigan Pier* his distance from those he observes, the fact that he is not 'one of them'.[208] The premise of the earlier text, that there is 'no difference between the mass of rich and poor' is replaced by the concept of constitutive and inflexible identities. Orwell insists that 'culturally I am different from the miner',[209] divided by different codes of behaviour and values. His emphasis upon such distinctions, and on his own '*middle-class* notions', undermines the idea that social exploration enables the accurate representation of the working class. Orwell cannot 'write as' one of the working class. His insistence that they possess positive, distinct value, moreover, prevents him simply or consistently adopting the position of a 'civilised' man reporting on 'primitive peoples' whose development has been retarded. He continues to describe details of housing, wages, and household budgets for the benefit of a middle-class readership, but his status as both a 'superior person',[210] and an impartial observer is repeatedly undermined. *The Road to Wigan Pier* is, in contrast to *Down and Out in Paris and London*, a self-reflexive work, focusing on the relation between observer and observed. It develops, moreover, an image of class as both constitutive and restrictive, as producing value and establishing divisions. In this context, 'class-breaking' is not an extension of 'civilisation', in which the 'primitive' poor attain 'culture', but a 'wild ride into the darkness',[211] both emancipating and destructive. In order to analyse these developments in his work, the rhetorical movement that enabled them and, in particular, the myth of working-class communities he formulates, it is necessary to examine in detail his complex and contradictory second work of social exploration.

IV

The Road to Wigan Pier is not only an important work of social exploration, but a revision of the genre that exposes some of the limitations and contradictions of earlier texts, including *Down and Out in Paris and London*. In contrast to this first study of poverty, it is a self-conscious, political book, and as such illustrates Orwell's evolving ideas of socialism. It was not until June 1937, after his experiences in Spain, that Orwell told Cyril Connolly that 'I have seen wonderful things & at last really believe in Socialism, which I never did before' (11:27–8:28). However, his account of his journey through the industrial north of England demonstrates a number of key developments in his thought. In particular, it focuses upon the working class, rather than disparate, often eccentric individuals. In addition, it represents class as a constitutive category, a source of identity as well as a method of classification. These changes both required and enabled a corresponding rhetorical shift. In contrast to *Down and Out in Paris and London, The Road to Wigan Pier* focuses upon communities defined not only by poverty, but also by shared values. It also emphasises research as well as personal observation, integrating his personal encounters with poverty into a broader critique of economic and social structures. These developments enabled Orwell to produce a myth of the working class that insists upon their stability, close integration and combination of 'traditional' values with political radicalism. However, the emphasis upon cohesive class identities exposes problems of political organisation, as it suggests that it is difficult to establish solidarity across class boundaries. In addition, as outlined above, it reveals contradictions in the genre of social exploration itself. It undermines the idea that it is possible to 'write as' a member of another class, or even report objectively upon them, as the explorer occupies a position within the social system that shapes his or her interpretations. *The Road to Wigan Pier* therefore not only establishes a foundation for Orwell's socialism, a powerful though problematic 'Myth of Proletariat', but exposes a series of political and generic tensions and, indeed, contradictions. In order to analyse these it is necessary first to explore the model of class Orwell develops in the text.

The concept of class dominates *The Road to Wigan Pier* and the political ideas it contains. Indeed, Orwell argues that 'before you can be sure whether you are genuinely in favour of Socialism, you have got to decide whether things at present are tolerable or not tolerable, and you have got to take up a definite attitude on the terribly difficult issue of class'.[212] His own attitude, however, is far from 'definite', and David Cannadine claims that his attempts to describe 'the social structure of his native land' are 'disappointingly confused'.[213] The statement does not value or indeed recognise Orwell's insights into 'the nature of class distinctions', which Hoggart describes as 'a constant delight'.[214] However, it does emphasise the tensions in his writing on class. *The Road to Wigan Pier* moves between distinct, sometimes contradictory interpretations of the social structure, exposing complexities rather than producing a 'definite' conclusion. It does not, for example, represent an individual's class as the determined by a single factor, such as income, education, or relation to the means of production, but multiple aspects of their financial position, social status, background, and beliefs. The text suggests that material and cultural factors, economic realities and myths, all shape the social structure. Even Orwell's attitude to class is ambiguous, as he represents it as both divisive and a basis of community. As an ideological form, class identities shape ' "lived" experience', providing a structure within which solidarities and relationships emerge.

In his study of Orwell, Richard Rees wrote that

> a friend in Sheffield who had introduced him to a militant Communist propagandist told me the following story. The Communist started in on his routine vilification of the bourgeoisie but was interrupted by Orwell who said: 'Look here, I'm a bourgeois and my family are bourgeois. If you talk about them like that I'll punch your head'.[215]

The anecdote exposes Orwell's ambiguous position in the working-class communities he visited. His aggressive response demonstrates his view that his class is established, identifiable and, indeed, an integral part of his identity. The fact that he was born into the 'lower-upper-middle-class'[216] defines him even as an adult. To change this, he argues, he would have to 'alter myself so completely that at the end I should hardly be recognisable as the same person'.[217] The image of a stable identity suggests that there is a persistent, even insoluble barrier between the narrator and those he encounters. However, it also implies that class forms a potential basis for communities. Orwell's status as 'bourgeois', for example, divides him from the working class, but means that he shares certain values and traditions with others members of the 'bourgeoisie'. It is therefore paradoxically both a source of impoverishment and plenitude.

This concept of class distinguishes and indeed divides Orwell's two works of social exploration. Its increasing importance reflects the conditions of the later book's production. Orwell based *The Road to Wigan Pier*, like *Down and Out in Paris and London*, on his direct observations. As Crick observes, he spent around two months 'living with working people in Wigan, Barnsley and Sheffield, from 31 January to 30 March'. On this occasion, however, he travelled as 'an established writer and a journalist, engaged on research, carrying letters of introduction from Richard Rees, Middleton Murry [...] and from ILP members in London'.[218] As Beatrix Campbell argues, 'he didn't pretend to be other than he was, a writer in exile from his own class, setting out to see with his own eyes the state of emergency among the Northern unemployed'.[219] He continued to use cheap lodging-houses on his journey north, but in the industrial areas themselves he stayed predominantly in working-class homes. Most of these, as Ian Hamilton observes, were 'relatively comfortable (what he would call "clean and decent") lodgings',[220] although he appears on occasion to have chosen unusually squalid houses, such as that used as the model for the Brookers'.[221] His research itself was structured by his political connections. On 15 February 1936, for example, he *'Went with N.U.W.M.* [National Unemployed Workers' Movement] *collectors on their rounds with a view to collecting facts about housing conditions'* (10:426–9:426). He even attended a number of political meetings in the north of England. Joe Kennan, for example, recalls that he took him to the Market Square in Wigan, where there were speakers from 'the ILP [...] the Communist Party [...] the National Unemployed Workers Movement'.[222] In his diary, Orwell recalls hearing both Oswald Mosley, a 'very good speaker' who delivered the 'usual claptrap' (10:452–8:456) and Wal Hannington, a 'poor speaker, using all the padding and cliches of the Socialist orator, and with the wrong kind of cockney accent (once again, though a Communist entirely a bourgeois)' (10:422–4:424).

In both his research and text, therefore, Orwell engaged with political debates of the period, in particular those on the Left. As a result, *The Road to Wigan Pier* focused not on *plongeurs* and tramps, but on the industrial proletariat, the group central to Marxist theory and described by Michael Roberts as the only class 'not utterly corrupted by capitalist spoon-feeding'.[223] It also attempted a broader analysis of social conditions and made far greater use of textual sources than *Down and Out in Paris and London*. This in turn demanded a new method of research. In his diary of 14 March 1936, for example, Orwell wrote that he did

> not think I shall pick up much of interest in Barnsley. [...] Cannot discover whether there is a branch of the N.U.W.M. here. The public library is no good. There is no proper reference library and it seems no separate directory of Barnsley is published. (10:452–8:455)

Libraries were essential as his observations of poverty were supplemented by his reading. As Christopher Hitchens writes, the 'notebooks and research for *The Road to Wigan Pier* would not have disgraced Friedrich Engels'.[224] The shift in perspective between the two texts of social exploration is reinforced by a change in rhetorical technique, and, indeed, narrator. As J. R. Hammond argued, the ' "I" of *Down and Out* is a different person from the "I" of *Wigan Pier*: in both the narrator, the shaping presence, is a deeply idiosyncratic personality, but from 1936 onwards the personality becomes much more overtly political'.[225] All these developments enabled Orwell to represent his views as the product of methodical, logical inquiry into poverty.

These differences between the texts have obvious political implications. As Storm Jameson argued, in documentary writing it is by 'choosing this detail, this work rather than another from the mass offered to us, we make our criticism, our moral judgements'.[226] Both *Down and Out in Paris and London* and *The Road to Wigan Pier* claim to represent 'typical' poverty, but they focus upon very different social groups, and consequently reach very different conclusions. The former bases its analysis of poverty on the experience of *plongeurs* and tramps and suggests reforms that address their immediate concerns. Orwell later argued, however, that 'social outcasts' such as tramps were 'very exceptional beings and no more typical of the working class as a whole than, say, the literary intelligentsia are typical of the bourgeoisie'.[227] *The Road to Wigan Pier* consequently concentrates on the urban working class in the north of England, who were the most conspicuous victims of the Depression. Orwell insisted that his journey was an attempt not only to 'see what mass-unemployment is like at its worst', but also to encounter the 'most typical section of the English working class at close quarters'.[228] His ideas of 'typical' poverty changed dramatically in the four years between the books' publication, and this shift in perspective reflected broader changes in his ideas and political commitments.

Orwell analyses the difference between the two texts in the autobiographical second section of *The Road to Wigan Pier*. He figures his early investigations as part of a process of atonement for his involvement in oppression, both as an individual and member of a class, and insists that after he resigned from the Imperial Indian Police he 'was conscious of an immense weight of guilt that I had got to expiate'. He believed that failure was 'the only virtue', and that 'even to "succeed" in life to the extent of making a few hundreds a year' was 'spiritually ugly, a species of bullying'. His social exploration, he argues, resulted from this and his consequent desire to 'escape' from 'every form of man's dominion over man'.[229] Many critics accept this interpretation. Meyers, for example, argues that 'Blair's tramping was certainly penitential',[230] Malcolm Muggeridge claims that Orwell believed the poor 'had been wronged by his class, and he must somehow make it up',[231] and Campbell insists that Orwell 'tried to purge himself of privilege by becoming a tramp'.[232] Mark Benney argues that Orwell retained this 'guilt' into later life and 'wanted to believe that he and his upper-middle-class kind were inescapably corrupt and evil'.[233] Atonement is obviously an unusual basis for social exploration, and some have challenged this explanation of his investigations into poverty. Glasser, for example, describes Orwell as a 'middle-class voyeur',[234] though he concedes that he 'had the courage to acknowledge his ignorance and try to remedy it'.[235] Terry Eagleton also condemns what he describes as Orwell's 'callously Romantic "low-life" explorations'.[236] This latter comment simplifies his investigations, suggesting a conscious cynicism for which there is little evidence. In addition, and perhaps more importantly, it implies that the motivation it attributes to Orwell invalidates his text. Nonetheless, *The Road to Wigan Pier* undermines the notion that *Down and Out in Paris* is a record of involuntary deprivation.

In his reflections on *Down and Out in Paris and London*, Orwell emphasises that when he wrote the book he 'knew nothing about working-class conditions' and concentrated upon 'the extreme cases, the social outcasts: tramps, beggars, criminals, prostitutes'.[237] In his descriptions of London in particular, he was primarily concerned with destitution and the most conspicuously impoverished. However, he later argued that such groups were not representative of the poor, as a tramp, for instance, 'is not a typical working-class person', but a member of a 'sub-caste'.[238] His examination of the industrial working class is consequently a revision of his earlier text, an attempt to describe the 'normal working class'.[239] William Empson's claim that Orwell continued to believe that 'only tramps and other down- and-outs were genuinely working-class'[240] is not only inaccurate, but obscures his political development. The later text does not represent tramps, but uses ideas of class to politicise its accounts of deprivation and develop a positive myth of working-class community.

Orwell justifies his claim that *The Road to Wigan Pier* describes the 'normal working class' by insisting that it represents the experience of 'enormous blocks of the working class',[241] and an '*under-fed* population of well over ten millions'.[242] He reinforces his argument by using statistical sources, surveys of wages and benefit payments, and analyses of household budgets that attempt to establish the 'typical' material position of this population. Like the concept of class, this concern with broad economic conditions enables him to comment on the social, political and economic system, rather than simply comment on individual hardship. The technique is obviously not peculiar to either Orwell or the 1930s. Engels, for example, based his text upon personal experiences, such as his walks through Manchester and 'repeated visits'[243] to Bolton, but also upon a variety of documents that provided anecdotal and statistical information. Jack London similarly reinforced his descriptions of deprivation with statistics, and made use of 'clippings from newspapers, selections from court transcripts'[244] as well his own observations. Orwell's sustained use of the technique is not unique, but it indicates the increasing sophistication of his sociological analyses, and his interest in economic and political problems, rather than simply the state of the beds in common lodging houses.

The later text also shows a greater interest in working-class culture. As Orwell argues, 'the essential point about the English class-system is that it is *not* entirely explicable in terms of money', but retains a 'shadowy caste-system'.[245] He reinforces this argument in a review of Alec Brown's *The Fate of the Middle Classes* when he describes the attempt to classify individuals upon the basis of 'economic status' as 'like watching somebody carve a roast duck with a chopper' (10:478).[246] Income was obviously important, but an individual's social status also depended upon their family, education, profession, and even, to some extent, perception of themselves. As McKibbin observes, the

> wealth criterion, for example, would include the country's richest man in this period, Sir John Ellerman (1862–1933), who neither by birth, education, cultivation, nor inclination was actually a member of the upper class. Yet, while some of the very wealthy would not have been considered upper-class by contemporaries, many of the wealthy were, and of all attributes of upper-classness wealth was probably the most important. But wealth alone was not sufficient.[247]

The ambiguities do not only apply to the upper-class, as 'you find petty shopkeepers whose income is far lower than that of the brick-layer and who, nevertheless, consider themselves (and are considered) the bricklayer's social superiors'.[248] Although 'Economically, no doubt, there are only two classes, the rich and the poor [...] socially there is a whole hierarchy of classes.'[249] These two conceptions of the social structure are obviously interwoven, but they cannot easily be reduced to a single model. The notion of social status derives largely from the kind of ideological myths of cultural value that underpin, for example, Gissing's representation of the 'masses'. These myths, however, encoded in customs and practices, shape individual's experience, identity and solidarities. In this sense, they are 'real'. As Day Lewis argued,

> In every village there is a social scale of infinite delicacy and exactitude; the titled; the wealthy retired; the professional class; big farmers; small farmers; shopkeepers; labourers and artisans of various grades. It all seems very silly, but try asking Class E to tea with Class F and you'll find it's real enough.[250]

A variety of social codes, from Old School ties, to accent, to more intangible qualities such as a knowledge of 'high' culture, reproduced such distinctions, though subtle shades of meaning could be difficult to interpret. In her account of growing up in working-class family in the 1920s and 1930s, for example, Angela Rodaway wrote that

> my sisters regarded 'the vegetable man' as a person who was socially superior to us. He sold 'King Edwards' which were a superior kind of potato.[251]

Despite such difficulties, however, codes performed a definite function, enabling members of imagined class communities to recognise and identify with one another.

The ability to manipulate these codes, of course, often depended on income, even if they were not themselves material. The etiquette of the upper classes, for example, relied upon access to certain social, cultural and educational opportunities denied to those on low incomes. In theory, particular codes, such as 'manners' or cultural knowledge could be adopted or abandoned as a result of consciousness choices. In practice, they tended to be the product of upbringing. This is both because, being largely internalised, their seamless adoption or abandonment was difficult, and because they formed an interlocked system, in which the position of an individual could not be changed by altering a single term. Orwell's references to 'millionaires who cannot pronounce their aitches',[252] or to the imagined 'Comrade X', an old Etonian who 'would be ready to die on the barricades, in theory anyway, but [...] still leaves his bottom waistcoat button undone',[253] illustrate his perception that the patterns of individual behaviour which determined social placement were relatively inflexible.

H. G. Wells, who was an important formative influence on Orwell, explores the difficulties of altering an individual's social status throughout his work. In *Tono-Bungay*, for example, Teddy Ponderevo attempts to master the codes of the upper classes after he has made his fortune from 'Tono-Bungay', a patent medicine described by the narrator, his nephew, as 'mischievous trash, slightly stimulating, aromatic and attractive'.[254] Teddy insists,

> Got to the get the hang of etiquette [...] Horses even. Practise everything. Dine every night in evening-dress.... Get a brougham or something. Learn up golf and tennis and things. Country gentleman. Oh Fay.[255]

In this assessment, membership of the upper classes demands not only wealth, but also a command of certain knowledge and manners. Teddy, along with his wife and nephew, 'recognised our new needs as fresh invaders of the upper levels of the social system, and set ourselves quite consciously to the acquisition of Style and *Savoir Faire*'.[256] Kipps shares this desire for social elevation, and has the 'pervading ambition of the British young man to be, if not a "gentleman", at least mistakably like one'.[257] His inherited wealth, which is substantial if more modest that Ponderevo accumulates, does not itself provide this status. He is haunted by his

> secret trouble. He knew that he wanted refinement – culture. It was all very well – but he knew. But how was one to get it?[258]

The novel traces his attempt, and failure, to achieve 'refinement', to 'get with educated people who know 'ow to do things – in the regular proper way'.[259] The people from whom Kipps attempts to acquire this knowledge, in the main the Walsinghams and Chester Coote, are, significantly, less wealthy than himself. In both these instances, money is a necessary but insufficient foundation for social mobility. Cultural knowledge, or the ability to behave 'in the regular proper way', is also essential, and this is not simply or immediately produced by wealth.

The notion that society is structured by cultural as well as financial differences shapes *The Road to Wigan Pier*. The text is further complicated by the idea that class is both a system of classification and a basis of identity. Individuals, Orwell suggests, identify with other members of their class, with whom they share traditions, beliefs and values. These establish common forms of behaviour and interpretation, a distinctive culture or 'way of life'. Classes can therefore be analysed as distinct entities rather than collections of separate individuals. There are problems with this approach, and Raymond Williams argued that in 'thinking, from his position, of the working class primarily as a class, he assumed too readily the observation of particular working-class people was an observation of all working-class behaviour'.[260] This is implicit, for example, in his claim to describe the 'most typical section of the English working class'. The interpretation of classes as cohesive units is one way of resolving the problem of selection in documentary writing, as it implies that particular examples are 'representative' and can be used to legitimise broad conclusions. In contrast to the *Down and Out in Paris and London*, *The Road to Wigan Pier*, as Williams observed, recognises 'the realities and consequences of a class society'.[261] However, its emphasis upon the 'typical' also obscures difference, insofar as it suggests working-class cultures and communities are internally homogeneous.

The representation of urban, industrial workers as the representative section of their class does not simply enable a broader analysis of the condition of England than had been possible in *Down and Out in Paris and London*. It also, as previously observed, locates the text within a specific political debate. Marx and Engels argued that of 'all the classes which today oppose the bourgeoisie, the only truly revolutionary class is the proletariat'.[262] The proletariat consists of workers who have been organised for the purposes of modern capitalist production. This and their education, which is necessary for advanced methods of production, enable them to become conscious of their exploitation. It is the industrial sector, the most advanced part of the economy, that demands such organisation, and Marxist theory therefore focuses on the proletariat rather than, for example, agricultural workers. Lenin reinforced this point when he insisted that the ability to initiate a socialist revolution 'is possessed by the proletariat *alone* [...] first, because it is the strongest and most advanced class in civilised societies; secondly, because in the most developed countries it constitutes the majority of the population',[263] and is therefore in a position to impose its will. Orwell's account of the industrial working class in *The Road to Wigan Pier* consequently means that his work intersects with that of Marxist writers. His interpretations of this group are, however, distinct from those of 'orthodox' Communists. Firstly, he does not at this stage represent them as actively revolutionary. He emphasises their organisational ability and radical potential, but insists that during 'the past dozen years the English working class have grown servile with a rather horrible rapidity' due to the 'frightful weapon of unemployment'.[264] More importantly, he represents their culture and communities as a potential model for a future socialist society. His emphasis is therefore different from that of Marx and Engels, who focus primarily on the shared economic position and interests of the proletariat. Whilst they recognise the importance of working-class solidarity, organisation and rebellion against oppression, they also draw attention to the ways in which industrial wage-labour constrains individuals, preventing their development. They therefore warn against those who 'regard the proletarian as *gods*'. The proletariat is important not because of any present virtues, but because it experiences 'all the conditions of life of society today in their most inhuman form'. As a result, it has 'not only gained theoretical consciousness' of its oppression but through 'absolutely imperative *need* – the practical expression of *necessity* – is driven directly to revolt against this inhumanity'. This revolt abolishes '*all* the inhuman conditions of life of society today which are summed up in its own situation',[265] and establishes new social, economic, and political structures. The proletariat is central to Marxist thought not because it has achieved a better way of life under capitalism, but because it responds to its exploitation by emancipating society as a whole. It does not develop towards bourgeois models, as liberal theorists and commentators suggest, but redefines previous 'forms of consciousness'[266] and structures of production. Its present virtues lie primarily in its capacity for revolution.

In contrast, Orwell attaches considerable value to existing working-class culture. In a 1940 review of Jack Hilton's *English Ways*, for example, he argues that 'English working-class life in the late capitalist age' was 'a good civilisation while it lasted, and the people who grow up in it will carry some of their gentleness and decency into the iron ages that are coming' (12:202–4:204). In *The Road to Wigan Pier*, he similarly insists that

> it is *not* the triumphs of modern engineering, nor the radio, nor the cinematograph, nor the 5000 novels which are published yearly, nor the crowds at Ascot and the Eton and Harrow match, but the memory of working-class interiors – especially as I sometimes saw them in my childhood before the war, when England was still prosperous – that reminds me that our age has not been altogether a bad one to live in.[267]

These passages reveal some of the characteristics and complexities of his 'Myth of the Proletariat'. In the first place, they celebrate a 'civilisation' that is either lost or coming to an end. They illustrate Orwell's belief that, as Bernard Crick argues, 'a good and decent way of life already existed in tradition: an egalitarian or genuine post-revolutionary society would not transfigure values or expect them to be different (his anti-Marxism comes out here) but would simply draw on the past'.[268] This view of the Edwardian world of his 'childhood' is, of course, idealised, and obscures the hardship endured by many who inhabited such 'working-class interiors'. Nonetheless, the passage not only recognises a value in impoverished communities, but establishes a foundation for his critique of social conditions in the 1930s and 1940s. The belief that a 'good and decent way of life' exists enables Orwell to attack capitalism for preventing its attainment. In addition, as Crick suggests, it provides an image of future socialist society based not on abstractions or speculation, but on an established culture.

The Road to Wigan Pier constructs a powerful, selective myth of the industrial proletariat. As Campbell observes, this ignores 'manifestations of instability in the culture', such as the 'tension between the roughness of the ghettos and the respectability of the well-paid, skilled working class',[269] and produces instead an image of a relatively homogeneous strata of society. It does this, in part, by focusing on a particular group, male manual workers and especially miners. As Crick argues, although the 'miners were not sociologically typical, only symbolically', they nevertheless personified for Orwell 'both the fate and the hopes of the whole working class'.[270] Indeed, Irving Howe describes *The Road to Wigan Pier* as 'his classic report on the condition of the English miners'.[271] They are, as Campbell writes, 'the core of his chronicle',[272] and are 'mythologised' in the text 'as archetypal proletarian men'.[273] Orwell was not, of course, the only writer of the period to describe the miners in these terms, and for many others on the Left they were representatives of exploited labour as such. Their work was essential, but difficult, dangerous and ill-rewarded. They also had a well-established reputation for bravery, mutual support and political radicalism. As a result, they represented both the failure of capitalism and the forces that would overcome it. For Orwell, mining communities were, moreover, stable, cohesive structures, founded upon 'traditional' values, which provided their members with stable identities.

Orwell justifies his focus on the miners by emphasising the importance of their work. Their labour, he argues, is essential because almost 'everything we do, from eating an ice to crossing the Atlantic, and from baking a loaf to writing a novel, involves the use of coal, directly or indirectly'.[274] The miners are, therefore, 'second in importance only to the man who ploughs the soil'.[275] This vital work is, however, difficult and dangerous, as they are at constant risk from accidents such as rock falls and explosions. The miner and writer B. L. Coombes observes that 'danger is always lurking'[276] underground, and recalls that in 'one week' during the First World War, when there was intense pressure on coal production, 'I was completely buried on three occasions'.[277] It continued to be a dangerous profession during the 1930s. Indeed, Orwell calculated that 'if a miner's working life is forty years the chances are nearly seven to one against his escaping injury and not much more than twenty to one against his being killed outright'.[278] The considerable human cost of extracting coal was prominent in other texts written in the period, particularly those by left-wing writers. Harold Heslop, for example, describes the 'drenched, blood-vivid coal thrown into the domestic grates and the fire-holes of factories and ships',[279] and in Lewis

Jones' novel *We Live*, Len tells the son of Lord Cwmardy to see 'the blood on every pound-note you change, taste the battered bodies on every bit of food you eat, see the flesh sticking on the coal you burn'.[280] Even when there were no accidents, mining was a hard, physically demanding job. Orwell's account of his visit to a working mine, for example, concludes with the image of the 'poor drudges underground blackened to the eyes, with their throats full of coal dust, driving their shovels forward with arms and muscles of steel',[281] and Coombes similarly describes men working 'in a crushing darkness with sweat running down their backs to make their singlets like a wet cloth'.[282]

Despite the fact that the miners' work was difficult, dangerous and essential to society, however, it was poorly paid. The anonymous author of *Miners, Owners and Mysteries* argued that there was 'possibly, no really large industry paying low wages to such a large number of men as the coal industry'.[283] Orwell himself calculated that a miner's wage did not 'average more, perhaps slightly less, than two pounds a week'.[284] J. B. Priestley supports this figure, and adds that

> if your supply of coal depended on my walking several miles to a pithead, descending in a cage for half a mile, walking again to the dwindling tunnel where I had to work, then slogging away for about seven hours in that hell, all for something like two pounds a week, your grates would be empty.[285]

The miners were conspicuous victims of the economic crises that followed the First World War. During the war, the mines had been under government control. Disputes within the industry began almost immediately after they were returned to private hands on 31 March 1921. The following day, as Laybourn states, 'the coal owners locked out those miners who would not work at [...] lower rate of pay'.[286] Wages were forced down, and, as McKibbin writes, 'Almost alone among the working classes miners suffered real-wage losses between 1920 and 1923, which is why industrial relations in the coalfields were so bitter and sympathy for the miners so widespread.'[287] This pattern continued into the 1930s, when the industry suffered high levels of unemployment, with some 41.2 per cent of workers unemployed by 1932.[288] Rates in certain areas, such as South Wales, were considerably higher. The result was a continuous series of industrial disputes, the most prominent of which was the General Strike of 1926, which Laybourn describes as 'simply an attempt to support the miners against a wage reduction'.[289] As McKibbin observes, in 'seven years' during the 1920s, 'days lost by miners' strikes represented more than half the total number of days lost: in 1926, of the 162 million working days lost no less than 146.5 million were lost by miners, and of the remainder nearly all were lost by those who struck in sympathy with them'.[290] These conflicts, along with the strong tradition of unionisation amongst miners, gave them a reputation for political organisation and radicalism.

Orwell's representation of miners as the 'type of the manual worker', whose labour 'keeps us alive' despite our being 'oblivious of its existence',[291] therefore constructs a particular image of the proletariat. It insists upon the importance of their work and their poverty, their suffering and their solidarity. As Campbell argues, they are figured as both 'victim and hero',[292] and Orwell argues against their exploitation on moral rather than economic grounds. However, his use of miners as symbols of the proletariat as a whole means that *The Road to Wigan Pier* locates working-class culture, experience, and value in male manual workers. He consequently marginalises or even ignores other forms of work and poverty. For example, although, as Campbell observes, 'there were as many cotton workers in Wigan as miners, many of them women',[293] they are not represented in the text. In the same manner, while he observes that newspaper-canvassers also earn just 'two pounds a week' doing work 'so hopeless, so appalling I wondered how anyone could put up with such a thing when prison was a possible altern-ative', he does not regard them as working class. They are excluded not merely by the fact that they are often 'out-of-work clerks and commer-cial travellers',[294] and therefore rooted in lower-middle-class culture, but by a model of work that focuses on manual labour. Most signific-antly, Orwell marginalises the experience of women, whether working in industry or the home, a problem explored in detail in the next chapter.

Orwell was not the only writer of this period to argue that heavy manual work had a particular value. Indeed, this idea was integral to the complex network of beliefs and desires that led a variety of middle-class commentators to explore industrial areas. As Gary Cross wrote, the

> industrial Northern environment produced an honest proletariat, an inspiration for the soft, jaded Southerner. The act of observation expressed a complex of feelings – guilt, social concern, curiosity, and a search for the 'authentic' in the hardy North.[295]

Working-class writers themselves frequently argued that their labour had a particular value. J. H. Watson, for instance, insisted that the labourer, by virtue of his labour, has a dancing blood stream, a rich zest for life, denied to the sedentary worker. Always excepting genius, his life is of more value than, please God, what we call the brain worker; the clerk, typist, civil servant, teacher, and the commercial traveller.[296]

These ideas permeated left-wing culture in the thirties, to the extent that Willie Gallacher felt it necessary to inform Communist students in Cambridge who 'denigrated their own academic work' that 'it's point-less to run away to the factories'.[297] Orwell challenges the notion that 'the industrial work done in the North is the only "real" work',[298] and that 'in some subtle way I am an inferior person because I have never worked with my hands'.[299] This builds upon his resistance in *Down and Out in Paris and London* to the way 'we have made a sort of fetish of manual work'.[300] Nonetheless, despite this scepticism, the miners, as archetypal skilled manual labourers, are central to his myth of working-class culture. As the next chapter explains in detail, this forms part of his identification with a particular form of working-class socialism that is interwoven with well-established ideas of masculinity.

This focus upon the miners also shapes Orwell's representations of working-class communities. Mining areas were widely regarded as tightly integrated, and the anonymous author of *Miners, Owners and Mysteries* argued that

> Miners are clannish. This is natural, as collieries are most frequently situated away from large centres of population, and the colliery village or township is a social unit in which the miners' lodge, the clubs, and, in these days, the Welfare Hall are the gathering grounds for men who work dangerously underground, and who are born, educated, married and die, amongst a comparatively limited number of people in a comparatively small place.[301]

Orwell figures the inhabitants of such areas, and indeed of the industrial north of England as a whole, as forming close communities that provide secure identities to those within them. He insists that London

> is so vast that life there is solitary and anonymous. Until you break the law nobody will take any notice of you, and you can go to pieces as you could not possibly do in a place where you had neighbours who knew you. But in the industrial towns the old communal way

of life has not yet broken up, tradition is still strong and almost everyone has a family – potentially, therefore, a home.[302]

For Orwell, the persistence of 'traditional', strictly gendered roles reinforces this stable, though threatened, social structure. In the working-class family, he insists, 'it is the man who is the master, and not, as in a middle-class home, the woman or the baby'.[303] His famous image of an interior in which 'Father, in shirt-sleeves, sits in the rocking-chair at one side of the fire reading the racing finals, and Mother sits on the other with her sewing, and the children are happy with a pennorth of mint humbugs, and the dog lolls roasting himself on the rag mat', emphasises the 'sane and comely shape' of the household, its 'perfect symmetry'.[304] As Campbell observes, 'Not surprisingly, given the ideological universe he inhabited in interwar England, there is no sense in Orwell of the family as one of the sites of sexual division in the working class, because he takes the standpoint of men, not women.'[305] Instead, he represents it as a 'natural' structure, a belief founded on his broader assumptions about gender. This enables him to figure it as an essential source of value and model for broader forms of community. He also argues that the working class has retained an active commitment to the family that other social groups have lost. As Crick observes, he emphasises 'homely contentments and fraternal virtues which contrast vividly with both middle-class acquisitiveness, competitiveness and prosperity and with the restless power-hungry arrogance of the intellectuals'.[306] He insists, however, that these virtues are threatened by unemployment and even by rehousing projects. The new council estates, he argues, not only have higher rents, but an 'uncomfortable, almost prison-like atmosphere'[307] that undermines social networks. Nevertheless, he represents the working class as sustaining, even under adverse conditions, forms of community lost to the middle classes.

In constructing this 'Myth of the Proletariat', Orwell drew upon a variety of images and stereotypes, many of which remain influential. As Peter Gurney argues, there is, for example, a widespread belief that 'working-class community' was 'characterized by warm face-to-face social relationships between individuals, traditions of solidarity and mutuality strengthened by scarcity, and was firmly rooted in the local and the particular'.[308] A number of critics have exposed Orwell's relatively uncritical reproduction of such images in *The Road to Wigan Pier*. Hoggart, for example, argues that Orwell 'never quite lost the habit of seeing the working-classes through the cosy fug of an Edwardian

music-hall'.[309] The criticism implies a sentimental attachment to established stereotypes, particularly those prominent during Orwell's childhood. Hynes emphasises the importance of older social models to his
work. He argues that the 'political implications' of this

> are essentially conservative – just keep the working classes working,
> and they will be happy, happier than *we* are; and second, the secure
> and cheerful life that they live is one from which middle-class intel-
> lectuals are excluded – *we* can never be *them*, and *they* can never be
> *us*. The fictional tradition operating here is no longer the proletarian
> novel: this passage is in the Dickensian tradition of the sentimental
> poor.[310]

This view is supported by Muggeridge, who claims that 'his data was
derived much more from the *News of the World* and seaside picture
postcards – two of his ruling passions – and even from Dickens,
than from direct observation'.[311] Cunningham insists on his use of
still older tradition, and argues that Orwell discovered 'pastorals by
working-class firesides'.[312] As these statements illustrate, Orwell used
a variety of inherited images to represent the working class as practising communal values that provided a source of stability and content-
ment. Indeed, he argues that 'the manual worker, if he is in steady
work and drawing good wages – an "if" which gets bigger and bigger –
has a better chance of being happy than an "educated" man'.[313]
As Hynes observed, this implies that the worker is basically satis-
fied with 'his' position. It also emphasises, however, both the value
of working-class communities and social consequences of economic
hardship.

The representation of a distinctive working-class culture centred
around work and the family, however, excludes Orwell from the
communities that he admires. Firstly, he is unable to do the necessary
kind of work. In Paris, his position as a *plongeur* made him part of the
'floating population' of the 'Hôtel X'. In his description of the Wigan
miners, however, he writes that

> I am not a manual labourer and please God I never shall be one, but
> there are some kinds of manual work that I could do if I had to. At a
> pinch I could be a tolerable road-sweeper or an inefficient gardener
> or even a tenth-rate farm hand. But by no conceivable amount of
> effort or training could I become a coal-miner; the work would kill
> me in a few weeks.[314]

The problem, however, is not merely one of skill or physical strength, as he argues that 'You couldn't get a job as a navvy or a coal-miner even if you were equal to the work.'[315] There is a persistent cultural difference between Orwell, the middle-class narrator, and those he observes. In a famous passage he writes that

> For some months I lived entirely in coal-miners' houses. I ate my meals with the family, I washed at the kitchen sink, I shared bedrooms with miners, drank beer with them, played darts with them, talked to them by the hour together. But though I was among them, and I hope and trust they did not find me a nuisance, I was not one of them, and they knew it even better than I did.[316]

The difference is indissoluble. Despite his admiration for the working class, Orwell is simply 'not one of them', just as he equally simply is 'a bourgeois'. The complex network of practices and values that defines the communities he visits prevents his integration. It also undermines his position as a social explorer. The text represents him as neither an 'objective' reporter nor a temporary 'native', but an outsider shaped by a particular set of beliefs and values. He is a 'member of the bourgeoisie', albeit a 'down-at-heel member',[317] a 'degenerate modern semi-intellectual'[318] with 'middle-class origins'.[319] He cannot write 'as' a member of the working class, or as an 'objective', 'scientific' reporter, but only as a 'bourgeois' observer. The second half of the book, which Hoggart describes as 'partly cultural autobiography, partly opinionation about socialism by a man who had then a patchy idea of the nature of socialism',[320] provides a critical context for reading the reportage of the first. It exposes his background and beliefs, revealing the narrator as a figure defined by particular historical and social ideologies.

Hoggart argues that Orwell 'always respected certain characteristic virtues of his class, such as fairmindedness and responsibility'.[321] There is, however, little explicit discussion of these virtues in *The Road to Wigan Pier*, although they are illustrated elsewhere in his work.[322] Instead, he simply defends his right to follow the conventions of his class. He insists, for example, that

> I cannot proletarianise my accent or certain of my tastes and beliefs, and I would not if I could. Why should I? I don't ask anyone else to speak my dialect; why should anybody else ask me to speak his?[323]

This statement demonstrates an active, even aggressive desire to preserve his 'tastes and beliefs'. It also suggests that, in any case, they cannot be changed. This supports his claim that the 'manners and traditions' peculiar to each class 'generally persist from birth to death'[324] in its members. The idea that such traditions are not chosen by individuals obscures questions as to their value. It also suggests that an individual's class identity depends upon a series of internalised beliefs and patterns of behaviour that resist analysis and alteration.[325] The inherited characteristics that prevent Orwell from being perceived as 'one of' the miners, originate in his childhood, and, as such, are resistant to change. Indeed, they persist even in individuals, like the 'thrice-bankrupt drapers in the country towns', who have the same income as many members of the working class. This has significant political implications, as it undermines the idea that there can be any straightforward identification between classes.

This problem attracted considerable attention in the period. In what Cunningham describes as a 'famous passage'[326] of the *Manifesto of the Communist Party*, Marx and Engels appeared to offer a solution. They argued that as the contradictions in capitalism become increasingly obvious, 'a part of the bourgeoisie goes over to the proletariat, in particular, a part of the bourgeois ideologists who have worked out a theoretical understanding of the whole historical development'.[327] If, however, as Orwell insists, background determines even 'the characteristic movements of my body', this identification could only be theoretical, as relations between individual members of the middle class and working class would still be constrained by residual differences in their habits, attitudes and values. Indeed, he argues that this is illustrated by the fact that a 'bourgeois' socialist 'still habitually associates with his own class; he is vastly more at home with a member of his own class, who thinks him a dangerous Bolshie, than with a member of the working class who supposedly agrees with him; his tastes in food, wine, clothes, books, pictures, music, ballet, are still recognisably bourgeois tastes; most significantly of all, he invariably marries into his own class'.[328] T. R. Fyvel insisted that this was the case for Orwell himself, as 'more than half the later acquaintances with whom he rubbed along were fellow-Etonians or Jewish intellectuals, while the women he liked were pretty classy: not much going native there'.[329] This does not imply that members of different classes cannot like, appreciate, sympathise with, or even admire one another. Orwell insists that it 'is not a question of dislike or distaste, only of *difference*', but this 'is enough to make real intimacy impossible'.[330] As Gary Day argues, 'in contrast to other writers of the period' Orwell 'appreciates how the differences between the middle and the working class prohibit any real alliance between them'.[331] The distinctions between the classes, Orwell insists, cannot be 'shouted out of existence with a few scoutmasterish bellows of good will', because they are embedded in the detail of day-to-day life, in lived experience.

Orwell valued and even celebrated the working-class communities he visited in the north of England, despite knowing that he could not become part of them. In a letter to Cyril Connolly, dated 14 February 1936, for example, he writes that

> The miners here are very nice people, very warm-hearted & willing to take one for granted. I would like to stay a good long time in the North, 6 months or a year, only it means being away from my girl & also I shall have to come back & do some work after about a couple of months. (10:425–6:426)[332]

In *The Road to Wigan Pier* itself, he insists that the 'the Lancashire and Yorkshire miners treated me with a kindness and courtesy that were even embarrassing; for if there is one type of man to whom I do feel myself inferior, it is a coal-miner'.[333] The working-class home was central to his 'Myth of the Proletariat' and, thereby, to his wider political thought. His idealised images contrast with the impoverished households he actually visited and described, but illustrate the 'way of life' he believed socialism would establish. In particular, he represents a stable structure that provides its members with an identity, a basis for their individuality. A working-class home, Orwell insists, is 'a good place to be in, provided that you can not only be in it but sufficiently *of* it to be taken for granted',[334] but he is aware that he is 'not one of them', not '*of*' it. It is consequently a utopian location in which he cannot participate.

In the concluding chapter of *The Road to Wigan Pier*, Orwell insists that, as concerns,

> the terribly difficult issue of class-distinctions, the only possible policy for the moment is to go easy and not to frighten more people than can be helped. And above all, no more of those muscular-curate efforts at class-breaking. If you belong to the bourgeoisie, don't be too eager to bound forward and embrace your proletarian brothers; they may not like it, and if they show they don't like it you will probably find that your class-prejudices are not so dead as you imagined. And if you belong to the proletariat, by birth or in the sight of God,

don't sneer too automatically at the Old School Tie; it covers loyalties which can be useful to you if you know how to handle them.[335]

The passage proposes a collaboration between classes rather than an attempt to dissolve them, a policy that, he implies, is, in any case, not feasible in the immediate future. Indeed, the text exposes the ambiguous function of the class-system, which divides individuals from one another but produces the working-class communities he idealises. Orwell argues that he could not alter his 'bourgeois' values even if he wished to, but also questions whether the dissolution of class boundaries would be as positive as it might initially appear, arguing it might produce 'a bleak world in which all our ideals, our codes, our tastes – our "ideology" in fact – will have no meaning'.[336] For this reason, although 'We all rail against class-distinctions [. . .] very few people seriously want to abolish them.'[337] For the immediate future, he proposes instead a tolerant collaboration between these 'alien cultures',[338] a recognition of difference. The eventual solution, he implies, is the establishment of a socialist society. In arguing that 'there is some hope that when Socialism is a living issue, a thing large numbers of Englishman care about, the class-difficulty may solve itself more rapidly than now seems thinkable',[339] Orwell speculates that a socialist revolution would resolve the divisions and contradictions that his narrative exposes. This socialism would be founded upon the values of the working class, but would dissolve 'class-distinctions' without producing a 'bleak world' stripped of productive ideologies and identities. In the absence of such a revolution, he remains ambiguous as to whether any such dismantling of class is possible, or, indeed, even desirable.

2
Gender

I

In a letter to Brenda Stalker, dated 27 July 1934, Orwell wrote that

> I had lunch yesterday with Dr. Ede. He is a bit of a feminist and thinks that if a woman was bought up exactly like a man she would be able to throw a stone, construct a syllogism, keep a secret etc. He tells me that my anti-feminist views are probably due to Sadism! I have never read the Marquis de Sade's novels – they are unfortunately very difficult to get hold of. (10:344–5:344)

The passage is a characteristic example of Orwell's treatment of feminism and, indeed, of gender. The subject of his 'anti-feminist views' is introduced, but then trivialised and dismissed. He denies Dr Ede's accusation of 'Sadism', for example, simply but illogically, insisting that this is impossible as he has not read de Sade's work. The diversion enables him to evade the broader question of his view of women. This pattern, in which issues of gender and feminism are denigrated or ignored, is repeated throughout his work. In *Keep the Aspidistra Flying*, for instance, the exchange between Rosemary and Gordon on the subject is represented in the series of comic stereotypes that insist,

> Men are brutes and women are soulless, and women have always been kept in subjection and they jolly well ought to be kept in subjection, and look at the Patient Griselda and what about polygamy and Hindu widows, and what about Mother Pankhurst's piping days when every decent woman wore mousetraps on her garters and couldn't look at a man without feeling her right hand itch for a castrating knife.[1]

The essential irrelevance of the debate is confirmed in the authorial comment that

> Gordon's diatribes against women were in reality a kind of perverse joke; indeed, the whole sex-war is at bottom only a joke. For some reason it is great fun to pose as a feminist or an anti-feminist according to your sex.

The series of displacements, in which Gordon is first exonerated from serious intent before the subject itself is dismissed as absurd, obscures the content of the 'sex-war'. The relationship between the sexes is, however, paradoxically the focus of the novel. Gordon's insistence that women 'want a safe income and two babies and a semi-detached villa in Putney with an aspidistra in the window',[2] figures his revolt against the 'money-code' as an attempt to escape his conventional gender role. His rebellion is, in one sense, directed against the dominant social model of heterosexual marriage and male wage labour, the perceived obligation of a man to 'provide'. Indeed, at the end of the novel, marriage and paternity serve to relocate Comstock within the social structure he attempted to reject. His identity is, therefore, defined and redefined in terms of the dominant ideas of gender the text itself dismisses as irrelevant. As a result, the novel is the site of a repressed conflict between the authorial comments and other elements of the narrative. As Daphne Patai argues, it is an example of a text in which the 'authorial voice one hears through the third-person narrative thus comes to judgement at odds with the information made available by the text'.[3]

The simultaneous dismissal and enactment of the 'sex-war' is repeated throughout Orwell's writing. The process is founded upon the well-established ideas that gender is a 'natural' component of individual identity, and that men and women are separated by differences in their behaviour, perceptions, values and intellect.[4] This notion of essential masculine and feminine identities underpins the 'anti-feminist views' incorporated in the texts, which are exhibited in a number of interrelated representational strategies. In the first place, his female characters, with the prominent exception of Dorothy Hare, are marginal figures. As Rees argued, most are 'no more than sketches of features in the human landscape surrounding the hero'.[5] In *Coming Up for Air*, for example, Hilda Bowling functions primarily as a constraint upon her husband, and in particular his attempt to return to Lower Binfield. She is not merely peripheral to his rebellion against the 'slick and streamlined'[6] modern world, but, indeed, unaware of it, and he concludes upon returning that even if 'I spent a week explaining to Hilda *why* I'd been to Lower Binfield, she'd never understand.'[7] Hilda represents the world that George Bowling attempts to escape, or at least temporarily evade. Her innate conservatism, obsession with money and jealousy, however, are figured as the product, not only of her upbringing in one of the 'decayed middle-class families',[8] but also of her femininity. She is a caricature of the restrictive wife, located within what Patai terms the 'antiwife, long-suffering-husband routine of the Donald McGill comic postcards'.[9]

The description of Hilda Bowling incorporates various qualities, such as conservatism, that are figured as characteristically 'feminine'. This is one example of a recurrent process in which stereotypical images of women are used to naturalise particular conceptions of female 'character' that, amongst other things, legitimise their peripheral position in the texts. This process also operates in reverse, as conventional images of active, productive men are mobilised to produce a stable, valued model of 'manliness'. Individual characters do not, of course, always conform to these roles. Gordon Comstock, for example, as previously noted, rejects the form of middle-class masculinity that he associates with providing for a family, and attaining 'some beastly little semi-detached villa in Putney, with Drage furniture and a portable radio and an aspidistra in the window'.[10] His insistence that in a restaurant a 'man pays for a woman, a woman doesn't pay for a man',[11] however, indicates a persistence of these traditional values, which reassert themselves at the conclusion of the novel. The categories of masculine and feminine themselves, in this as in other instances, are retained in spite of individual refusal or failure to adhere to them. Indeed, Patai argues that they underpin Orwell's criticisms of social structures and institutions. In *The Road to Wigan Pier*, for example, the form of Utopian socialism founded upon industrial progress is characterised by Orwell as a desire to make the world 'safe and soft',[12] so that, Patai insists, it appears 'as female – it is soft, enveloping, emasculating'.[13] This is implicitly contrasted to valued 'masculine' qualities such as 'strength, courage, generosity, etc.',[14] exhibited, for example, in mining communities. The association of the feminine with the 'soft' and 'passive' provides a representational structure for an attack on a mechanical 'mass-culture'.

The model of gender employed by Orwell is, therefore, the basis of a network of images, associations and values that are exploited for a variety of critical purposes. This use of these ideas of the 'masculine' and the 'feminine' is, however, not peculiar to his work. Indeed, this chapter argues that in using these categories to structure and legitimise his criticisms of the established order, Orwell aligns himself with a widespread form of socialism that perceived capitalist society as restricting or even violating masculinity. The analysis of his representation of gender is consequently divided into two parts. The first examines the use of categories of 'masculine' and 'feminine' in his work. It not only explores some of the ways in which these concepts are established, replicated and deployed, but also the moments in his work when their stability is undermined. The second section is concerned with how these ideas relate to those developed in other texts of the period. This approach locates his texts within their historical context and reveals the close parallels between Orwell's work and that of other writers who integrated 'traditional' patriarchal ideas into their critique of advanced capitalism. It does not 'exonerate' Orwell, but instead explores the political function of his concepts of 'masculinity' and 'femininity'. By analysing his texts' manipulation of certain pervasive forms of rhetoric, the chapter exposes the importance of established models of gender to much of the 'radical' culture of the 1930s. It therefore focuses, not simply upon individual prejudice or 'failure', but the broader issue of the ways in which much left-wing writing of the period reproduced, and in fact used, patriarchal categories and values.

Orwell's 'anti-feminist views' are prominently illustrated in his representation of female characters as committed to the established social order. The novels feature numerous conservative women. In *Nineteen Eighty-Four*, Winston Smith considers, on seeing Julia, that it 'was always the women, and above all the young ones, who were the most bigoted adherents of the Party, the swallowers of slogans, the amateur spies and nosers-out of unorthodoxy'.[15] This adherence to the established values is not, of course, restricted to Oceania. In *Coming Up for Air*, for example, Hilda's 'feeling that you *ought* to be perpetually working yourself up into a stew about lack of money'[16] not only prevents her from having 'any kind of joy in life, any kind of interest in things for their own sake',[17] but demonstrates a commitment to what is described in *Keep the Aspidistra Flying* as the 'money-code'.[18] This places pressure upon her husband, and Bowling represents himself as 'one of them with the boss twisting his tail and the wife riding him like the nightmare and the kids sucking his blood like leeches',[19] an individual oppressed by the demands of employer and spouse who together restrict him to the position of an exploited provider. The association of women with the 'money-code' is also demonstrated in *Burmese Days*, in which Elizabeth Lackersteen is described as one for whom 'the Good ("lovely" was her name for it) is synonymous with the expensive, the elegant, the aristocratic; and the Bad ("beastly") is the cheap, the low, the shabby, the laborious'.[20] Elizabeth's association of the moral and economic makes her indifferent to other criteria of worth. Her eventual position as the wife of Mr Macgregor and a typical 'burra memsahib' is the result of this commitment to dominant economic and social hierarchies. She is a representative of British imperialism, indifferent to local culture and a woman whose 'servants live in terror of her, though she speaks no Burmese'. Indeed, she enforces social divisions within the Anglo-Indian community itself, aided by an 'exhaustive knowledge of the Civil List'.[21] These characteristics are in part the result of her indoctrination in 'a very expensive boarding-school',[22] but are also represented as the product of an inherent and implicitly 'feminine' conservatism. Her eventual position is, the text insists, one 'for which Nature had designed her from the first'.[23] She is, moreover, only one of a number of female characters figured as responsible for the perpetuation of restrictive social systems. In *Keep the Aspidistra Flying*, Gordon interprets Rosemary and his sister Julia as being in 'feminine league against him' in their efforts to persuade him to 'go back to the New Albion'[24] and accept the values against which he has rebelled.

The eventual position of Elizabeth Lackersteen as a typical 'burra memsahib', however, is not only a result of her character, but of her sexual vulnerability. As an English tutor for the children of a bank manager in Paris, she finds herself 'struggling and struggling to keep' his 'ferret-like hand away from her'.[25] In Burma, she is subject to more serious assaults from her uncle, culminating in an occasion on which he 'celebrated his return to the house by manoeuvring Mrs Lackersteen out of the house, coming into Elizabeth's bedroom and making a spirited attempt to rape her'.[26] His sexual aggression make her aware of her precarious position, that she 'was penniless and had no home except her uncle's house'. In this context, marriage provides a measure of protection. She concludes that

> Whatever happened, she had got to escape from her uncle's house, and that soon. Yes, undoubtedly she would marry Flory when he asked her![27]

In the end, it is, of course, Mr Macgregor rather than Flory who actually provides an escape from Mr Lackersteen, who is 'pestering Elizabeth unceasingly', restrained only by her threat to 'tell her aunt; happily, he was too stupid to realize that she would never dare do it'.[28] The stable, recognised protection of a specific, and in this instance, prestigious man, is one practical method of resisting general male sexual aggression and establishing a definite position in society. This pragmatic compromise with the dominant system illustrates a broader process identified by Andrea Dworkin, who argues that women 'fight for meaning just as women fight for survival: by attaching themselves to men and the values honored by men'.[29] Urmila Seshagiri's claim that Elizabeth is a 'willing recipient of sexual assault'[30] is a misreading of the text, obscuring the extent to which it is her resistance to such an assault that determines her manoeuvring within the 'Indian marriage-market'.[31] The narrator's claim that her conservatism is the result of her 'Nature' is therefore undermined by the details of the text which imply that it is instead a response to her precarious position within the imperial community, and, indeed, patriarchal society. In this, as in other instances, there is a productive division between the 'authorial voice' and the 'information made available by the text'.

The idea of a 'feminine' conservatism makes opposition to the established order, by implication, a 'masculine' prerogative. Even on those occasions in the texts when women do escape this association, the form of their revolt is, in contrast to their male counterparts, determined by their gender. In *Nineteen Eighty-Four*, for example, Julia's rebellion is primarily sexual, in contrast to Winston's more intellectual opposition. She is, in Winston's words, as 'a rebel from the waist downwards', and the narrator observes that in 'the ramifications of Party doctrine she had not the faintest interest'.[32] This is demonstrated when she falls asleep as Winston reads aloud from 'the book' attributed to Goldstein. Fredric Warburg commented, in his initial report on the novel, that

> It is a typical Orwellism that Julia falls asleep while Winston reads part of the book to her. (Women aren't intelligent in Orwell's world.)[33]

Julia's rebellion is founded upon her promiscuity, which contravenes the sexual prohibitions of the Party demonstrated, for example, in the 'Junior Anti-Sex League'[34] for whom she does 'voluntary' work. Her belief that 'You wanted a good time; "they", meaning the Party, wanted to stop you having it; you broke the rules as best you could'[35] is the inverse of Katherine's commitment to Party doctrines governing sexual relations, but in both instances the character of the women is defined in terms of their sexual practice. Julia is, by her own admission, 'not clever', and 'didn't much care for reading'.[36] For Anthony Easthope, she is a figure of masculine fantasy, not unlike Honeychile in Fleming's *Dr No*, the tomboy stereotype of woman, less rational, less conscientious, less aware, less committed to culture, less concerned with absolute truth.[37]

This insistence that Orwell represents women as 'less rational' is paralleled in Leslie Tentler's statement that he figures 'Real women' as 'submissive, giving, nonintellectual'.[38] Indeed, the idea that Julia is 'nonintellectual' is a component of even Rees' more positive description of her as 'intelligent but completely unintellectual, determined, practical, unscrupulous, capable of generosity but rather narrowly single-minded'.[39]

The most important intellectual relationship of the novel is, as a consequence, that between two men, Winston Smith and O'Brien. Indeed, Patai argues that this is the focus of the text, and that 'Winston's true alliances are clear from the beginning of the novel: He hates, fears and desires Julia and is unambivalently drawn to O'Brien.'[40] The conventional association of women with emotional rather than rational motivations means that Julia's rebellion is peripheral and limited in scope. This does not, of course, mean that it is valueless, and indeed Newsinger insists that 'Orwell makes through Julia a powerful declaration for sexual liberation.'[41] It is, however, constrained by a particular concept of the 'feminine'. The perception that Julia's revolt is limited and does not have a firm intellectual foundation is implicitly shared by Winston himself, who accepts, or at least does not question O'Brien's statement that

> She betrayed you Winston, immediately – unreservedly. I have seldom seen anybody come over to us so promptly.[42]

The main intellectual exchange of the text is that between the two men, and Julia is consequently silenced, not just by the Party, but by the novel itself.

The peripheral status of female rebellion in *Nineteen Eighty-Four* can be explored by comparing the text with one of its sources, Yevgeny Zamyatin's *We*. In contrast to Julia, I-330, the heroine of *We*, formulates an intellectual, emotional and sexual opposition to the state she inhabits. In the homogenous, mechanised 'OneState', I-330 insists upon individuality and diversity, arguing that

> A person is like a novel. Up to the very last page you don't know how it's going to end. Otherwise there'd be no point in reading...[43]

In contrast to the principle male character, D-503, who accepts the official principle that 'to assert that "I" has certain "rights" with respect to the State is exactly the same as asserting that a gram weighs the same as a ton',[44] I-330 emphasises the importance of personal integrity, a quality she demonstrates in both her political analysis and activism. She raises her hand in opposition on the Day of Unanimity, speaks to those at the Mephi meeting beyond the Green Wall, and is present in the 'radio telephone room' of the INTEGRAL, 'like one of the ancient Valkyries'.[45] In *Nineteen Eighty-Four*, Julia is a function of Winston's attempted opposition to Big Brother. In *We*, it is I-330 who is the focus of the rebellion against OneState, destabilising the boundaries that D-503 cannot transgress, or, indeed, comprehend.

We both uses and transforms qualities associated with the 'feminine', such as fluidity and emotion, mobilising them in opposition to the instrumental rationality of OneState.[46] I-330 is the figure of a suppressed diversity, and the inexplicable pattern of her appearance and disappearance itself illustrates her emancipation from the 'Table of Hours' imposed by the State. Indeed, even maternity is integrated in the female opposition to mechanical rationalism. For O-90, for example, pregnancy is a form of illicit plenitude, and she insists that

I'm so happy, so happy. . . . I'm full you see. Full up to the brim![47]

D-503 interprets her contravention of the imposed program of reproduction as a criminal offence, as 'there's no difference between a woman that gives birth illegally—O—and a murderer, and that madman who dared aim his poem at OneState',[48] but he himself later desires an independent relationship with his mother that would legitimise his personal experience. He wishes for

a mother, the way the ancients had. I mean my *own* mother. And if for I could be – not the Builder of the INTEGRAL, and not the number D-503, and not a molecule of OneState, but just a piece of humanity, a piece of her own self – trampled, crushed, outcast.[49]

The relationship between mother and child is interpreted as an alternative to the forms of commitment authorised to the State, which are designed to efface individual difference. Indeed, the violent suppression of this relationship emphasises its subversive potential. The desire for maternity, punishable by the 'Benefactor's Machine',[50] is figured as integral to the principles of individual love and personal responsibility promoted by I-330. The decision to protect O-90 from OneState is therefore a political act.

The rebellion of women against OneState is, of course, not only located in their status as potential mothers. I-330 acts in direct opposition to the 'Benefactor', and indeed in so doing demonstrates a physical courage conventionally represented as peculiar to men. At the close of the novel, for example, she is tortured by the administrators of OneState:

> When they started pumping the air out of the Bell, she threw her head back, and half closed her eyes and pressed her lips together, which reminded me of something. She was looking at me, holding on tight to the arms of the chair, until her eyes closed completely. They pulled her out, quickly bought her to with the help of electrodes, and put her back under the Bell. This happened three times, and she still didn't say a word.

The silence, contrasted with the actions of 'Others that they brought in with that woman',[51] emphasises her commitment to her principles. In *Nineteen Eighty-Four*, O'Brien insists that Julia, whose rebellion is 'instinctive', submits under torture 'immediately – unreservedly'. I-330 is a conscious revolutionary who constructs a positive alternative to the mechanical logic of OneState. This opposition deploys 'feminine' qualities, such as plurality, the maternal bond and instinctive action, but does not, however, represent these as restrictive. In contrast to Julia's rebellion, which is limited by a conventional model of female behaviour, I-330 develops a broader politics that transforms but does not abandon the notion of distinct feminine strengths.

In *Homage to Catalonia*, his most sustained account of revolution, Orwell, however, associates resistance to oppression with masculinity. There were, he notes,

> still women serving in the militias, though not very many. In the early battles they had fought side by side with the men as a matter of course.

'Traditional' gender roles are, however, reinforced as the military situation stabilises, and Orwell observes that only a few months after the outbreak of war women who remained in the militias had to be drilled in isolation from the men 'because they laughed at the women and put them off'.[52] His account of Spain constructs the image of a male community produced by the shared experience of hardship. Warfare, in this account, reinforces a conventional ideal of masculinity, founded upon qualities such as physical courage and endurance. This is implicitly offered as a basis upon which to assess the actions of the narrator himself. Orwell records that when he first faces enemy bullets, for example,

> Alas! I ducked. All my life I had sworn that I would not duck the first time a bullet passed over me; but the movement appears to be instinctive, and almost everybody does it at least once.[53]

A similar experience follows his first exposure to heavy fire, when he notes that 'to my humiliation I found out that I was horribly frightened'.[54]

The emphasis upon physical courage figures the conflict as, in part, a trial of masculinity. In his description of an attack on a Fascist trench, Orwell states that

> I took it for granted that there would be a Fascist waiting for me at the top. If he fired at that range he could not miss me, and yet somehow I never expected him to fire, only to try for me with his bayonet. I seemed to feel in advance the sensation of our bayonets crossing, and I wondered whether his arm would be stronger than mine.[55]

In the event, there is, of course, 'no Fascist waiting'.[56] However, the repeated interpretation of actions in terms of 'masculine' qualities such as strength, courage and endurance, figures the war as an example of what Cunningham describes as the 'Test'.[57] The term is taken from Isherwood's *Lions and Shadows*, in which the narrator describes the 'Test of your courage, of your maturity, of your sexual prowess: "Are you really a Man?"'[58] The idea was also used by Auden, who questioned, in 'Ode (to my pupils)', 'Are you taking care of yourself, are you sure of passing/The endurance test?'[59] This trial is, Isherwood insists, founded upon the 'complex of terrors and longings connected with the idea "War"',[60] specifically the First World War, which his generation had lived through but not fought in. Indeed, Auden's poem also features the image of 'Daddy/Far away fighting'.[61] As Cunningham argues, Spain was an important site for the exploration of this obsession, as when 'the Spanish Civil War broke out many of the young [...] seized on it as the chance to catch up with their fathers, their older brothers and the dead Old Boys, to wipe out their guilt over having missed the First War'.[62]

The comparison between the two conflicts is made repeatedly throughout Orwell's account of the war in Spain. When he arrives at the front line, for example, he notes that

> In secret I was frightened. I knew the line was quiet at present, but unlike most of the men about me I was old enough to remember the Great War, though not old enough to have fought in it. War, to me, meant roaring projectiles and skipping shards of steel; above all it meant mud, lice, hunger and cold.[63]

This is paralleled in 'My Country Right or Left', in which he describes the war as 'a bad copy of 1914–18, a position war of trenches, artillery, raids, snipers, mud, barbed wire, lice and stagnation' (12:269–72:271). In Spain, Orwell identifies himself, not only with the masculine ideal of the partially militarised culture he was raised in,[64] or that of the militia, but also with those who died at the Somme and Ypres. Indeed, Rees insists that Orwell, when speaking 'of the first world war', said that 'his generation must be marked for ever by the humiliation of not having taken part in it'.[65] This image of guilt at having not 'taken part', and interpretation of service in Spain as a compensation for it, is paralleled in the notes Orwell made for a novel to be called *The Quick and the Dead*. In these, he wrote that

> Suddenly H. knows that the war is going on, that people older & more responsible than he are fighting it & think is supremely important to win it. He has a sudden terrible vision of the life of the trenches going on & on while he & his kind are [...] safe in the background & forget that the war is happening. His death in Spain in 1937 is the direct result of this vision. (15:361–7:366)

These examples provide a context within which to interpret his representations of the war in Spain. In the first place, they suggest that for Orwell the war was a 'Test' of whether he was 'really a Man'. In addition, they link this 'Test' to the pivotal event for Britain in early twentieth century, the First World War, which devastated a generation of men only a few years older than Orwell. As Martin Green argues, 'the dead were most of the starry spirits of the generation born between 1890 and 1900, the leaders and the elder brothers of those who survived',[66] and the image of these 'older & more responsible' men haunted the generation writing in the 1930s. Henry Green, for example, wrote that 'I had a feeling it is hard to explain almost as though I had missed something through being too young to fight'.[67] The experience of war was, in particular, a proof of masculinity, and Orwell insists that 'You felt yourself a little less than a man, because you had missed it' (12:270).

Homage to Catalonia figures the war in Spain as providing a version of this experience, and thereby a connection to the 'leaders and elder brothers' who formed a prevalent image of authentic 'manhood'. The notion that the militias were masculine communities is, however, undermined by the periodic presence in the text of revolutionary women, some of whom have been directly involved in the fighting. Orwell writes, for example, that it 'was rather humiliating that I had to be shown how to put on my new leather cartridge-boxes by a Spanish girl, the wife of Williams, the other English militiaman'. The woman disrupts the image of fixed gender roles, as, although she is 'a gentle, dark-eyed, intensely feminine creature who looked as though her life-work was to rock a cradle', she has 'fought bravely in the street-battles of July'. Her experience of active revolution contradicts the notion of an inherent female passivity or conservatism. The 'girl' is 'intensely feminine', and indeed is 'carrying a baby which was born just ten months after the outbreak of war and had perhaps been begotten behind a barricade',[68] but her participation in the revolution modifies the traditional associations of both femininity and motherhood. This perceived transformation is, however, partially contained, insofar as it is interpreted as a result of the unusual conditions in socialist Spain. Orwell states that the girls living in a village near to Huesca, for example, were 'splendid vivid creatures with coal-black hair, a swinging walk, and a straightforward, man-to-man demeanour which was probably a by-product of the revolution'.[69] The description retains the categories of 'masculine' and 'feminine' insofar as it links the development of active, 'straightforward' behaviour to a 'man-to-man demeanour'. However, it also undermines the idea of an essential connection between 'female' and 'feminine' and holds out the possibility that a socialist revolution will transform, amongst other things, traditional gender roles.

The defence of the revolution in Spain is nonetheless identified in *Homage to Catalonia* with the masculine virtues, exhibited, in particular, in the male-dominated militias. The men who serve in these are therefore represented as 'real' men, and, as such, as figures of particular value. Even the 'battered face' of the Italian militiaman Orwell meets in the Lenin Barracks in Barcelona, for example, is described in 'Looking Back on the Spanish War' as 'Purer than any woman's!' (13:497–511:510). The periodic recognition that women had active roles in the revolution, however, dislocates the interpretation of it as the product of masculine values. Women, the text observes, were excluded from combat roles as the 'Popular Army' became dominant, and those who continued to serve in the militia frequently worked in traditional 'feminine' roles, as in the case of the 'militiamen's wives who did the cooking'[70] at the barracks. The 'Spanish girl', however, who is a more competent soldier than the narrator, illustrates an alternative image of the war, which destabilises the idea of heroism as a male prerogative.

The image of the woman holding a child who 'had perhaps been begotten behind a barricade' integrates motherhood in the image of revolution. In most instances, however, the mothers represented in the texts are used to reinforce the idea of 'natural' female behaviour. In *Nineteen Eighty-Four*, for example, Winston, when thinking of his mother, 'did not suppose, from what he could remember of her, that she had been an unusual woman, still less an intelligent one; and yet she possessed a kind of nobility, a kind of purity, simply because the standards that she obeyed were private ones'.[71] Her instinctive protection of her children, even at moments when this protection is irrational, because ineffective, is compared to the refugee mother in the propaganda film who 'had also covered the little boy with her arm, which was no more use against bullets than a sheet of paper'.[72] The texts encode an ideal of the mother as protective, devoted and content with the domestic sphere. This is most obvious in *Coming Up for Air*, in which George Bowling remembers his mother as 'a great splendid protecting kind of creature, a bit like a ship's figurehead and a bit like a broody hen'.[73] In this, as in other instances, maternal behaviour is held to be instinctive, rather than conscious. The mother provides the child with a safe environment and unconditional love, but does not determine his personal, and in particular his intellectual development. Bowling insists that his own mother 'was unbelievably ignorant',[74] and that 'I realised this even by the time I was ten years old.'[75] The development of male consciousness, as a consequence, involves a movement from the 'feminine' domestic realm to 'masculine' social networks.

Mothers are positive figures in the texts insofar as they provide the child with unconditional love and support. The 'protecting' mother, however, also acts as a constraint. Bowling, for example, insists that, 'According to Mother, everything that a boy wants to do was "dangerous".'[76] The text represents his development as dependent upon the evasion of maternal control. As Patai argues, for 'George Bowling, growing up meant escaping from his mother's petty domain.'[77] He describes this in terms of a movement away from the house, and indeed when he recalls his first day with the male gang to which his brother belongs, he states 'Thank God I'm a man, because no woman ever has that feeling.'[78] The 'escape' from the female spheres of the household, and 'dame-school' run by the Mother Howlett, 'an old impostor and worse than useless as a teacher',[79] results in a sensation of individual power. Bowling describes it as the moment when 'I knew that I wasn't a kid any more, I was a boy at last', the moment, in other words, when his gender is asserted, and becomes a dominant component of his identity. The transition is enacted in a series of violent acts that confirm his position within the 'gang', and realised in the 'strong, rank feeling, a feeling of knowing everything and fearing nothing', which is 'all bound up with breaking rules and killing things'.[80] His new, gendered identity is, moreover, social, as it is produced by his involvement with the 'Black Hand' gang, who 'broke windows, chased cows, tore knockers off doors and stole fruit by the hundredweight'.[81] The description of these activities parallels Simone de Beauvoir's description of male childhood development, in which she insists that

> The great advantage enjoyed by a boy is that his mode of existence in relation to others leads him to assert his subjective freedom. His apprenticeship for life consists in free movement towards the outside world; he contends in hardihood and independence with other boys, he scorns girls. Climbing trees, fighting with his companions, facing them in rough games, he is aware of his body as a means for dominating nature and as a weapon for fighting; he takes pride in his muscles as in his sex; in games, sports, fights, challenges, trials of strength, he finds a balanced exercise of his powers; at the same time he absorbs the severe lessons of violence; he learns from an early age to take blows, to scorn pain, to keep back the tears. He undertakes, he invents, he dares.[82]

The 'Black Hand' is the mechanism of precisely such a process of socialisation. His participation in the gang enables a movement from 'kid' to 'boy' that is pivotal to his production of an independent masculine consciousness.

The memories of Lower Binfield that Bowling presents, however, are ambiguous, open to alternative interpretation. The journey to Lower Binfield, in which Bowling attempts unsuccessfully to reconstruct a coherent, stable town within the amorphous city it has become symbolises, amongst other things, his failed efforts to organise and establish the boundaries of his memories. This excess of meaning in the text, its encoding of alternative narratives, is illustrated by the 'Black

Hand' gang itself. He remembers the group as exuberant, if destructive, and their excursions, in which they 'managed to make a nuisance of themselves',[83] as the product of their developing strength. The name 'Black Hand', however, is also that of the Serbian group responsible for training Gavrilo Princip and the others involved in the assassination of Archduke Ferdinand. The connection implies a continuum between 'childish' destruction and the adult violence sanctioned by states or by ideologies such as nationalism. The parallel is all the more significant because Bowling and others in the gang serve in the First World War, for which Princip's actions were the catalyst. When he returns home for his mother's funeral, on a visit that gives him a 'last glimpse' of his childhood home, he discovers that

> Sid Lovegrove was dead, killed on the Somme. Ginger Watson, the farm lad who'd belonged to the Black Hand years ago, the one who used to catch rabbits alive, was dead in Egypt.[84]

The use of the name 'Black Hand', therefore, questions the 'innocence' of the childhood allegiances, implying that the forms of identification these produce can be mobilised later in life for destructive purposes. It also, of course, undermines the idea that Bowling controls the 'meaning' of his narrative, exposing instead its unresolved tensions and ambiguities.

Coming Up for Air traces a process of masculine development that emphasises, in particular, the importance of male communities, which reinforce the identities of their individual members. In adult characters, however, ideas of 'masculine' and 'feminine' are also located and reproduced in the relations between the sexes. The descriptions of sexual intercourse in particular reinforce the image of a 'passive' female and 'active' male. In *Coming Up for Air*, for example, Bowling describes Elsie, as 'deeply feminine, very gentle, very submissive, the kind that would always do what a man told her'.[85] In their first sexual encounter, Winston similarly perceives Julia as 'utterly unresisting, he could do what he liked with her'.[86] The image is also employed in *Keep the Aspidistra Flying*, when Gordon asks Rosemary if she will 'Let me do what I want with you?'[87] It is even used in *Burmese Days* in the description of the relationship between Flory and Ma Hla May, who had 'been bought from her parents two years ago, for three hundred rupees',[88] when she 'lay and let him do as he wished with her'.[89] The repeated image figures sexual intercourse as an exhibition, and therefore consolidation, of male will.

The image is not, however, peculiar to Orwell. In a report on Worktown produced by Mass-Observation, an anonymous source reports that it *'takes some time to do anything you like with a girl, if it is possible – which it generally is'.*[90] In all these instances, masculinity is continually enacted upon the passive female body. As Judith Butler argues, 'gender proves to be performative – that is, always constituting the identity it is purported to be'.[91] The female body is an important site in which the biological male is naturalised as 'masculine'. The process, however, depends upon repetition, a continued sexual 'performance'. As a result, the female body becomes the paradoxical locus of male identity. This is implicit, for example, in the description, in *Last Cage Down*, of the relationship between Betty and the James Cameron. Cameron, the local miners' leader, reflects,

> Did he love her? That had never occurred to him. She was a likeable lass, one with whom a man could become a man because she was essentially a woman possessed of the rich virtues and treasures of a woman.[92]

Cameron's masculinity is, therefore, dependent upon his active heterosexuality, and, as a consequence, ultimately upon the female body.

The emphasis upon sexual intercourse as the transformation of the passive female body is reinforced by the emphasis upon procreation, and, in consequence, the opposition to contraception. The latter is a consistent element of the texts, although its precise basis varies. In *Coming Up for Air*, for example, Bowling criticises the modern economy, and by extension the modern world which produces 'portable radios, life-insurance policies, false teeth, aspirins, French letters and concrete garden rollers',[93] locating contraceptives amongst the other 'superfluous' products of a mass culture. In *The Road to Wigan Pier*, 'birth-control fanatics' are grouped with 'Marxists chewing polysyllables' and 'escaped Quakers'[94] as examples of inauthentic middle-class socialists, obsessed with technological progress. In *Keep the Aspidistra Flying*, however, birth-control is used as a symbol of the limitations imposed on the 'natural' desires of the poor. After he and Rosemary are unable to have sex in the countryside, because he has not brought contraceptives, Gordon exclaims,

> Money again! Even in the most secret action of your life you don't escape it; you've still got to spoil everything with filthy, cold-blooded precautions for money's sake.

For Gordon, avoiding pregnancy is a financial decision, and he insists to Rosemary that 'You'd *want* the baby if it wasn't for that.' The 'birth control business', in his interpretation, is 'just another way they've found out of bullying us'.[95] He persists in this attitude, and when he and Rosemary do consummate their relationship they do not use contraception. Gordon's return to 'decent, fully human life'[96] is both caused and symbolised by the resultant pregnancy. He represents the embryonic child as 'a bit of himself – indeed it *was* himself',[97] and the 'guarded seed, his baby'[98] enables him to assume a position in the 'stream of life'.[99]

The opposition to contraception exhibited in *The Road to Wigan Pier* was criticised by Victor Gollancz, who wrote, in his foreword to the Left Book Club edition, that

> In the first part of the book Mr Orwell paints a most vivid picture of wretched rooms swarming with children, and clearly becoming more and more unfit for human habitation the larger the family grows: but he apparently considers anyone who wishes to enlighten people as to how they can have a normal sexual life without increasing this misery as a crank! The fact, of course, is that there is no more 'commonsensical' work than that which is being done at the present time by the birth-control clinics up and down the country – and common sense, as I understand it, is the antithesis of crankiness.[100]

A similar resistance to methods of birth-control, however, was widespread in working-class communities themselves. As Roberts observed, 'Artificial checks on conception could be bought as early as the 1820s and rubber vaginal caps from 1881', yet in many working-class bedrooms, save for *coitus interruptus* 'any artificial interference with the will of God aroused nothing but abhorrence'.[101] Numerous texts written in the period nevertheless emphasise the problems unwanted pregnancies caused for working-class families and particularly, of course, working-class women. The results could be tragic. In *A Scots Quair*, for example, Chris Guthrie's mother Jean tells her husband *'Four of a family's fine; there'll be no more'*, only for him to insist that *'We'll have what God in His mercy may send to us, woman.'*[102] She later commits suicide, and the inquest reveals that she 'poisoned herself, her and the twins, because she was pregnant again and afraid with a fear dreadful and calm and clear-eyed'.[103] Working-class women who wished to avoid or terminate pregnancies often had few options, however, and chemically induced abortions were common. Oxley, for instance, wrote that 'I know plenty of women [...] who dreaded too virile a relationship and discussed among themselves methods of abortion which were almost suicidal', including one who induced a miscarriage by 'drinking hot stout and washing soda' and another who 'almost killed herself with a concoction of gin and nutmeg'.[104] This description is echoed in Walter Greenwood's *There Was a Time*, in which Mrs Boarder describes how a neighbour has drunk 'Bottle after bottle of pennyroyal' in an effort to induce a termination as she has 'Eleven of 'em, and now another, and him only bringing home eighteen shillings a week when he can get it'.[105] In *Jew Boy*, Olive, when pregnant, not only 'had a hot plunge every morning, as hot as she could bear', but also 'walked to work, ran up and down stairs, lifted heavy weights, dosed herself with Epsom salts', in spite of all which the 'seed still flourished in her womb'.[106] Indeed, Patricia Knight argues that, before 1914, abortion was 'probably the most prevalent form of contraception for working-class women'.[107] Mechanical contraception was relatively expensive compared with the drugs commonly used to induce abortion, and there was considerable confusion about, as well as resistance to, birth control, especially amongst the poor. As late as 1949, Mass-Observation concluded that, of those surveyed '26% of those earning less than £3 a week, are apparently ignorant of birth control'.[108] Despite the awareness of the economic problems caused by unplanned births, and the dangers of illegal abortions, there was nevertheless widespread opposition to contraception. In part this was attributed to the fact that, as Richard Hoggart wrote, 'Husbands tend not to like sheaths – "they take away the pleasure" '.[109] Indeed, even in Sillitoe's *Saturday Night and Sunday Morning*, published in 1958, Arthur believes that a 'frenchie' will 'spoil everything',[110] a view that results in his married lover, Brenda, using gin and a hot bath to induce a miscarriage. However, the widespread opposition to contraception also reflected the idea that it was 'emasculating', interfering with 'natural' male potency, and, therefore, with masculinity itself.

Heterosexual intercourse is, for Gordon, one of the private acts that enables the epiphany in which 'greed and fear are mysteriously transmuted into something nobler'.[111] In the consummation of his relationship with Rosemary, and her subsequent pregnancy, Gordon validates himself as an 'authentic', potent man. His return to the 'New Albion' advertising agency, and the consequent salary of 'Four ten a week', enables him to provide for 'his' family, although he acknowledges that it 'would be a tight pinch when Rosemary stopped working'.[112] He is able to establish his masculinity, therefore, only within the terms of the economic order he has previously attempted to evade. As Rees argued,

In *Keep the Aspidistra Flying* the money-god says, in effect: Obey me by getting a 'good' (i.e. an immoral, anti-social and degrading) job and you can afford to have a baby. Disobey me, by writing poetry or doing any disinterested work, and you will have to forgo sex altogether, because no woman will go with a pauper; or if you do have the luck to find a generous girl, you will have to resort to contraceptives or abortion.[113]

For Gordon, the 'money-god' is powerful partly because it 'gets at you through your sense of decency',[114] signified by the expected child. The statement evokes Ernest Everhard's insistence, in Jack London's *The Iron Heel*, that workers are 'tied to the merciless industrial machine' by their 'heart-strings', in particular through their 'children – always the young life that it is their instinct to protect'.[115] The emphasis, in both instances, is upon capitalist exploitation of sexual and familial relations. The ideas of 'masculine', 'feminine', and the relations between them are, therefore, used for a political purpose, in order to criticise the dominant economic and social system.

The 'money-god', in this account, determines the conditions under which it is possible to be a 'man'. The exclusion from, or even marginalisation in the economic system results in a similar exclusion from sexual life. For Gordon Comstock, contraception is one symbol of this, as the 'money-code' places,

> *the sleek, estranging shield,*
> *Between the lover and his bride.*[116]

His poverty not only excludes him from paternity, but from sexual intercourse itself. He insists that Rosemary 'won't sleep with me, simply and solely because I've got no money'.[117] The basis of this accusation is the idea of female conservatism outlined earlier in the chapter, as Gordon argues that a 'woman's got a sort of mystical feeling towards money', a 'deep-down mystical feeling that somehow a man without money isn't worthy of you', and is, indeed 'a weakling, a sort of half-man'.[118] The idea denies him agency, and hence responsibility for his failures. As Michael Carter writes,

He wants it to seem that she won't sleep with him because, as a woman in general, she is *obliged* to obey the money-code. In this way, if his sexual hunger goes unfed he can attribute it to being an effect of a cause of which he has no control: money.[119]

Gordon believes himself to be 'emasculated', and attributes responsibility for this to the 'money-code' and female identification with it. The association of women with conservatism means that Rosemary becomes the instrument of the capitalist order responsible for making him 'a sort of half-man'. This emphasis evokes his insistence, in his preparatory drafts for an essay on the work of George Gissing, that in his novels 'Money and women were [...] the two instruments through which society revenged itself on the courageous and the intelligent' (19:346–52:349).

The idea that impoverished men are excluded from the heterosexual 'market' recurs throughout his work. In *Down and Out in Paris and London*, for example, Orwell writes that the 'reasons are not worth discussing, but there is no doubt that women never, or hardly ever, condescend to men who are much poorer than themselves'.[120] He argues that the very poor suffer from the denial of a basic 'drive', the fulfilment of which is, moreover, the condition of their status as 'men'. For this reason, he insists, 'cut off from the whole race of women, a tramp feels himself degraded to the level of a cripple or a lunatic'.[121] According to this argument, women are one of the 'instruments' through which advanced capitalism oppresses impoverished men. Because they only regard the prosperous as sexually attractive, the destitute, such as tramps, are denied the possibility of 'normal' sexual fulfilment. This is a serious matter because desire, implicitly male desire, is 'a fundamental impulse' and the 'starvation of it can be almost as demoralising as physical hunger'.[122] In the notes on Sheffield Orwell made whilst researching *The Road to Wigan Pier*, he wrote that 'sexual starvation owing to unemployment is said to be rife and both insanity and suicide very common' (10:567–70:567). Capitalism prevents males from becoming, or remaining, 'men' with, he implies, destructive consequences. In *Down and Out in Paris and London*, he insists that 'is obvious what the results of this must be: homosexuality, for instance, and occasional rape'.[123] The statement figures both male 'deviation' and violence as a function of the dominant social and economic order.

Ideas of the 'masculine', and the sexual structures it is founded upon are therefore integrated into the text's attack on capitalism. This is demonstrated in particular in his representation of the working class. The working-class men that Orwell idealises are figured as heterosexual, virile and, as such, as 'real' men. In contrast, the middle classes are frequently figured as sterile or homosexual. In his description of the Comstock family, for example, he writes that

It was noticeable even then that they had lost impulse to reproduce themselves. Really vital people, whether they have money or whether they haven't, multiply almost as automatically as animals.[124]

This image associates power, or at least the potential for power, with paternity. Gordon considers even the lower-middle-class families with their aspidistras *'alive'* because they 'begot children'.[125] The 'traditional' family, with its defined, gendered roles, is integral to this emphasis on paternity. As Crick argues, Orwell represents it as 'the primary school of that "mutual trust" which is the precondition of a wider fraternity and general decency towards others'.[126] The persistence of these families, explored in the previous chapter, provides evidence for Orwell of a working-class 'vitality' absent from the 'dull, shabby, dead-alive, ineffectual'[127] middle-class families represented by the Comstocks. In *Nineteen Eighty-Four*, Winston Smith, watching the washerwoman, who is 'blown up to monstrous dimensions by child-bearing',[128] thinks to himself that 'Out of those mighty loins a race of conscious beings must one day come.'[129] In this, as in other instances, reproduction is itself a demonstration of value and potential.

Orwell also represents the persistence of 'traditional' heterosexual relationships, despite economic hardship, as a demonstration of working-class resilience. In *The Road to Wigan Pier*, for example, he writes,

Take, for instance, the fact that the working class think nothing of getting married on the dole. It annoys old ladies in Brighton, but it is a proof of their essential good sense; they realise that losing your job does not mean that you cease to be a human being.[130]

The statement represents the working class as maintaining 'human' values despite middle-class disapproval. It reinforces the narrator's statement in *Keep the Aspidistra Flying*,

Hats off to the factory lad who with fourpence in the world puts his girl in the family way! At least he's got blood and not money in his veins.[131]

Both passages represent heterosexual relationships as having a 'natural' value, and both draw a contrast between sexual desire and money, the symbol of an oppressive, sterile capitalism. The position parallels that of Owen in Robert Tressell's novel *The Ragged Trousered Philanthropists*, who insists that a 'man who is not married is living an unnatural life'.[132] The 'sexual starvation' identified in Sheffield is, in this account, a form of mutilation. The restriction of this 'fundamental impulse' denies impoverished men the status of a 'human being' and, more particularly, of 'real' men, imposing instead an 'unnatural' life.

Orwell represents masculinity as a natural determinant of identity, but one that is restricted or even denied by capitalism. It is integral to his conception of socialism, a positive value that provides a basis for many of his criticisms of established social structures. In this sense, as Patai writes, 'the essential ideology at the heart of Orwell's work as a writer and a thinker can be understood only by exploring his ideas about masculinity and femininity'.[133] His 'Myth of Masculinity' forms an implicit but unquestioned basis of his work and political thought. However, this use of gender is not, as Patai implies, peculiar to Orwell. As Newsinger argues, although *The Orwell Mystique* is 'one of the most interesting recent accounts of Orwell's work', and certainly one of the most influential, it 'too often topples over into a "get Orwell" exercise'.[134] In particular, she

> considers Orwell in too great isolation so that he appears to stand almost alone as the champion of traditional notions of masculinity in the 1930s. This reduces her critique almost to the level of a moral objection to him personally, whereas, of course, it needs to be expanded into a critique of the whole masculine culture to which Orwell belonged and which he never seems to have seriously questioned.[135]

Because she does not consider these 'traditional notions' within their cultural and historical contexts, Patai figures them as primarily the product of Orwell's personal weaknesses or prejudices. However, as Newsinger observes, this approach obscures broader cultural and political issues. The patriarchal values that underpin Orwell's work also shaped, not only the conservative establishment, but also many of the working-class communities he admired and numerous left-wing texts of the period. His representations of conservative women and active, virile men are symptomatic of a broader literary and political culture that used a variety of prejudicial models of gender to criticise and oppose industrial capitalism. Janet Montefiore has, for example, analysed the way in which images of the 'devouring Mother', 'enraged barren woman', and 'lovely Vamp' were used by writers of the 'Auden Generation' and others to attack targets including 'the psychopathology of Fascism' and 'class privilege'.[136] In addition, however, Orwell's 'anti-feminist views' aligned him within the political debates of the period and, specifically, within the socialist movement. His work identifies itself, as the next section of this chapter will argue, with what it perceives as working-class socialism, and in opposition to the 'bourgeois Socialist', satirised in the figure of 'Comrade X, member of the CPGB and author of *Marxism for Infants'*.

II

The importance of masculinity to the 'working-class' socialism Orwell admired is demonstrated in J. H. Watson's claim that

> Not for the painted bridge player who gives to her husband a dinner yielded from a gill saucepan, nor to the hipless clerkess with her assortment of contraceptives, both of whom devour the adverts for the latest fool-proof, comfortable methods of preventing B.O. or halitosis, or have a periodical Turkish bath, not for them the virtue of a clean skin and untroubled blood-stream. A placid blood-stream remains placid in an atmosphere of hot air or cold, damp or dry.[137]

The description is an example, albeit an extreme one, of a particular critical perspective upon advanced capitalism and 'mass' culture. It represents those who are not involved in material production as degraded and artificial, or as having deviated from their 'natural' identities. The bridge player is 'painted', or inauthentic, as well as non-productive, and the limited appetite of her husband implies that he is not a 'real' man. The word 'clerkess', with its conspicuous 'feminine' suffix, also suggests an ambiguous status, neither 'masculine' nor 'feminine', and indeed she is 'hipless', or asexual, rendered sterile by the 'assortment of contraceptives' that industrial society has made available to her. The women are both unhealthy, as neither possesses a 'clean skin' or 'untroubled blood-stream', and both resort to the cures or preventatives promoted in adverts. The women are contrasted with the male manual worker whom, Watson argues, 'by virtue of his labour, has a dancing blood stream, a rich zest for life, denied to the sedentary worker'.[138] His labour, the account implies, produces valuable qualities such as the 'strength, courage, generosity, etc.' that Orwell admired in *The Road to Wigan Pier*. In contrast, those working in 'sedentary' professions, or, like the 'bridge player', no profession at all are condemned to sterility, inaction and artificiality.

The image of masculinity developed in the essay focuses upon production and, in particular, manual labour. Watson insists that

> To labour at furnaces is a man's job. There is no problem of sacrificing one's masculinity as there is with clerical work, machine watching and the like.[139]

This interpretation of metal workers is not, of course, peculiar to those employed in the profession; and Priestley, for instance, argued in his description of the Tyne shipyards that 'bending iron and riveting steel to steel, is the real thing, man's work'.[140] The claim that manual labour defined masculinity was paralleled in descriptions of other professions, including Jack Hilton's essay 'The Plasterer's Life'. Hilton insists that he and his companions 'are natural men, and are often disgusted at the depraved femininity that other working-men have adopted'. The idea of authenticity is once more pivotal to the distinction, as he continues that amongst 'homely and genuine people we feel happy, among the superior and refined we feel like a sailor among land-lubbers'.[141] The sentence emphasises that the 'superior and refined' are neither 'homely' nor, more importantly 'genuine', and this lack of authenticity aligns them with the 'depraved femininity' identified in certain, unspecified working-men. This division, as the use of the word 'depraved' indicates, is always also an evaluative one. For Watson, for example, the 'man who labours, even if he suffers under the indignity of appearing before a committee for non-payment of rent, is always higher, cleaner, more vivid, than the committee who examines him',[142] and 'excepting genius, his life is of more value than, please God, what we call the brain worker; the clerk, typist, civil servant, teacher, and the commercial traveller'.[143] The passages illustrate what McKibbin describes as 'a kind of folk-Marxism, quite independent of actual party-political allegiances' founded upon the belief that 'their own work was the source of all value; the only work that mattered' and that 'Clerical workers "did nothing"'.[144] They also develop an image of the 'authentic' man whose identity is established in the workplace.

The miners, described in the previous chapter, are a prominent example of 'natural men', whose masculine identity is established and consolidated in the process of labour. It is, however, not confined to the workplace, but also defines domestic relations. The descriptions of mining communities produced in the period frequently emphasise a division between 'external' male labour, in the mines, and female work within the household.[145] These roles are clearly defined, and persist even when their practical basis is removed. In *The Road to Wigan Pier*, for example, Orwell writes that

> In the working-class home it is the man who is the master and not, as in a middle-class home, the woman or the baby. Practically never, for instance, in a working-class home, will you see the man doing a stroke of the housework. Unemployment has not changed this convention, which on the face of it seems a little unfair. The man is idle from morning to night but the woman is as busy as ever – more so, indeed, because she has to manage with less money. Yet so far as my experience goes the women do not protest. I believe that they, as well as the men, feel that a man would lose his manhood if, merely because he was out of work, he developed into a 'Mary Ann'.[146]

In his diary he noted this was the case even when '*the woman occasionally is working*' (10:448) and that the only forms of domestic work men would do were '*carpentering and gardening*' (449). This attitude was not, of course, peculiar to the 1930s. In *The Uses of Literacy*, for example, published 20 years after *The Road to Wigan Pier*, Hoggart observed,

> A husband is therefore not really expected to help about the house. If he does so, his wife is pleased; but she is unlikely to harbour a grudge if he does not. 'When all's said and done', most things about a house are women's work: 'Oh, that's not a man's job', a woman will say, and would not want him to do too much of that kind of thing for fear he is thought womanish.[147]

The dominance working-class men exercise in the home often contrasted with their relative powerlessness at work and in society in general. Indeed, Orwell's contemporary Maya Woodside described the home as 'one sphere in an increasingly mechanised and impersonal existence where one can still exercise sovereign power, if only over women and children'.[148] In all these instances, the home is interpreted as a site within which masculine identity and prestige are consolidated.

The division of labour within the household is integral to this process, and the description of the structure of 'normal' working-class homes in *The Road to Wigan Pier* is reflected in the work of other texts of the period. In Lewis Jones' *We Live*, for example, the miner 'Big Jim', when asked to help in the house, exclaims,

> What? Me light fire? Good God! What is coming over you, my gel.
> Don't forget I am a man, not a bloody dish-cloth. Huh! It has always
> been against my principles to do a 'ooman's work.[149]

In Walter Brierley's *Means Test Man*, the unemployed miner Jack Cook
does participate in the 'whole round of domestic labour', but is aware
that to 'the miners he would have become a woman, working in
the home, providing for it with money which came from a pool
into which all the bread-winners in the land threw a determined,
compulsory amount'.[150] His domestic work separates him from the
masculine community he inhabited as a mine worker, and indeed for his
former colleagues he has 'become a woman', redefined by his 'feminine'
labour.

The division of labour on the basis of gender was 'naturalised' in
many working-class communities of the period. As McKibbin insists,
the 'majority of women believed that they should not work after
marriage or were doubtful as to its propriety, a view usually reinforced by
their husbands'.[151] This formed a central component of a broader division between the 'masculine' and 'feminine' enacted throughout these
communities. Indeed, Stephen Ingle argues that it 'is certainly true that a
major characteristic of British working-class life, especially in the North
of England, has traditionally been its manifest inequality – between
the sexes'.[152] The division was a foundation for both the masculine
identity of working-class men and their 'folk-Marxism', which Orwell
celebrated for its combination of radicalism and traditionalism. Its maintenance, however, relied upon continued employment, which guaran-
teed the individual's status both as a productive man, and a breadwinner
who provided for 'his' family. The experience of unemployment, as a
consequence, is frequently represented as undermining the masculinity
of individual workers. Andy Croft argues in his examination of Danny,
a character in Fred Boden's novel *Miner*,

> The language of masculinity connects Danny's sense of the emas-
> culating effect of unemployment to his inability to marry without
> secure full-time work. Without work he cannot be a married man, a
> family man, a bread winner – cannot be fully human. The force of his
> bitterness is expressed by appeals to the masculinity of the miner's
> work. Without that work Danny isn't a real man.[153]

The image of emasculation recurs in numerous other texts of the period.
Priestley, for example, wrote that men who 'knew they were idle and

useless through no fault of their own' nevertheless felt 'tainted', partly because their 'very manhood was going'.[154] Indeed, the idea that work provided a necessary foundation for masculinity persisted long after the 1930s. In her account of poverty in Britain in the 1980s, for example, Beatrix Campbell argued that because 'unemployment for men means their exclusion not only from work but from the environment that makes them men' it 'makes them feel unmanned'.[155] The masculine ideal that operated in working-class communities consequently provided one basis upon which to interpret and criticise the economic system that imposed this humiliation.

As Croft observes, certain ideas recur 'again and again in all these novels about unemployment – the difficulty of maintaining family life according to its conventional pattern, the greater responsibility borne by women, the acute humiliation of the unemployed men – their *emasculation* – and the subsequent strain on love and marriage'.[156] The latter issue, the perceived exclusion of unemployed men from 'normal' emotional and sexual relations, provides one basis upon which to explore the concept of '*emasculation*' and its integration within a radical politics. Despite Orwell's insistence in *The Road to Wigan Pier* that the working-class 'think nothing of getting married on the dole', many of his contemporaries argued that the economic hardship of the 1930s constrained or distorted 'normal' emotional and sexual development, particularly for the young. In *I Was One of the Unemployed*, for example, Max Cohen wrote that

> young people need that interchange of experience between the sexes known as 'romance'. Too often unemployment makes a romantic social life impossible; where it comes into being in spite of unemployment it is starved and stultified and poisoned, owing to the lack of elementary material needed to keep it alive and healthy.[157]

Wal Hannington also emphasised these limitations in his descriptions of families in which 'father, mother, and two or three sons and daughters' were 'all unemployed'. He insisted that as a result of these conditions, the 'sons have reached adult age and have avoided marriage because they see no prospects of security before them, and the daughters likewise have avoided marriage because they do not wish to take the risk of bringing children into the world in the conditions of poverty which surround their own lives'.[158] In *Grey Children*, an unemployed miner's son is quoted as saying,

I miss a lot of things since I fell out. I used to like going to the theatre in Cardiff, and I was in a photographic club and I had a girl, but all that's finished now. Many of us will never be able to marry at all.[159]

Lack of work, these texts insist, prevents working-class men from marrying, or maintaining a successful marriage, and thereby undermines their masculinity. In *Means Test Man*, for example, Jane Cook informs her unemployed husband that

I'm a woman first and a wife next. I want the decencies of life and I would have got them if I'd stopped single and in service. I married you and *you've* an obligation to provide them.[160]

The text suggests that his lack of work and consequent failure as a 'bread winner' undermines the stable roles on which their marriage is founded. The full realisation of her position as a 'woman', and, specifically, a married women, is dependent upon his ability to 'provide', and she informs him that, although 'she would hold on as long as she thought there was hope of him getting back to work', the 'moment after she should discover that her hope was vain, well, there was the reservoir down at Buttly, the canal at Nessfield, the river at Lingfall Park'.[161]

It was not, of course, only marriage that the unemployed were perceived as excluded from, but any sexual relationship. The idea of 'sexual starvation', used in Orwell's notes for *The Road to Wigan Pier*, is replicated in numerous descriptions of unemployed men from this period. Oxley, for example, wrote that

to many sex starvation is a real torture. The activity of sex is a rejuvenating process and many who are denied it have insufficient reserves to live upon themselves alone: they break down mentally and physically.[162]

In *Jew Boy*, Alec similarly reflects that he

had to be steadfast, a class-conscious proletarian, but it was hard. This woman business was getting him down. How could any young man be expected to lead a normal healthy life without some satisfactory sexual relationship? It was so necessary.[163]

For Alec it is his 'right as a man' to have 'some sort of home to go every night, where I'm welcome, where there's a woman'.[164] His exclusion from 'normal' sexual life therefore not only undermines the development of his class-consciousness, but also his position as a 'man'. The novel represents his 'starvation' as a contravention of his masculine 'right', a humiliation imposed upon him by the economic system. The interpretation of this as a form of oppression is widespread in the period. In *Keep the Aspidistra Flying*, for example, Ravelston is momentarily arrested in imagining 'Hermione's body, naked, like a ripe warm fruit' by the thought that 'Sexual starvation is awful among the unemployed'.[165] The image of 'sexual starvation' is integrated with that of the unemployed in 'frowzy beds, bread and marg. and milkless tea in their bellies'[166] to form a composite picture of capitalist failure.

In his essay on nineteenth-century Cleveland ironstone mining communities, Tony Nicholson argues that

> Each working-class community had its own unique character, but a common, deeply held set of codes which can be found everywhere clustered around the concept of masculine identity. This is not to say that working-class masculinity was monolithic and unchanging, but whatever forms emerged in particular places at particular times, there was always a powerful masculine presence at the very centre of working-class culture.[167]

A 'powerful masculine presence' continued to be an important determinant of working-class communities in the period in which Orwell wrote. It was integral to a particular critique of capitalism, often a form of 'folk-Marxism' founded, not upon an analysis of economic and social structures, but upon the interrelated ideals of male productive labour and stable gender roles. The unemployment of the 1930s was widely perceived as undermining both these bases of value, and as consequently 'emasculating' working-class men, who were unable to assume their expected economic or sexual status. The commitment to a particular 'masculine identity', conceived as inherently valuable, therefore enabled capitalism to be criticised as limiting or even violating the development of a 'natural' component of individual identity.

This 'folk-Marxism' and its use of masculinity are integral to Orwell's political thought. His work, as illustrated above, reproduces the idea that the impoverished male is forced into the position of 'a weakling, a sort of half-man'. It locates value in the fulfilment of idealised 'manhood' identified with heterosexual working-class men, such as the miners, who are also figured as practising an 'authentic' socialism. In *The Road to Wigan Pier*, he argues that the 'working man', whose 'vision of the Socialist future is a vision of present society with the worst abuses left out, and with interest centring round the same things as at present – family life, the pub, football, and local politics' was 'a truer Socialist than the orthodox Marxist'.[168] The distinction proposed is between a working-class socialism founded upon established values, including masculinity, and the 'picture of aeroplanes, tractors and huge glittering factories of glass and concrete',[169] which is associated with the middle-class socialist or 'orthodox Marxist'. This division parallels that between the 'masculine' and 'feminine' that operates throughout the texts. As Patai observed, Orwell represents the utopian vision of 'glittering factories' as 'female – it is soft, enveloping, emasculating'. His identification with working-class masculinity, therefore, aligns him within a socialist movement that he interprets as polarised between its 'masculine' and 'feminine' or 'effeminate' variants. In a letter to Jack Common, of April 1936, Orwell insisted that the 'socialist bourgeoisie' contained numerous individuals of

> the sort of eunuch type with a vegetarian smell who go about spreading sweetness and light and have at the back of their minds a vision of the working class all T.T., well washed behind the ears, readers of Edward Carpenter or some other pious sodomite and talking with B.B.C. accents. (10:470–1:471)

The caricature illustrates his belief that middle-class socialists were both emasculated and detached from the working class.

The association of the 'bourgeois Socialist'[170] with homosexuality reinforces the connection in the texts between 'authentic' socialism and the conception of 'manhood' outlined above. Homosexual men are represented throughout Orwell's work as effeminate. In *Keep the Aspidistra Flying*, for instance, the narrator states that a 'youth of twenty, cherry-lipped, with gilded hair, tripped Nancifully in' to the bookshop where Gordon works. His homosexuality determines, not only his 'R-less Nancy voice', but all other elements of his character. The text even connects it to his wealth and dilettantism, the latter demonstrated in his attributed position as a 'hanger-on of the arts'. The customer has 'the golden aura of money', and his physical appearance itself demonstrates his privileged position. Gordon insists that the young man is

> A nice looking boy, though, for all his Nancitude. The skin at the back of his neck was as silk-smooth as the inside of a shell. You can't have skin like that under five hundred a year.[171]

The association of homosexuality with wealth, privilege and a peripheral involvement in 'the arts' positions the customer as the object of Gordon's prejudices, a representative of the oppressive 'money-god'.

This form of the homophobia is in some respects similar to that Robert Roberts identified in working-class Salford in the early twentieth-century. Roberts argues that

> Amongst ignorant men any interest in music, books or the arts in general, learning or even courtesy or intelligence could make one suspect. This linking of homosexuality with culture played some part, I believe, in keeping the lower working-class as near-illiterate as they were.[172]

The emphasis in *Keep the Aspidistra Flying*, however, is not upon 'culture' as such, but upon a perceived cultural elite caricatured in Gordon's image of 'those moneyed young beasts from Cambridge'.[173] In *The Road to Wigan Pier*, Orwell represented them as parasites, emphasising their dependence on the labour of the working class, specifically the miners, as in order 'that the Nancy poets may scratch one another's backs, coal has go to be forthcoming'.[174] The contrast implies a series of further binary oppositions, between the active and passive, authentic and artificial, strength and weakness, that construct the 'Nancy poets' as the inverse of the virile masculinity represented by the miners. This association of a perceived cultural elite represented by such 'damp squibs' as 'Auden, Campbell, Day Lewis, Spender',[175] with homosexuality persists throughout his work. As he also associated these writers with what he describes as 'this utterly irresponsible intelligentsia, who "took up" Roman Catholicism ten years ago, "take up" Communism to-day and will "take up" the English variant of Fascism a few years hence' (11:242–6:244) their artistic and political commitments are implied to be similarly dilettante. He even represents Auden's poetry as emasculated, the product of a 'sort of gutless Kipling'.[176] The recurrent contrast between masculinity and 'effeminate' homosexuality is used to dismiss the 'Auden circle'.[177] As Patai wrote, throughout 'his writings he seems to feel that in order to discredit individuals and groups it is sufficient to attach to them the label of "Nancy boy" or "pansy" – two terms specifically designating the passive partner in a male homosexual dyad'.[178]

The image of male homosexuals as passive is reinforced in Orwell's unpublished response to the questionnaire 'Authors Take Sides on the Spanish War'. In this, he wrote that

I am not one of your fashionable pansies like Auden and Spender.
I was six months in Spain, most of the time fighting. I have a
bullet-hole in me at present and I am not going to write blah about
defending democracy or gallant little anybody. (11:66–8:67)[179]

The statement contrasts the 'blah', or empty pronouncements of the
'fashionable pansies' with Orwell himself, and represents his experience
of combat as a guarantee of the value of his views. The implication, that
'pansies', unlike more 'masculine' men, are not willing to fight for their
political beliefs, is replicated in 'As One Non-Combatant to Another',
written in response to a poem by Alex Comfort. In this, Orwell defended
his statements that 'at need/I'd fight to keep the Nazis out Britain', and
insists that it 'shocked' the 'pinks', although none of them 'would have
thought it odd of me/To write a shelf of books in praise of sodomy'
(15:142–5:143). The images of the 'pinks' and 'pansies' in these examples
serve to reinforce the active martial identities of the abstract masculine
communities with which Orwell identifies himself. As D. A. N. Jones
writes, in these statements 'Orwell has cast himself as lone Horatius,
being badly let down by a defeatist regiment of pink sodomites.'[180] The
figure of the homosexual, therefore, is used to establish the boundaries
of the idealised image of masculinity developed throughout the texts.

    This use of homophobia to consolidate or 'police' male communities
is, of course, not peculiar to Orwell. As Maud Ellmann writes,

Sedgwick points out that the homo*social* bonds of patriarchy depend
precisely on the disavowal of their homo*sexual* constituent, resulting
in the vicious persecution of gay men. Heterosexism is therefore
doubly fraudulent: the ostensible desire for women serves as a pretext
for affirming bonds with other men and for denying the sexual
component of those bonds.[181]

The simultaneous insistence upon the importance of male communities
and overt hostility to homosexual men is, in other words, a persistent
element of patriarchal societies. Indeed, Jonathan Dollimore argues that
'within a heterosexual economy generally, there tends to be a profound
separation between identification and desire, especially for males', who
are 'required to identify with other males but not allowed to desire
them; indeed *identification with* should actually preclude *desire for*'.[182]
This distinction operates throughout Orwell's work, in which homoso-
cial relations, such as those represented as central to working-class
communities, are divided from the homosexual relations associated

primarily, if not exclusively, with the 'degenerate' or 'sterile' middle class. The mobilisation of this dominant narrative forms one method of consolidating certain identities, and indeed certain forms of socialism, whilst marginalising or degrading others.

The use of homophobia to establish coherent male communities is illustrated in a number of Orwell's texts. In *Homage to Catalonia*, for example, Orwell insists that a 'half-witted little beast of fifteen' who served in the militia was 'known to everyone as the *maricón* (Nancy-boy)',[183] and that at the front, members of the POUM shouted '*Fascistas – maricones!*'[184] at their enemies. In this context, the term '*maricón*' does not denote sexual preference, but suggests that the individuals so described are not 'real' men or, indeed, competent soldiers. In other male, or male-dominated groups he represented, these attitudes resulted in more direct persecution. In his 'Hop-Picking Diary', for example, he writes that 'Young Ginger', a tramp,

> *related how he and some others on Trafalgar Square had discovered one of their number to be a 'Poof', or Nancy Boy. Whereupon they had instantly fallen upon him, robbed him of 12/6d, which was all he had, and spent it on themselves. Evidently they thought it quite fair to rob him, as he was a Nancy Boy.* (10:214–26:218)

In *Down and Out in Paris and London*, Orwell insists he was informed by a man who 'began making homosexual attempts upon me' that homosexuality was 'general among tramps of long standing'.[185] However, the belief that the theft from the '*Nancy Boy*' was '*quite fair*' suggests that he was not considered part of the community of male tramps. Even in more stable, established social networks, homosexual men occupied a precarious position. Roberts stated that, in Salford,

> Forming the base of the social pyramid we had bookies' runners, idlers, part-time beggars and petty thieves, together with all those known to have been in prison whatever might be their ostensible economic or social standing. Into this group the community lumped any harlots, odd homosexuals, kept men and brothel keepers.[186]

Homosexuals, according to this account, were perceived as outcasts, equivalent to thieves or those who have been in prison. Those listed mark the boundaries of the community and, as a result, establish the coherence of its 'respectable' members. What connects many of those excluded is their failure to adhere to the dominant conception of masculinity, and in particular, the ideal of productive labour. The thieves, beggars and kept men are all, in different ways, 'idlers', and their equation with 'odd homosexuals' figures the latter as parasitic. This exclusion of male homosexuals from 'respectable' male communities is, of course, not peculiar to Salford. Indeed, the fact that the word 'ponce' means both 'a man who lives off a prostitute's earnings' and 'an effeminate man',[187] demonstrates a widespread though irrational belief that there is an equivalence between 'homosexuals' and the 'kept man'.[188]

The homophobia and 'anti-feminism' exhibited in Orwell's texts obviously fulfil a multitude of functions, but both are used to construct a particular 'Myth of Masculinity'. Homosexual men, for example, are, as illustrated above, represented as deviating from a masculine ideal, whilst women are its inverse or negative term. Their association with conservatism, passivity and domesticity helps to establish the myth that 'real' men are radical and active in the 'external' worlds of work and politics. These oppositions recur throughout his work, and reproduce the idea of distinct, 'natural' masculine and feminine identities. The idealised conception of masculinity in particular is used as a measure of individual value. The working-class men described in *The Road to Wigan Pier* and the revolutionaries detailed in *Homage to Catalonia* are celebrated, in part, because of their fulfilment of their masculine roles, whether as workers or soldiers. These roles, which are inherently social, in turn illustrate the idea of gender as a potential basis of communities, and, therefore, also of political activism. Orwell suggests that masculinity connects individual men, and provides a set of shared values and perceptions capable of sustaining broader co-operation. It forms one basis upon which to construct 'imagined communities'. In particular, the 'traditional notions of masculinity', which, as Newsinger observed, Orwell 'never seems to have seriously questioned', are used to consolidate a specific image of the working-class, and of working-class radicalism.

Orwell's work identifies 'real' socialism with working-class men who embody 'traditional' masculine values, such as 'strength, courage, generosity, etc.' In contrast, it represents the established order as sterile, and associates it with figures such as the middle-class wife and 'burra memsahib', who reinforce present inequalities. It also interprets 'middle-class' socialism as 'effeminate', and identifies it with 'pansies', 'Nancy poets' and the 'pious sodomite'. The ideas of 'masculine' and 'feminine', and the values attached to them, inform a representational structure that underpins the texts' political analyses. This use of gender, however, is not peculiar to Orwell. As Nicholson observed, there was 'a powerful masculine presence at the very centre of working-class culture'.

Orwell's deployment of these 'traditional notions' illustrates, amongst other things, his identification with this culture. Watson's image of the 'hipless clerkess', Hilton's criticisms of the 'depraved femininity' of those workers not engaged in manual labour, and Brierley's observation that the domestic work undertaken by the unemployed Jack Cook meant that he would have 'become a woman' in the eyes of his former colleagues, all demonstrate the persistence of this 'powerful masculine presence' in working-class communities of the period. Indeed, it provided a basis for an influential criticism of capitalism, which, as Croft observes, argued that it 'emasculated' men by excluding them from their position as 'bread winners' and subjecting many to 'sexual starvation'. Orwell was therefore not alone in subscribing to a form of opposition to capitalism that encoded a simultaneous commitment to traditional form of masculinity.

In *The Orwell Mystique*, Patai writes that 'Orwell cares more for his continuing privileges as a male than he does for the abstractions of justice, decency and truth on behalf of which he claims to be writing.'[189] The statement identifies the extent to which his texts encode, and indeed, reinforce a polarised model of gender. However, this model is integral and not, as Patai suggests extraneous to the ideas of 'justice, decency and truth' Orwell supported. The problem is not simply one of personal weakness, but of the way these 'abstractions' themselves have been defined within a 'masculine culture' that extended, and indeed extends from the conservative establishment to many of its 'radical' opponents. The 'traditional notions' of gender Orwell mobilised in his writing were integral to various forms of socialism which argued, amongst other things, that capitalism distorted and undermined masculinity. Indeed, the idea of 'natural', invariant 'masculine' and 'feminine' identities permeated left-wing thought. Even Karl Marx, for example, listed his 'favourite virtue in man' as 'Strength', and his 'favourite virtue in woman' as 'Weakness'.[190] Most significantly for the purposes of this book, the 'ideas about masculinity and femininity' that Patai traces were central to the working-class socialism Orwell identified with. His homophobia and 'anti-feminism' were not, however unfortunately, distinct from his socialism, but inscribed within it, and, indeed, used to criticise a capitalist order he and others perceived as 'emasculating' working-class men.

3
Theories of Nationalism

I

In 'The Home Guard and You', published in 1940, Orwell wrote that 'We are in a strange period of history in which a revolutionary has to be a patriot and a patriot has to be a revolutionary' (12:309–12:311). The statement illustrates his attempt, following the outbreak of Second World War, to integrate patriotism in his political thinking. In part this was a pragmatic process, initiated by the 'strange' wartime conditions. England, the country with which Orwell himself identified, was the site of relative political freedom within Nazi-dominated Europe. As he insisted in 'Fascism and Democracy', its citizens at least possessed, for example, 'the knowledge that when you talk politics with your friends there is no Gestapo ear glued to the keyhole, the belief that "they" cannot punish you unless you have broken the law, the belief that the law is above the State' (12:376–82:378). This point was reinforced in *The Lion and the Unicorn*, in which he described England as a place where 'such concepts as justice, liberty and objective truth' (397) continued to determine popular opinion. His emphasis on patriotism in this period can, therefore, be identified with the defence of an England that retained civil liberties eradicated in occupied Europe. However, his insistence that the revolutionary must be a patriot implies that patriotism involves not only the defence of established freedoms but the potential for future social transformation. This aspect of his statement is concerned not only with his conception of England, but with patriotism as such and its political implications. As Stephen Lutman wrote, patriotism was both 'part of the defence against totalitarianism as Orwell saw it during the war, and a hope for the future'.[1]

The attempt to represent national identity as a basis for revolution relies upon the idea that nations are not fixed, but can be reinterpreted, and indeed reconstructed. This emphasis on mutability is of considerable importance in a period in which, Orwell insists, 'Old-fashioned patriotism is now a far stronger force that any kind of internationalism, or any ideas about the Socialist Fatherland' (12:546–53:547). The statement is founded upon the idea that, as Hosking and Schöpflin write, 'the beliefs a people holds about its shared fate represent one of the fundamental driving forces of modern society' and that 'National myths' are therefore 'crucial to understanding the world we live in'.[2] In essays such as 'Notes on Nationalism' and 'Anti-Semitism in Britain', he attempted to analyse the concept of the nation exploited by totalitarian movements and to propose an alternative to it. Pivotal to this is the argument outlined in 'Notes on Nationalism', that 'Nationalism is not to be confused with patriotism', and that 'two different and even opposing ideas are involved' (141–2). In this essay, and indeed elsewhere in his work, he distinguishes a revolutionary patriotism from a nationalism founded on the idea of fixed national identities. He, therefore, argues that patriotism can be used to construct the foundations of a future socialist society.

The analysis of Orwell's writing on patriotism and nationalism undertaken in this chapter is divided into two main sections. The first, concerned with concepts of nationality, outlines the work of a number of theorists in this area, and exposes some of the difficulties in defining and evaluating national identity. The second traces the evolution of Orwell's writing on the subject, from the jingoistic poems he wrote at St Cyprian's to his attempts to produce a model of radical patriotism in texts such as *The Lion and the Unicorn*. It then analyses this model, and examines whether he succeeded in establishing a stable, logical division between patriotism and nationalism. The chapter locates Orwell's writing on national identity within its historical and critical contexts. It therefore considers both the conditions of its production and other texts on the subject, many of which were written later. This enables the analysis of his writing both as a set of responses to developing events and as a contribution to a continuing debate on nationality and its political significance.

The nation is an evasive concept, which, in contrast to the state, cannot be defined in terms of its formal characteristics or institutions. The problem is illustrated in *Ulysses* when John Wyse asks Leopold Bloom 'do you know what a nation means?' Bloom replies that it 'is the same people living in the same place', but when Ned retorts that 'if that's so I'm a nation for I've been living in the same place for the past five years', Bloom modifies this definition, insisting that a nation also includes individuals 'living in different places'.[3] The revision, however, means that the nation becomes simply the 'same people'. The basis of this similitude, the term that connects members of the nation with one another, is absent. The distinction between the first and revised definitions, however, illustrates a tension between material and abstract descriptions of the nation. If the nation is defined as a group of individuals 'living in the same place', then it has a material foundation. Its membership is defined simply by residence, and it is therefore straightforward to become a member or leave the community. If, however, the nation consists of individuals who are 'the same' despite living 'in different places', then membership relies on less tangible connections, and is consequently more difficult to define or alter. This second possibility disrupts the connection between the nation and the nation-state. Germans, for example, need not be citizens of Germany to constitute a 'people'. The exchange in *Ulysses*, therefore, indicates one prominent difficulty in defining the nation. This tension, between formal criteria of nationality, such as residence in a particular area, and less tangible bases of similitude, such as those founded on ideas of shared culture, ethnicity or 'race', is apparent in the various critical attempts to define the nation.

In 'Marxism and the National Question', Stalin argued that the nation is '*a historically constituted, stable community of people, formed on the basis of a common language, territory, economic life, and psychological make-up manifested in a common culture*'.[4] These factors must all be present for a given 'community of people'[5] to constitute a nation. There is, therefore,

> no *single* distinguishing characteristic of a nation. There is only a sum total of characteristics, of which, when the nations are compared, sometimes one characteristic (national character), sometimes another (language), or sometimes a third (territory, economic conditions), stands out in sharper relief. A nation constitutes the combination of all these characteristics taken together.[6]

It cannot, for example, exist independent of a particular territory, as it is in part the product of 'lengthy and systematic intercourse, as a result of people living together generation after generation'.[7] The nation need not have sovereignty over this territory, which may be administered by a state incorporating several nations, but its members must inhabit it. Indeed, Stalin argued that Bauer's model, which claimed residence in a particular area was not essential, described 'not a living and active nation, but something mystical, intangible and supernatural', as it included communities 'the members of which do not understand each other (since they speak different languages), inhabit different parts of the globe, will never see each other, and will never act together, whether in time of peace or in time of war!'[8] His own definition, in contrast, has a material foundation, insisting upon residence in a particular area and a shared '*economic life*'. It also, however, incorporates the less precise notion of a '*common culture*' and is, therefore, neither simply a formal nor an 'intangible' category, but relies on a combination of factors. Their precise configuration varies between different nations, and, indeed, periods, as 'a nation, like every historical phenomenon, is subject to the law of change, has its history, its beginning and end'.[9]

Later definitions retain these basic categories, although the emphasis upon each varies. There is particular debate over the importance of territory. Anthony Smith, for example, argues that a nation is '*a named human population sharing a historic territory and historical memories, a mass, public culture, a common economy and common legal rights and duties for all members*'.[10] This definition, like Stalin's, insists that cultural, political and territorial criteria are all essential to a nation. Its geographical basis, for example, cannot be omitted as 'Nationalism is about "land", both in terms of possession and (literal) rebuilding, and of belonging where forefathers lived and where history demarcates a "homeland".'[11] David Miller, however, does not entirely support this analysis and argues that a nation is a 'community (1) constituted by shared belief and mutual commitment, (2) extended in history, (3) active in character, (4) connected to a particular territory, and (5) marked off from other communities by its distinct public culture'.[12] The fourth criterion implies, in contrast to Smith, that a community need not possess a territorial base in order to constitute a nation. For Miller, the two are not identical but 'connected', a word that suggests that even residence in a particular territory is not essential to the definition of nationhood. Benedict Anderson supports this distinction, arguing that a nation is 'an imagined political community' which is 'imagined as both inherently limited and sovereign'.[13] This interpretation implies that it is the imaginative connection with a territory, rather than residence in, or sovereignty over it that defines a nation. For James Kellas, a territorial basis, realised or otherwise, is only one of a number of possible characteristics. He claims that a nation is 'a group of people who feel themselves to be a community bound together by ties of history, culture, and common ancestry', and which may possess 'a territory, a language, a religion, or common descent (though not all those are always present)'.[14] It is, according to this account, the perception of a shared ancestry or culture that is decisive, and not material factors such as residence in a particular territory.

All these definitions have some common elements, but the relative importance of the various criteria is disputed. In particular, there is a distinction between those theories which insist that a nation must have a material foundation, and those that define it upon the basis of factors such as 'national character'. This parallels the division identified by Antony Easthope between 'two different materialities, nation as state and nation as culture'.[15] The tensions between these can be analysed by exploring in detail a particular theory of the nation, such as that produced by Ernest Gellner, and the various criticisms of it. Gellner focuses upon the development of the nation as a geographical and economic formation, insisting that the territorial state precedes nationalism, which 'emerges only in milieux in which the existence of the state is very much taken for granted'.[16] In this respect, his theories parallel those of Gasset, who argued that national identities were produced by the state itself. Gasset insisted that neither 'blood nor language gives birth to the national State', as states have 'been filled from the most heterogeneous blood streams' and 'peoples to-day brought together under one State spoke, or still speak, different languages'.[17] He also rejected the concept of 'natural frontiers', as the boundaries of the state instead 'served to consolidate at every stage the political unification already attained'.[18] Instead, Gasset argued 'it is the national State which levels down the differences arising from the red globule and the articulated sounds',[19] establishing 'a relative unification of races and tongues'.[20] Like Gellner, therefore, he argues that the modern state is a necessary condition for the development of the nation, rather than a product of it.

Gellner argues that technical developments, particularly in communication, lead to the emergence of a national culture, which replaces older, localised cultures. These developments enable the production of a standardised print language, educational system and judicial process, reinforcing the cultural as well as the institutional power of the state. He, therefore, constructs a materialist account of the nation, in which even the 'psychological' connections between its members are interpreted as the product of material networks. It is, therefore, 'not the case, as Elie Kedourie claims, that nationalism imposes homogeneity; it is rather that a homogeneity imposed by objective, inescapable imperative eventually appears on the surface in the form of nationalism'.[21]

The origins of nations, and therefore of nationalism, are 'not in human nature as such, but in a certain kind of now pervasive social order'.[22] The nation is not the realisation of an essential identity, but is enabled by advanced methods of production and the modern state.[23] Indeed, Gellner argues that 'Nations as a natural, God-given way of classifying men, as an inherent though long-delayed political destiny, are a myth',[24] and that they are instead the products of evolution or conscious policies, albeit policies that frequently utilise pre-existing ethnic cultures. This emphasis upon 'nation-building' contradicts the myth of inherent national identity. The model does not represent nationality as the passive reflection of new methods of production, but does insist that these form its historical basis. It is, therefore, distinct from accounts that perceive the nation as the product of a pre-existent culture.

The development of a national culture is, however, essential to the 'nation-building' instituted by the state. For Gellner, national identity is, in part, the result of 'the general imposition of a high culture on society, where previously low cultures had taken up the lives of the majority, and in some cases the totality, of the population'. A unified culture, legitimised by the state, therefore replaces 'folk cultures reproduced locally and idiosyncratically by the micro-groups themselves', and establishes 'a school-mediated, academy-supervised idiom, codified for the requirements of reasonably precise bureaucratic and technological communications'.[25] The control of education is particularly important to the development of both the nation and national identity. In contrast to Max Weber, who insisted that 'a state is a human community that (successfully) claims the *monopoly of the legitimate use of physical force* within a given territory',[26] Gellner argues that,

> At the base of the modern social order stands not the executioner but the professor. Not the guillotine, but the (aptly named) *doctorat d'état* is the main tool and symbol of state power. The monopoly of legitimate education is more important, more central than is the monopoly of legitimate violence.[27]

A national education system ensures the nation, rather than say, regional, ethnic or religious communities, defines knowledge. Indeed,

> Modern society is one in which no sub-community, below the size of one capable of maintaining an independent education system, can any longer reproduce itself. The reproduction of fully socialized

individuals itself becomes part of the division of labour, and is no longer performed by sub-communities for themselves.[28]

To a considerable extent, the control of education eradicates independent traditions and interpretative models. It also enables the state to naturalise the established social system and provide industry with a skilled, literate workforce. As Althusser argues the 'ideological State apparatus which has been installed in the *dominant* position in mature capitalist social formations', is 'the *educational ideological apparatus*',[29] which is essential to the production and reproduction of the nation-state.

This use of a homogeneous education system is complemented by the imposition of a standardised national language.[30] In principle at least, this enables communication between all members of the nation, in contrast to earlier societies in which, Gellner insists 'the language of the hunt, of harvesting, of various rituals, of the council room, of the kitchen and harem, all form autonomous systems'.[31] This official language, originating in the codification undertaken by the publishing industry, also emphasises boundaries between nations. As Anderson argues,

> Speakers of the huge variety of Frenches, Englishes, or Spanishes, who might find it difficult or even impossible to understand one another in conversation, became capable of comprehending one another via print and paper. In the process, they gradually became aware of the hundreds of thousands, even millions, of people in their particular language-field, and at the same time that *only those* hundreds of thousands, or millions, so belonged.[32]

The members of a nation therefore recognise one another, in part at least, because of their shared access to one, or on occasion more than one national language.[33] These are frequently represented as ancient, but are instead, as E. J. Hobsbawn observes, 'almost always semi-artificial constructs and occasionally, like modern Hebrew, virtually invented', as they 'are usually attempts to devise a standardized idiom out of a multiplicity of actually spoken idioms'.[34] This process of standardization relies on the codification of the language in national dictionaries and grammars, and is reinforced by publications, in particular national newspapers, that allow individuals to 'visualize in a general way the existence of thousands and thousands like themselves through print language'.[35] The production of an official language or languages is essential to the development of a distinct national 'public culture', the network of codes that enable members of a nation to recognise one another. As Miller observes, 'national communities are constituted by belief: nations exist when their members recognize one another as compatriots and believe that they share characteristics of the relevant kind'.[36] A shared culture enables such recognition. However, as Gellner argues, national cultures themselves are the product of a process of 'nation-building' that 'sometimes takes pre-existing cultures and turns them into nations', but also 'sometimes invents them, and often obliterates pre-existing cultures'.[37]

According to this theory, the modern state produces national identity, partly through its control of what Althusser terms the 'ideological State apparatus', which enables it to reproduce itself and to construct a shared 'public culture'. A standardised education system and language, in particular, establish a national community whose members can interact with one another but are divided culturally, and frequently linguistically, from those beyond its borders. The identification with the nation is, in this analysis, the product of state power, which it in turn legitimises. This is not, however, how the foundations of the nation are conceived by nationalists. For the nationalist, the object of his or her identification is not the product of comparatively recent material developments, but the realisation of an essential identity. Nationalism, therefore, is not constrained by the 'real' history of the nation. The powerful 'emotional' appeal of nationalism, often founded upon a mythical reinterpretation of national history, is central to several critical accounts of Gellner's model.

Kellas, for example, argues that whilst 'Gellner's theory is compelling', there is

> little here about the primordial roots of nationalism, and its powerful emotional appeal. Why should people be prepared to die for what is in this analysis an imperative of a rational economic and social system of industrialisation?[38]

In addition, he insists, were Gellner correct then 'as the economy internationalises, national characteristics fade into cosmopolitan ones, and with them fade the national culture'. Instead, in his assessment, although 'nationalism has weakened at the state level' there has been an increase in 'sub-state ethnic and social nationalism'.[39] The comment implies that Gellner represents the relationship between industrial society and nationalism as one obvious to nationalists themselves. It also suggests that nationalism remain dependent on its material base and does not develop independently from it. In fact, Gellner argues that nationalism practices 'basic deception and self-deception',[40] as it represents itself as a reflection of essential, ahistorical identities. It is, therefore, a form of ideology or 'false consciousness',[41] and like all ideologies it is, as Althusser observed, 'characterized [...] by the fact that *its own problematic is not conscious of itself*'.[42] It not only suppresses it own history, but replaces it with an alternative, mythical narrative, a false explanation of its own origins. As a result, as Gellner argues, the 'historic agents' of nationalist movements 'know not what they do'.[43] The fact that individual nationalists believe they are defending or furthering their essential identity does not disprove the idea that nationalism is 'an imperative of a rational economic and social system'.

Nonetheless, nationalism has a 'powerful emotional appeal', which Gellner does not analyse in any detail. He is not alone in this. As Easthope observes, 'Historical study frequently remarks upon the passionate subjective response to the nation but, in general, has little to say about it except that it is beyond reason and so probably beyond analysis.'[44] Even if, as Gellner and others argue, the nation is a product of 'nation-building' enabled by the modern state, nationalism obscures this material foundation, figuring itself instead as the realisation of an essential identity. This process of 'self-deception' involves, amongst other things, a process of historical revision in which a myth of antiquity is substituted for the more prosaic, complex national history. There is, as Anderson observes, a contradiction between the 'objective modernity of nations to the historian's eye' and their 'subjective antiquity in the eyes of nationalists'.[45] Nationalists use pre-existing texts, myths, traditions and rituals in order to manufacture this fictive antiquity, constructing a genealogy that connects the members of an imagined community upon the basis of perceived common historical, cultural, and often 'racial' origins.[46] This simultaneous suppression of the history and production of a myth of origin legitimised by the manipulation of historical records and artefacts ensures, as Anderson argues, that nations 'always loom out of an immemorial past, and, still more important, glide into a limitless future', in a continuous narrative that transforms 'chance into destiny'.[47] The nation paradoxically depends on both the suppression of its objective history and the production of a fictive history. It is therefore a product of myth. It utilises a symbolic process that 'transforms history into nature',[48] positing the essential existence of certain categories, values or methods of interpretation which are, in fact, the result of particular historical developments. This process of historical revision is both a function and a source of the 'powerful emotional appeal' of nationalism.

Habermas analyses the distance between the formal structure of the nation and the narratives that produce its 'emotional appeal' by distinguishing between the 'citizen' and the '*Volksgenossen*'. He argues that

> *Citizens* constitute themselves on their own as a political association of the free and equal; *Volksgenossen* see themselves as belonging to an ethnic community bound together by a common language and historical destiny. The tension between the universalism of an egalitarian community under law and the particularism of a historical community of destiny is built into the nation-state.

The passage identifies two co-existent bases of the nation and thereby exposes its inherent tension. The concept of citizenship is founded upon formal criteria, such as laws, and therefore incorporates the idea that new members can be admitted to the nation provided that these are adhered to. The *Volksgenossen*, however, is founded upon the idea of the 'same people', the belief that there are essential differences between individuals, and that nations are structured upon the lines of these pre-existent divisions. These concepts, for Habermas, illustrate 'the twofold nature of the nation – the desired nation of citizens which creates democratic legitimization, as well as the born nation of *Volksgenossen* which makes for national integration',[49] but their analytical separation exposes two distinct forms of identification built upon the material and ideological foundations of the nation itself. The relation between these elements determines the form and, indeed, political implications of national identities.

This idea of nationalism as a form of 'passionate' identification that obscures its own foundations is pivotal to Orwell's writing on nationality. In contrast to the materialist analysis proposed by writers such as Gellner, his work concentrates upon the 'nation as culture', and the 'emotional' commitment to the nation, rather than its historical origins or institutional forms. Nevertheless, it interprets the nation as an evolving community, in contrast to the idea of an inflexible 'born nation', associated in the period with the racial theories of National Socialism. His analysis of this 'passionate' commitment is, in other words, divided, in that it supports a radical patriotism whilst simultaneously condemning an irrational, aggressive nationalism. In so doing, his work obviously reflects the historical and political conditions under which it was produced. Indeed, as previously observed, he himself emphasised that his commitment to England during Second World War, for example, was a response to a 'strange period of history'. His writing on nationality intervenes in various contemporary debates, in particular those initiated by the Nazi manipulation of national identity.

The remainder of this chapter analyses Orwell's interest in the 'emotional' commitment to the nation, the distinction he draws between 'nationalism' and 'patriotism', and his idea that the latter could be integrated in a socialist politics. It traces the evolution of his thinking on nationality and concludes with a detailed analysis of his 1945 essay 'Notes on Nationalism'. This explores his ideas about the psychological basis of nationalism, its political function and its manifestations. It also analyses his attempt to produce a revolutionary patriotism that would combine commitment to tradition, tolerance of difference and openness to change. This exploration of his writing on national identity is, of course, complicated by his own active involvement in a process of myth-making, in particular in his writing on 'Englishness', which is examined in detail in the next chapter. The models of the nation outlined above, however, provide a theoretical context within which to read his work and a basis upon which to assess his various attempts to appropriate national identity for a radical politics, a process which itself formed part of a broader attempt to found a future socialist society in established forms of community.

II

George Orwell's first published work was the poem 'Awake Young Men of England'. It was written when he was 11 years old and printed on 2 October 1914 in the *Henley and South Oxfordshire Standard*, concluding with the lines,

> Awake! Oh you young men of England,
>   For if when your country's in need,
> You do not enlist in your thousands,
>   You truly are cowards indeed. (10:20)

This was followed by another patriotic poem, 'Kitchener', included in the same paper on 21 July 1916. This, as Crick observes, was 'to be his last publication for twelve years'.[50] As Hynes writes, of 'Awake Young Men of England',

> All the clichés are there – the evocation of England, the glorification of sacrifice, the image from medieval, romantic battle, the emotive

language of courage and cowardice. It is a poem written not so much by a boy as by a tradition, and a tradition that was at an end.[51]

The poem is the product of a 'traditional' form of patriotism integral to public and private schools of the period,[52] including St. Cyprian's, which Orwell attended from 1911 until December 1916. This was an ambitious preparatory school, and, as Crick observes, although 'only twelve years old in 1911' had already established 'a reputation for getting scholarships and places at Harrow or other leading public schools'.[53] It imposed the values of these schools on its students, and as Meyers argues 'stressed loyalty and patriotism, valued money and privilege above everything else' and 'was class-conscious and conformist'.[54] Cyril Connolly insisted that, even at this age, Orwell rejected 'the war, the Empire, Kipling, Sussex, and Character', and informed him that 'whoever wins this war, we shall emerge a second-rate nation'.[55] However, as Crick argues, this 'attributes views to 9- and 10-year-old boys only plausible in precocious 12- and 13-year-olds'. It seems probable that the description corresponds more closely to 'what they were like when they were at Eton.' The two poems suggest Orwell did not 'reject the War, Empire and Kipling in 1914',[56] but held more conventional views that reflected his class and education.

Patriotism was, of course, only one of the values promoted by British public schools. As Meyers observed, they also taught 'class-consciousness'. Indeed, Orwell insisted in *The Road to Wigan Pier* that

> there is no place in the world where snobbery is quite so ever-present or where it is cultivated in such refined and subtle forms as in an English public school. Here at least one cannot say that English 'education' fails to do its job. You forget your Latin and Greek within a few months of leaving school – I studied Greek for eight or ten years, and now, at thirty-three, I cannot even repeat the Greek alphabet – but your snobbishness, unless you persistently root it out like the bindweed it is, sticks by you till your grave.[57]

The position is reinforced in his insistence in *The Lion and the Unicorn* that a 'public-school education is partly a training in class prejudice' (424). Institutions such as St. Cyprian's and Eton, therefore, not only provided an academic education, but promoted the values of the dominant class, often encoded in the over-determined idea of 'character'. As Pierre Maillaud writes, 'is often said that English education lays emphasis on character rather than on intellect', and emphasises the 'importance of behaviour, and, above all, of social conduct and social codes'.[58] Patriotism was an important element of this, although the process of indoctrination was, of course, not always successful. Orwell insisted that there was, for example, a 'general revolt against orthodoxy and authority'[59] at Eton when he attended, albeit an inconsistent one in which pupils 'retained, basically, the snobbish outlook of our class', but 'derided the OTC, the Christian religion, and perhaps even compulsory games and the Royal Family'. The continued importance of patriotism to the school authorities is, however, illustrated in the very activities against which pupils rebelled. Orwell wrote that in 1919, for example, Eton organised 'so-called peace celebrations' in which 'We were to march into the school-yard, carrying torches, and sing jingo songs of the type of "Rule Britannia".' He insists that the 'boys – to their honour, I think – guyed the whole proceeding and sang blasphemous and seditious words to the tunes provided'.[60] Nonetheless, the event itself demonstrates an 'official' celebration of the nation, and, indeed, the 'nation as state'.[61]

It was not, of course, only public or private schools that attempted to instil patriotism in their pupils. Robert Roberts argued that

> Compulsory state education had been introduced with overt propaga-
> tion of the imperialistic idea: especially was this so after 1880.
> Schools – and none more than those belonging to the Church of
> England – set out with vigour to instil in their charges a stronger
> sense of national identity and a deeper pride in expanding empire.[62]

The public schools provided a model for this process, and indeed informed popular culture, as their 'ethos, distorted into myth and sold among us weekly in penny numbers, for good or ill, set ideals and standards'. This 'ethos' was encoded in the popular serial stories set in fictional public schools, and indeed Roberts argued that 'it may well be found that Frank Richards during the first quarter of the twentieth century had more influence on the mind and outlook of young working-class England than any other single person, not excluding Baden-Powell'.[63] As Orwell wrote, in 'Boys' Weeklies', the stories represented a secure, imperial identity and a nation in which

> The King is on his throne and the pound is worth a pound. Over
> in Europe the comic foreigners are jabbering and gesticulating, but
> the grim grey battleships of the British Fleet are steaming up the
> Channel and at the outposts of the Empire the monocled Englishmen
> are holding the niggers at bay. (67)

Despite the fact that the public schools served only a particular, albeit dominant section of the population, their values informed popular culture, and, therefore, the nation as a whole. The stories in the 'penny numbers', like the instruction in the schools themselves, interpolated individuals in a form of national identity that celebrated, amongst other things, its imperial project.

This emphasis upon schools, whether as actual institutions or sites of a particular ethos, supports Gellner's emphasis upon the importance of a 'monopoly of legitimate education' in constructing national identity, and Althusser's insistence upon the pivotal role of 'the *educational ideological apparatus*' in consolidating and diffusing the values of the dominant classes. Both Orwell and Roberts argue that schools encourage their students to identify with the nation. The national identity they promote is, however, interwoven with particular ideas about state power, social hierarchy, and, in this period, imperialism. Orwell argued, for example, that the various 'boys' weeklies' encoded, amongst other things, the idea that 'the British Empire is a sort of charity-concern which will last for ever' (12:74). The imposition of patriotism in schools was, therefore, part of a process by which the state reproduced itself.

In a review of Malcolm Muggeridge's *The Thirties*, Orwell wrote that the 'closing chapters' illustrated

> the emotion of the middle-class man, brought up in the military tradition, who finds in the moment of crisis that he is a patriot after all. It is all very well to be 'advanced' and 'enlightened,' to snigger at Colonel Blimp and proclaim your emancipation from all traditional loyalties, but a time comes when the sand of the desert is sodden red and what have I done for thee, England, my England?

It is a tradition with which Orwell declared he could 'sympathise' (12:149–52:151), and he demonstrated his renewed patriotism by attempting to take a direct part in the war. In a letter to Geoffrey Gorer, dated 10 January 1940, he complained that 'I have so far completely failed to serve HM. government in any capacity, though I want to, because it seems to be me that now we are in this bloody war we have got to win it & I would like to lend a hand' (12:6–7:6). The sentiment contrasts with the opposition to war he frequently expressed between his return from Spain and the outbreak of the Second World War. As late as 23 February 1939, he wrote to Lady Rees that the 'idea of war is just a nightmare to me, and I refuse to believe that it can do the slightest good or even that it makes that much difference who wins'

(11:329–30:330). Indeed, in a letter to Charles Doran, of 26 November 1938, he stated that, 'we have got perhaps two years' breathing space in which it may be possible to provoke a real popular anti-war movement in England, in France, and above all in the Fascist countries' (11:238–40:238). After the outbreak of war, however, Orwell declared his support for British military action, and in *The Lion and the Unicorn* condemned the 'familiar arguments to the effect that democracy is "just the same as" or "just as bad as" totalitarianism' (397), arguments that parallel his own earlier statement that it would not make 'that much difference who wins'. As previously observed, his support for the British war effort was in part a pragmatic reaction to the political and military situation. However, he claimed it was also an 'instinctive' patriotic response to the threat of invasion and conquest. Indeed, in 'My Country Right or Left', he represents it as a literal revelation, and insists that what 'I knew in my dream that night was that the long drilling in patriotism which the middle class go through had done its work, and that once England was in a serious jam, it would be impossible for me to sabotage' (271). The values of his family, class and in particular his education return in a moment of national crisis.

The patriotism Orwell describes is internalised and, as the phrase 'what have I done for thee England, my England' indicates, an emotional rather than a rational attachment. In this sense, as Easthope argues, identification with the nation is comparable to 'falling in love', insofar as 'in both cases an object (the loved one, nation) is put in the place of an ego ideal'.[64] The persistent, even irrational importance of the nation as a basis of individual identity was repeatedly demonstrated throughout the period. As Arendt argued, 'stateless people', for example, demonstrated 'a surprising stubbornness in retaining their nationality' and 'never banded together [...] to defend common interests'.[65] Even the prosecution of ostensibly international causes was frequently defined by national allegiances, as in the case of the Spanish Civil War, in which the 'International Brigade was organized into national battalions, in which the Germans felt they fought against Hitler and the Italians against Mussolini, just as a few years later, in the Resistance, the Spanish refugees felt they fought against Franco when they helped the French against Vichy'.[66] This interpretation of the conflict is supported by Hobsbawn, who writes that,

> support for Spain was not a simple act of international solidarity, like the anti-imperialist campaigns for India or Morocco, which had a much more restricted appeal. In Britain the fight against fascism and

war concerned the British, in France the French – but after July 1936 the main front on which it was waged happened to be near Madrid. Issues which were essentially domestic in each country were, by the accidents of history, being fought out on battlefields in a country so remote and unknown to most workers that it had virtually no association for the average Briton other than those of the struggle which concerned them.[67]

Indeed, nationality sustained a limited solidarity even when efforts had been made to deprive individuals of all identity. In 'The Gypsy', Primo Levi wrote that, in Auschwitz,

> There was little feeling of *camaraderie* among us. It was confined to compatriots, and even towards them it was weakened by the minimal life conditions.[68]

Even under the most extreme conditions, therefore, the nation persisted as the dominant basis of identification. Indeed, in *The Lion and the Unicorn*, Orwell insisted that

> a *positive* force there is nothing to set beside it. Christianity and international Socialism are as weak as straws in comparison with it. (392)

According to Orwell, the problem for socialism was to appropriate or at least accommodate national identity. The position parallels that of Crick, who argues that some 'writers on nationalism need to be reminded, as Tocqueville said of democracy to the French conservatives of the 1830s, that it has come to stay, and that the problem is not how best and most elegantly to deplore it, but how to work with it so that it can be politicized'.[69]

In order for patriotism to be integrated into a socialist politics, however, it must be distinguished from both its traditional forms, such as those imposed in the public schools, and the nationalism of fascist states. To this end, Orwell insists that it is not a commitment to maintain the nation as it exists, but to 'liberate' or improve it. In 'Our Opportunity', for example, he defends 'the patriotism of the middle classes' but argues that commitment to Britain requires the fundamental transformation of the country, as 'a victory over Hitler demands the destruction of capitalism' (347). He insists that such a transformation is possible, in part because 'the patriotism of the middle classes' can be 'made use of', and the 'people who stand to attention during "God Save the King" would readily transfer their loyalty to a Socialist regime, if they were handled with the minimum of tact' (12:352–7:352–3). He figures patriotism as a mechanism of social change rather than an impediment to it. Indeed, Lutman argues that Orwell saw the possibilities of radical patriotism himself in Spain, where he experienced the 'feeling of belonging to a political community which could combine both traditional and revolutionary loyalties in terms of actual physical existence'.[70] In these examples, he figures patriotism as a force that can be integrated in a radical politics, rather than as being inherently subservient to the dominant order.

Orwell argues that patriotism is valuable to socialists because it connects diverse individuals and enables them to act together, to recognise their responsibilities to one another. He is not alone in this view. Indeed, Miller argues that nations are 'ethical communities', encoding the idea that 'I owe special obligations to fellow members of my nation which I do not owe to other human beings.'[71] Because people believe that they all belong to a specific community, he insists, 'the scheme of co-operation can be based on loose rather than strict reciprocity, meaning that redistributive elements can be built in which go beyond what the rational self-interest of each participant would dictate'.[72] This transcendence of 'rational self-interest', therefore, is founded, not upon a contractual or economic notion of citizenship, but upon a belief in shared membership of a community, an 'emotional' commitment that legitimises 'special obligations'. Orwell's claim in *The Lion and the Unicorn*, for example, that 'in moments of supreme crisis' the English 'can suddenly draw together' (393), illustrates his idea that that patriotism enables the kind of collective action and co-operation essential to 'democratic Socialism'.

This representation of patriots as committed to an evolving nation corresponds to what Hobsbawn describes as 'the original sense of the word', a sense that is 'the opposite of those who believed in "my country, right or wrong"'. He argues that 'the French Revolution, which appears to have used the term in the manner pioneered by Americans and more specially the Dutch Revolution of 1783, thought of patriots as those who showed the love of their country by wishing to renew it by reform or revolution'.[73] The nation was not perceived as the realisation of an essential identity, but as an evolving community. This usage provides a historical precedent for Orwell's ideas, but their methodological basis and practical operation are nevertheless problematic. The idea of 'reform' implies a rational, or at least conscious, assessment of the nation and its actions. This form of analysis is demonstrated in Orwell's writing on the 'nation as state', such as in the 'six point programme' (422)[74] for the alteration of institutions and policies outlined in *The Lion and the Unicorn*. His work on national identity, however, concentrates on the 'passionate subjective response' to the nation. It is, therefore, the 'intangible' network of myth, ritual and cultural tradition that forms the site of his struggle to construct a radical patriotism. The production of a revolutionary commitment to the nation is complicated by its unconscious, even irrational basis, the extent to which it exceeds the formal relations of citizenship.

In 'The Rediscovery of Europe', Orwell observes that

> Themes like revenge, patriotism, exile, persecution, race hatred, religious faith, loyalty, leader-worship, suddenly seem real again. Tamerlane and Genghis Khan seem credible figures now, and Machiavelli seems a serious thinker, as they didn't in 1910. (13:209–21:216)

The passage recognises a connection between 'patriotism', 'race hatred' and 'leader-worship'. In order to construct a radical patriotism, however, these terms had to be disentangled. 'Notes on Nationalism' attempts to do this. In this essay, Orwell argues that

> Nationalism is not to be confused with patriotism. Both words are normally used in so vague a way that any definition is liable to be challenged, but one must draw a distinction between them, since two different and even opposing ideas are involved. By 'patriotism' I mean devotion to a particular place and a particular way of life which one believes to be the best in the world but has no wish to force upon other people. Patriotism is of its nature defensive, both militarily and culturally. Nationalism, on the other hand, is inseparable from the desire for power. (141–2)

He insists that it 'can be plausibly argued, for instance – it is even probably true – that patriotism is an inoculation against nationalism' (154). Perhaps paradoxically, the essay represents patriotism as both revolutionary and defensive. It is committed to improving the nation but it also maintains cultural traditions without seeking to impose them on others. As Woodcock insisted, Orwell 'wished to defend his country at the cost of no other people'.[75] In contrast, Orwell claims nationalism is inherently aggressive, a form of 'power-hunger tempered by self-deception' (17:142). It involves 'identifying oneself with a single nation or unit, placing it beyond good and evil and recognizing no other duty than that of advancing its interests' (141). This analysis of what he describes in 'Anti-Semitism in Britain' as the 'disease of nationalism' (17:64–70:68) figures the division between the two forms of identification as fundamental and stable. Both their manifestations and indeed bases are quite distinct.

In 'Notes on Nationalism', Orwell argues that nationalism is primarily defined by three qualities, obsession, instability and indifference to reality. The first, he insists, is demonstrated by the fact that as 'nearly as possible, no nationalist ever thinks, talks or writes about anything except the superiority of his own power unit', and that it is 'difficult if not impossible for any nationalist to conceal his allegiance'. This results in their interpreting all events and societies in terms of this commitment. The nationalist, he argues, will insist upon the superiority of his or her nation 'not only in military power and political virtue, but in art, literature, sport, the structure of languages, the physical beauty of its inhabitants, and perhaps even in climate, scenery and cooking' (145). This obsessive connection, however, need not be with the state or culture that the nationalist actually inhabits, and Orwell describes this as the 'instability' of nationalism. The fact that they are not bound by immediate ties, such as residence or citizenship, illustrates the fact that nationalism is not determined by rational self-interest. Indeed, he insists the object of their devotion need not even be stable, as what 'remains constant in the nationalist is his own state of mind: the object of his feelings is changeable, and may be imaginary' (146). The third category, that of an 'indifference to reality', is, Orwell claims, demonstrated in the interpretation of historical and contemporary events. He argues that, for the nationalist, actions 'are held to be good or bad, not on their own merits, but according to who does them, and there is almost no kind of outrage – torture, the use of hostages, forced labour, mass deportations, imprisonment without trial, forgery, assassination, the bombing of civilians – which does not change its moral colour when it is committed by "our" side' (147). Indeed, the 'nationalist is haunted by the belief that the past can be altered' (148), as they select, represent, interpret, suppress and even alter historical facts in accordance with their political objectives. This exploitation and distortion of history is, of course, fully realised in Oceania, where 'the past was bought up to date'[76] in order to provide support for the policies of the state. However, Orwell insisted that the manipulation of the past was a feature of the contemporary world, and indeed in a letter to Noel Wilmett, of 18 May 1944, he argued that 'history has in a sense ceased to exist, i.e. there is no such thing as a history of our own times which could be universally accepted'

(16:190–2:191). Nationalism, in this account, appropriates, adapts and reinterprets historical narratives in order to legitimise present actions.

This description of nationalism parallels that of Isaiah Berlin, who argues that for the nationalist the

> essential human unit in which man's nature is fully realised is not the individual, or a voluntary association which can be dissolved or altered or abandoned at will, but the nation; that it is to the creation and maintenance of the nation that the lives of subordinate units, the family, the tribe, the clan, the province, must be due, for their nature and purpose, what is often called their meaning are derived from its nature and its purposes; and that these are revealed not by rational analysis, but by a special awareness, which need not be fully conscious, of the unique relationship that binds individual human beings into the indissoluble and unanalysable organic whole which Burke identified with society, Rousseau with the people, Hegel with the state, but which for nationalist is, and can only be, the nation, whether in social structure or form of government.[77]

This 'unit' is closed, and able to suppress or displace its contradictions.[78] It is also, Berlin insists, 'unanalysable', resistant to rational criticism. The assessment is broadly similar to that of Orwell, but Berlin argues that the commitment described is 'indissoluble', a position that contrasts with the emphasis on 'instability' in 'Notes on Nationalism'. This distinction emphasises Orwell's interpretation of nationalism as a structure of thought or 'state of mind'. For Berlin, the nation is a particular type of 'human unit', 'defined in terms of common territory, customs, laws, memories, beliefs, language, artistic and religious expression, social institutions, ways of life, to which some add heredity, kinship, racial characteristics'.[79] For Orwell, however, these codes and connections are not essential to its definition, and indeed he concedes that 'I have chosen the word "nationalism", but it will be seen in a moment that I am not using it in quite the ordinary sense, if only because the emotion I am speaking about does not always attach itself to what is called a nation – that is, a single race or a geographical area.' It is instead defined as a 'habit of mind' (17:141). Nationalism does 'not necessarily mean loyalty to a government or country, still less to *one's own* country, and it is not even strictly necessary that the units in which it deals should actually exist' (142). It is, in this analysis, a structure of interpretation that incorporates a particular conception of power, commitment and collective action.

The irrational or mythic definition of the nation is demonstrated in a speech delivered by Adolf Hitler on 1 May 1937, in which he examined 'what it is which the nation shares in common'. Despite the racial doctrines of National Socialism, he insisted that it was not 'blood' that was of primary importance, as although this 'is a common possession' it had 'not prevented men who spoke one language from being at loggerheads with one another for centuries'.[80] Nor was it 'common economic interests', as these had not 'prevented the hardest struggles from taking place precisely in this sphere', or even a common history, as, in Germany, this was 'a sad tale of war and dissension'. Instead, Hitler insisted,

> it is something quite different which not merely brings us to this community but even makes it unavoidable. It is our common fate, that common fate which none can escape and which is the lot of all life upon this earth.[81]

The statement figures nationality as an inevitable component of individual identity. Indeed, in a speech 1 May 1935 Hitler stated,

> may you one and all forget what life has made out of you as individuals, may you remember that in spite of these barriers you are members of one nation, and that you are so not by human will but God's will. It was He who made us members of this nation, He who gave us our mother tongue, He who implanted in us that being with which we are filled, which we must obey if we are to be more on earth than mere worthless chaff.[82]

In this earlier speech, nationality is represented as both 'indissoluble' and 'unanalysable'. The image of a community formed by 'God's will' resists rational analysis, positing an ahistorical essence that is not produced or even affected by human actions. In this account national identity is always already present.

These examples provide a potential basis upon which to examine the distinction Orwell makes between patriotism and nationalism. In both instances the identification is 'emotional'. However, whilst nationalism is aggressive, intolerant and concerned with power, he defines patriotism as a simultaneous defence of tradition and commitment to renewal. It interpellates individuals within a specific set of historical and cultural narratives, and produces an 'imagined community' that links the 'nation as state' to the 'nation as culture'. Indeed, as Easthope writes, 'national desire runs across that disjunction, responding to the promise that all may be synthesised into a single national characterisation, in the case of England, for example, allowing both state and culture – and their mixed components – to be marked as "English".'[83] The identification with 'English' culture can be mobilised in defence of the state with which this culture is identified, and therefore forms a basis for political activism. In contrast to 'nationalism', however, patriotism, as Orwell conceives it, is stable, inseparable from a network of specific, and therefore limited, traditions, institutions and territories. It is a 'devotion to a particular place and a particular way of life' and cannot be transferred. In contrast nationalism, a 'habit of mind', is characterised by 'instability', and its object may alter even if its structure persists.

The division between patriotism and nationalism is, of course, most obvious when the distance between their objects is at its widest.[84] It becomes more problematic when they use the same symbols or myths, revealing the potential for movement between the two terms. The patriotism imposed on Orwell as a child, for example, and which underpins the popular school stories, demonstrates the very 'indifference to reality' he represents as characteristic of nationalism. Despite his insistence in 'Boys' Weeklies' that it 'has nothing whatever to do with power-politics or "ideological" warfare', it incorporates the related idea that 'England is always in the right and England always wins'. It is defensive, insofar as its adherents 'do not feel that what happens in foreign countries is any of their business', but nevertheless interprets events, policies and institutions in national terms. Indeed, this process is satirised in the descriptions of *A Hundred Page History of Britain*, the textbook used in 'Ringwood House', the private school run by Mrs Creevy in *A Clergyman's Daughter*. The book, dated 1888, has for its 'frontispiece, a portrait of Boadicea with a Union Jack draped over the front of her chariot', an image that appropriates an evocative, pre-national figure to produce a fictive national 'antiquity'. The text itself promotes a sense of British superiority by distorting the past, and continually contrasting British 'success' with foreign 'failure'. It informs its readers, for example, that

After the French revolution was over, the self-styled Emperor Napoleon Buonaparte attempted to set up his sway, but though he won a few victories against continental troops, he soon found that in the 'thin red line' he had more than met his match. Conclusions were tried upon the field of Waterloo, where 50,000 Britons put to flight 70,000 Frenchmen – for the Prussians, our allies, arrived too late for the battle.

It also describes the 'Great Reform Bill of 1832' as 'the first of those bene-
ficent reforms which have made British liberty what it is and marked us
off from less fortunate nations'.[85] The text conceals the ambiguities of
British history, figuring it instead as a series of successes that legitimise
the imperialist Victorian state.

Orwell's satirical description of teaching at 'Ringwood House' parallels
autobiographical accounts of education in this period. Richard Hoggart,
for example, recalls that

> we were taught by those teachers to be unthinking little latter-day
> imperialists. Our history, when external to Britain, was imperial
> history – Wolfe dying on the Plains of Abraham, above all; the
> paradigm of a gallant English soldier and gentleman (an officer, of
> course), with Nelson at Trafalgar a close second and no mention of
> Emma; and little about Napoleon, except that he was a French villain.
> We heard much about Crusades, much about the benefits of British
> rule later brought to benighted natives everywhere, much about the
> warrior statesmen and little about the missionaries except for Living-
> stone and he was presented chiefly as an explorer.[86]

History teachers and textbooks interpreted their subject within terms
of a particular myth of the nation, which they in turn reinforced. This
manipulation of history sustained various widespread forms of nationalism, such as 'Neo-Toryism', and indeed Orwell argued that in 'England,
if one simply consider the number of people involved, it is probable that
the dominant form of nationalism is old-fashioned British jingoism'
(17:143). These examples expose two distinct problems in the division
Orwell proposes. In the first place, there is simply a characteristic slip-
page in the meaning of key terms between the various essays concerned
with national identity. The forms of 'patriotism' referred to in 'The Rediscovery of Europe', 'Boys' Weeklies' and 'Notes on Nationalism' have
quite different connotations and significance. In addition, however, the
examples to 'Neo-Toryism' and 'old-fashioned British jingoism' illustrate, nationalists are capable of using the codes, traditions and rituals
upon which patriotism relies. Indeed, nationalist movements can use
patriotism itself. The Nazi exploitation of German patriotism is one
prominent example of this process in the period. The distinction in
these instances, therefore, is one of interpretation or usage. The symbols
of the nation are contested, potential objects of both forms of identification, as illustrated by the permeable boundary between patriotism and
jingoism in the public school.

The example of a national language illustrates, not only this ambiguity of usage or interpretation, but the recurrent problem of defining the nation, and the importance of myth to Orwell's notion of patriotism. Access to a common language, as Hobsbawm insisted, is essential to 'nation-building' as it enables individuals to 'visualize in a general way the existence of thousands and thousands like themselves'. It not only provides a connection between current members of a national community, but also links them to their predecessors and successors. As Orwell writes in 'Culture and Democracy',

> I can't tell you what our civilization will be like in A.D. 2200, but I think I could probably prophesy some of its characteristics. I think I can fortell, for instance, that we shall still be using the English language and that it will have something in common with the English of Shakespeare, always assuming that we have escaped conquest from without. (13:67–79:76)

The passage figures language as connecting the living and the dead. In addition, it uses a reference to Shakespeare to suggest the inherent value of English. The use of language to define 'our civilization' is problematic, in that American English, for example, also has 'something in common with the English of Shakspeare'. Nevertheless, language is central to the definition of 'Englishness', and Shakespeare is integral, not only to the national literature, but to the culture as a whole. Orwell himself insists, in 'The English People', that

> The belief that we resemble our ancestors – that Shakespeare, say, is more like a modern Englishman than a modern Frenchman or German – may be unreasonable, but by existing it influences conduct. Myths which are believed tend to become true, because they set up a type, or 'persona', which the average person will do his best to resemble. (16:199–228:204)[87]

Shared access to a common language and literature provides a basis for integration, and is therefore important to Orwell's conception of patriotism. However, he connects language to the process of national renewal, arguing that it 'ought to be the joint creation of poets and manual workers', and that when these sections of the population are able to meet on more equal terms 'English may show more clearly than at present its kinship with the language of Shakespeare and Defoe' (221). The passage appropriates the myths surrounding national language, redeploying them to support a demand for social transformation. Orwell represents the future aesthetic value of the English language as dependent upon the development of a classless, socialist society.

The political connotations of a national language, however, are ambiguous, as it can also be used to consolidate or extend dominance. In colonial countries, for example, the imposition of a language upon a dominated population is used to 'prove' the cultural superiority of the imperial power. As Orwell argues in 'Notes on Nationalism', nationalists will 'consider it a duty to spread their own language to the detriment of rival languages' (145), a desire illustrated in Hitler's insistence that in 'a hundred years, our language will be the language of Europe'.[88] The linguistic competence of a subject people, however, is simultaneously constrained in order to retain the prestige of the dominant group. The imperial language is used for administrative purposes and amongst elites, but there is frequently an opposition to the colonised population attaining too high a proficiency in its use. Hitler, for example, favoured only an 'elementary instruction in reading and writing in German'[89] for the population of the occupied 'Eastern territories'. This paradoxical position is demonstrated in *Burmese Days*, in which Ellis responds to the butler's statement 'I find it very difficult to keep ice cool now' by exclaiming,

> Don't talk like that, damn you – 'I find it very difficult!' Have you swallowed a dictionary? 'Please master, can't keeping ice cool' – that's how you ought to talk. We shall have to sack this fellow if he gets to talk English too well. I can't stick servants who talk English.[90]

The polyglossia of the butler transgresses the linguistic boundaries that sustain the imperialist community, and therefore threatens the idea that a common identity 'unites' the diverse members of the European Club. These members, despite their individual differences, are connected by their use of signifiers that enable them to recognise one another as 'British'. The ability of the butler to manipulate English exposes these codes as learned, and erodes the idea of an essential distinction between the imperial and colonial populations. This forms part of a broader process in which the dominant status of the British community in Burma is exposed as the product of material power, rather than essential superiority, and therefore as potentially subject to change. Ellis' racism depends upon the concept of an inherent difference between the Burmese and the British, of which language is one signifier. As Orwell writes, in his 'As I Please' column of 20 October 1944, the 'endless emphasis on the differences between the "natives" and yourself is one of the necessary props of imperialism' (16:434–6:435).

Hobsbawm argues that it 'is important to distinguish between the exclusive nationalism of states or right-wing political movements which substitutes itself for all other forms of political and social identification, and the conglomerate nation/citizen, social consciousness which, in modern states, forms the soil in which all other political sentiments grow'.[91] In his work on national identity, particularly that produced during Second World War, Orwell attempted to establish precisely such a division.[92] He insisted that whilst the nation could be the object of an absolute identification it could also be the site of political reform, and, therefore, the democratic Socialism he supported. The distinction is in practice, however, political rather than methodological, in spite of his claims that patriotism and nationalism are founded upon 'two different and even opposing ideas'. The codes, symbols and myths utilised by 'old-fashioned British jingoism' and the English patriotism Orwell promoted, for example, are similar if not identical. As Easthope argues, 'identification and hostility appear as different sides of a single piece of paper'.[93] The distinction then, is one of their interpretation and deployment, and, indeed, of the presence or absence of politics itself. As Crick insists, 'Nationalism is at this time perhaps the most compelling of all motives that can lead men to abandon or to scorn politics',[94] as it posits a series of essential identities that render politics superfluous. Patriotism, in contrast, is political, established by argumentation, and by interventions such as that of Orwell. His own attempts to represent the nation as the object of both an 'emotional' commitment and of politics, to construct patriotism as the 'devotion to something that is changing but is felt to be mystically the same' (12:271) are illustrated in his writing on Englishness, which is analysed in the next chapter.

4
Englishness

The idea of 'Englishness' is integral to numerous accounts of Orwell. Paul Potts, for example, insisted that he was 'very English, as English as the grass that grows along the Thames at Runnymede'.[1] For Hammond, he was,

> first of all, a quintessentially *English* writer. This was a man who loved coal fires and English cooking, Victorian furniture and high tea, a man who delighted in the novels of Dickens, Wells and Gissing, who loved the countryside and the open air and appreciated the quirkiness of such institutions as the monarchy, public schools and the Church of England.[2]

Christine Berberich describes him as, 'not only a patriot', but an '*English patriot*'.[3] Indeed, Orwell is represented by numerous critics as not only English, but a typical, even archetypal English figure. Bradbury, for example, insists that Orwell was 'as deeply English as Koestler was European'.[4] This comparison was also made by John Strachey, who wrote that

> Arthur Koestler, if you meet him in the street, is Central Europe. George Orwell, walking down the road, was England – not, of course, the England of convention, of John Bull: just the contrary. He was one of the least bluff or hearty men who ever lived. He was another England: subtle, retired, but very sharp. He was the England of the major eccentrics, the major satirists.[5]

Even his adopted name is held by some to encode a certain 'Englishness'. Crick, for example, argues that it has 'a manly, English, indeed country-sounding ring to it',[6] and Peter Lewis observes that it 'has been suggested that "George Orwell" appealed to him because of its Englishness – the patron saint's Christian name followed by the name of an East Anglian river'.[7]

The notion of 'Englishness' not only pervades accounts of Orwell himself, however, but also interpretations of his work. Easthope, for example, analyses his writing in terms of distinctive English literary and philosophical traditions. *Nineteen Eighty-Four* is consequently viewed as 'a Lockeian novel',[8] the product of an 'empiricist discourse' that 'constantly retrieving attitudes from some half-forgotten precedent in Locke, continues to define the limits for English culture'.[9] This 'discourse', founded upon the idea that 'reality can be experienced more or less directly by the unprejudiced observer and that knowledge derives more or less directly from that experience',[10] is illustrated when, for example, Winston Smith reassures himself that

> Truisms are true, hold on to that! The solid world exists, its laws do not change. Stones are hard, water is wet, objects unsupported fall towards the earth's centre.[11]

The idea that such empiricism demonstrates the 'Englishness' of Orwell's writing is reinforced by Christopher Norris, who argues that his texts show a 'bluff disregard of theoretical problems' that 'has always been the hallmark of that "English" ideology which thinkers from the "other", Continental traditions have treated with alternating wonder and despair'.[12] Lionel Trilling similarly insists that

> Orwell is an intellectual to his fingertips, but he is far removed from both the Continental and the American type of intellectual. The turn of his mind is what used to be thought of as peculiarly 'English.' He is indifferent to the allurements of elaborate theory and of extreme sensibility. The medium of his thought is common sense, and his commitment to intellect is fortified by an old-fashioned faith that the truth can be got at, that we can, if we really want to, see the object as it really is.[13]

Edmund Wilson also wrote that Orwell 'has the good English qualities that, in the literary field at any rate, are beginning to seem old-fashioned: readiness to think for himself, courage to speak his mind, the tendency to deal with concrete realities rather than theoretical positions, and a prose style that is both downright and disciplined'.[14] These qualities are illustrated by, for example, Orwell's statement, in a letter to Henry Miller of August 1936, that 'I have a sort of belly to earth attitude and always feel uneasy when I go away from the ordinary world where grass is green, stones hard etc.' (10:495–7:496).

The interpretation of Orwell's texts as the product of a distinct national 'discourse' or 'turn of mind' is reinforced by their critical location within a particular English literary tradition. For Hammond, Orwell combined in his essays 'the two great traditions of English letters', the 'solid *belles lettres* tradition of Hazlitt and Stevenson' and the 'radical questioning tradition of Defoe and Swift'.[15] The latter, in particular, is frequently invoked in critical accounts of Orwell. Woodcock, for example, argued that not 'since Swift, his great master, has there been a prose more lucid, flexible, exact and eloquent than Orwell's',[16] whilst Crick insists that his 'debt to Swift has often been noted [...] but his deliberate choice of rhetoric, his adopted style and conscious persona as a writer may owe more to Daniel Defoe; and he wrote for much the same kind of audience'.[17] For Irving Howe, Orwell was 'the best English essayist since Hazlitt, perhaps since Dr Johnson',[18] and for Potts 'a journalist, but only if Swift and Hazlitt were journalists'.[19] The recurrent comparison with these writers locates Orwell within English literary tradition, as 'heir' to Swift, Defoe and Hazlitt, whilst his own essays on writers such as H. G. Wells, Rudyard Kipling, George Gissing, Charles Dickens and Jonathan Swift implicitly reinforce the notion of a distinctive national 'canon'.

Critical interpretations of Orwell's socialism also frequently locate him within English 'radical tradition'. Crick, for example, describes Orwell as 'a pretty typical English left-wing socialist in the tradition of Morris, Blatchford, Carpenter, Cole, Tawney, Laski, Bevan and Foot'.[20] Gordon Beadle emphasises his inheritance from English nineteenth-century radicalism, arguing that whilst many of 'Orwell's intellectual contemporaries yielded, at least for a time, to the authoritarian, dogmatic ideologies of the inter-war years' he 'remained stubbornly faithful to the Victorian tradition of radicalism, with its emphasis on democracy, pragmatism, morality and individual freedom.[21] Orwell himself, in his introduction to *British Pamphleteers*, locates English radicals within a broader socialist tradition, insisting that the 'English Diggers and Levellers [...] are links in a chain of thought which stretches from the slave revolts of antiquity, through various peasant risings and heretical sects of the Middle Ages, down to the Socialists of the nineteenth century and the Trotskyists and Anarchists of our own day' (19:106–15:109). His own work nevertheless incorporates features, such as the emphasis upon a '*moral* subject, self-conscious, responsible for choice',[22] which East-hope argues are distinctively English. The emphasis upon 'individual freedom', or, as Crick terms it, the belief that there are 'some areas of life which have to be preserved from politics',[23] is also interpreted in these accounts as characteristic of the English and English socialism. This does not, of course, indicate parochialism, but instead a distinctive national contribution to the 'vision of a world of free and equal human beings, living together in a state of brotherhood' (19:109).

The idea of 'Englishness' provides an interpretative context for Orwell's work, which draws upon inherited intellectual, literary and political traditions for its form and values. 'Englishness', however, is not only a discourse within which the texts operate but a concept reinter-preted within them. Orwell attempted, particularly after 1939, to figure patriotism as a component or even basis of 'democratic Socialism'. The focus of this was the concept of 'Englishness', the particular narrative within which he perceived himself as embedded and which he used to illustrate his ideas. The exploration of this form of identification and its radical potential, most visible in *The Lion and the Unicorn* and *The English People*, therefore formed an important element of his political writing in this period. This attempt to use the nation and national identity for political purposes was, however, not peculiar to Orwell. Croft argues that much of the historical fiction of the 1930s, for example,

> was directed at showing the radical and democratic traditions of British history, at emphasising the struggles by which these liberties were won. All of this involved a re-working of notions of 'English-ness'. Abroad the National government was palpably betraying the national interest by its appeasement of European fascism and its collusion in the defeat of Spanish, Austrian and Czech democracy. At home the British Union of Fascists were trying hard to appropriate national sentiment against Jews and Communists. The Left was thus drawn unavoidably into a struggle over definitions.[24]

England and 'Englishness' consequently became central to a political conflict centring on the meaning and use of 'English culture'. Their centrality to contemporary literary and intellectual debates is emphas-ised by Hynes, who refers to 'two of the generation's myths: the Myth of Revolution and the Myth of England'.[25] In texts produced by the Left, these two myths are frequently interwoven, with the nation figured as the site of potential revolution.

Images and invocations of both England and revolution recur in Left-wing texts from this period. In *The Magnetic Mountain*, for example, Day Lewis addresses 'You that love England, have an ear for her music', whilst implying, in his image of the 'entrance of a new theme'[26] that this England is not fixed but changing. The poem positions itself in opposition to those who 'tell you all's well with our lovely England',[27] whom it characterises as the 'Scavenger barons and your jackal vassals', instructing them to 'quit the country before it's too late'.[28] It therefore distinguishes 'our pleasant land'[29] from its present dominant class, locating 'authentic' dedication to the nation in a commitment to renewal and a 'new theme'. Such commitment was common on the Left in the period. Even Harry Pollitt celebrated Britain as 'one of the love-liest countries in the world, the genius, craftsmanship, initiative and magnificent fighting traditions of its people going back for hundreds of years'.[30] These and other references to Britain or, more commonly, England, figure it as a potential basis of what Lewis describes as a 'new world'.[31] Those on the Left are represented as the legitimate inher-itors of 'Englishness', and indeed in his preface to *New Country* Michael Roberts comments that although 'our sympathies turn toward revolu-tionary change',[32] nevertheless 'we have indeed greater faith in England than you'.[33] The position is reflected in the collection itself, and Hynes comments that

> *England* also appears again and again in both the prose and verse in *New Country*, in ways that suggest that these writers were as nation-alistic in their way as the Georgian poets were. Their England is a curious mixture of contradictory elements, pastoral and derelict, loveable and sick, and their attitude towards their country is equally mixed, part love and part social criticism.[34]

Orwell's exploration of 'Englishness' is, therefore, produced within the context of a broader 'struggle over definitions' in which England becomes a contested, political site. For the Left, the basis of this, Croft argues, was the belief that

> Patriotism could be rescued from embarrassment and the Right. Part of a crucial political relocation in the Left's thinking in the 1930s, it ceased to be a dirty word and was successfully mobilised against fascism, British and German.[35]

The manipulation of national identities by the Right, in this interpretation, is countered in the attempt to use the nation as the basis of resistance to fascism, and indeed to figure it as the potential site of a future socialist practice.

The reinterpretation of English patriotism undertaken by Orwell after 1939 was, according to this account, part of a broader 'relocation in the Left's thinking'. His exploration and use of the 'Myth of England' is nevertheless a distinctive and indeed characteristic intervention in this debate. As Lutman argues, Orwell interprets patriotism 'as part of the connective tissue between the individual and society', consisting 'of a whole network of loyalties, emotions, feelings, and values' that provide the individual with 'identity and meaning'.[36] It is also a basis for collective action. Indeed, as Easthope argues, this is a feature of national identities as such, as they involve not only 'identification with the idea of nation', but also 'a simultaneous identification with others'[37] who are also committed to this 'idea'. The precise contours of the 'network' upon which patriotism is founded define this identification and consequently the kind of co-operation it enables. The 'loyalties, emotions, feelings and values' upon which 'Englishness', for example, is founded, determine to a considerable extent the range of purposes for which it can be mobilised. Its reinterpretation is, therefore, a political act. Orwell's attempt to figure 'Englishness' as the basis of a socialism that would not abandon traditional identities illustrates a distinct form of radicalism also exhibited, for example, in his discussions of class. Indeed, for Hynes, his representations of class and nationality are linked, as 'Orwell mythologized his idea of ordinariness in two related ways: in a Myth of the Proletariat (where ordinariness was given a class identity), and in a Myth of the English People (where it was made a national characteristic).'[38]

The development of this form of 'Englishness', which incorporates both revolutionary and traditional values, relies on the construction of a coherent narrative from the diverse images of the English, and indeed of England itself. Even establishing who the 'English' are, however, could be problematic, as illustrated in a passage from Doris Lessing's *In Pursuit of the English*, in which Rose discusses her landlady, Flo, with the narrator, who has been raised in colonial Africa. Rose explains that

> 'I'm not saying anything against her, don't think it. She's English really. She was born here. But her grandmother was Italian, see? She comes from a restaurant family. So she behaves different. And then the trouble is, Dan isn't a good influence – not that I'm saying a word against him.'

'Isn't he English?'

'Not really, he's from Newcastle. They're different from us, up in places like that. Oh no, he's not English, not properly speaking.'

'And you?'

She was confused at once. 'Me, dear? But I've lived in London all my life. Oh, I see what you mean – I wouldn't say I was English so much, as a Londoner, see? It's different.'[39]

For Lessing, despite the fact that the 'Press, national institutions, the very flavour of the air we breathe indicate their continued and powerful existence'[40] the English are 'hard to meet',[41] obscured by a plethora of other identities. As Easthope argues 'no matter what national identity claims for itself, it can never be more than one among many', as 'identities extend in overlapping circles'.[42] The formulation of a distinct 'Englishness' therefore depends, to an extent at least, on its separation from these other identities with which it co-exists. It also, obviously, depends upon the successful representation of the nation itself as a distinct unit. The problem is emphasised in *The English People*, in which Orwell imagines an 'intelligent observer' questioning,

is there such a thing as 'the English character'? Can one talk about nations as though they were individuals? And supposing that one can, is there any genuine continuity between the England of today and the England of the past? (203)

In *The Lion and the Unicorn*, he notes the difficulty of even a synchronic account of the English, inquiring,

Are we not forty-six million individuals, all different? And the diversity of it, the chaos! The clatter of clogs in the Lancashire mill towns, the to-and-fro of the lorries on the Great North Road, the queues outside the Labour Exchanges, the rattle of pin-tables in the Soho pubs, the old maids biking to Holy Communion through the mists of the autumn morning – all these are not only fragments, but *characteristic* fragments, of the English scene. How can one make a pattern out of this muddle? (392)

The statement exposes the 'diversity' and 'chaos' of the material upon which accounts of 'Englishness' are founded. It also, however, illustrates one method by which it can be represented. The use of a list of 'representative' features of English life to describe the national 'character' and to posit a relation between its diverse elements is a persistent feature of accounts of 'Englishness'. The distinctions between such lists, however, illustrate the use of selection to impose particular conceptions of the nation. The series of images produced in this period by, for example, T. S. Eliot, A. L. Rowse and J. B. Priestley, illustrate three distinct conceptions of English culture, and provide a point of comparison for the 'Myth of the English People' Orwell himself formulates.

In *Notes Towards the Definition of Culture*, Eliot writes that

> the reader must remind himself as the author has constantly to do, of how much is here embraced by the term *culture*. It includes all the characteristic activities and interests of a people: Derby Day, Henley Regatta, Cowes, the twelfth of August, a cup final, the dog races, the pin table, the dart board, Wensleydale cheese, boiled cabbage cut into sections, beetroot in vinegar, nineteenth-century Gothic churches and the music of Elgar. The reader can make his own list.[43]

The series illustrates a particular view of English society that includes, for example, a 'naturalisation' of established class structures. Henley Regatta, Cowes and the twelfth of August are all events associated with the upper classes, whilst the 'cup final' and 'dog races' are images, even clichés of working-class life in the period.[44] The list, therefore, both posits a national culture that transcends divisions of income or class, and implies that such divisions structure this culture. This acceptance of a traditional hierarchy is in accordance with Eliot's argument that what 'is important is a structure of society in which there will be, from "top" to "bottom", a continuous gradation of cultural levels',[45] and that a 'nation which has gradations of class seems to me, other things being equal, likely to be more tolerant and pacific than one which is not so organized'.[46] The list is, therefore, not neutral, but uses the idea of 'characteristic' features to naturalise a particular set of values.

A similar use of a series of images of English culture to represent certain values as inherent in the national character is illustrated in Rowse's *The English Spirit*. In his preface, Rowse writes that, in 'bringing these essays together – composed over a number of years – I am a little surprised to find how consistent and strong is the theme that runs through them: something more than pride in, a deep love for, English things, for our countryside and towns, with their memories of the people who inhabit them and of the things that took place there – all so much alive for me; for places associated with names that are the very stuff of our tradition, Thomas More and Elizabeth, George Herbert and Hampden and Clarendon, Swift and Horace Walpole, William and Dorothy Wordsworth, the Tower and Hampton Court, Rycote and Great Tew, Trinity Great Court and the High, Wilton, the Close at Salisbury; our tradition itself and the literature in which it is expressed and handed on'.[47] The 'deep love' for 'English things' is here located in a series of prominent historical figures, the places associated with them, and the literature some of them produced. The insistence upon these figures as representative of the national 'character', or indeed as its realisation, is continued in the essays themselves. In 'The Idea of Patriotism', for example, Rowse emphasises the 'great achievements and great men whom this country has produced – Shakespeare, Newton, Milton, Darwin, Cromwell, Nelson, the Pitts – our tradition of political freedom, the triumphs of modern industry, the British Commonwealth of Nations'.[48] In 'The English Spirit', he focuses on the 'astounding achievement of the English, a people who have contributed such names to the roll of the world's great men, to take a few at random: Shakespeare, Newton, Milton, Darwin, Dickens, Drake, Nelson, Malborough, Swift, the Pitts – to say nothing of our kith and kin across the seas, Washington, Franklin, Abraham Lincoln'.[49] These passages reinforce the idea that the 'English Spirit' inheres primarily in 'great men' rather than in, for example, national institutions.[50] The various lists dispersed throughout the text endorse the idea of individual genius and, moreover, describe 'Englishness' primarily in terms of literature, politics and warfare. This attempt to 'define the indefinable',[51] the national character, encodes a particular idea of history and nationality, representing them as determined by an elite who operate in certain privileged spheres.

The list, in these examples, is a rhetorical device used to establish a relation between diverse objects. It is employed by Rowse and Eliot in their descriptions of 'Englishness' to make 'a pattern out of this muddle', to connect a series of images which are then figured as representative of England or the English. The list are both diverse and incomplete, as Eliot concedes when he writes that the 'reader can make his own list'. Nonetheless, both writers imply that there is a distinctive, coherent national character that these series of images expose. In *English Journey*, however, Priestley uses three quite different lists to represent what he describes as the 'three Englands I had seen, the Old, the Nineteenth Century and the New'.[52] 'Old England', for Priestley, is the 'country of the cathedrals and minsters and manor houses and inns, of Parson and Squire; guide-books and quaint highways and byways of England', the landscape which 'our railway companies' describe to the 'readers of American magazines'.[53] The 'nineteenth-century England', in contrast, is the

> industrial England of coal, iron, steel, cotton, wool, railways; of thousands of rows of little houses all alike, sham Gothic churches, square-faced chapels, Town Halls, Mechanics' Institutes, mills, foundries, warehouses, refined watering-places, Pier Pavilions, Family and Commercial Hotels, Literary and Philosophical Societies, back-to-back houses, detached villas with monkey-trees, Grill Rooms, railway stations, slag-heaps and 'tips,' dock roads, Refreshment Rooms, doss-houses, Unionist or Liberal Clubs, cindery waste grounds, mill chimneys, slums, fried-fish shops, public-houses with red blinds, bethels in corrugated iron, good-class drapers' and confectioners' shops, a cynically devastated countryside, sooty dismal little downs, and still sootier grim fortress-like cities.[54]

The third England is described as the

> new post-war England, belonging far more to the age itself than to this particular island. America, I supposed, was its real birthplace. This is the England of arterial and by-pass roads, of filling stations and factories that look like exhibition buildings, of giant cinemas and dance-halls and cafés, bungalows with tiny garages, cocktail bars, Woolworths, motor-coaches, wireless, hiking, factory girls looking like actresses, greyhound racing and dirt tracks, swimming pools, and everything given away for cigarette coupons.[55]

These 'three Englands' are, to an extent, geographically divided. The description of the Cotswolds, for example, which he insists is the 'most English and the least spoiled of all our countrysides',[56] is, implicitly, part of 'Old England', whilst Birmingham, with its 'many miles of ugliness, squalor, and the wrong kind of vulgarity'[57] forms part of 'nineteenth-century England'. Priestley insists, however, that although it 'would be possible, though not easy, to make a coloured map of them', the 'three were variously and most fascinatingly mingled in every part of the country I had visited'.[58] The north of England, for example, is not entirely 'nineteenth-century', despite the concentration of 'traditional' industries, any more than the south-east is entirely 'Old'.

The three models of England emphasise a series of social and economic divisions within England that undermine the idea of a unified, or even coherent nation. Indeed, Priestley insists that

> It was all very puzzling. Was Jarrow still in England or not? Had we exiled Lancashire and the North-east coast?[59]

The tripartite model exposes the various contradictory associations of both England and Englishness. The insistence that the nation incorporates such distinct characteristics is not, of course, peculiar to Priestley. In *Lady Chatterley's Lover*, for example, Lawrence, describing the co-existence of mines and stately homes, writes,

> England my England! But which is *my* England?

The division in this instance is a binary one, a progression in which the 'industrial England blots out the agricultural England'.[60] Lawrence collapses the distinction between the 'nineteenth-century' and the 'New', between modern and 'traditional' industries, to represent a polarised nation. This contrast, frequently traced upon the landscape itself, is a recurrent element of images of England. Pierre Maillaud, for example, insists that most 'foreigners and especially Frenchmen have a preconceived vision of England as the land of mechanical power, blast furnaces, cotton mills, foundries, steelworks and the like, with somewhere in between a few pictures of a lovely and minute conservative countryside'.[61] This distinction is, again, in part a geographical one located in the contrast between, for example, the Cotswolds and Jarrow, or between the agricultural towns of the southern counties and the impoverished industrial cities of northern England. In *In England Now*, the American Mary Ellen Chase also constructs such an opposition when she contrasts the 'southern cathedral towns', which she represents as 'mellow and venerable, beautiful, content, and secluded', with the 'northern towns', which she insists are 'harsh, ugly, restless, discontented, with no past that is discernible in their bleak present'.[62] The distinction, however, is not only one of environment or economic status, but one between different conceptions of 'England' and 'Englishness'. This focuses upon the binary opposition of the rural and industrial, a variant of the older division between country and city. As Raymond Williams argues, a 'contrast between country and city, as fundamental as ways of life, reaches back into classical times', and,

On the country has gathered the idea of a natural way of life: of peace, innocence, and simple virtue. On the city has gathered the idea of an achieved centre: of learning, communication and light. Powerful hostile associations have also developed: on the city as a place of noise, worldliness and ambition; on the country as a place of backwardness, ignorance and limitation.[63]

The precise associations and their significance, however, change across periods and cultures. Williams insists, for example, that 'Old England, settlement, the rural virtues', all aspects of the idea of the 'country', 'mean different things at different times, and quite different values are being brought to question'.[64] The opposition, although well established, is always realised within particular social, economic and political contexts that determine its precise significance. In Orwell's writing, it forms a basis of the contradictory commitment to both established and revolutionary values embedded in his work on 'Englishness' and, indeed, his writing as a whole. The binary model of town and country, and the tripartite model developed by Priestley, provide a basis for a political analysis of Orwell's writing on the English and its significance for his socialism.

Orwell's idea of 'Englishness' as a potential component of 'democratic Socialism' is most prominently developed in *The Lion and the Unicorn* and *The English People*. In these texts, he uses lists, the rhetorical device employed by Eliot and Rowse, to construct the image of an English character that is simultaneously diverse and coherent. In *The Lion and the Unicorn*, for example, he insists that the English 'are not gifted artistically', 'not intellectual' in comparison with other Europeans, 'have a horror of abstract thought', and possess 'a certain power of acting without taking thought' (12:393). In *The English People*, he argues that a 'foreign observer, new to England, but unprejudiced' would 'Almost certainly... find the salient characteristics of the English common people to be artistic insensibility, gentleness, respect for legality, suspicion of foreigners, sentimentality about animals, hypocrisy, exaggerated class distinctions, and an obsession with sport' (16:200). These images, which Orwell claims 'would be accepted by almost all observers' (12:393), parallel those in other accounts of the national character. The insistence that the English 'have a horror of abstract thought', for example, evokes Easthope's description of a prevalent English empiricism that maintains 'reality can be experienced more or less directly', as well as Trilling's reference to a 'peculiarly "English"' intellectual tradition, 'indifferent to the allurements of elaborate theory'. Chase also comments that the 'English are not an analytical people',[65] whilst in

Storm Jameson's *The Moment of Truth*, Emil Breuner considers 'the English trick of reconciling contradictions by sending them to play in different rooms', and concludes that they 'have wisdom and no logic'.[66] Paul Cohen-Portheim argued that 'the Englishman is the least analytical of men',[67] whilst his insistence that 'Intellectual things are as little in the average Englishman's line as they are in the average schoolboy's',[68] supports Orwell's statement that the English are 'not intellectual'. The claim that a 'suspicion of foreigners' is a national characteristic is also paralleled in the accounts of other commentators. Cohen-Portheim, for example, argues that the English have a 'distrust of anything foreign or over-clever',[69] whilst Drew Middleton remarks that one 'of the most interesting contrasts in British life is between the nation's world-wide interests and responsibilities and the strong strain of xenophobia in the national character'.[70] The 'salient characteristics' that Orwell identifies, therefore, are not simply the product of a personal analysis, but recurrent images, or indeed myths, of 'Englishness'.

These widespread, even conventional images of the English are, however, linked by Orwell to the idea of radical social transformation and, in particular, socialism. Indeed, in *The Lion and the Unicorn*, he insists that it 'is only by revolution that the native genius of the English people can be set free' (415). This 'native genius' is located by Orwell in various characteristics, perceived as distinctively English, that he interprets as forming a potential basis of 'democratic Socialism'. These include, for example, the 'respect for legality' listed above, but also other qualities, such as a belief in 'justice, liberty and objective truth' (397), and what he describes as the 'outstanding and – by contemporary standards – highly original quality of the English', their 'habit of *not killing one another*' (16:222). The latter feature is interpreted as the product of a national cohesion that ensures that in

> any circumstances we can foresee, the proletariat of Hammersmith will not arise and massacre the *bourgeoisie* of Kensington: they are not different enough. Even the most drastic changes will have to happen peacefully and with a show of legality, and everyone except the 'lunatic fringes' of various political parties is aware of this. (210)

This interpretation of the English parallels that of other commentators. Middleton, for example, insists upon the 'essential homogeneity'[71] of the British, whilst D. W. Brogan argues that although the 'English are both the most united and the most divided of great peoples' in 'moments of great crisis they discover hidden though not unexpected sources of national strength in their mutual trust'.[72] The idea of a commitment to 'liberty' as a feature of 'Englishness' is also common to numerous accounts of the national character, although it is often interpreted as dependent upon individual adherence to a shared code of conduct. Maillaud, for example, comments that it is interwoven with 'English social conformity',[73] Chase that it is 'only possible through the strict adherence to certain laws within and without oneself',[74] and Cohen-Portheim that it is 'inextricably connected' to the 'inclination of conventionality'.[75] The idea of a widespread English belief in the 'liberty of the individual', however constituted, is nevertheless a persistent one. The characteristics that Orwell identifies, therefore, are recurrent images of the English, reinterpreted within the context of his political commitments. This forms one example of the 'struggle over definitions', an attempt to mobilise various existing national myths in order to construct a revolutionary 'Myth of the English People'.

The Lion and the Unicorn is explicitly concerned with the 'rise of something that has never existed before, a specifically *English* Socialist movement', a national radicalism which is contrasted with both the 'Labour Party, which was the creation of the working class but did not aim at any fundamental change, and Marxism, which was a German theory interpreted by Russians and unsuccessfully transplanted to England' (426). This movement is figured as the product of a pre-existent 'Englishness' which it in turn reinforces, as by 'revolution we become more ourselves, not less' (432). The model is, amongst other things, used to distance socialism from the 'English intelligentsia', whom Orwell insists are 'Europeanized', detached from the 'common culture of the country', taking their 'cookery from Paris and their opinions from Moscow' (406). The emphasis of the text, however, is not simply upon the national character, but also upon a particular section of the English population that broadly corresponds to the 'New' England described by Priestley. Orwell insists that the

> place to look for the germs of the future England is in the light-industry areas and along the arterial roads. In Slough, Dagenham, Barnet, Letchworth, Hayes – everywhere, indeed, on the outskirts of great towns – the old pattern is gradually changing into something new.

These areas contain 'the people who are most at home in and most definitely *of* the modern world, the technicians and the higher-paid skilled workers, the airmen and their mechanics, the radio experts, film producers, popular journalists and industrial chemists' (408), representatives of the 'whole classes of necessary people, factory managers, airmen, naval officers, farmers, white-collar workers, shopkeepers, policemen', who have previously been 'frightened away' by 'left-wing propaganda' (420). In particular, Orwell emphasises the 'technical experts', including 'airmen, destroyer commanders, etc., etc.', without whom 'we could not survive for a week' (421). The idea of 'a specifically *English* Socialist movement' developed in the text therefore relies upon both the reinterpretation of a 'traditional' image of the English character, and an appeal to the 'New' England of the 'technical experts'.

The connotations of this 'New' England are, of course, ambiguous. Priestley, for example, interpreted it, not as the basis of an *'English* Socialist movement', but of conformity or indifference, insisting that 'too many of the people in this new England are doing not what they like but what they have been told they would like'.[76] Orwell himself describes the areas as the site of

> a rather restless, cultureless life, centring round tinned food, *Picture Post*, the radio and the internal combustion engine. It is a civilisation in which children grow up with an intimate knowledge of magnetoes and in complete ignorance of the Bible. (12:408)

In contrast to Priestley, however, who argues that because this 'latest England' is 'not politically-minded' it may produce 'an iron autocracy',[77] Orwell represents its inhabitants as 'necessary', the representatives of 'something new'. This perception of 'airmen' and 'managers' as figures of a new order recurs throughout the literature of the period. As Cunningham argues, the 'man in the aeroplane', for example, was for numerous writers the 'quintessential man of action',[78] a distinctively modern hero. His flight is frequently associated with the idea of the journey, described by Hynes as the 'most insistent of 'thirties metaphors', which traces a passage 'out of the familiar and secure into the unknown and frightening, which had to be taken if one was to reach the new life'.[79] The significance of the 'airman' is ambiguous, insofar as the 'aerial position' is 'natural and ideal for that recognizably totalitarian strain of giving orders, hectoring, advising, preaching sermons, being schoolmasterly'.[80] His privileged status is, however, a product of his association with modernity and, Orwell claims, that 'indeterminate stratum' of the population 'at which the older class distinctions are beginning to break down' (12:408).

Indeed, even 'managers', despite their obvious association with capitalism, are perceived as integral to such new social developments.

James Burnham, for example, insists on the increasing dominance of a 'managerial' class expert in 'the technical direction and co-ordination of the process of production'.[81] These individuals, he argues, rather than the owners of capital, exercise 'control over the instruments of production',[82] with 'their rights belonging to them not as individuals, but through the position of actual directing responsibility which they occupy'.[83] The significance of the 'managerial' class is, however, like that of the 'airman', ambiguous. Burnham observes that those 'nations – Russia, Germany, and Italy – which have advanced furthest toward the managerial social structure are all of them, at present, *totalitarian* dictatorships',[84] and the Party described in *Nineteen Eighty-Four* is a recognisably a 'managerial' elite. The incorporation of such figures in the image of a 'future England', therefore, demonstrates, not only a commitment to integrating the middle classes within a theory of socialism, but an attempt to define and appropriate these evocative, contested symbols of the modern age.

The idea of 'Englishness' expounded in Orwell's works is, however, not located only in this 'New' England, but also in a more traditional, pastoral landscape. Stephen Ingle, for example, comments on Orwell's 'love of the countryside and his sentimental, nostalgic attachment to the certainties of pre-1914 English family and community life, which were used as yardsticks to measure the horrors of life on Animal Farm and in Oceania'.[85] This emphasises a commitment to 'Old' England, a rural order located before what Orwell described in 'Inside the Whale' as an 'age' of 'concentration-camps, rubber truncheons, Hitler, Stalin, bombs, aeroplanes, tinned food, machine-guns, putsches, purges, slogans, Bedaux belts, gas-masks, submarines, spies, provocateurs, press-censorship, secret prisons, aspirins, Hollywood films and political murders' (12:86–115:91). This point is reinforced by Hammond, who insists that 'Orwell shared with a number of other radical English novelists, most notably H. G. Wells, a nostalgia for the unchanging rural order he had known and loved as a child',[86] and Berberich, who argues that 'Orwell's essays, his journalism and his letters are interspersed with nostalgia, notions of Englishness, a longing for the seemingly safe and stable world of his childhood.'[87] This 'safe and stable' world is represented in *Coming Up for Air*, for example, in the Lower Binfield of 1900, when 'Vicky's at Windsor, God's in heaven, Christ's on the cross'[88] and people 'didn't think of the future as something to be terrified of'.[89] It is a time and place contrasted with the inauthentic 'modern world', which is 'slick and streamlined, everything made out of something else', a world of 'Celluloid, rubber, chromium-steel everywhere, arc-lamps blazing all night, glass roofs over your head, radios all playing the same tune, no vegetation left, everything cemented over'.[90] The description is, of course, close to that of the 'cultureless life, centring round tinned food, *Picture Post*, the radio and the internal combustion engine' in the areas of 'New' England interpreted elsewhere as the potential basis of a socialist society.

The commitment to the rural, and indeed agricultural, is widely interpreted as a distinctive characteristic of 'Englishness'. Chase, for example, comments upon the 'Englishman's insistence upon the countryside as his birthright' which 'triumphs over brick and mortar, city dumps and railway tracks, which places flowers in tubs from Mayfair to Southwark, which decorates even the bare spaces between the chimney pots on the roofs of Stepney and Shoreditch, Lambeth and Bethnal Green'.[91] Priestley similarly writes that there 'is this to be said about the English people; give them even a foot or two of earth, and they will grow flowers in it; they do not willingly let go of the country – as the foreign people do – once they have settled in a town; they are all gardeners, perhaps country gentlemen, at heart'.[92] The comments emphasise a commitment to the 'countryside' that persists even amongst the urban population, and indeed Cohen-Portheim argues that 'Love of the country is the most fundamental thing about the English and can alone make their character and their history intelligible.'[93] The statements suggest a close relationship with the countryside, or 'nature', peculiar to the English. Indeed, Rowse claims that there is a 'secret compact that the Englishman has entered into with nature' and that 'of all modern people it is the English who provide the best example of a people in harmony with their environment'.[94] The artistic representation of the countryside is figured as an important component of this 'love', a tradition interwoven with the idea of the 'natural' itself. David Gervais, for example, insists that 'Englishness' 'derives from landscape and poetry (especially Shakespeare's) more than from pride in political institutions', observing that 'Dickens, the most English of writers, rhapsodised about the English countryside, but caricatured Parliament as a long-running farce'.[95] Hilaire Belloc also makes this connection between art and 'nature', writing that

Nowhere are men so moved by the aspect of Nature as are Englishmen. In the pictorial arts you find that continually, from Turner to the woodcuts of Whymper, which for my part I have always thought to be a high example of the national genius.[96]

In his commitment to the English countryside, therefore, and to its literary representation, Orwell positions himself within a popular narrative of 'Englishness'.

The idealised image of 'Old' England, is, however, distinguished from images of modern rural pursuits, such as hiking, and the new, 'inauthentic' residents of the countryside. As Cunningham argues, it is 'not true rural yearnings that annoy him, it's the social and historical forces that hamper their fulfilment or fob the yearners off with bogus diversions and sentimental substitutes (hiking, simple-life-isms, Joadified Mortonizings)'.[97] In *The Road to Wigan Pier*, hikers, for example, are caricatured in the figures of 'two dreadful-looking old men', wearing 'pistachio-coloured shirts and khaki shorts into which their huge bottoms were crammed so tightly that you could study every dimple', who are travelling to the I.L.P. 'summer school at Letchworth'. The men are dismissed by a 'commercial traveller' as 'Socialists', and are used by Orwell to illustrate his claim that, to the 'ordinary man, a crank meant a Socialist, and a Socialist meant a crank'.[98] The hikers are figured as 'inauthentic', equated with the 'fruit-juice drinker, nudist, sandal-wearer, sex-maniac, Quaker, "Nature Cure" quack, pacifist and feminist',[99] which socialism also attracts. Their presence in the countryside is, it is implied, the result of eccentricity or fashion, rather than of 'love' or 'genuine' commitment. The condemnation of such 'cranks' is still more overt in *Coming Up for Air*. It is illustrated, for example, when George Bowling returns to Lower Binfield to discover that Binfield House has been converted into a 'loony-bin',[100] and the area around it, which he remembers from childhood as deserted woodland, is now dominated by 'arty-looking houses, another of those sham-Tudor colonies'.[101] Bowling is shown the new development by 'one of those old men who've never grown up',[102] and who insists, despite the fact almost all the trees have been cut down, that the residents are living in 'the midst of Nature up here', with the 'primeval forest brooding round us'.[103] The pool that Bowling has come to look for, which used to be 'hidden away in the woods' with 'monstrous fish sailing round it',[104] has been drained for a rubbish-tip, already 'half-full of tin cans', whilst the remaining 'little bit of copse' has been renamed the 'Pixy Glen'. As he drives down to Lower Binfield, Bowling concludes

God rot them and bust them! Say what you like – call it silly, childish, anything – but doesn't it make you puke sometimes to see what they're doing to England, with their bird-baths and their plaster gnomes, and their pixies and tin cans, where the beech woods used to be?[105]

The 'vegetarians' and 'Professor Woad, the psychic research worker',[106] are caricatured representatives of those whose 'bogus diversions and sentimental substitutes' for traditional rural life deface and destroy the countryside they believe themselves to be protecting. As Cunningham argues, in *Coming Up for Air* the 'local naturists make a poor substitute for a natural life formerly conducted in real touch with nature'.[107]

The countryside, and particularly the English countryside, is imbued with value throughout Orwell's writing, and is central to his socialism. In 'Some Thoughts on the Common Toad', for example, he writes that

> I have always suspected that if our economic and political problems are ever really solved, life will become simpler instead of more complex, and that the sort of pleasure one gets from finding the first primrose will loom larger than the sort of pleasure one gets from eating an ice to the tune of a Wurlitzer. I think that by retaining one's childhood love of such things as trees, fishes, butterflies and – to return to my first instance – toads, one makes a peaceful and decent future a little more probable, and that by preaching the doctrine that nothing is to be admired except steel and concrete, one merely makes it a little surer that human beings will have no outlet for their surplus energy except in hatred and leader-worship. (18:238–41:240)

This commitment to the pleasures of 'nature' is explicitly defended against the 'Left-wing', and Orwell states that 'I know by experience that a favourable reference to "Nature" in one of my articles is liable to bring me abusive letters' (239). This constructs an image of 'Nature' that is both integral to his own political thought, insofar as it is figured as a source of inherent value displaced by advanced capitalism, and distinct from what he perceives as the position of the majority of the 'Left'. In this sense, the emphasis upon 'trees, fishes, butterflies' is part of a broader to opposition to the idea of a future 'Socialist world' as a 'completely mechanised, immensely organised world',[108] or, indeed, to the notion of a 'central-heated, air-conditioned, strip-lighted Paradise' (16:37–45:42) as such. The essay instead suggests that the resolution of 'economic and political problems' will enable a return to 'Nature', the source of authentic pleasure and value. This point is reinforced in 'Pleasure Spots', in which he insists upon the 'instinctive horror which all sensitive people feel at the progressive mechanization of life', and concludes that 'man only stays human by preserving large patches of simplicity in his life, while the tendency of many modern inventions – in particular the film, the radio and the aeroplane, is to weaken his consciousness, dull his curiosity, and, in general, drive him nearer to the animals' (18:29–32:32).

Orwell's use of images of the English countryside is nevertheless problematic. In the first place, the mechanised world represented as encroaching upon the English countryside has numerous parallels to his 'future England'. The town in which the old 'Lower Binfield had been swallowed up and buried like the lost cities of Peru',[109] for example, is compared to 'these new towns that have suddenly swelled up like balloons in the last few years, Hayes, Slough, Dagenham and so forth',[110] that are also used as examples of a 'New' England. In addition, the 'Old' England Orwell describes is the product, not only of a particular image of the English countryside, but of what Berberich describes as the 'seemingly safe and stable world of his childhood', a world which he himself refers to as 'that lost paradise "before the war" – that is, before the other war' (19:395–8:397). In *Coming Up for Air*, Bowling insists the period was one in which 'people had something that we haven't got now',[111] a 'feeling of security, even when they weren't secure', a 'feeling of continuity',[112] but the novel nevertheless emphasises that the 'old life's finished, and to go about looking for it is just a waste of time'.[113] 'Old' England, a world in which it is 'summer all the year round',[114] is an inaccessible contrast to the 'modern' world, its 'security' emphasising the instability of the era which succeeded it. There is, Orwell insists, no method of reviving this particular 'safe and stable world', as 'there can be no more question of restoring the Edwardian age than of reviving Albigensianism' (19:396).

The commitment to the 'rural order', and to the 'lost paradise' of Edwardian England, is therefore tempered by the knowledge that it cannot be recovered. Indeed, Orwell even writes in a 1943 review that 'all praise of the past is partly sentimental, because we do not live in the past' (14:279–89:283). The idea of 'Nature' nevertheless continues to form a pivotal element of his socialism, which he argues will institute a 'simpler' way of life. There is, therefore, a tension between the 'future England', with its 'restless, cultureless life', and a valued 'Old' England. Indeed, it is this to which Cyril Connolly refers in a famous passage from his 1945 review of *Animal Farm*, when he argues that,

> Mr Orwell is a revolutionary who is in love with 1910. This ambivalence constitutes his strength and his weakness.[115]

This simultaneous commitment to the rural and urban, mechanical and natural, is, of course, not peculiar to Orwell. Indeed, Crick claims that 'the attempt to strike a balance between the interests of humanity in nature and in manufacture, or between town and country' is a 'characteristic of English socialism'.[116] The attachment to a 'nature' identified primarily with Edwardian England, however, results in a tension most obvious in *Coming Up for Air*.

The paradoxical interaction of the 'Old' and 'New' is further complicated by the importance Orwell attaches to the 'traditional' industrial working class, the inhabitants of what Priestley described as 'nineteenth-century England'. Industrial landscapes are condemned throughout his writing, and in *The Road to Wigan Pier* he claims that Sheffield, for example, 'could justly claim to be called the ugliest town in the Old World', with 'fewer decent buildings than the average East Anglian village of five hundred'.[117] The working class themselves, however, and in particular figures such the miners, are idealised. 'Nineteenth-century' England is figured as the site of 'authentic' communities, 'real' men and a set of values that provide a potential basis for a future egalitarian society. In contrast, the rural population is conspicuously absent from his texts.[118] These focus instead upon members of the lower middle class, such as Bowling, who works for 'The Flying Salamander'[119] insurance company, and the 'traditional' working class. It is these, rather than the 'airmen and their mechanics' or the inhabitants of 'Old' England, the texts value and even celebrate. In a 1940 review, for example, Orwell praised 'English working-class life in the late capitalist age', the 'England of tote, dog-races, football pools, Woolworth's, the pictures, Gracie Fields, Wall's ice cream, potato crisps, celanese stockings, dartboards, pin-tables, cigarettes, cups of tea, and Saturday evenings in the four ale bar', insisting that it was a 'good civilisation while it lasted, and the people who grew up in it will carry some of their gentleness and decency into the iron ages that are coming' (12:202). This conception of working-class life as the site of virtues such as 'decency' illustrates the importance of 'nineteenth-century England' to his political thought, despite the 'ugliness'[120] of the industrial towns themselves.

The 'three Englands' identified by Priestley, and the values associated with them, co-exist within the various images of 'Englishness' Orwell develops, although their relative importance alters from text to text, example to example. Their interaction is still further complicated by the idea of 'Englishness' as a fluid identity, founded upon inherited traditions but subject to alteration and renewal. This idea is central to both *The Lion and the Unicorn* and *The English People*, which posit the reform, not only of national institutions, but of the English 'character' itself. Indeed, in *The English People* he insists that such a transformation is essential, and that the English must

> breed faster, work harder, and probably live more simply, think more deeply, get rid of their snobbishness and their anachronistic class distinctions, pay more attention to the world and less to their own backyards. Nearly all of them already love their country, but they must learn to love it intelligently.

The persistence of inherited characteristics limits the scope of this reconstruction, so that, for example, the 'English will never develop into a nation of philosophers' (227), but the texts nevertheless insist upon the potential for a radical transformation of 'Englishness' that would eradicate established social and economic hierarchies. This negotiation between past and present is emphasised by Berberich, who argues that

> Orwell was nostalgic about the past, yes. But he also, more than anything, wanted social changes. He wanted people in England to wake up and take political responsibility, he wanted a reshuffling of the political and class system and to do away with old hierarchies. But he did not want to do so at all costs, he wanted to keep certain forms, certain values that had proved valuable in the past and wanted to apply them to the present.[121]

'Englishness', in this account, is not invariant, and the values of the 'three Englands' can be utilised and transformed to enable national renewal. Indeed, Orwell suggests that the production of a radical patriotism involves precisely such a selection and even transformation of inherited myths and discourses.

The process is figured, however, not as one in which a new form of 'Englishness' is produced, but one of revelation, a release of an existent but suppressed 'native genius'. In *The Lion and the Unicorn*, Orwell writes that

> England has got to assume its real shape. The England that is only just beneath the surface, in the factories and the newspaper offices, in the aeroplanes and the submarines, has got to take charge of its own destiny. (415)

The statement locates the 'authentic' England, not in the 'great men' emphasised by Rowse, but in the broader English public. This position is reinforced at the conclusion of the text, when Orwell insists that the heirs of Nelson and Cromwell are not in the House of Lords. They are in the fields and the streets, in the factories and in the armed forces, in the four-ale bar and the suburban back garden; and at present they are still kept under by a generation of ghosts. (432)

The form and site of this 'real' England, however, remain ambiguous. The image of England and the English developed within the texts incorporates a simultaneous commitment to Edwardian country-towns, the population, if not the architecture, of the industrial north, and the 'future England' of the technical experts and arterial roads. These three distinct 'Englands' are, as in *English Journey*, 'variously and most fascinatingly mingled' in Orwell's writing. The concept of an English character is used to connect them, to figure them as elements of a particular nation and as founded upon a common set of values or single 'genius'. The resolution is, however, incomplete, and there remains a tension between, for example, the values of Lower Binfield and those of the 'future England' destined to replace it, between the home counties and the industrial north, between traditional hierarchies and potential radicalism. The rhetorical strategies that produce the image of 'the English people' are counterbalanced by a proliferation of examples of difference that resist the notion of a single 'character'. The result is the idea of a 'specifically *English* Socialist movement' that would incorporate elements of these distinct narratives or traditions, resolving their divisions. The 'England beneath the surface' is for Orwell both exposed and produced by socialism. The myth of 'Englishness' enables him to figure the 'future England' as inherited as much as constructed, as a realising an 'authentic' nation that has hitherto been 'kept under by a generation of ghosts' (432), who choke it like a 'necklace of corpses' (413). In an interview with Raymond Williams on Orwell, published in *New Left Review*, the interviewer condemned the '*regressive social patriotism he stoked up in war-time England and post-war England*'.[122] The patriotism he developed, however, is far from regressive. It is instead integral to his vision of the future, and to a socialism inseparable from the commitment to both the 'England beneath the surface' and the 'future England' it will produce.

5
Totalitarianism

In 'Worlds Without End Foisted Upon the Future', Andy Croft writes that

> Much of the left's response to *Nineteen Eighty-Four*, and to its political marketing has been simply hostile, going to great lengths to attack both the novel and its author. Understandable though this may be, particularly during the worst years of the Cold War when many reviewers were recommending *Nineteen Eighty-Four* precisely as an anti-socialist novel and an attack on the Atlee Government, this has meant in practice abandoning the novel to the literary right.[1]

The hostility of many on the Left is, indeed, obvious from the reviews that followed its first publication. For James Walsh, for example, writing in *Marxist Quarterly*, the text 'is merely one weapon in the war of many fronts that has been waged against the progressive movement and the Soviet Union since 1945 and before'.[2] In *Masses and Mainstream*, Samuel Sillen argued that its 'moral is that if capitalism departs the world will go to pot',[3] and that the text itself was a demonstration that 'surrounded by burgeoning socialism' the 'bourgeoisie' was 'capable only of hate-filled, dehumanized anti-Utopias'.[4] This interpretation of the text as anti-socialist was replicated in later critical studies. A. L. Morton, for example, claimed that Orwell had attempted 'not to argue a case but to induce an irrational conviction in the mind of his readers that any attempt to realise socialism must lead to a world of corruption, torture and insecurity'.[5] Isaac Deutscher similarly argued that the novel 'is a document of dark disillusionment not only with Stalinism but with every form and shade of socialism'.[6] Indeed, Raymond Williams insisted that all 'Orwell's later works' were 'written by an ex-socialist'.[7] This hostility persisted in later studies, and informed a number of essays in the 1984 collection *Inside the Myth*, in which Croft's article is included. For Alaric Jacob, for example, *'Nineteen Eighty-Four* is one of the most disgusting books ever written – a book smelling of fear, hatred, lies and self-disgust by comparison with which the works of the Marquis de Sade are no more than the bad dreams of such a mind'.[8] The approach of many of the writers who contributed to the collection is illustrated in Christopher Norris' introduction, in which he writes that it 'is too much to hope that *Nineteen Eighty-Four*, like 1984, will soon be consigned to the dusty annals of Cold-War cultural propaganda'.[9] The statement delimits the significance of Orwell's text, representing it as a function of Cold War politics.

There are a number of problems with these criticisms of the novel. In the first place, as Croft argued, they abandon it to the 'literary right', implying that the Left cannot use what Gorman Beauchamp describes as 'as one of the half dozen most important books of this century, arguably – for all its artistic and ideological limitations – the most influential one'.[10] In addition, the description of the text as simply an example of 'Cold-War cultural propaganda' represents its use by particular groups in a particular historical period as determining its meaning and significance. The deficiencies of this method of criticism are obvious if one considers the parallel, if more extreme, examples of the interpretation of Marx in terms of his deployment by the Stalinist regime, or Wagner in terms of his position within the culture of Nazi Germany. The consensus with the 'literary right', therefore, is reinforced by a critical structure that fixes the novel within a particular context, restricting its interpretation to the polarised categories of the Cold War.

The hostile response of many left-wing critics to the text and their emphasis upon the use made of it following publication, obscures, amongst other things, its relation to Orwell's earlier writing. This provides an alternative context within which to read *Nineteen Eighty-Four*, as an attempt to defend a particular model of socialism conceived as founded on, rather than superseding, 'traditional' communities. The text is concerned in particular with the threat posed to this idea of socialism by what Orwell described, in a statement issued after its publication, as 'totalitarian ideas' that have 'taken root in the minds of intellectuals everywhere'. It was, he claimed, an attempt to 'draw these ideas out to their logical consequences' (20:134–6:136),[11] an exploration of the concept of totalitarianism rather than of its realisation in a particular state. The text satirises elements of a number of contemporary societies, including not only Stalinist Russia but post-war Britain.

Oceania does not correspond to a particular modern state, but is, as Beauchamp argued, 'the logical consequence, the pure idea, of the totalitarian mentality – the truly Caesarean environment where power operates without constraint – and not an attempt at historical mimesis'.[12] There is therefore a movement in the novel between the particular and the abstract, between the satirical use of details from existent or historical societies and a broader examination of a distinctive modern form of authoritarianism. The continuous movement between 'pure idea' and political practice demanded a different, more flexible narrative form to that used in the realist novels Orwell had written before Second World War.

In *Animal Farm*, his first substantial work of fiction to be published after the war, Orwell developed a new narrative form to explore both political ideas and historical developments. Its sub-title classifies it as 'A Fairy Story', and in a letter to his agent Leonard Moore of 6 December 1943 he describes it as 'a fairy story but also a political allegory' (16:59). As this description of the text as 'allegorical' indicates, it is structured around a particular historical narrative, that of the Russian Revolution and subsequent Bolshevik regime. It transposes this narrative to the farmyard, but there are continuous parallels between the fictive and historical worlds that extend even to apparently minor details of the text. This is illustrated in Orwell's letter of 17 March 1945 to Roger Senhouse, the director at Secker & Warburg who dealt with his work. In this he requests that if *Animal Farm*

> has not actually been printed yet, there is one further alteration of one word that I would like to make. In Chapter VIII (I think it is VIII), when the windmill is blown up, I wrote 'all the animals including Napoleon threw themselves on their faces.' I would like to alter it to 'all the animals except Napoleon.' If the book has already been printed it's not worth bothering about, but I just thought the alteration would be fair to J.S., as he did stay in Moscow during the German advance. (17:90)[13]

The insistence that the text should accurately represent the developments in Russia following the revolution means that it is an intervention in a particular political debate and indeed a commentary upon a particular regime. Orwell describes it in a letter to Moore of 19 March 1944 as 'strongly anti-Stalin in tendency' (16:126–7:126), and similarly insists in a letter written on the same day to Victor Gollancz, to whom he was still contracted, that it was 'completely unacceptable politically from your point of view (it is anti-Stalin)' (16:127). The decision to write *Animal Farm* as a 'fairy story' produces an explicitly fictional space in which revolution can be explored in relative isolation from the historical, political and economic contexts in which it actually occurred. Its allegorical method, however, means that it is always also a critical commentary on a particular state and its development. The narrative form adopted enables a selective use of contemporary history that attempts to isolate the 'essential' features of the Stalinist regime, and to use this as an illustration of the inherent dangers of a particular type of revolution. This process is outlined by Orwell himself in a letter to Dwight Macdonald of 2 December 1946, in which he writes,

> Of course I intended it primarily as a satire on the Russian revolution. But I did mean it to have a wider application in so much that I meant *that kind* of revolution (violent conspiratorial revolution, lead by unconsciously power-hungry people) can only lead to a change of masters. I meant the moral to be that revolutions only effect a radical improvement when the masses are alert and know how to chuck out their leaders as soon as the latter have done their job. The turning point of the story was supposed to be when the pigs keep the milk and apples for themselves (Kronstadt). (18:506–8:507)

The passage illustrates the use of detailed parallels to Russian history in the 'fairy story' to underpin a broader commentary on '*that kind* of revolution' and thereby to suggest alternatives to it.

The technique of displacement used in *Animal Farm* is paralleled in *Nineteen Eighty-Four*, although the narrative form of the later novel is, of course, quite different. It is, in the first place, utopian rather than allegorical. Oceania is not a transposition of a particular past or contemporary society, but an explicitly non-existent location used to extrapolate tendencies in several such societies. Orwell himself, in a letter to Julian Symons of 4 February 1949, describes his 'new book' as 'a Utopia in the form of a novel' (20:35).[14] He emphasises the critical method of utopian literature in a talk on Samuel Butler's *Erewhon*, in which he states that

> All Utopia books are satires or allegories. Obviously if you invent an imaginary country you do so in order to throw light on the institutions of some existing country, probably your own. (17:168–73:169)

In *Animal Farm* satire and allegory are combined, but in *Nineteen Eighty-Four* the precise schema used in the latter is abandoned. The novel is primarily a satire, using a utopian society, Oceania, to explore various elements of contemporary political theory and practice. As Robert Elliott wrote, 'the two modes – utopia and satire – are linked in a complex network of genetic, historical, and formal relationships',[15] and Orwell uses the critical potential of this relationship to explore elements of the real world, most prominently totalitarianism, in relative isolation of the complex, particular historical, political and economic conditions under which they in fact occurred. He was not, of course, the only writer of the period to exploit the possibilities of this form or indeed to adopt it for this purpose. As Croft observes, 'non-realist ways of writing', including utopias, were popular amongst 'anti-fascist novelists',[16] as methods of exploring authoritarian regimes and theories. These 'non-realist' methods were intended to examine aspects of contemporary political problems that, for a variety of reasons, were not perceived as accessible to more conventional literary forms. A wide range of techniques was adopted for this purpose, with the form of individual texts both shaping and shaped by their political perspective. *Nineteen Eighty-Four*, for instance, retains the narrative style of Orwell's earlier realist works, is set only 35 years after publication, in contrast to the distant, futuristic societies described in texts such as Aldous Huxley's *Brave New World* and Katherine Burdekin's *Swastika Night*, and incorporates features of a variety of contemporary societies. The significance of these characteristics of the text, and their function in producing a critical utopia at once abstract and specific, can be analysed by comparing Orwell's text with contemporary works that employed a similar form.

In 1937, Katherine Burdekin published *Swastika Night*,[17] a novel set in a Europe that has been controlled by the Nazis for more than 700 years. Hitler is worshipped as a God, and his successors have enforced the 'Reduction of Women',[18] a policy that restricts them to their reproductive role. They are deliberately degraded, having 'naked shaven scalps' and 'no grace, no beauty, no uprightness'. Romantic relationships exist only between men and boys, as to 'love a woman, in the German mind, would be equal to loving a worm, or a Christian'.[19] The Nazis have also 'killed all the Jews off'.[20] The location of the narrative centuries after the text itself was produced enables certain perceived elements of National Socialism to be extrapolated to their logical conclusion. The precise form of the projected regime is, admittedly, problematic as a reading of National Socialism, despite Croft's claim that the novel is 'undoubtedly the most sophisticated and original of all the many anti-fascist dystopias of the late 1930s and 1940s'.[21] The text's emphasis upon sexuality, for example, focuses attention upon Nazism's misogyny, but does so to such an extent that it obscures the movement's historical origins in the economic crises that followed First World War, the history of anti-Semitism in Germany and the absence of a well-established democratic tradition, figuring the movement instead as primarily the result of a pervasive sexual complex. It also identifies the Nazi movement with homosexual men, ignoring the ways in which they were persecuted and murdered by the regime. However, as Croft observes, in a number of details '*Swastika Night* clearly anticipated Orwell's *Nineteen Eighty-Four* by several years'.[22] It used the utopian form to examine an authoritarianism characterised by the rewriting of history, involvement in perpetual warfare, manipulation of sexuality and deification of a leader. The method enabled the theoretical premises of the Nazi regime to be detached from the historical conditions under which it in fact operated, and particular elements of their political beliefs to be isolated for the purposes of analysis.

This method of displacement contrasts with that used in another text from the period concerned with Nazism, H. V. Morton's *I, James Blunt*. First published in 1942, it is set only a few years later, between late 1944 and early 1945. Its premise is the Nazi occupation of Britain following the conclusion of a peace treaty. The text is, therefore, explicitly concerned with immediate political events, in particular the possibility that Britain would seek a separate peace. Hitler himself, in private, argued this might occur, stating on 7 January 1942 that if 'a nation were to quit the war before the end of the war, I seriously think it would be England'.[23] In contrast to Burdekin, who uses a narrative distance of over 700 years in order to explore the Nazi movement, Morton addresses immediate political concerns. Indeed, the diary form he employs necessarily locates the text within an extremely specific time period. *I, James Blunt* is a utopian text insofar as it represents a non-existent society, a 'no-place', but the narrative displacement it practices is relatively minimal. It nevertheless shares some features with both *Swastika Night* and, indeed, *Nineteen Eighty-Four*. The Nazis suppress records of British history, for example, in order to prevent the maintenance of a distinct national identity that could be used as a basis of opposition. This entails the renaming of Waterloo Station as 'Goebbels Station', as 'the names of all British military victories are now banned',[24] the destruction of a pub sign 'showing Charles II hiding in the oak', because 'it is against the law to show pictures of English historical characters',[25] and the banning of the legends of 'Arthur and his Knights', which are condemned as 'nationalistic stories'.[26] The critical method of the text, however, is quite different from that of *Swastika Night*. In contrast to Burdekin's emphasis upon the theoretical and psychological foundations of Nazism, Morton concentrates on its policies as exhibited in occupied Europe. His text is explicitly an intervention in an immediate political debate, and indeed, in a remark quoted in the publisher's blurb he dedicates it to 'all complacent optimists and wishful thinkers, and to those who cannot imagine what life would be like if we lost the war'.[27]

The use of displacement to explore authoritarianism and oppression is also demonstrated in Winifred Ashton's novel *The Arrogant History of White Ben*, first published in 1939 under the pseudonym Clemence Dane. It is set at the conclusion of the 'disastrous war of the nineteen-fifties',[28] which has ended in stalemate and widespread impoverishment, and focuses upon the figure of White Ben, a scarecrow who comes to life when a young girl places a mandrake root in his chest. He is, as Croft writes 'filled with a mission to revenge himself on the crows who have preyed on his fields for so long'.[29] His denunciation of crows is, however, continually reinterpreted by those around him, despite his insistence that 'I said crows and I mean crows',[30] and he quickly becomes a popular leader in a dispirited, fragmented England. Lady Pont, for example, one of his earliest supporters, concludes that 'by "crows" you mean the exploiters, the destructive, the hangers-on, the war-mongers, the middle-men, don't you?',[31] whilst the liberal parliamentarian Edgar Swete concludes simply that 'I know what he means'.[32] He himself later revises his own ideas, concluding that 'if men could become birds of prey, then birds of prey could become men',[33] and the violence he initiates is increasingly directed, not at the 'little crows in the fields', but at the 'men-crows'.[34] The 'crows' become an amorphous target, a fluid group of scapegoats, figured as responsible for the various social and economic problems of the country. In his speech in Trafalgar Square immediately before he seizes power, Ben informs the crowd that

> You are a fine, handsome people, but you are not clever. You never once guessed, when your taxes grew heavier and your profits light, when they made you die for them on the battle-fields, in the heaving seas, or made you go cap-in-hand for work, when they paid you for it such a pitiful wage that you could scarcely eat or keep a roof over your head [...] when they let your children grow up in the slums and sweat-shops like plants forced in a cellar [...] that you were being preyed upon by crows disguised as men.[35]

The persecution this rhetoric initiates after Ben has assumed power is enormous. In a report, his deputy, Illico Smith, who later succeeds him, records that after four months the 'Total bag of crows' numbers 700,000. Another 1,600,000 are still being held in 'cages', whilst the number who have already died in such captivity 'owing to food difficulties, illness and under discipline' has reached 30,000.[36]

In contrast to *Swastika Night* and *I, James Blunt*, *The Arrogant History of White Ben* does not explicitly represent a contemporary political movement in either its present or future form. There are, however, clear parallels between Ben and Adolf Hitler. Ben establishes 'concentration cages',[37] has a popular appeal based on his abilities as a public speaker, and is backed by a powerful, wealthy elite, including Bothering, who believe that he is a 'mad little Messiah'[38] whose popularity can be exploited. Even his image of the 'men-crows', founded on Lady Pont's description of the 'Norman type' of 'Black hair, beak noses',[39] suggests the anti-Semitic caricatures used in National Socialist propaganda. Indeed, the definition of 'crows' used by the regime after it comes to power is in part racial, incorporating 'those of alien blood or descent within three generations'.[40] The focus of the text upon the figure of the animated scarecrow, therefore, satirises Hitler, transposing his characteristics onto a literal straw man described even by Illico Smith as 'a lunatic'.[41] Nevertheless, the process of displacement and absence of an explicit target indicates an exploration of broader issues, such as the idea of charismatic leadership, the persecution of minorities and the political exploitation of irrational prejudice. White Ben is in part a mythic figure, and in the final sentence of the novel, Ashton states that

> Time-travellers report indeed that the savants of a thousand years hence have proved beyond all further doubt or disputation that White Ben was no more than the wish fulfilment of a backward people, and that he personifies in their folk-lore the natural human instinct to maltreat the harmless and destroy the happy.[42]

The Arrogant History of White Ben uses 'non-realist ways of writing' to explore ideas of authoritarianism, and whilst its methods are quite different from those employed in *Swastika Night* and *I, James Blunt*, the texts all use non-existent states to establish a critical distance between the narratives and the societies or ideas upon which they comment.

These examples provide a context within which to examine *Nineteen Eighty-Four*. One distinctive characteristic of the text is the insistent and overt connection between the utopia and the society from which it extrapolates. In contrast to the world described in *Swastika Night*, Oceania retains many features of contemporary society, and, as Crick argues, the 'opening pages' of the novel 'are full of images of immediate post-war London, albeit with grim but not gross exaggeration'.[43] This aspect of the novel was identified by its first reviewers, and Philip Rahv, for example, wrote in *Partisan Review* that 'If it inspires dread above all, that is precisely because its materials are taken from the real world as we know it, from conditions now prevailing in the totalitarian nations, in particular the Communist nations, and potentially among us too.'[44] This use of a familiar environment, like that of Morton, located the text within contemporary political debates, most prominently, of course, those concerning the Stalinist regime. Indeed, the relation of the society described in the text to twentieth-century states is emphasised in O'Brien's reference to 'the totalitarians, as they were called', the 'German Nazis and the Russian Communists'[45] who were the precursors of the Party. The interconnections between Oceania and familiar societies also fulfilled a distinct narrative function, in that, as Julian Symons wrote, by 'creating a world in which the "proles" still have their sentimental songs and their beer, and the privileged consume their Victory gin, Mr Orwell involves us most skilfully and uncomfortably in the story, and more readily our belief in the fantasy of thought-domination that occupies the foreground of his book'.[46]

The text is not, however, restricted to its immediate context, as either an exercise in 'Cold-War cultural propaganda' or 'historical mimesis'. Oceania is not a portrait, or even caricature, of a single state. It incorporates features of Stalinist Russia, Nazi Germany and indeed post-war Britain, but is also an exploration of the 'pure idea' of totalitarianism. *Nineteen Eighty-Four*, Orwell insists, is concerned with 'the direction in which the world is going at the present time' (20:134),[47] a statement that implies both a foundation in the present and a process of extrapolation from it. The novel incorporates elements 'taken from the real world', but also explores authoritarian theories and practices by representing their complete realisation. As Irving Howe wrote,

> To capture the totalitarian spirit, Orwell had merely to allow certain tendencies in modern society to spin forward without the brake of sentiment or humaneness. He could thus make clear the relationship between his model of totalitarianism and the societies we know in our experience, and he could do this without resorting to the clap-trap of science fiction or the crude assumption that we already live in 1984.[48]

The text therefore exploits the methods of other 'non-realist' works, representing a society insistently linked to the present, but nevertheless distant enough from it to enable the exploration of 'totalitarian ideas' in relative isolation from specific historical conditions.

In Arthur Koestler's *Darkness at Noon*, Rushabov writes that '*We admitted no private sphere: not even inside a man's skull.*'[49] The elimination of privacy also dominates *Nineteen Eighty-Four*. In principle, a Party member in Oceania 'had no spare time, and was never alone except in bed'.[50] Indeed, *The Theory and Practice of Oligarchical Collectivism*, attributed to Emmanuel Goldstein, states that a

> Party member lives from birth to death under the eye of the Thought Police. Even when he is alone he can never be sure that he is alone.[51]

The State dominates all aspects of personal existence and even proves capable of redefining or eliminating individual beliefs and allegiances. After his release, Winston, recalling Julia's earlier assertion that 'They can't get inside you',[52] concludes that

> they could get inside you. 'What happens to you here is *for ever*,' O'Brien had said. That was a true word.[53]

The control of the personal is a central objective of Party policy, and defines much of life in Oceania. It leads Winston to admire his mother, whom he believes possessed 'a kind of nobility, a kind of purity, simply because the standards she obeyed were private ones',[54] and determines the form of his opposition to the state. He rebels by reasserting his independent existence, and, as Ingle writes, 'trying to create a private realm – through purchasing and keeping a diary and by indulging in a love affair'.[55] In *Nineteen Eighty-Four*, Orwell, as Howe insisted, 'is trying to present the kind of world in which individuality has become obsolete and personality a crime'.[56] This emphasis in the novel on the eradication of diversity and the construction of a homogeneous, regulated population demonstrates a continued concern with the ideas of individual liberty central to the model of socialism Orwell developed in his earlier writing. As Crick argues, the socialist tradition he inherited maintained that 'there are some areas of life which have to be preserved from politics: a good politics even sets up barriers of laws, institutions and customs against itself'.[57] The Party, in contrast, determines all areas of individual existence, for its members at least, and as such represents the opposite of the 'democratic Socialism' with which Orwell identified himself. His satirical attack on the intrusion of the State in the 'private realm' illustrates a continued commitment to the 'barriers' that preserve individual freedom.

The Party in *Nineteen Eighty-Four* is, however, not only concerned with the *'private sphere'*, but with the relation between individuals. It attempts to eliminate independent communities, including those founded upon class, ethnicity or nation, that form potential sites of allegiance and validate individual identities. In his diary, Winston refers to Oceania as a state in which men *'live alone'*, and the period as the *'age of solitude'*.[58] The description indicates, not only the repression of relationships such as that between Winston and Julia, but also of broader communities. In the Ministry of Love, O'Brien informs Winston that the Party has

> cut the links between child and parent, and between man and man, and between man and woman. No one dare trust a wife or a child or a friend any longer. But in the future there will be no wives and no friends.[59]

The forms of community suppressed or manipulated by the state extend from the family, which 'had become in effect an extension of the Thought Police',[60] to national and ethnic identities, which are subsumed in the three dominant States. The old nation-states have been eliminated, and Britain, for example, is renamed 'Airstrip One',[61] separating it from its previous history. The concept of national identity is absent from Oceania, a multinational state which, *The Theory and Practice of Oligarchical Collectivism* states, 'has no capital', and except 'that English is its chief lingua franca and Newspeak its official language, it is not centralised in any way'.[62] Only a 'primitive patriotism' is retained, largely amongst the 'proles', to 'be appealed to whenever it was necessary to make them accept longer working-hours or shorter rations'.[63] The eradication of traditional communities is combined with an emphasis upon collective activity administered by the Party itself. Indeed, involvement in these authorised social networks is perceived as demonstrating conformity. Julia, for example, 'spent an astonishing amount of time in attending lectures and demonstrations'[64] in order to disguise her transgression of Party principles, whilst the zealous Parsons 'would inform you with quiet pride, between whiffs of his pipe, that he had put in an appearance at the community centre every evening for the past four years'.[65] The implicit object is to control to the contexts within which individuality is formed and validated. As Marx wrote 'Man is in the most literal sense a *zoön politikon*, not only a social animal, but an animal which can individuate itself only in society.' The centralised control of social networks makes this individuation a function of state doctrine.

The conscious destruction of independent communities contrasts with the form of oppression represented in *Animal Farm*. The pigs use both propaganda and terror to consolidate and even extend their power, but do not eradicate the solidarity between those they exploit. Indeed, the persistence of this is demonstrated when, following the first executions on the farm, the 'remaining animals, except for pigs and dogs, crept away together' and 'made their way onto the little knoll where the half-finished windmill stood, and with one accord they all lay down as though huddling together for warmth – Clover, Muriel, Benjamin, the cows, the sheep and a whole flock of geese and hens – everyone, indeed, except the cat, who had suddenly disappeared just before Napoleon ordered the animals to assemble'.[66] The image is compared to the occasion when Clover 'protected the lost brood of ducklings with her foreleg on the night of Major's speech',[67] indicating the continuation of the mutual dependence and support that ironically enabled their initial rebellion. In the course of the purge, or as Squealer terms it the 'execution of the traitors',[68] the animals killed, significantly, confess to their 'crimes', and are not testified against by their companions. The farm is structured by the division between the pigs and dogs, on the one hand, and the remainder of the animals on the other, both of which form relatively cohesive groups. Indeed, Napoleon informs the neighbouring farmers that the

> farm which he had the honour to control [...] was a co-operative enterprise. The title-deeds, which were in his own possession, were owned by the pigs jointly.[69]

The oppressed animals also remain a community, albeit one that is threatened at the conclusion of the text as the pigs introduce animals from 'farms ten or twenty miles away'.[70] Indeed, even the idea of equality persists, insofar as 'the tune of "Beasts of England" was perhaps hummed secretly here and there: at any rate it was a fact that every animal on the farm knew it, though no one would have dared to sing it aloud'.[71]

The Party in *Nineteen Eighty-Four*, in contrast, attempts to destroy all independent communities, including those represented in Orwell's earlier work as the structures within which individuals establish a positive identity and stable commitment to one another. The 'Englishness' explored in *The Lion and the Unicorn* and *The English People*, for example, has been dissolved by the State in Oceania, which has erased the historical records, literature and values upon which it was based. The suppression of these communities also destroys the notion of politics that underpins Orwell's conception of socialism. Crick defines politics as 'the activity by which differing interests within a given unit of rule are conciliated by giving them a share in power in proportion to their importance to the welfare and the survival of the whole community'.[72] It is therefore inevitably pluralist, founded upon 'at least some tolerance of different truths, some recognition that government is possible, indeed best conducted, amid the open canvassing of rival interests',[73] and, as such, distinct not only from totalitarianism, which attempts 'to reconstruct society utterly according to the goals of an ideology',[74] but even from the 'democratic doctrine of the sovereignty of the people',[75] which has the potential to establish a coercive or oppressive state. Politics is founded upon the co-existence of multiple 'group interests'[76] established by the perception of shared values, histories and objectives. Communities, therefore, are not only social units but also potential bases of political activism. The continual attempt in Orwell's writing to mobilise networks founded on shared class, nationality or gender as the basis of a socialist practice is analysed in the previous chapters of this book, and demonstrates a commitment, however problematic, to the notion of politics outlined by Crick. This is reinforced by his representation of the possible consequences of eliminating the multiple independent traditions and communities upon which the political process depends. This process is founded upon the interaction of different social networks with their particular histories and values, and therefore contrasts with what Howe described as the 'world of total integration',[77] in which history is uniform, if constantly redefined, and communities are controlled by the state.

The concept of 'total integration' can be explored with reference to the work of Adolf Hitler. The extent to which Orwell's work is concerned with Nazi movement has been disputed by critics and commentators. Fyvel, for example, argued that his 'one serious reference to Nazism, which he there overrated, was in his essay on H. G. Wells' and that there 'is almost no mention in his writings of Goebbels, Goering, and the other larger-than-life Nazi leaders'. Indeed, Fyvel insists, there is 'no mention in the index of Orwell's collective writings of Auschwitz, that hell on earth; indeed, very few references at all to the Nazi concentration camps'.[78] He describes Orwell's 'one journalistic piece' on the subject, a review of *Mein Kampf* published in *New English Weekly* on 21 March 1940, as 'pretty silly'.[79] The comments underestimate the various direct and indirect references to Nazism in his work.[80] Bowling's conception of the 'after-war' in *Coming Up for Air*, for example, with its 'coloured shirts, the barbed wire, the rubber truncheons'[81] evokes images of the Nazi state. In *The Third Reich*, Michael Burleigh argues that *Nineteen Eighty-Four* uses the 'distilled characteristics of Nazism and Stalinism' and that the 'Rumpelstiltskin figure preaching hate with an outstretched fist is derived from the Nazi propagandist Joseph Goebbels.'[82] Other details from the Nazi movement are used in the text, including, for example, the 'black overalls of an Inner Party member',[83] which suggest, amongst other things, the uniforms of the S. S. Even O'Brien's description of the projected future in terms of 'a boot stamping on a human face'[84] implies such a parallel, insofar as it evokes the argument in *The Lion and the Unicorn* that the 'goose-step' used by the German military is 'simply an affirmation of naked power; contained in it, quite consciously and intentionally, is the vision of a boot crashing down on a face' (396). The texts utilise details of Nazism and its practices as the basis of a composite image of totalitarianism.

In addition to this use of particular details, there is also, of course, a close parallel between the structure of Nazi Germany and that of Oceania. Indeed, Melvyn New insists that these connections define the text, and although 'it would be foolish to suggest that Orwell's long campaign against Stalin was not operating in *1984*, I maintain that the imaginative core of the work, and most especially its last, most often criticized section, derives directly from Orwell's response to, and attempt to explain, what happened to the Jews under Hitler.'[85] According to New, Oceania is organised, for members of the Outer Party in particular, upon the same basis as concentration camps, insofar as it is a 'world which exists only by and for its capacity to create victims'.[86] Particularly after Second World War, Orwell's work focuses on Stalinism, not least because, as he wrote in his 'As I Please' column of 14 January 1944, 'the Nazi régime has succeeded in smashing itself to pieces within a dozen years' (16:60–4:61), and did not, therefore, pose a direct threat to the ideas of freedom he valued. Its methods, however, provided only one example of the 'totalitarianism' examined in the novel.

The Nazi movement provided both a concrete example of a totalitarian state and a source of details that could be utilised in *Nineteen Eighty-Four*. Hitler's work also, however, provides a theoretical framework within which to read the novel. Despite historical accounts that describe Hitler as an opportunist or 'adventurer', he was, Hugh Trevor-Roper argued, a 'systematic thinker'[87] who formulated 'in advance a complete blue-print of his intended achievement'.[88] This interpretation is supported by Primo Levi, who describes Hitler as 'a coherent fanatic whose ideas were extremely clear'.[89] The 'blueprint' he produced was not, however, as

Trevor-Roper claimed, largely identical with 'its ultimate actual form',[90] but a theoretical model of a regime that was, in practice, always more fragmented and contradictory. There were, as Burleigh argues, 'inevitable discrepancies between ideal and reality'[91] in totalitarian societies, and much of Hitler's work is a utopian projection of a future Nazi state rather than a description of its existent form. Indeed, Carey states that Hitler has 'a unique place in the history of utopianism', and can even 'be seen as the culmination of the great utopian tradition that starts with Plato', a tradition which 'he terminated'.[92] As previously observed, Orwell reviewed *Mein Kampf* in 1942, emphasising the irrational component of Hitler's thought, the fact that he 'knows that human beings *don't* only want comfort, safety, short working-hours, hygiene, birth-control and, in general, common sense; they also, at least intermittently, want struggle and self-sacrifice, not to mention drums, flags and loyalty-parades' (12:116–18:117). He could not, however, have known of *Table Talk*, the summaries of Hitler's conversation recorded under the instructions of Martin Bormann, which were not published in English until 1953. These summaries must, of course, be treated with caution, but they nonetheless provide an additional perspective from which to interpret both Hitler's published writing and his government's actions. Though Hitler's work was not necessarily a dominant influence on *Nineteen Eighty-Four*, it is nevertheless valuable to an interpretation of the novel, as it contains a contemporary model of the totalitarian state. It represents a simultaneous if disconnected attempt to map, from the opposite perspective, the structure and basis of a distinctive modern form of authoritarianism. Both Orwell and Hitler suggest that the elimination of independent identities, control of legitimate knowledge and manipulation of history are pivotal to the construction of a totalitarian society.

In *Mein Kampf* and *Table Talk* Hitler not only described his ideal racial state, but detailed the various methods that would be used to construct it. The process of transformation he outlined illustrates the distinctions between his utopia and the societies from which it was to be developed. He insisted, for example, that the Nazis would 're-write history, from the racial point of view', moving from 'isolated examples' to a 'complete revision'.[93] This would form part of a broader attempt to produce an internally homogeneous state. The development of this unified society would be enforced by state policies, a process he argued was essential because,

> Without organisation – that is to say, without compulsion – and, consequently, without sacrifice of the part of individuals, nothing can work properly. Organised life offers the spectacle of a perpetual renunciation by individuals of a part of their liberty.[94]

It was, he stated, the 'limitation of this liberty, within the framework of an organisation which incorporates men of the same race, which is the real pointer to the degree of the civilisation attained', and, as a consequence, to 'give more liberty to the individual' is to drive 'the people along the road to decadence'.[95] The racial interpretation of history and value was one basis of this elimination of individuality, as he argued that the 'right of personal freedom recedes before the duty to preserve the race'.[96] The objective was to construct a unified population, under the control of single leader and legitimised by an essentialist historical narrative. This involved the eradication of older, more fluid principles of association, organisation and indeed privilege. He condemned the English class system, for example, observing that one 'can be the son of a good family and have no talent',[97] and argued that the identities of the individual states within Germany should be broken down. The 'autobahnen' were used for this purpose, and had a 'political' function, insofar as they 'swept away the internal frontiers of the Reich'.[98] Even national identities were held to be of limited importance, as once 'the conditions of the race's purity are established, it's of no importance whether a man is a native of one region rather than another – whether he comes from Norway or from Austria'.[99] The old forms of allegiance and loyalty were to be eradicated among the 'Germanic' peoples, and replaced by the concept of 'race' conceived as a unity of perspective as well as of 'blood'.

The utopian Nazi 'nation', therefore, extended beyond the boundaries of established nation-states, which were founded on a complex network of historical, cultural, institutional and geographical criteria.[100] The homogeneity of its population, theoretically determined by shared race, was to be enforced and regulated through the control of information, and, in particular, of the press. In a secret speech to representatives of the German press on 10 March 1938, Hitler insisted the press would become a 'means to an end' and an 'enormously powerful instrument' only when 'it is no longer possible for newspaper A to contradict newspaper B or for newspapers C, B and A to contradict each other'.[101] This control enabled, amongst other things, a binary division to be established between the members of the utopian state and its perceived enemies. The 'art of all truly great national leaders at all times', for Hitler, consisted 'in not dividing the attention of a people, but in concentrating it upon a single foe'.[102] This concentration relied upon a monopoly of the means of communication, a control of information that prevented the population at large from perceiving 'so much as a glimmer of right on the other wise'.[103] The control of the press also enabled shifts in policy to be legitimised by both preparing public opinion and by eliminating the communication of alternative perspectives. He insisted that

> We have frequently found ourselves compelled to reverse the engine and to change, in the course of a couple of days, the whole trend of imparted news, sometimes with a complete *volte face*. Such agility would have been quite impossible, if we had not had firmly in our grasp that extraordinary instrument of power which we call the press – and know how to make use of it.[104]

The 'little Rumpelstiltskin figure'[105] in *Nineteen Eighty-Four*, identified by Burleigh with Goebbels, provides a fictive example of such a reversal and of the importance of propaganda to the totalitarian state. His ability to alter the target of his speech from Eurasia to Eastasia 'in mid-sentence, not only without a pause, but without even breaking the syntax', satirises in particular the rapid alteration of propaganda in both Germany and Russia following first the signing and later the collapse of the Nazi-Soviet pact. It also, however, indicates more broadly the importance of the control of information to the popular acceptance of such a shift, enabling, in this instance, the 'Hate' to continue 'exactly as before, except that the target had been changed'.[106]

The construction of a binary relationship between the state and its perceived opponents implies that both terms are internally homogeneous, even if their referents are, paradoxically, variable, redefined on the basis of political expediency or ideological objectives. The attempt by Hitler to construct a uniform domestic population with a single enemy, however, is accompanied by an insistence on the practical importance of a proliferation of divisive identities and allegiances in the occupied 'Eastern territories'. He argued that the Nazis must 'meet, to the best of our ability any and every desire for individual liberty which they may express, and by so doing deprive them of any form of State organisation'.[107] The explicit objective was to prevent the development of wider forms of allegiance, and he insisted that 'village communities must be organised in a manner which precludes any possibility of fusion with neighbouring communities'.[108] The objective in religious matters, for example, was for 'each petty little district to have its own Pope'.[109]

As in *Nineteen Eighty-Four*, in which the Party encourages the proles to focus their attention on immediate communities and 'petty specific grievances',[110] the elimination of sub-cultures or allegiances within the dominant section of the population is counterbalanced by an excess amongst the oppressed majority. In both instances, the measures are intended to eradicate political practice, establishing a divide between a dominant population from which diversity has been eliminated, and an oppressed subject people fragmented by the proliferation of limited and divisive communities.

The model Hitler outlined is, of course, an abstract conception of the Nazi state, rather than a faithful representation of it. The 'Eastern territories' were not in practice characterised during the Nazi occupation by officials who accepted 'any and every desire for individual liberty' on the part of the inhabitants. His discussion of the future Reich does, however, expose the basis of a complete totalitarian state, and, in particular, emphasise the importance of eliminating previous communities. It insists upon a uniformity reinforced by the control of the media, 'revision' of history and eradication of subsidiary identities, including those founded upon shared class, region or even nationality. As Easthope writes, fascism 'it can be argued, aims to solve the problem of politics by eradicating politics as political conflict; in order to do this it seeks to abolish the necessary and inescapable differences that inhere within even the most apparently unified culture'.[111] Indeed, for 'totalitarian' states, as Arendt observed, even nationalism, founded upon a complex network of territorial, cultural, historical, linguistic and institutional factors, was finally a limitation upon its development, however much it might be exploited in propaganda. In particular, 'a development toward nationalism would frustrate its exterior expansion, without which the movement cannot survive'.[112] The National Socialist regime was instead, as Crick observes, increasingly founded upon 'racialism', which 'as a principle of allegiance cut right through nations'.[113] Despite the patriotic and nationalist rhetoric employed by the National Socialists, the traditional concept of the nation was in practice a constraint upon its actions.

The image Hitler formulates, of an authoritarian utopia in which the multitude of 'traditional' communities have been eliminated, is paralleled in *Nineteen Eighty-Four*, and connects the novel with Orwell's earlier work. The idea of community permeates his writing, and its most prominent forms, particularly those founded upon class, gender and nationality, are examined in the earlier chapters of this book. The communities he validates are independent of the state, in the main the product of particular, localised histories, and, he argues, provide the potential basis of a diverse, political socialism. His final novel is a utopian satire that implicitly defends, not only the 'private sphere', but the value of communities against political models that attempt to determine all aspects of social practice. In particular, it is concerned with the idea of 'totalitarianism', a form of government which, as Burleigh argued, 'did not confine itself to the usual realms allotted the state, but sought to control the family and private morality, and to direct the arts and sciences in ways which exceed the mere exertion of influence'.[114] The 'totalitarian ideas' that Orwell identified were, as the work of Hitler illustrates, not a literary construct, but an active structure of thought that informed contemporary authoritarian regimes, even if their practices were, inevitably, always more fragmented and contradictory than the theories upon which they were founded. *Nineteen Eighty-Four* is therefore in the tradition of the 'English socialism' described by Crick, which establishes 'barriers' to regimentation. Despite the critical insistence that the text was written by an 'ex-socialist', that it is a 'document of dark disillusionment not only with Stalinism but with every form and shade of socialism', and significant only as an example of 'Cold-War cultural propaganda', *Nineteen Eighty-Four* demonstrates a continued concern with a particular conception of socialism and defends the traditional communities upon which Orwell perceived it to be founded. The utopian structure of the text enables it to explore the concept of totalitarianism, whilst its use of familiar detail enables it to connect these abstract ideas to present social and political forms, mobilising it against more limited threats. This method of displacement, used by numerous other writers of the period, and exploited by Orwell in *Animal Form*, is used to continue to explore the political ideas that had occupied him in much of his previous writing. As John Wain argued, '*Animal Farm* and *Nineteen Eighty-Four*' are 'two mighty blows for the things he loved against the things he hated'.[115] In his final novel, he defended, amongst other things, the notion of community he had developed and tried to radicalise in his earlier work by constructing a utopia from which it was absent, a world in which individuals '*live alone*'.

Conclusion

In *Keep the Aspidistra Flying*, Gordon Comstock imagines London as 'Mile after mile of mean lonely houses, let off in flats and single rooms; not homes, not communities, just clusters of meaningless lives drifting in a sort of drowsy chaos to the grave!'[1] He is not, of course, the only one of Orwell's characters to experience 'the ever-recurrent thing – loneliness'.[2] Flory, for example, has 'existed to the brink of middle age in bitter loneliness',[3] whilst Dorothy Hare, returning to her father, contemplates a future dominated by what Mr Warburton terms 'those deadly little jobs that are shoved off on to lonely women'.[4] Winston Smith, writing his diary, also considers himself 'a lonely ghost uttering a truth that nobody would ever hear'.[5] These characters, all members of what Woodcock described as the 'lower ranks of the ruling elite',[6] are outside the 'stream of life',[7] unable or unwilling to become integrated in their societies. Gordon, however, interprets his own condition as a general one, 'objectifying his own inner misery' to produce the image of a London populated by 'corpses walking',[8] 'meaningless' individuals not validated by families or communities. His own family, which is 'dull, shabby, dead-alive, ineffectual',[9] consists of precisely such people, typified by his sister Julia, whose only social interaction outside work consists of 'occasional foregatherings with spinster friends as lonely as herself'.[10] The image, despite originating in Gordon's 'inner misery', posits a broader social fragmentation which is, indeed, a recurrent motif in Orwell's fiction as a whole.

The isolation of Orwell's protagonists is, however, frequently juxtaposed with images of active communities. These vary from temporary support networks, such as those amongst the hop-pickers, whom Dorothy finds 'extraordinarily kind',[11] to more stable, 'traditional' communities. Bowling's memories of the Lower Binfield of his childhood, with its 'feeling of continuity',[12] provide an idealised example of the latter. These communities persist even in Oceania. The 'proles' adhere to older values Winston associates with his mother, who represents for him a society 'governed by private loyalties'. Their commitment to one another, and to 'traditional' social institutions such as the family, emphasises Winston's isolation. The 'proles' have preserved attitudes 'he himself had to re-learn by conscious effort',[13] their communities and relative freedom from state doctrine providing them with the productive, secure identities Party members cannot attain. In this instance, as throughout Orwell's writing, images of community are figured as a positive alternative to societies conceived as chaotic, oppressive, or even 'meaningless and intolerable'.[14] For Comstock, it is the 'ruck of men' that convinces him of the value of a society he earlier wished 'to see blown to hell by bombs'.[15] For Orwell himself, it was 'working-class interiors' and his 'foretaste of Socialism' during the Spanish Civil War.

For Orwell, therefore, 'traditional' communities were a source of value in an 'epoch of fear, tyranny and regimentation' (12:91). Their centrality to his work is in part the product of his belief, described earlier, that individuals are formed within determinate social contexts. As Crick argues, 'Orwell's individualism' was 'either of a republican sort (sometimes called "civic humanism") or of a modern socialist kind: a person cannot be truly human except in relationships with others, my uniqueness consists not in my "personality" but in the "identity" by which others recognise my actions – a mutual, social process, not solitude'.[16] In their existent form, however, these constitutive processes are, as the texts reveal, ideological. Society is not reproduced as a seamless whole within which individual identities are flexible and chosen, but according to pre-existent narratives, such as those of class, gender and nation, which ultimately reflect material relations. Orwell does not suggest that all forms of socialisation produce 'real' communities. Dorothy Hare, Flory and Winston Smith are all defined by their upbringing and the values it instils in them, but none are represented as inhabiting a community that provides a stable, constructive basis for their personal identity. Despite his recognition that all human beings are socially constituted, therefore, Orwell's work focuses on particular communities that are figured as enabling such individual development. These are integral to his socialism, both as models for a future society and potential foundations of revolutionary activism. Indeed, the myths that structure such communities are, this conclusion will argue, the focus of his own political practice.

The most prominent communities in Orwell's writing are those formed by 'common men',[17] whether the miners of *The Road to Wigan Pier*, the militiamen of *Homage to Catalonia*, the 'proles' of *Nineteen Eighty-Four*, or even, symbolically, the oppressed animals of *Animal Farm*. His texts focus in particular upon the English working class. He was not, of course, the only writer of the 1930s and 1940s concerned with this section of the population, and his two major works of social exploration, containing his most sustained, direct analyses of this class, were, moreover, produced within an established literary tradition. The texts are nevertheless a distinctive contribution to this tradition. His account of class identities in *The Road to Wigan Pier* figures them as determinants of experience, realised in differences of values, mannerisms and 'taste'. This undermines the notion of 'going over', in that, as Woodcock writes, Orwell argues that 'Political conversion [. . .] does not give a man the cultural attributes of another class, nor does any glib intellectual acceptance of the desirability of a classless society.'[18] It figures class, however, not only as an abstract system of economic classification, but as a productive basis of identity, informing experience itself.

The working-class communities Orwell encountered in the north of England were produced, in part, by 'objective' factors such as the shared experience of labour and economic hardship. He also interpreted them, however, as the product of a distinctive tradition and, indeed, 'culture'. For Orwell, these communities maintained 'decent' values such as solidarity, mutual support and a commitment to the 'traditional' family. The 'sane and comely shape' of working-class life he describes in *The Road to Wigan Pier* persists even in Oceania, where Winston believes it is the proles alone who have the potential to create a 'world of sanity'.[19] The values attributed to these communities are also those integral to Orwell's notion of socialism. Indeed, Ingle argues that he

> has a view of socialism as a living value system, a system which forms the basis of working-class life in the North of England. It is a system which is rooted in equality and which emphasises what might be called the basic Judaeo-Christian civic virtues of decency and justice.[20]

Orwell interprets the 'folk-Marxism' of these communities, as McKibbin describes it, as an enactment of socialist values. Despite his insistence that the beliefs which structure a 'working-class home' are 'not necessarily better but are certainly different' from 'middle-class ideals and prejudices',[21] his conception of 'working-class life' provides, in practice, a positive foundation for his political thought.

Orwell's representations of the working-class are, however, 'mythic', founded, not only upon his exploration of impoverished areas, but upon the stereotypes and associations he inherited. The comparison with contemporary and earlier texts undertaken in this book demonstrates the extent to which Orwell selected from and adapted the images his society made available to him. The 'Myth of the Proletarian', to which Hynes refers, was not produced in a vacuum, nor, indeed, from a position of 'objective' critical detachment, but was an intervention in a prominent debate of the period. The specific myth Orwell developed has a number of distinct functions. In the first place, as described above, it figures the working class as sustaining the close-knit communities both he and his characters lack. It is in this sense a response to what Wager describes as Orwell's 'insatiable need for roots'.[22] These stable, 'traditional' social networks represent an alternative to both the 'drowsy chaos' of middle-class life and the ' "realism" and power-politics' he associated with the 'modern intellectual' (12:20–57:55). Orwell figures the working class as possessing qualities, such as the commitment to mutual support, 'traditional' morality, and 'family values', that would characterise a future socialist state. He not only represents 'socialist values' as feasible, but as existing in embryonic form. Working-class communities were, he suggested, a provisional model for a socialist society, and indeed his 'foretaste of Socialism' occurred in Barcelona in the brief period when the 'working class was in the saddle'.[23]

The political significance of Orwell's 'Myth of the Proletariat' is reinforced in his insistence that the working-class 'know how to combine'[24] and have a 'wonderful talent for organisation'.[25] In addition to encompassing 'socialist values', therefore, the working class are perceived as possessing the solidarity necessary to operate as an effective political force. This is, however, a potential rather than a realised power, as illustrated by the unemployed, whom he wrote had 'grown servile', or the 'proles' of Oceania who 'need only to rise up and shake themselves like a horse shaking off flies'[26] to remove the Party, but who nevertheless remain oppressed. Orwell was not, of course, the only writer to attribute qualities such as solidarity and mutual support to this section of the population. His is, nevertheless, an important contribution to the 'myth-making' of the period, and is used to sustain a distinctive form of 'moral' socialism.[27] Despite Beatrix Campbell's claim that 'what he feels for the common people edges on contempt',[28] and Rees' insistence that in his last two novels Orwell represents the 'common man' as 'helpless, inert, and almost imbecile',[29] the working-class demonstrate, for Orwell, the 'ordinary human decency' (18:60–3:60) upon which any egalitarian, just future society will be founded.

The ideas of masculinity and Englishness developed in his texts are both interwoven with this myth of 'common men', and both rely on a similar, selective use of existing conventions and stereotypes. His conception of active, heterosexual masculinity, for example, evokes that of even politically radical working-class communities, and is constructed in opposition to middle-class figures frequently represented as sterile, effeminate or homosexual. His discussion of 'Englishness' involves a similar process of alignment, identifying the nation with those in 'the fields and the streets, in the factories and in the armed services', rather than those in the 'House of Lords'. In both instances, moreover, the myths developed reinforce values also integral to his discussion of the working class. His representations of masculinity, for example, natur-alise the 'traditional' family structure, emphasise productive labour, and focus on qualities such as strength, physical courage and solidarity which he associates, in particular, with the miners. It is a form of 'manli-ness' primarily expounded through manual workers and militiamen, rather than, for example, 'gentlemen' and officers. His interpretation of 'Englishness' also focuses on qualities such as 'respect for legality' and the 'habit of *not killing one another*' that reinforce the notion of a tolerant co-operation enabled by adherence to established values. In these instances, as in his representation of the working-class, the myths Orwell develops are used to naturalise an image, however contentious, of 'ordinary human decency'.

The three myths explored in this book are, therefore, interlocked. Indeed, a composite image of the English working-class man emerges from the texts, conceived as simultaneously the victim of present inequalities, practitioner of 'socialist values' and instrument of social transformation. The myths Orwell constructs are, however, neither simple exercises in 'romantic' idealisation nor, indeed, static. His images of Englishness, for example, are, as previously observed, critical and reformist, concerned with renewal as much as with preservation. As Hitchens argues, his 'version of St George was also able and willing to slay national dragons, and to take on – rather than to transmit or represent – national myths'.[30] His descriptions of the working-class contain a similar emphasis on renewal, focusing on the need to mobilise their potential power. In this respect, his work supports the claim of Marx and Engels, that the role of 'socialist writers' is not to 'regard the proletarians as *gods*' but to demonstrate their capacity to abolish '*all* the inhuman conditions of life of society today which are summed up' in their 'own situation'.[31] Orwell's comparatively uncritical use of the masculine culture he inherited is the exception to this pattern. His persistent emphasis upon social transformation, however, provides a basis upon which to assess the political implications of myth-making itself.

In 'The Proletarian Writer', Orwell wrote that 'every artist is a propagandist', in the sense that 'he is trying, directly or indirectly, to impose a vision of life that seems to him desirable' (12:294–9:297). This point is reinforced in his claim, in 'Why I Write', that all literature is ' "political" in the widest possible sense', because it is motivated by the desire 'to push the world in a certain direction, to alter other people's idea of the kind of society that they should strive after' (18:316–21:318). These statements locate literature's political significance in its ability to 'impose a vision of life', to reinterpret the myths that define social values and ideals. As Schöpflin argues, myths are 'one of the ways in which collectivities [...] establish and determine the foundations of their own beliefs, their own systems of morality and values'.[32] Their reinterpretation is consequently always also a reinterpretation of the communities, and indeed individuals, they define. For Orwell, literature was integral to both the construction and the reconstruction of myths, and in a letter to Geoffrey Gorer of 23 May 1936 he argues that 'people's habits etc. are formed not only by their upbringing & so forth but also very largely by books' (10:481–2:482). This position is supported by Ingle, who states that

> the imaginative instinct of a writer can enable him to make concrete a whole ideology in an unforgettable character or situation. This image, once having influenced a person's thinking, may prove highly resilient. It seems possible to state that imaginative writers influence principally as a result of their ability to create symbols which people can identify with their own experience and value system, and which therefore serve as a synthesis and reinforcement.

In essence, the 'imaginative writer's ability to capture in miniature a whole landscape of political and social comment – this, it seems, is what gives them influence'.[33] In this context, Orwell's adaptation and reinterpretation of 'myths of collectivity' is a political process, an attempt to 'push the world in a certain direction' by using and transforming the narratives that define ' "lived" experience'.

Orwell's representations of the working-class, masculinity and Englishness are, as this book has demonstrated, frequently paradoxical, incorporating a simultaneous commitment to tradition and radical change. There are, nevertheless, consistent elements of his political thought, and, it is fitting to conclude by outlining the most important of these. In the first place, his work is characterised by a moral focus, a persistent concern with 'decency and justice'. Indeed, in a letter to Humphrey House, of 11 April 1940, he condemns the 'inherently mechanistic Marxist notion that if you make the necessary technical advance the moral advance will follow of itself' (12:139–42:141). This emphasis distanced him from the 'power-politics' he associated with 'intellectuals', and is interwoven with a commitment to the 'common man', whom he perceived as the site of such moral value. Despite Williams' claim that Orwell sees the 'proles', his last portrait of such men, as 'a shouting, stupid crowd in the streets',[34] they are in fact the representatives of a 'decency' lost to Party members. The 'proles'

> were not loyal to a party or a country or an idea, they were loyal to one another [...] The proles had stayed human. They had not become hardened inside.[35]

It is the 'proles' alone who have the potential to construct a 'world of sanity'. The text, as Crick observes, uses them to satirise 'what the mass media, poor schools, and the selfishness of the intelligentsia was doing to the actual working class of Orwell's time'.[36] It nevertheless emphasises the positive value of their communities, beliefs and culture. Indeed, a commitment to 'common men' is demonstrated even in his use of 'Oranges and Lemons' in *Nineteen Eighty-Four*. In *Brave New World*, Huxley uses the work of Shakespeare, a prominent representative of 'high' culture, as the symbol of lost cultural values. Orwell's use of a childhood 'nursery rhyme' to evoke the past validates, in contrast, a 'traditional' popular culture.

The most important element of Orwell's political thought, however, is, of course, his socialism. As Crick argues,

> Orwell never changed his values after 1936. There is no biographical evidence that his socialism waned; on the contrary there is much that it matured.[37]

This political radicalism was, moreover, not incompatible with his 'nostalgia for the Edwardian shabby-genteel or the under-dog'. As Hitchens observes, 'George Orwell was conservative about many things, but not about politics.'[38] After his visits to the north of England, and experience in Spain, Orwell defined himself as a socialist, and his political ideas shaped his work. Indeed, he famously wrote that 'Every line of serious work that I have written since 1936 has been written, directly or indirectly, *against* totalitarianism and *for* democratic Socialism, as I understand it' (18:319). His 'understanding' of socialism, as this book demonstrates, could be idiosyncratic, contradictory and illogical. It was founded, however, on the belief 'that human nature is fairly decent to start with' (18:62), and that 'Socialism is a *better* way of life but not necessarily, in its first stages, a more comfortable one' (17:245–59:248). These 'moral' and 'utopian' elements, however, were combined with a focus on immediate problems, and a commitment to the 'best' of 'tradition'. In locating Orwell within his historical context, and demonstrating his attachment to many of the values he inherited, this book traces a distinctive form of socialism committed to both past and future, preservation and renewal. Ironically Orwell, like Lenin, did not propose to abandon the 'valuable achievements of the bourgeois epoch', but to integrate them within a new society committed to 'decency and justice'. His use and reinterpretation of myth is an example of this. Orwell's 'new country' would abandon class distinctions but retain 'working-class interiors', dissolve nationalism but retain Englishness. It would mobilise the communities of the past to create a future 'world of free and equal human beings'. His is not, perhaps, a logical or consistent form of socialism, but it is nevertheless a distinctive and valuable contribution to that a radical tradition Orwell believed led 'back through Utopian dreamers like William Morris and mystical democrats like Walt Whitman, through Rousseau, through the English diggers and levellers, through the peasant revolts of the Middle Ages, and back to the early Christians and the slave rebellions of antiquity' (18:62).

Notes

Introduction

1. S. Hynes, 'Introduction' in Samuel Hynes, ed., *Twentieth Century Interpretations of 1984* (Englewood Cliffs: Prentice Hall, 1971), pp. 1–19, p. 10. In *The Auden Generation: Literature and Politics in England in the 1930s* (London: Bodley Head, 1976), Hynes writes that, in using the word 'myth' he is 'thinking of the way ideas gather about them certain images and feelings, and then tend to be treated in terms of those accumulations' (p. 109). Myth, therefore, is used to signify the encoding of an idea or value within particular images, a concept that has obvious parallels to the definition formulated by Roland Barthes, which is examined later in this chapter.

2. The association of the working class with stupidity is illustrated, for example, in George Gissing's novel *The Nether World* (1889; repr. Oxford: Oxford University Press, 1999), in which the narrator insists that 'Irony is not a weapon much in use among working people; their wits in general are too slow' (p. 32), and describes the 'London poor' as the 'least original and least articulate beings within the confines of civilisation' (p. 41).

3. P. Macherey, *A Theory of Literary Production* (1966; repr. London: Routledge, 1986), p. 100.

4. K. Bluemel, *George Orwell and the Radical Eccentrics: Intermodernism in Literary London* (Basingstoke: Palgrave Macmillan, 2004), p. 5.

5. Ibid., p. 147.

6. A. Easthope, *Englishness and National Culture* (London: Routledge, 1999), p. 23.

7. G. Schöpflin, 'The Functions of Myth and a Taxonomy of Myths' in Geoffrey Hosking and George Schöpflin, eds, *Myths and Nationhood* (New York: Routledge, 1997), pp. 19–35, p. 22.

8. R. Williams, 'Introduction' in Raymond Williams, ed., *George Orwell: A Collection of Critical Essays* (Englewood Cliffs: Prentice Hall, 1974), pp. 1–9, p. 2.

9. R. Williams, *Orwell* (London: Fontana, 1971), p. 87.

10. B. Anderson, *Imagined Communities: Reflections on the Origins and Spread of Nationalism* (London: Verso and NLB, 1983), p. 31.

11. D. Miller, *On Nationality* (Oxford: Clarendon, 1995), p. 22.

12. Easthope, *Englishness and National Culture*, p. 10.

13. L. Althusser, 'Philosophy as a Revolutionary Weapon' in *On Lenin and Philosophy and Other Essays* (London: New Left Books, 1971), pp. 13–25, p. 25.

14. K. Marx, 'Introduction to the *Grundrisse*' in Terrell Carver, ed., *Marx: Later Political Writing* (Cambridge: Cambridge University Press, 1996), pp. 128–57, p. 129.

15. K. Marx, 'The Paris Notebooks' in Joseph O' Malley, ed., *Marx: Early Political Writings* (Cambridge: Cambridge University Press, 1994), pp. 71–96, p. 80.

16. Ibid., pp. 80–1.
17. K. Marx, ' "The German Ideology": Chapter One, "Feuerbach" ', ibid., pp. 119–81, p. 129.
18. J. Habermas, *Moral Consciousness and Communicative Action* (1983; repr. Cambridge: Polity, 1990), p. 199.
19. Marx argues that the 'modes of production of material life conditions the social, political and intellectual life-processes generally. It is not the consciousness of men that specifies their being, but on the contrary their social being that specifies their consciousness.' (' "Preface" to *A Contribution to the Critique of Political Economy'*, *Later Political Writings*, pp. 158–62, p. 160).
20. Schöpflin, 'The Functions of Myth', p. 22.
21. L. Althusser, 'Marxism and Humanism' in *For Marx* (1965; repr. London: Allen Lane, 1969), pp. 219–47, p. 231.
22. L. Althusser, 'Ideology and the Ideological State Apparatuses (Notes Towards an Investigation)' in *On Lenin and Philosophy*, pp. 121–73, p. 149.
23. L. Althusser, 'A Letter on Art in Reply to André Daspre', ibid., pp. 203–8, p. 204.
24. Ibid., p. 123.
25. R. Moĕnik, 'Ideology and Fantasy' in E. Ann Kaplan and Michael Sprinkler, eds, *The Althussarian Legacy* (London: Verso, 1993), pp. 139–56, p. 144.
26. F. Jameson, *Postmodernism, or, the Cultural Logic of Late Capitalism* (London: Verso, 1991), p. 273.
27. Ibid., pp. 263–4.
28. 'Class', in this context, is conceived as a system of economic classification, rather than a broader model, used elsewhere in his work, in which the term refers to a network of economic and cultural determinants.
29. In his essay 'To My English' readers, for example, Althusser observes that 'as Marx says, it is in ideology that men "become conscious" of their class conflict and "fight it out" ' (*For Marx*, pp. 9–15, p. 11).
30. F. Engels, 'Engels to Joseph Block, September 21–22, 1890' in Marx and Engels, eds, *On Literature and Art* (Moscow: Progress Publishers, 1976), p. 57.
31. R. Barthes, 'Myth Today' in Annette Lavers, ed., *Mythologies* (1975; repr. London: Vintage, 2000), pp. 109–59, p. 114.
32. Ibid., p. 129.
33. Ibid., p. 116.
34. Ibid., p. 143.
35. Ibid., p. 117.
36. Ibid., p. 140.
37. Barthes, 'Myth Today', p. 146. Barthes argues that the revolution will strip away ideology, of which myth is an integral part, as well as reconstructing the material basis of society. Myth is therefore 'absent' from post-revolutionary society because it has disposed of the inequalities and, indeed, inefficiencies that ultimately engendered and sustained this 'false consciousness'. Myth is absent, in other words, simply because it is no longer required.
38. Ibid., p. 157.
39. B. Crick, 'Introduction' in George Orwell, *Nineteen Eighty-Four* (1949; Oxford: Clarendon, 1984), pp. 1–136, p. 13.

1　Class

1. F. Engels, *The Condition of the Working Class in England* (1845; repr. London: Penguin, 1987), p. 27.
2. P. Keating, 'Introduction' in Peter Keating, ed., *Into Unknown England 1866– 1913: Selections from the Social Explorers* (London: Fontana, 1976), pp. 11–32, p. 13.
3. M. A. Crowther, 'The Tramp' in Roy Porter, ed., *Myths of the English* (Cambridge: Polity, 1992), pp. 91–113, p. 100.
4. Cunningham, *British Writers of the Thirties*, p. 239.
5. K. Marx and Friedrich Engels, 'Manifesto of the Communist Party' in Terrell Carver, ed., *Marx: Later Political Writings* (Cambridge: Cambridge University Press, 1996), pp. 1–30, p. 10.
6. G. Woodcock, *The Crystal Spirit: A Study of George Orwell* (London: Jonathan Cape, 1967), p. 125.
7. C. Day Lewis, 'Letter to a Young Revolutionary' in Michael Roberts, ed., *New Country: Prose and Poetry by the Authors of New Signatures* (London: Hogarth, 1933), pp. 25–42, p. 41.
8. J. Hanley, *Grey Children: A Study in Humbug and Misery* (London: Methuen, 1937), p. 22.
9. R. Glasser, *Gorbals Boy at Oxford* (1988; repr. London: Pan Books, 1990), p. 19.
10. P. Macherey, *A Theory of Literary Production* (1966; repr. London: Routledge, 1986), p. 49.
11. Ibid., p. 100.
12. C. Booth, 'Life and Labour of the People of London' in *Into Unknown England*, 112–40, p. 137.
13. V. Woolf, 'Introductory Letter to Margaret Llewelyn Davies' in Margaret Llewelyn Davies, ed., *Life as We Have Known It, by Co-operative Working Women* (1931; repr. London: Virago, 1977), pp. xvii–xli, p. xxx.
14. Ibid., p. xxiii.
15. Ibid., p. xxx.
16. Orwell, *The Road to Wigan Pier*, p. 149.
17. Ibid., p. 215.
18. Ibid., p. 211.
19. J. Greenwood, 'A Night in the Workhouse' in *Into Unknown England*, pp. 33– 54, p. 46.
20. G. Sims, 'How the Poor Live', ibid., pp. 65–90, p. 65.
21. W. Booth, 'In Darkest England and the Way Out', ibid., pp. 141–73, p. 145.
22. P. J. Keating, *The Working Classes in Victorian Fiction* (London: Routledge & Kegan Paul, 1971), pp. 32–3.
23. Ibid., p. 33.
24. Engels, *The Condition of the Working Class*, p. 73.
25. [C. F. G. Masterman], *From the Abyss: Of Its Inhabitants by One of Them* (London: R. Brimley Johnson, 1902), p. 23.
26. Orwell, *Down and Out in Paris and London*, p. 215.
27. C. Dickens, 'The Noble Savage' in John Carey, ed., *The Faber Book of Utopias* (London: Faber, 1999), pp. 239–45, p. 239.
28. J. McLaughlin, *Writing the Urban Jungle: Reading Empire in London from Doyle to Eliot* (London and Charlottesville: University of Virginia Press, 2000), p. 21.

29. Ibid., p. 80.
30. Sims, 'How the Poor Live', pp. 86–7.
31. H. Mayhew, *London Labour and the London Poor* (1861–2; repr. Harmondsworth: Penguin, 1985), p. 43.
32. J. Carey, *The Intellectuals and the Masses* (London: Faber, 1992), p. 21.
33. Ibid., p. 160.
34. Masterman, *From the Abyss*, p. 2.
35. Ibid., p. 12.
36. Ibid., p. 24.
37. Ibid., p. 20.
38. Ibid., p. 25.
39. Ibid., p. 26.
40. J. O. y Gasset, *The Revolt of the Masses* (1930; repr. New York: Mentor, 1951), p. 83.
41. Ibid., pp. 83–4.
42. Ibid., p. 10.
43. Ibid., p. 46.
44. H. Arendt, *The Origins of Totalitarianism* (1951; repr. London: Allen & Unwin, 1967), p. 311.
45. G. Orwell, *Nineteen Eighty-Four* (1949; repr. London: Secker & Warburg, 1997), p. 274.
46. Ibid., p. 282.
47. Ibid., p. 56.
48. Ibid., p. 74.
49. Ibid., p. 156.
50. G. Orwell, *Animal Farm* (1945; repr. London: Secker & Warburg, 1997), p. 92.
51. Ibid., p. 37.
52. D. Bradshaw, 'Introduction' in A. Huxley, *The Hidden Huxley* (1994; repr. London: Faber, 1995), pp. vii–xxvi, p. x.
53. Keating, *The Working Classes in Victorian Fiction*, p. 136.
54. Gissing, *The Nether World*, p. 107.
55. G. Gissing, *New Grub Street* (1891; repr. Harmondsworth: Penguin, 1980), p. 116.
56. G. Gissing, *Demos: A Story of English Socialism* (1866; repr. Brighton: Harvester, 1972), p. 367. Adela belongs by birth to a 'higher' social class.
57. R. Williams, *Culture and Society: Coleridge to Orwell* (1958; repr. London: Hogarth, 1993), p. 178.
58. G. Gissing, *The Unclassed* (1895; repr. Brighton: Harvester, 1983), p. 114.
59. J. London, *The People of the Abyss* (1903; repr. [London?]: Joseph Simon, 1980), p. 51.
60. Gissing, *The Nether World*, p. 11.
61. Ibid., p. 109.
62. D. Grylls, *The Paradox of Gissing* (London: Allen & Unwin, 1986), p. 66.
63. Ibid., p. 50.
64. Gissing, *The Unclassed*, p. 53.
65. Orwell, *Down and Out in Paris and London*, p. 120.
66. Ibid., p. 121.
67. Ibid., p. 122.
68. Ibid., p. 213.

69. McLaughlin, *Writing the Urban Jungle*, pp. 106–7.
70. R. R. Marett, 'Preface' in J. B. M. McGovern, *Among the Headhunters of Formosa* (1922; repr. Taipei: SMC, 1997), pp. 9–14, p. 13.
71. McGovern, *Among the Headhunters of Formosa*, p. 31.
72. McLaughlin, *Writing the Urban Jungle*, p. 22.
73. This is related to the widely held idea that there is an intimate connection between Orwell's life and work, and that the two reinforce one another. Lionel Trilling, for example, writes in 'George Orwell and the Politics of Truth' (*George Orwell: A Collection of Critical Essays*, pp. 62–79) that he was a 'figure', a term he used to denote 'men who live their visions as well as write them, who *are* what they write' (p. 65). Richard Hoggart also argues in 'George Orwell and the Art of Biography' (*An English Temper: Essays on Education, Culture & Communication* (London: Chatto & Windus, 1982), pp. 111–18) that 'He's someone whose work we find hard to separate from his personality. We do not often feel "negative capability" in him; we meet an exceptional personality, whose life and art were one and who, we feel, *lived out* his beliefs' (p. 113).
74. Orwell, *Down and Out in London and Paris*, p. 12. The original of this thief may have been somewhat different. In 'A Great Feeling for Nature' (Audrey Coppard and Bernard Crick, eds, *Orwell Remembered* (London: Ariel, 1984), pp. 94–8), Mabel Fierz insists that Orwell had told her of 'a little trollop he picked up in a café in Paris', who later 'decamped with everything he possessed' (p. 95). As Crick argues, in *George Orwell*, 'Orwell may have favoured the Italian over the girl in order not to upset his family too much' (p. 199).
75. Orwell, *Down and Out in Paris and London*, p. 116.
76. Ibid., p. 128.
77. Anonymous, 'Unsigned Notice, *Nation*' in Jeffrey Meyers, ed., *George Orwell: The Critical Heritage* (London: Routledge & Kegan Paul, 1975), pp. 45–6, p. 45.
78. W. H. Davies, 'W. H. Davies, *New Statesman and Nation*', ibid., pp. 43–5, p. 44.
79. D. Murphy, 'Introduction' in *Down and Out in Paris and London* (1933; repr. Harmondsworth: Penguin, 1989), pp. v–xv, p. viii.
80. D. Jacobson, 'Orwell's Slumming' in *The World of George Orwell*, pp. 47–52, p. 48.
81. M. Bradbury, *The Modern British Novel* (London: Secker & Warburg, 1993), p. 238.
82. J. Montefiore, *Men and Women Writers of the 1930s: The Dangerous Flood of History* (London: Routledge, 1996), p. 11.
83. Woodcock, *The Crystal Spirit*, p. 32. This division between Orwell and the narrator of the texts is further complicated by the fact that 'Orwell' himself is a constructed literary persona.
84. Orwell, *The Road to Wigan Pier*, p. 142.
85. Orwell, *Down and Out in Paris and London*, p. 13.
86. Ibid., p. 203.
87. J. Newsinger, *Orwell's Politics* (Basingstoke: Macmillan, 1999), pp. 24–5.
88. Orwell, *Down and Out in Paris and London*, p. 13.
89. Ibid., p. 15.

90. Newsinger, *Orwell's Politics*, p. 20.
91. Woodcock, *The Crystal Spirit*, p. 72.
92. Orwell, *The Road to Wigan Pier*, p. 138.
93. Orwell, *Down and Out in Paris and London*, p. 118.
94. Ibid., p. 121.
95. Ibid., p. 128.
96. Ibid., p. 129.
97. Ibid., p. 130.
98. London, *The People of the Abyss*, pp. 9–10.
99. Crick, *George Orwell*, p. 184.
100. Orwell, *Down and Out in Paris and London*, p. 130.
101. Orwell, *The Road to Wigan Pier*, p. 144.
102. Ibid., p. 106.
103. T. Harrisson, 'Introduction' in Humphrey Spender, *Britain in the 30s* (London: Lion and Unicorn Press, 1975), not paginated.
104. McKibbin, *Classes and Cultures*, p. 37.
105. P. Gurney, ' "Intersex" and "Dirty Girls": Mass-Observation and Working Class Sexuality in England in the 1930s' *Journal of the History of Sexuality*, 8: 2 (October 1997), pp. 256–90, p. 261.
106. Orwell, *The Road to Wigan Pier*, p. 113.
107. Orwell, *Down and Out in Paris and London*, p. 197.
108. Ibid., p. 2.
109. Ibid., p. 71.
110. Ibid., p. 72.
111. Ibid., p. 117.
112. Ibid., p. 69.
113. Ibid., p. 63.
114. Ibid., p. 151.
115. Ibid., p. 160.
116. Ibid., p. 159.
117. Ibid., p. 196.
118. Orwell, *The Road to Wigan Pier*, p. 144.
119. A. Zwerdling, *Orwell and the Left* (New Haven: Yale University Press, 1974), p. 165.
120. Orwell, *Down and Out in Paris and London*, p. 3.
121. Ibid., p. 21.
122. Ibid., p. 102.
123. Ibid., p. 166.
124. Ibid., p. 82.
125. Ibid., p. 83.
126. Crick, *George Orwell*, p. 201.
127. Orwell, *Down and Out in Paris and London*, p. 176.
128. Ibid., p. 203.
129. Ibid., p. 210.
130. J. R. Hammond, *A George Orwell Companion: A Guide to the Novels, Documentaries and Essays* (1982; repr. Chippenham: Anthony Rowe, 1994), p. 81.
131. Orwell, *Down and Out in Paris and London*, p. 167.
132. Zwerdling, *Orwell and the Left*, p. 165.
133. Orwell, *Down and Out in Paris and London*, p. 3.

134. Rai, *Orwell and the Politics of Despair* (Cambridge: Cambridge University Press, 1998), p. 31.
135. Newsinger, *Orwell's Politics*, pp. 30–1.
136. Crick, *George Orwell*, p. 201.
137. Ibid., p. 213.
138. K. Laybourn, *Britain on the Breadline: A Social and Political History of Britain 1918–1939* (1990; repr. Stroud: Sutton Publishing, 1998), p. 9.
139. R. Croucher, *We Refuse to Starve in Silence: A History of the National Unemployed Workers' Movement, 1920–46* (London: Lawrence and Wishart, 1987), p. 14.
140. Orwell, *Down and Out in Paris and London*, p. 208.
141. Ibid., p. 117.
142. Ibid., p. 120.
143. Ibid., p. 216.
144. H. Massingham, *I Took Off My Tie* (London: Heinemann, 1936), pp. 2–3.
145. M-O A: FR 2465 'Pseudo-Personality in Prostitution', March 1945, p. 27.
146. T. Harrisson and C. Madge, *Britain by Mass-Observation* (1939; repr. London: Cresset Library, 1986), p. 12.
147. Cunningham, *British Writers of the Thirties*, p. 333.
148. A. Calder, 'Introduction' in *Britain by Mass-Observation*, pp. vii–xv, p. xiii.
149. G. Cross, 'Introduction: Mass-Observation and Worktowners at Play' in *Worktowners at Blackpool: Mass-Observation and Popular Leisure in the 1930s* (London: Routledge, 1990), pp. 1–15, pp. 6–7.
150. Engels, *The Condition of the Working Class in England*, p. 150.
151. Massingham, *I Took Off My Tie*, p. 1.
152. T. Harrison, 'Preface' in Mass-Observation, *The Pub and the People: A Worktown Study* (London: Victor Gollancz, 1943), pp. 7–14, p. 7.
153. Cunningham, *British Writers of the Thirties*, p. 266.
154. A. Hitler, *Mein Kampf* (1925–6; repr. London: Pimlico, 1997), p. 435.
155. S. Blumenfeld, *Jew Boy* (London: Jonathan Cape, 1935), p. 223.
156. M. Cohen, *I Was One of the Unemployed* (London: Gollancz, 1945), p. 19.
157. Ibid., p. 20.
158. L. G. Gibbon, *A Scots Quair* (1946; repr. London: Penguin, 1986), p. 395.
159. Marx and Engels, 'Manifesto of the Communist Party', p. 20.
160. Ibid., p. 348.
161. L. Jones, *We Life: The Story of a Welsh Mining Village* (London: Lawrence and Wishart, 1939), p. 243.
162. R. E. Warner, 'Hymn' in *New Country*, pp. 254–6, p. 254.
163. J. B. Priestley, *English Journey, Being a Rambling But Truthful Account of What One Man Saw and Heard and Felt and Thought During a Journey Through England During the Autumn of the Year 1933* (1934; repr. London: Heinemann, 1937), p. 29.
164. G. Garrett, 'The First Hunger March' in *The Penguin New Writing: 1* (Harmondsworth: Penguin, 1940), pp. 62–75, p. 69.
165. Harrisson and Madge, *Britain by Mass-Observation*, p. 145.
166. Ibid., pp. 190–1.
167. Mass-Observation, *Worktowners at Blackpool*, p. 173.
168. Harrisson and Madge, *Britain by Mass-Observation*, pp. 170–1.
169. Orwell, *The Road to Wigan Pier*, p. 101.
170. Massingham, *I Took Off My Tie*, p. 12.

171. Woolf, 'Introductory Letter to Margaret Llewelyn Davies', p. xxiv.
172. Ibid., p. xxvii.
173. Ibid., p. xxx.
174. Ibid., pp. xxxix–xl.
175. V. Woolf, 'The Leaning Tower' in *Collected Essays: Volume Two* (London: Hogarth, 1966), pp. 162–81, p. 168.
176. V. Woolf, *A Room of One's Own* (1928; repr. Harmondsworth: Penguin, 2000), p. 106.
177. London, *The People of the Abyss*, p. 143.
178. Ibid., p. 27.
179. Ibid. pp. 72–3.
180. Ibid., p. 32.
181. C. Chesterton, *In Darkest London* (1926; repr. London: Stanley Paul, 1927), p. 110.
182. Gissing, *The Nether World*, p. 340.
183. W. Brierley, *Sandwichman* (London: Methuen, 1937), p. 49.
184. Ibid., p. 201.
185. W. Greenwood, *Love on the Dole* (1933; repr. London: Vintage, 1993), p. 150.
186. Hanley, *Grey Children*, p. 126.
187. J. Common, *Freedom of the Streets* (1938; repr. Newcastle upon Tyne: People's Publications, 1988), p. 29.
188. Glasser, *Gorbals Boy at Oxford*, p. 1.
189. Ibid., p. 19.
190. W. Hannington, *The Problem of the Distressed Areas* (London: Gollancz, 1937), pp. 51–2.
191. A. F. Brockway, *Hungry England* (London: Gollancz, 1932), p. 50.
192. Orwell, *The Road to Wigan Pier*, p. 15.
193. G. Orwell, *Coming Up for Air* (1939; repr. London: Secker & Warburg, 1997), p. 41.
194. M. P. Reeves, *Round About a Pound a Week* (1913; repr. London: Virago, 1999), p. 64.
195. J. Campbell, 'Introduction' in Margery Spring Rice, ed., *Working-Class Wives: Their Health and Condition* (Harmondsworth: Penguin, 1939), pp. vii–xii, p. ix.
196. B. L. Coombes, *Miners Day* (Harmondsworth: Penguin, 1945), p. 76.
197. R. Roberts, *The Classic Slum: Salford Life in the First Quarter of the Century* (1971; repr. Harmondsworth: Penguin, 1987), p. 41.
198. Rice, *Working-Class Wives*, p. 18.
199. Brieley, *Sandwichman*, p. 49.
200. A. Brown, 'December 1934' in David Margolies, ed., *Writing the Revolution: Cultural Criticism from* Left Review (London: Pluto, 1998), pp. 27–9, p. 28.
201. V. I. Lenin, 'On Proletarian Culture' in *On Culture and Cultural Revolution* (1966; repr. Moscow: Progress Publishers, 1970), pp. 147–8, p. 148.
202. Orwell, *The Road to Wigan Pier*, p. 106.
203. Ibid., p. 107.
204. Ibid., p. 105.
205. Ibid., p. 68.
206. Orwell, *Nineteen Eighty-Four*, p. 172.
207. Woodcock, *The Crystal Spirit*, p. 125.
208. Orwell, *The Road to Wigan Pier*, p. 145.

209. Ibid., p. 213.
210. Ibid., p. 30.
211. Ibid., p. 156.
212. Orwell, *The Road to Wigan Pier*, p. 113.
213. D. Cannadine, *Class in Britain* (1998; repr. Harmondsworth: Penguin, 2000), p. 144.
214. R. Hoggart, 'Introduction' in *The Road to Wigan Pier* (1937; repr. Harmondsworth: Penguin, 1989), pp. v–xii, p. vii.
215. R. Rees, *George Orwell: Fugitive from the Camp of Victory* (London: Secker & Warburg, 1961), p. 146.
216. Orwell, *The Road to Wigan Pier*, p. 113.
217. Ibid., p. 150.
218. Ibid., p. 279. The I.L.P. is the Independent Labour Party, which Orwell joined on 13 June 1938.
219. B. Campbell, *Wigan Pier Revisited* (London: Virago, 1984), p. 2.
220. Ian Hamilton, 'Along the Road to Wigan Pier' in *The World of George Orwell*, pp. 53–61, p. 55.
221. For an analysis of the controversy surrounding Orwell's stay in the tripe shop and his account of it, see Crick, *George Orwell*, pp. 281–2.
222. J. Kennan, 'With the Wigan Miners' in *Orwell Remembered*, pp. 130–2, p. 131.
223. M. Roberts, 'Preface' in *New Country*, pp. 9–21, p. 16.
224. C. Hitchens, *Orwell's Victory* (Harmondsworth: Penguin, 2002), p. 26.
225. Hammond, *A George Orwell Companion*, p. 128.
226. S. Jameson, 'Documents' in *Fact*, 4 (July, 1937), pp. 9–18, p. 17.
227. Orwell, *The Road to Wigan Pier*, p. 143.
228. Ibid., p. 113.
229. Ibid., p. 138.
230. Meyers, *Orwell*, p. 79.
231. M. Muggeridge, 'A Knight of Woeful Countenance' in *The World of George Orwell*, pp. 165–75, p. 171.
232. Campbell, *Wigan Pier Revisited*, p. 2.
233. M. Benney, *Almost a Gentleman* (London: Peter Davies, 1966), p. 168.
234. Glasser, *Gorbals Boy at Oxford*, p. 41.
235. Ibid., p. 44.
236. T. Eagleton, 'Orwell and the Lower-Middle-Class Novel' in *George Orwell: A Collection of Critical Essays*, pp. 10–33, p. 22.
237. Orwell, *The Road to Wigan Pier*, p. 139.
238. Ibid., p. 142.
239. Ibid., p. 144.
240. W. Empson, 'Orwell at the BBC' in *The World of George Orwell*, pp. 93–9, p. 97.
241. Ibid., p. 158.
242. Ibid., p. 70.
243. Engels, *The Condition of the Working Class in England*, p. 83.
244. McLaughlin, *Writing the Urban Jungle*, p. 106.
245. Orwell, *The Road to Wigan Pier*, p. 114.
246. Brown's book is mentioned in *The Road to Wigan Pier*, where it is described as 'in some ways interesting', as an example of the work of an 'orthodox Marxist' (p. 208).
247. McKibbin, *Classes and Cultures*, p. 1.

248. Orwell, *The Road to Wigan Pier*, p. 209.
249. Ibid., p. 208.
250. Lewis, 'Letter to a Young Revolutionary', p. 32.
251. A. Rodaway, *A London Childhood* (1960; repr. London: Virago, 1985), p. 74.
252. Orwell, *The Road to Wigan Pier*, p. 209.
253. Ibid., p. 126.
254. H. G. Wells, *Tono-Bungay* (1909; repr. London: Pan, 1972), p. 112.
255. Ibid., p. 203.
256. Ibid., p. 206.
257. H. G. Wells, *Kipps* (1905; repr. London: Fontana, 1973), p. 40.
258. Ibid., p. 112.
259. Ibid., p. 113.
260. Williams, *Culture and Society*, p. 292.
261. Williams, *Orwell*, p. 22.
262. Marx and Engels, 'Manifesto of the Communist Party', p. 10.
263. Lenin, 'A Great Beginning. Heroism of the Workers in the Rear. "Communist Subbotniks"' in *On Culture and Cultural Revolution*, pp. 84–116, pp. 98–9.
264. Orwell, *The Road to Wigan Pier*, p. 118. The idea of a revolutionary working class emerges, in a very different form, in his writing after the outbreak of Second World War.
265. K. Marx and F. Engels, 'The Holy Family, or Critique of Critical Criticism: Against Bruno Bauer and Company' in F. Teplov and V. Davydov, eds, *The Socialist Revolution* (1978; repr. Moscow: Progress, 1981), pp. 38–9, p. 39.
266. Marx and Engels, 'Manifesto of the Communist Party', p. 19.
267. Orwell, *The Road to Wigan Pier*, p. 109.
268. Crick, 'Introduction', p. 13.
269. Campbell, *Wigan Pier Revisited*, p. 220.
270. Crick, *George Orwell*, p. 291.
271. I. Howe, 'George Orwell: "As the Bones Know"' in *Decline of the New* (London: Gollancz, 1971), pp. 269–79, p. 271.
272. Campbell, *Wigan Pier Revisited*, p. 99.
273. Ibid., p. 223.
274. Ibid., p. 29.
275. Ibid., p. 18.
276. Coombes, *Miners Day*, p. 15.
277. B. L. Coombes, *These Poor Hands: The Autobiography of a Miner Working in South Wales* (London: Gollancz, 1939), p. 120.
278. Orwell, *The Road to Wigan Pier*, p. 39.
279. H. Heslop, *Last Cage Down* (London: Wishart, 1935), pp. 104–5.
280. Jones, *We Live*, p. 113.
281. Orwell, *The Road to Wigan Pier*, p. 31.
282. Coombes, *Miners Day*, p. 126.
283. 'An Observer', *Miners, Owners and Mysteries* (London: Waterloo & Sons, [1936?]), p. 8.
284. Orwell, *The Road to Wigan Pier*, p. 38.
285. Priestley, *English Journey*, p. 330.
286. Laybourn, *Britain on the Breadline*, p. 113.

287. McKibbin, *Classes and Cultures*, p. 115.
288. Layourn, *Britain on the Breadline*, p. 8.
289. Ibid., p. 139.
290. McKibbin, *Classes and Cultures*, pp. 144–5.
291. Orwell, *The Road to Wigan Pier*, p. 30.
292. Campbell, *Wigan Pier Revisited*, p. 97.
293. Ibid., p. 223.
294. Orwell, *The Road to Wigan Pier*, p. 8.
295. Cross, 'Introduction: Mass-Observation and Worktowners at Play', p. 7.
296. J. H. Watson, 'The Big Chimney' in J. Common, ed., *Seven Shifts* (London: Secker & Warburg, 1938), pp. 205–45, p. 240.
297. J. Klugman, 'The Crisis in the Thirties: A View from the Left' in Jon Clark et al., eds, *Culture and Crisis in Britain in the Thirties* (London: Lawrence and Wishart, 1979), pp. 13–36, p. 32.
298. Orwell, *The Road to Wigan Pier*, p. 101.
299. Ibid., p. 213.
300. Orwell, *Down and Out in Paris and London*, p. 118.
301. 'An Observer', *Miners, Owners and Mysteries*, p. 4.
302. Ibid., p. 73.
303. Ibid., p. 75.
304. Ibid., p. 108.
305. Campbell, *Wigan Pier Revisited*, p. 222.
306. Crick, *George Orwell*, pp. 288–9.
307. Ibid., p. 65. This opinion was not peculiar to Orwell. In Mark Benney's, *The Big Wheel* (London: Peter Davies, 1940), for example, Harry Carne, commenting on some new buildings intended to house the poor, insists that 'They not only impose a standardised pattern of shelter, but a standardised pattern of life as well. And it isn't even a pleasant pattern. But variation from its own norm is discouraged and even penalised. In the old slums you got what you could from life. In Pimstone Buildings you get what you're given' (p. 95).
308. P. Gurney, ' "Measuring the Distance": D. H. Lawrence, Raymond Williams and the Quest for "Community" ' in Keith Laybourn, ed., *Social Conditions, Status and Community 1860–c.1920* (Stroud: Alan Sutton, 1997), pp. 160–83, p. 160. Gurney is, in this instance, referring predominantly to social historians whom, he argued, have uncritically accepted ideas of community. His comments are, however, of obvious relevance to social explorers, whose work represents itself as a form of anecdotal history or sociology, describing social 'realities'.
309. R. Hoggart, *The Uses of Literacy* (London: Chatto & Windus, 1957), p. 17. In *The Classic Slum*, Roberts warns against such romanticised images of the Edwardian period, observing that many working-class women, for example, 'remember the spoiled complexions, the mouths full of rotten teeth, the varicose veins, the ignorance of simple hygiene, the intelligence stifled and the endless battle merely to keep clean. Unlike many in the middle and upper classes, fondly looking back, they see no "glory gleaming" ' (p. 41).
310. Hynes, *The Auden Generation*, p. 276.
311. Muggeridge, 'A Knight of Woeful Countenance', p. 171.

312. Cunningham, *British Writers of the Thirties*, p. 238.
313. Orwell, *The Road to Wigan Pier*, p. 108.
314. Ibid., p. 29.
315. Ibid., p. 144.
316. Ibid., p. 145.
317. Ibid., p. 44.
318. Ibid., p. 195.
319. Ibid., p. 213.
320. Hoggart, 'Introduction to *The Road to Wigan Pier*', p. 34.
321. Ibid., p. 36.
322. The qualities of honesty and dedication to work are demonstrated in a number of characters in his fiction, such as George Bowling's father, in *Coming Up for Air*, and, arguably in Dorothy, the heroine of *A Clergyman's Daughter* (1935; repr. London: Secker & Warburg, 1997), who persists in doing 'what is customary, useful and acceptable' (p. 295) even after losing her faith. Orwell also repeatedly insists, for example, on the value of the patriotism of the middle-classes during World War II, arguing in a review of Malcolm Muggeridge's *The Thirties* (12: 149–52), that 'even at its stupidest and most sentimental it is a comelier thing than the shallow self-righteousness of the leftwing intelligentsia' (pp. 151–2).
323. Orwell, *The Road to Wigan Pier*, p. 213.
324. Ibid., p. 208.
325. These internalised structures are, of course, not 'value-neutral', a matter only of, for example, table manners and accent. They are also integral to the reproduction of labour relations, defining the social distinctions between different economic classes. This point is explored by Louis Althusser, who argued in 'Ideology and the Ideology State Apparatuses' that 'the reproduction of labour power requires not only a reproduction of its skills, but also, at the same time, a reproduction of its submission to the rules of the established order, i.e. a reproduction of submission to the ruling ideology for the workers, and a reproduction of the ability to manipulate the ruling ideology correctly for the agents of exploitation and repression, so that they, too, will provide for the domination of the ruling class "in words" ' (pp. 127–8).
326. Cunningham, *British Writers of the Thirties*, p. 211.
327. Marx and Engels, 'Manifesto of the Communist Party', p. 10.
328. Orwell, *The Road to Wigan Pier*, p. 126. For an account of the privileged circles with which many left-wing writers moved in period, see Cunningham, *British Writers of the Thirties*, especially pp. 133–5.
329. T. R. Fyvel, *George Orwell: A Personal Memoir* (London: Weidenfeld and Nicolson, 1982), pp. 175–6.
330. Orwell, *The Road to Wigan Pier*, p. 145.
331. G. Day, *Class* (London: Routledge, 2001), p. 172.
332. The 'girl' is Eileen O'Shaughnessy, whom Orwell married on 9 June 1936.
333. Orwell, *The Road to Wigan Pier*, p. 105.
334. Ibid., p. 108.
335. Ibid., pp. 214–15.
336. Ibid., p. 156.

337. Ibid., p. 146.
338. Ibid., p. 154.
339. Ibid., p. 215.

2   Gender

1. Orwell, *Keep the Aspidistra Flying*, p. 128.
2. Ibid., p. 127.
3. D. Patai, *The Orwell Mystique: A Study in Male Ideology* (Amherst: University of Massachusetts Press, 1984), p. 37.
4. In *Sexual/Textual Politics* (1985; repr. London: Routledge, 1994), Toril Moi argues that 'patriarchal oppression consists of imposing certain social standards of femininity on all biological women, in order precisely to make us believe that the chosen standards for "femininity" are *natural*. Thus a woman who refuses to conform can be labelled both *unfeminine* and *unnatural*. It is in the patriarchal interest that these two terms (femininity and femaleness) stay thoroughly confused' (p. 65).
5. Rees, *George Orwell*, pp. 106–7.
6. Orwell, *Coming Up for Air*, p. 24.
7. Ibid., p. 246.
8. Ibid., p. 141.
9. Patai, *The Orwell Mystique*, p. 194.
10. Orwell, *Keep the Aspidistra Flying*, p. 126.
11. Ibid., p. 131.
12. Orwell, *The Road to Wigan Pier*, p. 181.
13. Patai, *The Orwell Mystique*, p. 93.
14. Orwell, *The Road to Wigan Pier*, p. 180.
15. Orwell, *Nineteen Eighty-Four*, p. 12.
16. Orwell, *Coming Up for Air*, p. 142.
17. Ibid., p. 141.
18. Orwell, *Keep the Aspidistra Flying*, p. 47.
19. Orwell, *Coming Up for Air*, p. 10.
20. G. Orwell, *Burmese Days* (1934; repr. London: Secker & Warburg, 1997), p. 92.
21. Ibid., p. 300. In a letter to F. Tennyson Jesse, dated 7 March 1946, Orwell wrote that his own 'grandmother lived forty years in Burma and at the end could not speak a word of Burmese – typical of an ordinary Englishwoman's attitude' (18:126–8:128).
22. Orwell, *Burmese Days*, p. 92.
23. Ibid., p. 300.
24. Orwell, *Keep the Aspidistra Flying*, p. 238.
25. Orwell, *Burmese Days*, p. 94.
26. Ibid., p. 238.
27. Ibid., p. 181.
28. Ibid., pp. 275–6.
29. A. Dworkin, *Right Wing Women: The Politics of Domesticated Females* (London: The Women's Press, 1983), p. 21.

30. U. Seshagiri, 'Misogyny and Imperialism in George Orwell's *Burmese Days*' in Alberto Lázaro, ed., *The Road from George Orwell: His Achievement and Legacy* (Bern: Peter Lang, 2001), pp. 105–19, p. 117.
31. Orwell, *Burmese Days*, p. 113.
32. Orwell, *Nineteen Eighty-Four*, p. 163.
33. F. Warburg, *All Authors Are Equal* (London: Secker & Warburg, 1973), p. 105.
34. Orwell, *Nineteen Eighty-Four*, p. 127.
35. Ibid., p. 137.
36. Ibid., p. 136.
37. A. Easthope, 'Fact and Fantasy in "Nineteen Eighty-Four"' in Christopher Norris, ed., *Inside the Myth: Orwell: Views from the Left* (London: Lawrence and Wishart, 1984), pp. 263–85, p. 274.
38. L. Tentler, '"I'm Not Literary, Dear": George Orwell on Women and the Family' in Ejner Jensen, ed., *The Future of Nineteen Eighty-Four* (Ann Arbor: University of Michigan Press, c.1984), pp. 47–63, p. 53.
39. Rees, *George Orwell*, p. 107.
40. Patai, *The Orwell Mystique*, p. 227. The statement is, of course, polemical in form, but is nevertheless valuable insofar as it emphasises the importance of the relationship between Winston and O'Brien. Winston, even whilst he is being tortured considers that in 'some senses that went deeper than friendship, they were intimates: somewhere or other, although the actual words might never be spoken, there was a place where they could meet and talk' (*Nineteen Eighty-Four*, p. 264).
41. Newsinger, *Orwell's Politics*, p. 132.
42. Orwell, *Nineteen Eighty-Four*, p. 271.
43. Y. Zamyatin, *We* (1924; repr. Harmondsworth: Penguin, 1993), p. 156.
44. Ibid., p. 111.
45. Ibid., p. 192.
46. The association with fluidity persists in later radical feminist texts. In 'Volume with Contours', for example, Luce Irigarey writes that 'woman is neither closed nor open. Indefinite, unfinished/infinite, *form is never complete in her*. She is not infinite, but nor is she *one* unit: a letter, a figure, a number in a series, a proper name, single object (of a) sensible world, the simple ideality of an intelligible whole, the entity of a foundation, etc. This incompleteness of her form, of her morphology, allows her to become something else at any moment, which is not to say that she is (n)ever unambiguously anything.' (Margaret Whitford, ed., *The Irigaray Reader* (1991; repr. Oxford: Blackwell, 1994), pp. 53–67, p. 55.)
47. Zamyatin, *We*, p. 163.
48. Ibid., p. 112.
49. Ibid., pp. 204–5.
50. Ibid., p. 109.
51. Ibid., p. 221.
52. Orwell, *Homage to Catalonia*, p. 5.
53. Ibid., p. 21.
54. Ibid., p. 44.
55. Ibid., pp. 68–9.
56. Ibid., p. 69.
57. Cunningham, *British Writers of the Thirties*, p. 171.

58. C. Isherwood, *Lions and Shadows: An Education in the Twenties* (1938; repr. London: Four Square, 1963), p. 46.
59. W.H. Auden, 'Ode (to my pupils)' in Michael Roberts, ed., *New Signatures* (London: Hogarth, 1932), pp. 23–39, p. 25.
60. Isherwood, *Lions and Shadows*, p. 46.
61. Auden, 'Ode (to my pupils)', p. 25.
62. Cunningham, *British Writers of the Thirties*, p. 49. Isherwood's own father was killed in action during the First World War, an event described in *Kathleen and Frank* (1971; repr. London: Vintage, 2000).
63. Orwell, *Homage to Catalonia*, pp. 17–18.
64. This is demonstrated, for example, the training given in English public schools, and his later experience as a Military Policeman in Burma. Indeed, in 'My Country Right or Left' he wrote that 'On and off, I have been toting a rifle ever since I was ten' (p. 270).
65. Rees, *George Orwell*, p. 154.
66. M. Green, *Children of the Sun: A Narrative of 'Decadence' in England after 1918* (1976; repr. London: Pimlico, 1992), p. 66.
67. H. Green, *Pack My Bag: A Self-Portrait* (1940; repr. London: Hogarth, 1952), p. 196.
68. Orwell, *Homage to Catalonia*, p. 12.
69. Ibid., p. 55.
70. Ibid., p. 5.
71. Orwell, *Nineteen Eighty-Four*, p. 171.
72. Ibid., p. 172.
73. Orwell, *Coming Up for Air*, p. 117.
74. Ibid., p. 49.
75. Ibid., pp. 49–50.
76. Orwell, *Coming Up for Air*, p. 52.
77. Patai, *The Orwell Mystique*, p. 169.
78. Orwell, *Coming Up for Air*, p. 66.
79. Ibid., p. 56.
80. Ibid., p. 66.
81. Ibid., p. 57.
82. S. de Beauvoir, *The Second Sex* (1949; repr. London: Vintage, 1997), p. 307.
83. Orwell, *Coming Up for Air*, p. 57.
84. Ibid., p. 118.
85. Ibid., pp. 106–7.
86. Orwell, *Nineteen Eighty-Four*, p. 126.
87. Orwell, *Keep the Aspidistra Flying*, p. 155.
88. Orwell, *Burmese Days*, p. 52.
89. Ibid., p. 53.
90. Mass-Observation, 'Little Kinsey' in L. Stanley, ed., *Sex Surveyed 1949–1994: From Mass-Observation's 'Little Kinsey' to the National Survey and the Hite Report* (London: Taylor and Francis, 1995), pp. 65–203, p. 186.
91. J. Butler, *Gender Trouble: Feminism and the Subversion of Identity* (New York: Routledge, 1990), pp. 24–5.
92. Heslop, *Last Cage Down*, p. 55.
93. Orwell, *Coming Up for Air*, p. 11.
94. Orwell, *The Road to Wigan Pier*, p. 201.

95. Orwell, *Keep the Aspidistra Flying*, p. 157.
96. Ibid., p. 265.
97. Ibid., p. 261.
98. Ibid., p. 254.
99. Ibid., p. 266.
100. V. Gollancz, 'Foreword' in *The Road to Wigan Pier*, pp. 216–25, p. 220.
101. Roberts, *The Classic Slum*, p. 51. There were, of course, exceptions to this. Roberts describes, for example, a 'young journeyman of the new type, an ex-sailor' who tested 'every new packet of his own sheaths on the compressed air blower in the foundry' and assured his colleagues that no woman 'at the "Crown", our dance hall, needed to fear the consequences of his manly ardour, and he wanted the fact generally known' (p. 231).
102. Gibbon, *A Scots Quair*, p. 34.
103. Ibid., p. 59.
104. W. Oxley, 'Are You Working' in *Seven Shifts*, 103–44, p. 138.
105. W. Greenwood, *There Was a Time* (1967; repr. Harmondsworth: Penguin, 1969), p. 50.
106. Blumenfeld, *Jew Boy*, p. 270.
107. P. Knight, 'Women and Abortion in Victorian and Edwardian England' in *History Workshop* (Autumn 1977), pp. 57–68, p. 57.
108. Mass-Observation, 'Little Kinsey', p. 96.
109. R. Hoggart, *The Uses of Literacy* (London: Chatto & Windus, 1957), p. 41.
110. A. Sillitoe, *Saturday Night and Sunday Morning* (1958; repr. London: Flamingo, 1994), p. 69.
111. Orwell, *Keep the Aspidistra Flying*, p. 267.
112. Ibid., p. 270.
113. Rees, *George Orwell*, p. 38.
114. Orwell, *Keep the Aspidistra Flying*, p. 258.
115. J. London, *The Iron Heel* (1907; repr. Harmondsworth: Penguin, 1945), p. 41.
116. Orwell, *Keep the Aspidistra Flying*, p. 168.
117. Ibid., p. 127. It is significant that in the one section of the text in which Gordon *does* have some money, after his payment by the *Californian Review*, his method of reasserting his masculinity is in the commercial and predatory form of a visit to a prostitute. Here, however, as elsewhere, his resort to the conventional association of money and potency is not successful, and his expenditure, especially that upon alcohol, is the cause of his impotence.
118. Ibid., pp. 126–7.
119. M. Carter, *George Orwell and the Problem of Authentic Existence* (London: Croom Helm, 1985), p. 125.
120. Orwell, *Down and Out in Paris and London*, p. 206. The statement is one example of Orwell's coercive rhetoric, in that its basis is 'not worth discussing'.
121. Ibid., p. 207.
122. Ibid., p. 206.
123. Orwell, *Down and Out in Paris and London*, p. 206.
124. Orwell, *Keep the Aspidistra Flying*, p. 41.

125. Ibid., p. 268.
126. Crick, 'Introduction', p. 26.
127. Orwell, *Keep the Aspidistra Flying*, p. 40.
128. Orwell, *Nineteen Eighty-Four*, p. 228.
129. Ibid., p. 230.
130. Orwell, *The Road to Wigan Pier*, p. 81.
131. Orwell, *Keep the Aspidistra Flying*, p. 47.
132. R. Tressell, *The Ragged Trousered Philanthropists* (1955; repr. London: Granada, 1982), p. 27.
133. Patai, *The Orwell Mystique*, p. 1.
134. Newsinger, *Orwell's Politics*, p. 8.
135. Ibid., p. 47.
136. Montefiore, *Men and Women Writers of the 1930s*, p. 85.
137. Watson, 'The Big Chimney', p. 209. The image of the 'hipless clerkess' evokes the 'typist home at teatime' described in *The Waste Land*. Here the 'food in tins' and the 'Stockings, slippers, camisoles, and stays' imply a life framed, indeed shaped, by industrial products. (T. S. Eliot, 'The Waste Land' in *Collected Poems: 1909–1963* (1963; repr. London: Faber, 1974), pp. 61–86, p. 71.) This mechanisation extends to her sexual encounter with the aggressive 'young man carbuncular', after which 'She smooths her hair with automatic hand, / And puts a record on the gramophone' (p. 76), her body melding with the machines which, as a typist, form the basis of her economic role in society.
138. Watson, 'The Big Chimney', p. 240.
139. Ibid., p. 226.
140. Priestley, *English Journey*, p. 311.
141. J. Hilton, 'The Plasterer's Life' in *Seven Shifts*, pp. 1–49, p. 22.
142. Watson, 'The Big Chimney', p. 239.
143. Ibid., p. 240.
144. McKibbin, *Classes and Cultures*, p. 139.
145. There were, of course, numerous working-class women in work, and they were employed across a wide range of industries. Nevertheless, as McKibbin observes, 'the female proportion of the total workforce scarcely changed at all in the first half of the twentieth century – in 1911, 29.7 per cent of the whole workforce was female; in 1951, 30.8 per cent – and never reached the levels of the mid-nineteenth century'. For working-class women 'paid work' was, in any case, 'though both inferior to and preparatory to marriage' (p. 111). The static position of female labour in the period meant that there was little pressure to change conventional attitudes to it.
146. Orwell, *The Road to Wigan Pier*, p. 75. The phrase 'Mary Ann' is an example of the homophobia explored later is this chapter, not only because it implies an 'effeminate' man, but because as Martin Gardner observed, in his notes to Lewis Carroll's *The Annotated Alice: The Definitive Edition* (Harmondsworth: Penguin, 2000), it 'became a vulgar term for sodomites' (p. 40).
147. Hoggart, *The Uses of Literacy*, p. 49.
148. M. Woodside, 'Courtship and Mating in an Urban Community', *The Eugenics Review* (April 1946), pp. 29–39, p. 32.

149. Jones, *We Live*, p. 77.
150. W. Brierley, *Means Test Man* (London: Methuen, 1935), p. 23.
151. McKibbin, *Classes and Cultures*, p. 133.
152. S. Ingle, *George Orwell: A Political Life* (1993; repr. Manchester: Manchester University Press, 1994), p. 119.
153. Croft, *Red Letter Days*, pp. 68–9.
154. Priestley, *English Journey*, p. 407.
155. Campbell, *Wigan Pier Revisited*, pp. 189–90.
156. Croft, *Red Letter Days*, p. 112.
157. Cohen, *I Was One of the Unemployed*, p. 159.
158. Hannington, *The Problems of the Distressed Areas*, p. 74.
159. Hanley, *Grey Children*, p. 13.
160. Brierley, *Means Test Man*, p. 201.
161. Ibid., p. 48.
162. Oxley, 'Are You Working?', p. 120.
163. Blumenfeld, *Jew Boy*, p. 96.
164. Ibid, pp. 201–2.
165. Orwell, *Keep the Aspidistra Flying*, p. 105.
166. Ibid., p. 110.
167. Nicholson, 'Masculine Status and Working-Class Culture', p. 145.
168. Orwell, *The Road to Wigan Pier*, p. 164.
169. Ibid., p. 201.
170. Orwell, *The Road to Wigan Pier*, p. 126.
171. Orwell, *Keep the Aspidistra Flying*, pp. 12–13.
172. Roberts, *The Classic Slum*, p. 55.
173. Orwell, *Keep the Aspidistra Flying*, p. 8.
174. Orwell, *The Road to Wigan Pier*, p. 29.
175. Orwell, *Keep the Aspidistra Flying*, p. 12. This association was not, of course, peculiar to Orwell. In *The Strings Are False: An Unfinished Autobiography* (1965; repr. London: Faber, 1982), Louis MacNeice wrote that he 'discovered that in Oxford homosexuality and "intelligence", heterosexuality and brawn, were almost inexorably paired' (p. 103). Martin Green also observed, in *Children of the Sun*, that the 'ambience' in Oxford during the period 'was quite generally homoerotic' and that 'as late as 1938 John Betjeman felt free to say, in *An Oxford University Chest*, "State subsidised undergraduates are generally heterosexual. Probably they will have a fine romance with an undergraduate and will marry her when they go down. In that case the undergraduate has performed a better service than by getting her usual second after three years' unremitting work...."' (p. 203).
176. Orwell, *The Road to Wigan Pier*, p. 170.
177. This is not to suggest that the homophobia exhibited in the text was a consciously pragmatic manipulation of various images and prejudices associated with male homosexuality. It is, rather, to expose various functions that homophobia served, both in the work of Orwell, and in broader social structures.
178. Patai, *The Orwell Mystique*, p. 84.
179. For further details of the questionnaire, and the responses to it, see John Miller, ed., *Voices Against Tyranny: Writings of the Spanish Civil War* (New York: Scribner, 1986), pp. 139–47.

180. D. A. N. Jones, 'Arguments Against Orwell' in *The World of George Orwell*, pp. 153–63, p. 156.
181. M. Ellmann, 'Introduction' in Maud Ellmann, ed., *Psychoanalytic Literary Criticism* (London: Longman, 1994), pp. 1–35, p. 15. The work Ellmann comments upon in this passage is Eve Kosofsky Sedgwick's 1985 study *Between Men*.
182. J. Dollimore, *Sexual Dissidence: Augustine to Wilde, Freud to Foucault* (Oxford: Clarendon, 1991), p. 305.
183. Orwell, *Homage to Catalonia*, p. 17.
184. Ibid., p. 42.
185. Orwell, *Down and Out in Paris and London*, p. 148.
186. Roberts, *The Classic Slum*, pp. 21–2.
187. Judy Pearsell, ed., *The New Oxford Dictionary of English* (1998; repr. Oxford: Oxford University Press, 1999), p. 1440.
188. Homosexuals were also regarded as comic. In *Worktowners at Blackpool*, Mass-Observation noted that the 'Punch and Beauty' show playing in Blackpool included 'comedy and parody of politicians, lawyers, artists, teachers, doctors, homosexuals, teetotallers, dead royalty and dictators' (p. 129).
189. Patai, *The Orwell Mystique*, p. 266.
190. K. Marx, 'Confessions' in *On Literature and Art*, p. 436. This may be a joke, but it is a revealing one.

3   Theories of Nationalism

1. S. Lutman, 'Orwell's Patriotism' in *Journal of Contemporary History*, 2:2 (April 1967), pp. 149–58, p. 158.
2. G. Hosking and G. Schöpflin, 'Preface' in *Myths and Nationhood*, p. v.
3. J. Joyce, *Ulysses* (1922; repr. Oxford: Oxford University Press, 1998), p. 317.
4. J. Stalin, 'Marxism and the National Question' in Bruce Franklin, ed., *The Essential Stalin: Major Theoretical Writings 1905–52* (London: Croom Hill, 1973), pp. 54–84, p. 60.
5. Ibid., p. 57.
6. Ibid., p. 64.
7. Ibid., p. 58.
8. Ibid., p. 64.
9. Ibid., p. 60.
10. A. D. Smith, *National Identity* (London: Penguin, 1991), p. 14.
11. Ibid., p. 70.
12. Miller, *On Nationality*, p. 27.
13. Anderson, *Imagined Communities*, p. 15.
14. J. Kellas, *The Politics of Nationalism and Ethnicity* (Basingstoke: Macmillan, 1991), p. 2.
15. Easthope, *Englishness and National Culture*, p. 46.
16. E. Gellner, *Nations and Nationalism* (Oxford: Blackwell, 1983), p. 4.
17. Gasset, *The Revolt of the Masses*, p. 123.
18. Ibid., p. 124.
19. Ibid., p. 123.

20. Ibid., p. 125.
21. Gellner, *Nations and Nationalism*, p. 39.
22. Ibid., p. 34.
23. In spite of the obvious parallels between this and the materialist interpretation of history proposed by Marxist writers, Gellner rejects the categorisation of his work as 'Marxist'.
24. Ibid., pp. 48–9.
25. Ibid., p. 57.
26. M. Weber, 'Politics as a Vocation' in H. H. Gerth and C. Wright Mills, eds, *From Max Weber: Essays in Sociology* (1946; repr. Oxford: Oxford University Press, 1978), pp. 77–128, p. 78.
27. Gellner, *Nations and Nationalism*, p. 34.
28. Ibid., p. 32.
29. Althusser, 'Ideology and the Ideological State Apparatuses', pp. 144–5.
30. This language may be that used by an elite group instrumental in establishing the state, but it does not have to be. Even when an existing dialect or language is the basis of an official language, it is adapted in its diffusion throughout the nation as a whole.
31. Gellner, *Nations and Nationalism*, p. 21.
32. Anderson, *Imagined Communities*, p. 47. This language does not need to have a long-established historical connection with the region, although it often does have, nor need it be the exclusive property of a single country. As Anderson observed 'If radical Mozambique speaks Portuguese, the significance of this is that Portuguese is the medium through which Mozambique is imagined (and at the same time limits its stretch into Tanzania and Zambia)' (p. 122).
33. There are, of course, states that recognise two or more languages, such as Switzerland, Belgium, India and Canada. There are a number of strategies used to maintain these multilingual countries, from the meticulous balancing of language claims (as in Canada) to the use of one or more languages valid throughout the state as a whole (for example, the use of English in India). This, however, does not always prevent the development of internal 'nationalist' movements, such as that for the independence of Quebec, based upon linguistic divisions.
34. E. J. Hobsbawn, *Nations and Nationalism Since 1780: Programme, Myth, Reality* (Cambridge: University of Cambridge Press, 1990), p. 54.
35. Ibid., p. 112.
36. Miller, *On Nationality*, p. 22.
37. Gellner, *Nations and Nationalism*, p. 49.
38. Kellas, *The Politics of Nationalism and Ethnicity*, p. 43.
39. Ibid., p. 67.
40. Gellner, *Nations and Nationalism*, p. 57.
41. The reading of nationalism as ideological is disputed by Easthope, who insists in *Englishness and National Culture* that this implies that it is 'a way of thinking designed to promote the interests of a particular group' (p. 6), although he nevertheless uses Althusser's theories to support his idea of how individuals 'are "interpellated" by the practices and discourses of the particular culture they arrive into so that, as speaking subjects, they come to see its constructedness as obvious and natural' (p. 19). It is, of course,

true that nationalism is 'spontaneously supported from below', but this does not contradict the notion that it is an ideology, as the success of ideology is predicated on precisely such a support, and upon the fact that it is itself 'something actually lived into' (p. 7). Ideology, for Althusser, legitimises domination, insofar as it 'naturalises' particular structures of hierarchy and oppression, but this is only one aspect of a broader effect that is constructive as well as limiting.

42. L. Althusser, 'On the Young Marx' in *For Marx*, pp. 49–86, p. 69.

43. Gellner, *Nations and Nationalism*, p. 49.

44. Easthope, *Englishness and National Culture*, p. 50.

45. Anderson, *Imagined Communities*, p. 14. This modernity of the nation is admittedly disputed by some theorists, including Kellas, who argued that 'The idea of a nation is to be found as far back as the ancient world, although it is not clear that there was then what we understand as a nation today.' However, this concession that the commitment was not founded upon 'what we understand as a nation today' itself exposes the distinction between these identities in the ancient world and 'nationalism'. Greek or Jewish consciousness of 'their identity as peoples' (p. 22) is not identical with the concept of the nation. Instead, these can be seen as networks of connected ethnic, religious and linguistic allegiances, albeit networks that informed later nationalist movements. Jewish identity, for example, was, and continues to be, fragmented by the different societies and classes that individual Jews inhabit, with the result that Zionism, developed in the nineteenth century, can be seen as the first form of Jewish nationalism.

46. An example of this is the use of Tacitus' *Germania* and of images of Teutonic knights' orders in the German nationalism of the first half of the twentieth-century.

47. Anderson, *Imagined Communities*, p. 19.

48. Barthes, 'Myth Today', p. 129.

49. J. Habermas, '1989 in the Shadow of 1945: On the Normality of a Future Berlin Republic' in *A Berlin Republic: Writings on Germany* (1995; repr. Cambridge: Polity, 1998), pp. 161–81, p. 173.

50. Crick, *George Orwell*, p. 87.

51. Hynes, *The Auden Generation*, pp. 18–9.

52. Patriotism frequently developed into intolerant nationalism during First World War. In *Pack My Bag*, for example, Henry Green insisted that this involved representing the Germans as fundamentally different and of less value than the British. He wrote that 'We hated Germans and at school we did believe they were so short of food they boiled the dead down to get the fats, that they crucified Australians, and that they were monsters different from us' (p. 72).

53. Crick, *George Orwell*, p. 60.

54. Meyers, *Orwell*, p. 20. This is not to imply that St. Cyprian's was, by the standards of its time, either a bad or unusual preparatory school. Indeed, Robert Pearce argues, in 'Truth and Falsehood: George Orwell's Prep School Woes' (*Review of English Studies*, XLIII: 171 (1992), pp. 367–86) that it 'was not nearly as bad as it was portrayed' and even 'gave a good academic education and in many ways a well-balanced education' (p. 382).

55. C. Connolly, *Enemies of Promise* (1938; repr. Harmondsworth: Penguin, 1961), p. 179. Connolly renames St. Cyprian's as St. Wulfric's.

56. Crick, *George Orwell*, p. 85.
57. Orwell, *The Road to Wigan Pier*, p. 128.
58. P. Maillaud, *The English Way* (London: Oxford University Press, 1945), p. 36.
59. Orwell, *The Road to Wigan Pier*, p. 129.
60. Ibid., p. 130. This description, Crick observed in *George Orwell*, is supported by others at Eton at the time, and some 'go further and speak of it as a riot to demand the resignation of the officer in charge of the OTC that spread into the streets of the town' (p. 121).
61. Crick observed that 'Blair's election of 1916' was in any case unusual, as it 'was far more liberal and relaxed', an attitude demonstrated within by the fact that it 'used the cane very little, and almost dismantled the privileges of Sixth Form and College Pop' (p. 132). The resistance he describes cannot, therefore, be regarded as 'typical'.
62. Roberts, *The Classic Slum*, p. 143.
63. Ibid., p. 161.
64. Easthope, *Englishness and National Culture*, p. 36.
65. Arendt, *The Origins of Totalitarianism*, p. 282.
66. Ibid., pp. 282–3.
67. Hobsbawn, *Nations and Nationalism Since 1780*, p. 147.
68. P. Levi, 'The Gypsy' in *Moments of Reprieve* (1981; repr. Harmondsworth: Penguin, 1987), pp. 63–71, p. 67.
69. B. Crick, *In Defence of Politics* (1962; repr. Harmondsworth: Penguin, 1976), p. 77.
70. Lutman, 'Orwell's Patriotism', p. 151. Lutman argues that '*Homage to Catalonia* is Orwell's most patriotic book' (p. 150).
71. Miller, *On Nationality*, p. 49.
72. Ibid., p. 73.
73. Hobsbawn, *Nations and Nationalism Since 1780*, p. 87.
74. The programme is described in more detail in pp. 422–6.
75. Woodcock, *The Crystal Spirit*, p. 202.
76. Orwell, *Nineteen Eighty-Four*, p. 42.
77. I. Berlin, 'Nationalism: Past Neglect and Present Power' in Henry Hardy, ed., *Against the Current: Essays in the History of Ideas* (1979; repr. London: Pimlico, 1997), pp. 333–55, p. 342.
78. This apparent internal coherence is a condition of ideology as such. As Macherey wrote, in *A Theory of Literary Production*, 'In so far as ideology is the false resolution of a real debate, it is always adequate to itself *as a reply*' (p. 131).
79. Berlin, 'Nationalism', p. 341.
80. Race, realised in 'blood', is nevertheless the dominant determinant of identity elsewhere in Hitler's work. Hitler, although an extremely valuable source, must obviously be treated with caution, as his work is not only defined by the theories of nationality and race that he consistently pursued, but by a political expediency that led to certain elements being emphasised at particular times. His public speeches in this period, however, are concerned primarily with nationality, and are therefore appropriate material for such analyses. For further information on Hitler's critique of nationality and his use of racial theories, see, for example, Hitler, *Mein Kampf*, *Hitler's Table Talk 1941–44: His Private Conversations* (1953; repr. London: Pheonix, 2000) and

H. Rauschning, *Hitler Speaks: A Series of Political Conversations with Adolf Hitler* (London: Thornton Butterworth, 1939).

81. A. Hitler, 'May 1, 1937' in Richard Mönnig, ed., *Adolf Hitler: From Speeches 1933–1938* (Berlin: Terramare Office, 1938), pp. 64–5, p. 65.
82. A. Hitler, 'May 1, 1935' in ibid., p. 66.
83. Easthope, *Englishness and National Culture*, p. 55.
84. For example, there is an obvious structural distinction between traditional English patriotism and, for example, 'Trotskyism', one of the 'purely negative' (p. 142) forms of nationalism listed by Orwell.
85. Orwell, *A Clergyman's Daughter*, p. 211. The textbook is, significantly, concerned with 'Britain' rather than with 'England'. The implicit emphasis is upon the United Kingdom as a 'natural', homogeneous political unit, an idea also encoded in the Union Jack that ornaments the chariot of Boadicea.
86. R. Hoggart, *A Local Habitation: Life and Times, Volume 1: 1918–1940* (London: Chatto & Windus, 1988), p. 147.
87. In *Nineteen Eighty-Four*, Orwell figures Shakespeare as a potential locus of opposition to a totalitarianism which dissolves traditional identities, as Winston, after dreaming of Julia, 'woke up with the word "Shakespeare" on his lips' (p. 33).
88. Hitler, *Table Talk*, p. 110. This future dominance is legitimised in part by the perception of an innate superiority of the German language, which Hitler insisted possessed, in contrast to English, 'the ability to express thoughts that surpass the order of concrete things', something which made Germany 'the country of thinkers' (p. 357). In contrast, William Gerhardi insisted in 'Climate and Character' (Hugh Kingsmill, ed., *The English Genius* (London: Right Book Club, 1939), pp. 57–80), that it 'is apparent to anyone knowing German that the English language is a more intelligent German language' (p. 63).
89. Hitler, *Table Talk*, p. 589.
90. Orwell, *Burmese Days*, p. 23.
91. Hobsbawm, *Nations and Nationalism Since 1780*, p. 145.
92. He was not, of course, alone in doing so. As Hobsbawm points out, 'Nationalism thus acquired a strong association with the left during the antifascist period, an association which was consequently reinforced by the experience of anti-imperial struggle in colonial countries' (p. 148). The term 'nationalism' obviously has a different meaning in this passage than it does in, for example, 'Notes on Nationalism'.
93. Easthope, *Englishness and National Culture*, p. 216.
94. Crick, *In Defence of Politics*, p. 74.

4 Englishness

1. P. Potts, *Dante Called You Beatrice* (London: Eyre and Spottiswoode, 1960), p. 79.
2. Hammond, *A George Orwell Companion*, p. 27.
3. C. Berberich, 'A Revolutionary in Love with the 1900s: Orwell in Defence of "Old England" ' in *The Road from George Orwell*, pp. 33–52, p. 34.
4. M. Bradbury, *The Modern British Novel* (London: Secker & Warburg, 1993), p. 236.

5. J. Strachey, 'The Strangled Cry' in *Twentieth Century Interpretations of 1984*, pp. 54–61, p. 54.
6. Crick, *George Orwell*, p. 234.
7. P. Lewis, *George Orwell: The Road to 1984* (London: Heinemann/Quixote Press, 1981), p. 29.
8. Easthope, *Englishness and National Culture*, p. 156.
9. Ibid., p. 86.
10. Ibid., p. 63.
11. Orwell, *Nineteen Eighty-Four*, p. 84.
12. C. Norris, 'Language, Truth and Ideology: Orwell and the Post-War Left' in *Inside the Myth*, pp. 242–62, p. 256.
13. L. Trilling, 'Orwell on the Future' in *Twentieth Century Interpretations of 1984*, pp. 24–8, p. 24.
14. E. Wilson, 'Edward Wilson, *New Yorker*' in *George Orwell: The Critical Heritage*, pp. 224–6, p. 224.
15. Hammond, *A George Orwell Companion*, p. 227.
16. Woodcock, *The Crystal Spirit*, p. 275.
17. B. Crick, 'Orwell and English Socialism' in Peter Buitenhuis and Ira B. Nadal, eds, *George Orwell: A Reassessment* (Basingstoke: Macmillan, 1988), pp. 3–19, p. 3.
18. I. Howe, 'George Orwell: "As the Bones Know"' in *Decline of the New* (London: Gollancz, 1971), pp. 269–79, p. 270.
19. Potts, *Dante Called You Beatrice*, p. 72.
20. Crick, 'Orwell and English Socialism', p. 4.
21. G. Beadle, 'George Orwell and Charles Dickens: Moral Critics of Society' in *Journal of Historical Studies*, 2:4 (Winter 1969–70), pp. 245–55, p. 255.
22. Easthope, *Englishness and National Culture*, p. 91.
23. Crick, 'Orwell and English Socialism', p. 16.
24. Croft, *Red Letter Days*, p. 207.
25. S. Hynes, *The Auden Generation: Literature and Politics in England in the 1930s* (London: Lawrence and Wishart, 1990), p. 109.
26. C. D. Lewis, 'The Magnetic Mountain' in *The Complete Poems* (London: Sinclair-Stevenson, 1992), pp. 131–75, p. 169.
27. Ibid., p. 155.
28. Ibid., p. 156.
29. Ibid., p. 170.
30. H. Pollitt, 'Will it be War?' in *Selected Articles and Speeches: Vol II* (London: Lawrence and Wishart, 1954), pp. 130–44, p. 130. Indeed, he even insisted that there is 'nothing in the world lovelier than our valleys, dales, fields and villages' (139), linking the radicalism he represented to a defence, or even revitalisation of the English countryside. The emphasis is here, of course, on Britain, rather than England, the wider compass of his remarks being in keeping with the emphasis upon broad consensus inherent in the idea of the 'Popular Front'.
31. Lewis, 'The Magnetic Mountain', p. 165.
32. Roberts, 'Preface', p. 10.
33. Ibid., p. 15.
34. Hynes, *The Auden Generation*, p. 112.
35. Croft, *Red Letter Days*, p. 194.

36. Lutman, 'Orwell's Patriotism', p. 154.
37. Easthope, *Englishness and National Culture*, p. 18.
38. S. Hynes, 'Introduction' in *Twentieth Century Interpretations of 1984*, pp. 1–19, p. 10.
39. D. Lessing, *In Pursuit of the English* (1960; repr. London: Sphere Books, 1968), p. 60.
40. Ibid., p. 9.
41. Ibid., p. 8.
42. Easthope, *Englishness and National Culture*, p. 23.
43. T. S. Eliot, *Notes Towards the Definition of Culture* (1948; repr. London: Faber, 1962), p. 51.
44. In his discussion of the various attempts of writers in the 1930s to 'transcend class differences', Cunningham observes that 'Auden, at Oxford, usually (it's claimed) relaxed by frequenting the dog-races, boxing matches, and speedways' (*British Writers of the Thirties*, p. 249) The 'dog-races' are figured as a stereotypical working-class entertainment, in the minds of the middle-classes at least, and indeed in Henry Green's *Living* (1929; repr. London, 1970) the younger Mr Dupret complains of 'all you hear about the lower classes not being able to live decently when you see 10's of thousands there every night' (p. 51).
45. Eliot, *Notes Towards the Definition of Culture*, p. 48.
46. Ibid., p. 60.
47. A. L. Rowse, 'Preface' in *The English Spirit: Essays in History and Literature* (London: Macmillan, 1944), pp. v–viii, p. v.
48. A. L. Rowse, 'The Idea of Patriotism', ibid., pp. 45–51, p. 47.
49. A. L. Rowse, 'The English Spirit', ibid., pp. 35–40, pp. 35–6.
50. The emphasis upon 'great men' as representative figures is not, of course, peculiar to Rowse. In 'Conversations with a Lama', for example, Ralph Fox wrote that the 'real typical man of any nation is not the ordinary man, but the genius' (*Penguin New Writing: 1*, pp. 126–37, p. 127).
51. Rowse, 'The English Spirit', p. 35.
52. Priestley, *English Journey*, p. 406.
53. Ibid., p. 397.
54. Ibid., pp. 398–9.
55. Ibid., p. 401.
56. Ibid., p. 47.
57. Ibid., p. 86.
58. Ibid., p. 406.
59. Ibid., p. 411.
60. D. H. Lawrence, *Lady Chatterley's Lover* (1928; Harmondsworth: Penguin, 1999), p. 156.
61. Maillaud, *The English Way*, p. 18.
62. M. E. Chase, *In England Now* (London: Collins, 1937), pp. 116–8.
63. R. Williams, *The Country and the City* (1973; repr. St. Albans: Paladin, 1975), p. 9.
64. Ibid., pp. 21–2.
65. Chase, *In England Now*, p. 163.
66. S. Jameson, *The Moment of Truth* (London: Macmillan, 1949), p. 77.

67. P. Cohen-Portheim, *England, the Unknown Isle* (London: Duckworth, 1930), p. 42.
68. Ibid., p. 58.
69. Ibid., p. 23.
70. D. Middleton, *The British* (1957; repr. London: Pan Books, 1958), p. 137. Chase insists, in contrast, that the 'Englishman has no objection to foreigners' provided that 'they remain what they are and do not attempt any approximation to him' (*In England Now*, p. 36), but observes that, nevertheless, in 'England all who are not English are foreigners' (p. 35).
71. Middleton, *The British*, p. 272.
72. D. W. Brogan, *The English People: Impressions and Observations* (1943; repr. London: Hamish Hamilton, 1947), p. 27.
73. Maillaud, *The English Way*, p. 43.
74. Chase, *In England Now*, p. 89.
75. Cohen-Portheim, *England, the Unknown Isle*, p. 43.
76. Priestley, *English Journey*, p. 403.
77. Ibid., p. 405.
78. Cunningham, *British Writers of the Thirties*, p. 168. It was, in the vast majority cases, a man, as 'Very few women pilots are mentioned in '30s texts', (p. 172) and indeed 'there were in the West in the '30s comparatively few actual women pilots' (p. 173).
79. Hynes, *The Auden Generation*, p. 229.
80. Cunningham, *British Writers of the Thirties*, p. 192.
81. J. Burnham, *The Managerial Revolution, or What is Happening in the World Now* (1941; repr. Harmondsworth: Penguin, 1945), p. 70.
82. Ibid., p. 39.
83. Ibid., p. 109.
84. Ibid., p. 131.
85. Ingle, *George Orwell: A Political Life*, pp. 62–3.
86. Hammond, *A George Orwell Companion*, p. 151.
87. Berberich, 'A Revolutionary in Love with the 1900s', p. 41.
88. Orwell, *Coming Up for Air*, p. 31.
89. Ibid., p. 109.
90. Ibid., p. 24.
91. Chase, *In England Now*, pp. 218–19.
92. Priestley, *English Journey*, pp. 37–8.
93. Cohen-Portheim, *England, the Unknown Isle*, p. 11.
94. Rowse, 'The English Spirit', p. 38.
95. D. Gervais, 'Englands of the Mind' in *The Cambridge Quarterly*, 30:2 (2001), pp. 151–68, p. 152. The celebration of English poetry is itself an important element of a prevalent image of 'Englishness'. Rowse, for example, insists upon the 'naturally poetic character of the English', and argues that they have 'contributed the greatest poetic literature to the world – even greater than Greek, a distinguished Greek scholar assures me – more varied and of greater *envergure*' ('Preface', p. vii).
96. H. Belloc, 'English Verse' in *The English Genius*, 17–32, p. 23.
97. Cunningham, *British Writers of the Thirties*, p. 238. C. E. Joad wrote *The Horrors of the Countryside* (1931) and *A Charter for Ramblers* (1934), whilst H. V. Morton was the author of *In Search of England* (1927). Cunningham insists

Morton 'couldn't get rid of his irksomely condescending sentimentalities of tone and his sense that mining valleys and industrialized locations were a freakishly intrusive aberration from a more permanent rural normality' (229).

98. Orwell, *The Road to Wigan Pier*, pp. 161–2.
99. Ibid., p. 161. It is significant that in Oceania the Party encourages communal hiking.
100. Orwell, *Coming Up for Air*, p. 224.
101. Ibid., p. 225.
102. Ibid., p. 226.
103. Ibid., p. 227.
104. Ibid., p. 81.
105. Ibid., p. 229.
106. Ibid., p. 227.
107. Cunningham, *British Writers of the Thirties*, p. 238.
108. Orwell, *The Road to Wigan Pier*, p. 175.
109. Orwell, *Coming Up for Air*, p. 191.
110. Ibid., p. 192.
111. Ibid., p. 109.
112. Ibid., p. 110.
113. Ibid., p. 237.
114. Ibid., p. 37.
115. C. Connolly, 'C. C. (Cyril Connolly), *Horizon*' in *George Orwell: The Critical Heritage*, pp. 199–201, p. 199.
116. Crick, 'Orwell and English Socialism', p. 8.
117. Orwell, *The Road to Wigan Pier*, p. 98.
118. Hop-pickers are, of course, described in some detail in *A Clergyman's Daughter* (1935; repr. London: Secker & Warburg, 1997). These are, however, with a few exceptions, temporary workers, as 'quite half of them were gypsies' and 'most of the others were respectable East Enders' (p. 117). Few are either 'permanent' agricultural labourers, or, in fact, residents of a particular area of the countryside. Even in *Coming Up for Air*, farmers are peripheral figures, the emphasis being upon small shopkeepers such as Bowling's father.
119. Orwell, *Coming Up for Air*, p. 5.
120. Orwell, *The Road to Wigan Pier*, p. 99.
121. Berberich, 'A Revolutionary in Love with the 1900s', p. 51.
122. R. Williams, 'Orwell' in *Politics and Letters: Interviews with New Left Review* (London: NLB, 1979), pp. 384–92, p. 385.

5   Totalitarianism

1. A. Croft, 'Worlds Without End Foisted Upon the Future – Some Antecedents of Nineteen Eighty-Four' in *Inside the Myth*, pp. 183–216, p. 185.
2. J. Walsh, 'James Walsh, *Marxist Quarterly*' in *George Orwell: The Critical Heritage*, pp. 287–93, p. 293.
3. S. Sillen, 'Samuel Sillen, *Masses and Mainstream*', ibid., pp. 274–6, p. 274.

4. Ibid., p. 276.
5. A. L. Morton, 'The English Utopia' in *Twentieth Century Interpretations of 1984*, pp. 109–111, p. 110.
6. I. Deutscher, ' "1984" – The Mysticism of Cruelty', ibid., pp. 29–40, p. 35.
7. Williams, 'Orwell', p. 390.
8. A. Jacob, 'Sharing Orwell's "Joys" – But Not His Fears' in *Inside the Myth*, pp. 62–84, p. 81.
9. C. Norris, 'Introduction', ibid., pp. 7–11, p. 11.
10. G. Beauchamp, 'From Bingo to Big Brother: Orwell on Power and Sadism' in *The Future of Nineteen Eighty-Four*, pp. 65–85, p. 82.
11. The statement was drafted by Warburg, Orwell's publisher, under his directions.
12. Beauchamp, 'From Bingo to Big Brother', p. 75.
13. 'J. S.' is, of course, Joseph Stalin.
14. The word 'utopia' is obviously used here in its strict sense of a non-existent place, rather than, as in its popular usage, a 'good place'.
15. R. Elliott, *The Shape of Utopia: Studies in a Literary Genre* (Chicago: University of Chicago Press, 1970), p. 3. Elliott associates utopias primarily with 'the ideal' (ibid.), but nonetheless his comment illustrates the interrelationship of the two forms.
16. Croft, 'World's Without End Foisted Upon the Future', p. 196.
17. The novel was first published under the pseudonym Murray Constantine.
18. M. Constantine (pseud.), *Swastika Night* (London: Gollancz, 1937), p. 101.
19. Ibid., p. 15.
20. Ibid., p. 105.
21. Croft, 'World's Without End Foisted Upon the Future', p. 209.
22. Croft, *Red Letter Days*, p. 238.
23. Hitler, *Hitler's Table Talk*, p. 187. Hitler tended to refer to 'England' and the 'English', rather than 'Britain' and the 'British', although there are, of course, numerous exceptions to this pattern.
24. H. V. Morton, *I, James Blunt* (London: Methuen, 1942), p. 23.
25. Ibid., p. 17.
26. Ibid., p. 41.
27. Ibid. The blurb is printed on the inside front cover, which is not paginated.
28. C. Dane (pseud.), *The Arrogant History of White Ben* (London: Heinemann, 1939), p. 1.
29. Croft, *Red Letter Days*, p. 234.
30. Dane, *The Arrogant History of White Ben*, p. 269.
31. Ibid., pp. 75–6.
32. Ibid., p. 190.
33. Ibid., p. 279.
34. Ibid., p. 323.
35. Ibid., pp. 351–2.
36. Ibid., p. 363.
37. Ibid.
38. Ibid., p. 193.
39. Ibid., p. 78.
40. Ibid., p. 362.
41. Ibid., p. 296.

42. Ibid., pp. 419–20.
43. Crick, 'Introduction', p. 20.
44. P. Rahv, 'Philip Rahv, *Partisan Review*' in *George Orwell: The Critical Heritage*, pp. 267–73, p. 268.
45. Orwell, *Nineteen Eighty-Four*, p. 266.
46. J. Symons, 'Julian Symons, *Times Literary Supplement*' in *George Orwell: The Critical Heritage*, pp. 251–7, p. 253.
47. Orwell, 'Orwell's Statement on *Nineteen Eighty-Four*'.
48. I. Howe, 'Orwell: History as Nightmare' in *Politics and the Novel* (New York, 1957), pp. 235–51, p. 242.
49. A. Koestler, *Darkness at Noon* (1940; repr. Harmondsworth: Penguin, 1946), p. 93.
50. Orwell, *Nineteen Eighty-Four*, p. 85.
51. Ibid., p. 219.
52. Ibid., p. 174.
53. Ibid., p. 303.
54. Ibid., p. 171.
55. Ingle, *George Orwell: A Political Life*, p. 98.
56. Howe, 'Orwell: History as Nightmare', p. 237.
57. Crick, 'Orwell and English Socialism', p. 16.
58. Orwell, *Nineteen Eighty-Four*, p. 30.
59. Ibid., p. 280.
60. Ibid., p. 140.
61. Ibid., p. 5.
62. Ibid., p. 217.
63. Ibid., p. 75.
64. Ibid., p. 135.
65. Ibid., p. 24.
66. Orwell, *Animal Farm*, p. 57.
67. Ibid., p. 58.
68. Ibid., p. 59.
69. Ibid., p. 93.
70. Ibid., p. 87.
71. Ibid., p. 88.
72. Crick, *In Defence of Politics*, p. 21.
73. Ibid., p. 18.
74. Ibid., p. 34.
75. Ibid., p. 62.
76. Ibid., p. 127.
77. I. Howe, 'The Fiction of Antiutopia' in *Decline of the New*, pp. 66–74, p. 68.
78. Fyvel, *George Orwell*, pp. 177–8.
79. Ibid., p. 177.
80. A considerable number of the direct references to the Nazis occurred, of course, in the broadcasts Orwell made whilst working at the BBC. As these were prepared for the Eastern service, however, it is unlikely that Fyvel would have known in any detail what was contained in them.
81. Orwell, *Coming Up for Air*, p. 157.
82. M. Burleigh, *The Third Reich: A New History* (2000; repr. London: Pan Macmillan, 2001), p. 16.

83. Orwell, *Nineteen Eighty-Four*, p. 12.
84. Ibid., p. 280.
85. M. New, 'Orwell and Antisemitism: Toward *1984*' in *Modern Fiction Studies*, 21:1 (Spring 1975), pp. 81–105, p. 84.
86. Ibid., p. 101.
87. H. Trevor-Roper, 'The Mind of Adolf Hitler' in *Hitler's Table Talk*, pp. xi–xxxix, pp. xxii–iii.
88. Ibid., p. xxii.
89. P. Levi, *The Drowned and the Saved* (1986; repr. Harmondsworth: Penguin, 1988), p. 147.
90. Trevor-Roper, 'The Mind of Adolf Hitler', p. xxii. That Hitler's model was not achieved is illustrated by the fact that many of his pronouncements refer to the period after an anticipated Nazi victory, when he intended to reconstruct Europe upon the basis of his racial theories.
91. Burleigh, *The Third Reich*, p. 20.
92. Carey, *The Faber Book of Utopias*, p. 423.
93. Hitler, *Table Talk*, p. 88.
94. Ibid., p. 381.
95. Ibid., p. 423.
96. Hitler, *Mein Kampf*, p. 232. This opinion is replicated in his private conversation, and he insisted that whilst 'I would prefer not to see anyone suffer, not to do harm to anyone', when 'I realise the species is in danger, then in my case sentiment gives way to the coldest reason.' (*Table Talk*, p. 44).
97. Hitler, *Table Talk*, p. 255.
98. Ibid., p. 578.
99. Ibid., p. 106.
100. The term 'nation', in this context, refers to the 'Germanic' society that Hitler attempted to construct and not to more traditional conceptions of the nation.
101. A. Hitler, 'Appendix B: Hitler's Secret Address to Representatives of the German Press, Munich, 10 November 1938' in Z. A. B. Zeman, ed., *Nazi Propaganda* (1964; repr. London: Oxford University Press, 1973), pp. 212–25, p. 217.
102. Hitler, *Mein Kampf*, p. 108.
103. Ibid., p. 167.
104. Hitler, *Hitler's Table Talk*, pp. 480–1. The example he uses to illustrate such a reversal is, of course, the signing Russo-German Pact and subsequent invasion of Russia.
105. Orwell, *Nineteen Eighty-Four*, p. 188.
106. Ibid., p. 189.
107. Hitler, *Hitler's Table Talk*, pp. 423–4.
108. Ibid., p. 424.
109. Ibid., p. 671.
110. Orwell, *Nineteen Eighty-Four*, p. 75.
111. Easthope, *Englishness and National Culture*, p. 48.
112. Arendt, *The Origins of Totalitarianism*, p. 389. Hitler himself recognised the limitations of nationalism as a basis of political practice, and stated that 'what we're building is the Germanic Reich, or simply the Reich, with

Germany constituting merely her most powerful source of strength, as much from the ideological as from the military point of view' (*Hitler's Table Talk*, p. 403). He even proposed that Berlin should be renamed 'Germania', in order to help it function as a capital of the 'Germanic peoples' rather than simply of the German nation state.

113. B. Crick, 'On Rereading *The Origins of Totalitarianism*' in *Political Thoughts and Polemics* (Edinburgh: Edinburgh University Press, 1990), pp. 41–56, p. 47.
114. Burleigh, *The Third Reich*, p. 15.
115. J. Wain, 'In the Thirties' in *The World of George Orwell*, pp. 75–90, p. 89.

Conclusion

1. Orwell, *Keep the Aspidistra Flying*, p. 93.
2. Ibid., p. 69.
3. Orwell, *Burmese Days*, p. 120.
4. Orwell, *A Clergyman's Daughter*, p. 281.
5. Orwell, *Nineteen Eighty-Four*, p. 30.
6. Woodcock, *The Crystal Spirit*, p. 62.
7. Orwell, *Keep the Aspidistra Flying*, p. 266.
8. Ibid., p. 93.
9. Ibid., p. 40.
10. Ibid., p. 62.
11. Orwell, *A Clergyman's Daughter*, p. 118.
12. Orwell, *Coming Up for Air*, p. 110.
13. Ibid., p. 172.
14. Orwell, *Keep the Aspidistra Flying*, p. 16.
15. Ibid., p. 267.
16. Crick, 'Introduction', p. 27.
17. Orwell, *Keep the Aspidistra Flying*, p. 267.
18. Woodcock, *The Crystal Spirit*, p. 133.
19. Orwell, *Nineteen Eighty-Four*, p. 229.
20. Ingle, *George Orwell*, p. 54.
21. Orwell, *The Road to Wigan Pier*, p. 106.
22. W. W. Wager, 'George Orwell as Political Secretary of the Zeitgeist' in *The Future of Nineteen Eighty-Four*, pp. 177–99, p. 177.
23. Orwell, *Homage to Catalonia*, p. 2.
24. Orwell, *The Road to Wigan Pier*, p. 106.
25. Ibid., p. 77.
26. Orwell, *Nineteen Eighty-Four*, p. 73.
27. For a description of 'moral' socialism, see Stephen Ingle, *Socialist Thought in Imaginative Literature* (London: Macmillan, 1979), especially p. 10.
28. B. Campbell, 'Orwell – Paterfamilias or Big Brother?' in *Inside the Myth*, pp. 126–38, p. 127.
29. Rees, *George Orwell*, p. 88.
30. Hitchens, *Orwell's Victory*, p. 93.
31. K. Marx and F. Engels, 'The Holy Family' in *On Literature and Art*, pp. 156–9, pp. 158–9.

32. Schöpflin, 'The Functions of Myth', p. 19.
33. Ingle, *Socialist Thought in Imaginative Literature*, p. 187.
34. Williams, *Orwell*, p. 78.
35. Orwell, *Nineteen Eighty-Four*, p. 172.
36. Crick, 'Introduction', p. 30.
37. Crick, 'Orwell and English Socialism', p. 12.
38. Hitchens, *Orwell's Victory*, p. 73.

Selected Bibliography

Primary sources

[Anonymous]. 'Unsigned Notice, *Nation.*' Ed. Jeffrey Meyers. *George Orwell: The Critical Heritage*. London: Routledge & Kegan Paul, 1975. 45–6.

[An observer]. *Miners, Owners and Mysteries*. London: Waterlow & Sons, [1936?].

Auden, W. H. *Collected Poems*. Ed. Edward Mendelson. 1976. London: Faber, 1994.

——. *The English Auden: Poems, Essays and Dramatic Writings 1927–1939*. Ed. Edward Mendelson. London: Faber, 1977.

——. 'Ode (to my Pupils).' Ed. Roberts. *New Signatures*. London: Hogarth, 1932. 23–9.

Auden, W. H. and Christopher Isherwood. *The Ascent of F6 and On the Frontier*. 1958. London: Faber, 1961.

——. *The Dog Beneath the Skin or Where is Francis?* 1935. London: Faber, 1986.

Benney, Mark. *Almost a Gentleman*. London: Peter Davies, 1966.

——. *The Big Wheel*. London: Peter Davies, 1940.

Blumenfeld, Simon. *Jew Boy*. London: Jonathan Cape, 1935.

——. 'A Stall in the Market.' Ed. Jack Common. *Seven Shifts*. London: Secker & Warburg, 1938. 179–204.

Boden, F. C. *Miner*. London: J. M. Dent, 1932.

Booth, Charles. 'Life and Labour of the People of London.' Ed. Peter Keating. *Into Unknown England*. London: Fontana, 1976. 112–40.

Booth, William. 'In Darkest England and the Way Out.' Ed. Peter Keating. *Into Unknown England*. London: Fontana, 1976. 141–73.

Brierley, Walter. *Means Test Man*. London: Methuen, 1935.

——. *Sandwichman*. London: Methuen, 1937.

Brockway, A. Fenner. *Hungry England*. London: Gollancz, 1932.

Brown, Alec. 'December 1934.' Ed. David Margolies. *Writing the Revolution*. London: Pluto, 1998. 27–9.

Calder, Angus. Introduction. *Britain by Mass Observation*. By Tom Harrisson and Charles Madge. 1939. London: Cresset Library, 1986.

Campbell, Janet. Introduction. *Working Class Wives*. By Margery Spring Rice. Harmondsworth: Penguin, 1939. vii–xii.

Caudwell, Christopher [Christopher St.-John Sprigg]. *Illusion and Reality*. 1937. London: Lawrence and Wishart, 1973.

Chesterton, Mrs Cecil. *In Darkest London*. 1926. London: Stanley Paul, 1927.

Cohen, Max. *I Was One of the Unemployed*. London: Gollancz, 1945.

Common, Jack. *Freedom of the Streets*. 1938. Newcastle upon Tyne: People's Publications, 1988.

——, ed. *Seven Shifts*. London: Secker & Warburg, 1938.

Connolly, Cyril. 'C. C. (Cyril Connolly), *Horizon.*' Ed. Jeffrey Meyers. *George Orwell: The Critical Heritage*. London: Routledge & Kegan Paul, 1975. 199–201.

——. *Enemies of Promise*. 1938. Harmondsworth: Penguin, 1961.

Constantine, Murray [Katherine Burdekin]. *Swastika Night*. London: Gollancz, 1937.

Coombes, B. L. *Miners Day*. Harmondsworth: Penguin, 1945.

———. *These Poor Hands: The Autobiography of a Miner Working in South Wales*. London: Victor Gollancz, 1939.

Cross, Gary, ed. *Worktowners at Blackpool: Mass-Observation and Popular Leisure in the 1930s*. London: Routledge, 1990.

Dane, Clemence [Winifred Ashton]. *The Arrogant History of White Ben*. London: Heinemann, 1939.

Davies, Margaret Llewelyn, ed. *Life as We Have Known It, by Co-operative Working_Women*. 1931. London: Hogarth, 1977.

Davies, W. H. *The Autobiography of a Super-Tramp*. 1908. London: Jonathan Cape, 1940.

———. 'W. H. Davies, *New Statesman and Nation*.' Ed. Jeffrey Meyers. *George Orwell: The Critical Heritage*. London: Routledge & Kegan Paul, 1975. 43–5.

Demant, V. A. *The Miners' Distress and the Coal Problem*. London: Student Christian Movement Press, 1929.

Dickens, Charles. 'The Noble Savage.' Ed. John Carey. *The Faber Book of Utopias*. London: Faber, 1999. 239–45.

Eliot, T. S. *Collected Poems: 1909–1963*. 1963. London: Faber, 1974.

———. *Notes Towards the Definition of Culture*. 1948. London: Faber, 1962.

Engels, Friedrich. *The Condition of the Working Class in England*. 1845. London: Penguin, 1987.

Fox, Ralph. 'Conversations with a Llama.' *Penguin New Writing* 1 (1940): 126–37.

Garrett, George. 'The First Hunger March.' *Penguin New Writing* 1 (1940): 62–75.

Gibbon, Lewis Grassic. *A Scots Quair*. 1946. London: Penguin, 1986.

Gissing, George. *Demos: A Story of English Socialism*. 1866. Brighton: Harvester, 1972

———. *The Nether World*. 1889. Ed. Stephen Gill. Oxford: Oxford University Press, 1999.

———. *New Grub Street*. 1891. Harmondsworth: Penguin, 1980.

———. *The Unclassed*. 1884. Brighton: Harvester, 1983.

Glasser, Ralph. *Gorbals Boy at Oxford*. 1988. London: Pan Books, 1990.

Gollancz, Victor. Foreword. *The Road to Wigan Pier*. By George Orwell. 1937. London: Secker & Warburg, 1997. 216–25.

Green, Henry. *Living*. 1929. London: Hogarth, 1970.

———. *Pack My Bag: A Self-Portrait*. 1940. London: Hogarth, 1952.

Greenwood, James. 'A Night in the Workhouse.' Ed. Peter Keating. *Into Unknown England*. London: Fontana, 1976. 33–54.

———. *The Seven Curses of London*. 1869. Oxford: Blackwell, 1981.

Greenwood, Walter. *Love on the Dole*. 1933. London: Vintage, 1993.

———. *There Was a Time*. 1967. Harmondsworth: Penguin, 1969.

Hanley, James. *Grey Children: A Study in Humbug and Misery*. London: Methuen, 1937.

Hannington, Wal. *The Problem of the Distressed Areas*. London: Gollancz, 1937.

———. *Ten Lean Years: An Examination of the Record of the National Government in the Field of Unemployment*. London: Gollancz, 1940.

Harrisson, Tom and Charles Madge. *Britain by Mass-Observation*. 1939. London: Cresset Library, 1986.

Heslop, Harold. *Last Cage Down*. London: Wishart, 1935.

Hilton, Jack. 'The Plasterer's Life.' Ed. Jack Common. *Seven Shifts*. London: Secker & Warburg, 1938. 1–49.

Hitler, Adolf. *Adolf Hitler: From Speeches 1933–1938*. Ed. Richard Mönnig. Berlin: Terramare Office, 1938.

——. 'Appendix B: Hitler's Secret Address to Representatives of the German Press, Munich, 10 November 1938.' Ed. Z. A. B. Zeman. *Nazi Propaganda*. 1964. London: Oxford University Press, 1973. 212–25.

——. *Hitler's Table Talk: 1941–1944*. 1953. Trans. Norman Cameron and R. H. Stevens. London: Phoenix, 2000.

——. *Mein Kampf*. 1925–6. Trans. Ralph Manheim. London: Pimlico, 1997.

Hoggart, Richard. *A Local Habitation: Life and Times, Volume 1: 1918–1940*. London: Chatto & Windus, 1988.

Huxley, Aldous. *The Hidden Huxley*. Ed. David Bradshaw. 1994. London: Faber, 1995.

——. *Island*. London: Chatto & Windus, 1962.

Isherwood, Christopher. *Kathleen and Frank*. 1971. London: Vintage, 2000.

——. *Lions and Shadows: An Education in the Twenties*. 1938. London: Four Square, 1963.

Jameson, Storm. 'Documents.' *Fact* 4 (July 1937): 9–18.

——. 'To a Labour Party Official.' *Left Review* 1.2 (November 1934): 29–34.

——. *The Moment of Truth*. London: Macmillan, 1949.

Jones, Lewis. *Cwmardy*. 1937. London: Lawrence and Wishart, 1978.

——. *We Live: The Story of a Welsh Mining Village*. London: Lawrence and Wishart, 1939.

Joyce, James. *Ulysses*. 1922. Ed. Jeri Johnson. Oxford: Oxford University Press, 1998.

Keating, Peter, ed. *Into Unknown England 1866–1913: Selections from the Social Explorers*. London: Fontana, 1976.

——, ed. *Working-Class Stories of the 1890s*. London: Routledge & Kegan Paul, 1971.

Koestler, Arthur. *Darkness at Noon*. 1940. Harmondsworth: Penguin, 1946.

Lawrence, D. H. *England, My England*. 1922. Harmondsworth: Penguin, 1960.

——. *Lady Chatterley's Lover*. 1928. Harmondsworth: Penguin, 1999.

——. *The Prussian Officer*. 1914. Harmondsworth: Penguin, 1945.

——. *The Rainbow*. 1915. London: Heinemann, 1971.

——. *Sons and Lovers*. 1913. Ed. David Trotter. Oxford: Oxford University Press, 1998.

Lessing, Doris. *In Pursuit of the English*. 1960. London: Sphere Books, 1968.

Levi, Primo. *The Drowned and the Saved*. Trans. Raymond Rosenthal. 1986. Harmondsworth: Penguin, 1988.

——. *If This is a Man/The Truce*. Trans. Stuart Woolf. 1958, 1963. Harmondsworth: Penguin, 1979.

——. *Moments of Reprieve*. Trans. Ruth Feldman. 1981. Harmondsworth: Penguin, 1987.

Lewis, Cecil Day. *The Complete Poems*. London: Sinclair-Stevenson, 1992.

——. 'Letter to a Young Revolutionary.' Ed. Michael Roberts. *New Country: Prose and Poetry by the author of New Signatures*. London: Hogarth, 1933. 25–42.

——. 'The Road These Times Must Take.' *Left Review* 1.2 (November 1934): 35.

London, Jack. *The Iron Heel.* 1907. Harmondsworth: Penguin, 1945.
——. *The People of the Abyss.* 1903. [London?]: Joseph Simon, 1980.
MacNeice, Louis. *Collected Poems.* 1979. London: Faber, 1986.
——. *The Strings Are False: An Unfinished Autobiography.* 1965. London: Faber, 1982.
Mannion, Herbert. 'I Was in a Gas Works.' Ed. Jack Common. *Seven Shifts.* London: Secker & Warburg, 1938. 145–77.
Marett, R. R. Introduction. *Among the Headhunters of Formosa.* By Janet B. Montgomery McGovern. 1922. Taipei: SMC, 1997.
Margolies, David, ed. *Writing the Revolution: Cultural Criticism from* Left Review. London: Pluto Press, 1998.
Marshall, Arthur Calder. 'Fiction.' *Fact* 4 (July 1937): 38–44.
Massey, Philip. 'Portrait of a Mining Town.' *Fact* 8 (November 1937): 7–78.
Massingham, Hugh. *I Took Off My Tie.* London: Heinemann, 1936.
Mass-Observation. *First Year's Work: 1937–38.* Ed. Charles Madge and Tom Harrisson. London: Drummond, 1938.
——. *The Pub and the People: A Worktown Study.* London: Gollancz, 1943.
Masterman, Charles Frederick G. *England After War.* London: Hodder and Stoughton, [1922?]
——. [Pub. Anon.] *From the Abyss: of its Inhabitants by One of them.* London: R. Brimley Johnson, 1902.
Mayhew, Henry. *London Labour and the London Poor.* 1861–2. Selected Victor Neuberg. Harmondsworth: Penguin, 1985.
McCullock, T. A. 'Working on the Railway.' Ed. Jack Common. *Seven Shifts.* London: Secker & Warburg, 1938. 247–71.
McGovern, J. B. M. *Among the Headhunters of Formosa.* 1922. Taipei: SMC, 1997.
Meyers, Jeffrey, ed. *George Orwell: The Critical Heritage.* London: Routledge & Kegan Paul, 1975.
Miles, Hamish. 'Hamish Miles, *New Statesman and Nation.*' Ed. Jeffrey Meyers. *George Orwell: The Critical Heritage.* London: Routledge & Kegan Paul, 1975. 110–13.
Morrison, Arthur. *A Child of the Jago.* 1896. Harmondsworth: Penguin, 1946.
Morton, H. V. *I, James Blunt.* London: Methuen, 1942.
Orwell, George. *All Propaganda is Lies: 1941–1942.* Ed. Peter Davison. *The Complete Works of George Orwell.* Vol. 13. London: Secker & Warburg, 1998.
——. *Animal Farm: A Fairy Story.* 1945. Ed. Peter Davison. London: Secker & Warburg, 1997.
——. *Burmese Days.* 1934. Ed. Peter Davison. London: Secker & Warburg, 1997.
——. *A Clergyman's Daughter.* 1935. Ed. Peter Davison. London: Secker & Warburg, 1997.
——. *Coming Up for Air.* 1939. Ed. Peter Davison. London: Secker & Warburg, 1997.
——. *Down and Out in Paris and London.* 1933. Ed. Peter Davison. London: Secker & Warburg, 1997.
——. *Facing Unpleasant Facts: 1936–1939.* Ed. Peter Davison. *The Complete Works of George Orwell.* Vol. 11. London: Secker & Warburg, 1998.
——. *Homage to Catalonia.* 1938. Ed. Peter Davison. London: Secker & Warburg, 1997.
——. *I Belong to the Left: 1945.* Ed. Peter Davison. *The Complete Works of George Orwell.* Vol. 17. London: Secker & Warburg, 1998.

——. *I Have Tried to Tell the Truth: 1943–1944*. Ed. Peter Davison. *The Complete Works of George Orwell*. Vol. 16. London: Secker & Warburg, 1998.

——. *It Is What I Think: 1947–1948*. Ed. Peter Davison. *The Complete Works of George Orwell*. Vol. 19. London: Secker & Warburg, 1998.

——. *Keep the Aspidistra Flying*. 1936. London: Secker & Warburg, 1997.

——. *Keeping Our Little Corner Clean: 1942–1943*. Ed. Peter Davison. *The Complete Works of George Orwell*. Vol. 14. London: Secker & Warburg, 1998.

——. *A Kind of Compulsion: 1903–1936*. Ed. Peter Davison. *The Complete Works of George Orwell*. Vol. 10. London: Secker & Warburg, 1998.

——. *Nineteen Eighty-Four*. 1949. Ed. Peter Davison. London: Secker & Warburg, 1997.

——. *Our Job is to Make Life Worth Living: 1949–1950*. Ed. Peter Davison. *The Complete Works of George Orwell*. Vol. 20. London: Secker & Warburg, 1998.

——. *A Patriot After All: 1940–1941*. Ed. Peter Davison. *The Complete Works of George Orwell*. Vol. 12. London: Secker & Warburg, 1998.

——. *The Road to Wigan Pier*. 1937. Ed. Peter Davison. London: Secker & Warburg, 1997.

——. *Smothered Under Journalism: 1946*. Ed. Peter Davison. *The Complete Works of George Orwell*. Vol. 18. London: Secker & Warburg, 1998.

——. *Two Wasted Years: 1943*. Ed. Peter Davison. *The Complete Works of George Orwell*. Vol. 15. London: Secker & Warburg, 1998.

Oxley, Will. 'Are You Working?' Ed. Jack Common. *Seven Shifts*. London: Secker & Warburg, 1938. 103–44.

Pollitt, Harry. *Selected Articles and Speeches: Vol. II: 1936–1939*. London: Lawrence and Wishart, 1954.

Priestley, J. B. *English Journey, Being a Rambling but Truthful Account of What One Man Saw and Heard and Felt and Thought During a Journey Through England During the Autumn of the Year 1933*. 1934. London: Heinemann, 1937.

Rahv, Philip. 'Philip Rahv, *Partisan Review*.' Ed. Jeffrey Meyers. *George Orwell: The Critical Heritage*. London: Routledge & Kegan Paul, 1975. 267–73.

Reeves, Maud Pember. *Round About a Pound a Week*. 1913. London: Virago, 1999.

Rice, Margery Spring, *Working-Class Wives: Their Health and Condition*. Harmondsworth: Penguin, 1939.

Roberts, Michael, ed. *The Faber Book of Modern Verse*. 1936. London: Faber, 1948.

——. *New Country: Prose and Poetry by the Author of New Signatures*. London: Hogarth, 1933.

——, ed. *New Signatures*. London: Hogarth, 1932.

Roberts, Robert. *The Classic Slum: Salford Life in the First Quarter of the Century*. 1971. Harmondsworth: Pelican, 1987.

——. *A Ragged Schooling*. 1976. Manchester: Mandolin, 1984.

Rodaway, Angela. *A London Childhood*. 1960. London: Virago, 1985.

Rowse, A. L. *The English Spirit: Essays in History and Literature*. London: Macmillan, 1944.

Sillen, Samuel. 'Samuel Sillen, *Masses and Mainstream*.' Ed. Jeffrey Meyers. *George Orwell: The Critical Heritage*. London: Routledge & Kegan Paul, 1975. 274–76.

Sillitoe, Alan. *Saturday Night and Sunday Morning*. 1958. London: Flamingo, 1994.

Sims, George R. 'How the Poor Live.' Ed. Peter Keating. *Into Unknown England*. London: Fontana, 1976. 65–90.

Skelton, Robin, ed. *Poetry of the Thirties*. Harmondsworth: Penguin, 1964.

Spender, Humphrey. *Britain in the Thirties*. London: The Lion and the Unicorn Press, 1975.

Spender, Stephen. *Collected Poems: 1928–1985*. 1985. London: Faber, 1990.

——. 'Poetry.' *Fact* 4: (July 1937): 18–30.

——. *The Temple*. 1988. London: Faber, 1989.

——. *World Within World*. 1977. London: Faber, 1991.

Stalin, Joseph. *The Essential Stalin: Major Theoretical Writings 1905–52*. Ed. Bruce Franklin. London: Croom Hill, 1973.

Stirling, James. 'Steel Works.' Ed. Jack Common. *Seven Shifts*. London: Secker & Warburg, 1938. 51–101.

Strachey, John. 'Education of a Communist.' *Left Review* 1.3 (December 1934): 62–9.

Symons, Julian. 'Julian Symons, *Times Literary Supplement*.' Ed. Jeffrey Meyers. *George Orwell: The Critical Heritage*. London: Routledge & Kegan Paul, 1975. 251–7.

Toynbee, Philip. 'Philip Toynbee, *Encounter*.' Ed. Jeffrey Meyers. *George Orwell: The Critical Heritage*. London: Routledge & Kegan Paul, 1975. 115–18.

Tressell, Robert. [Robert Noonan] *The Ragged Trousered Philanthropists*. 1955. London: Granada, 1982.

Walsh, James. 'James Walsh, *Marxist Quarterly*.' Ed. Jeffrey Meyers. *George Orwell: The Critical Heritage*. London: Routledge & Kegan Paul, 1975. 290–1.

Warner, R. E. 'Hymn.' Ed. Roberts. *New Country*. London: Hogarth, 1933. 254–6.

Watson, J. H. 'The Big Chimney.' Ed. Jack Common. *Seven Shifts*. London: Secker & Warburg, 1938. 205–45.

Wells, H. G. *Kipps*. 1905. London: Fontana, 1973.

——. *Love and Mr. Lewisham*. 1899–1900. Harmondsworth: Penguin, 1946.

——. *Tono-Bungay*. 1909. London: Pan, 1972.

Williams-Ellis, Amabel. 'Not So Easy.' *Left Review* 1.1 (October 1934): 39–41.

——. 'Soviet Writers' Conference.' *Left Review* 1.2 (November 1934): 39–41.

Wilson, Edmund. 'Edmund Wilson, *New Yorker*.' Ed. Jeffrey Meyers. *George Orwell: The Critical Heritage*. London: Routledge & Kegan Paul, 1975. 224–6.

Woolf, Virginia. *Collected Essays: Volume Two*. London: Hogarth, 1966.

——. 'Introductory Letter to Margaret Llewelyn Davies.' Ed. Margaret Llewelyn Davies. *Life as We Have Known It, By Co-operative Working Women*. 1931. London: Hogarth, 1977. xvii–xxxxi.

——. *A Room of One's Own*. 1928. Harmondsworth: Penguin, 2000.

Zamyatin, Yevgeny. *We*. 1924. Trans. Clarence Brown. Harmondsworth: Penguin, 1993.

Secondary sources

Adelson, Joseph. 'The Self and Memory in Nineteen Eighty-Four.' Ed. Ejner J. Jensen. *The Future of Nineteen Eighty-Four*. Ann Arbor: University of Michigan Press, c.1984. 111–19.

Allen, Francis J. 'Nineteen Eighty-Four and the Eclipse of Private Worlds.' Ed. Ejner J. Jensen. *The Future of Nineteen Eighty-Four*. Ann Arbor: University of Michigan Press, c.1984. 151–75.

Althusser, Louis. *For Marx*. 1965. London: Allen Lane, 1969.

——. *On Lenin and Philosophy and Other Essays*. Trans. Ben Brewster. London: New Left Books, 1971.

Althusser, Louis and Etienne Balibar. *Reading Capital*. Trans. Ben Brewster. 1968. London: NLB, 1970.

Anderson, Benedict. *Imagined Communities: Reflections on the Origins and Spread of Nationalism*. London: Verso and NLB, 1983.

Arendt, Hannah. *The Origins of Totalitarianism*. 1951. London: Allen & Unwin, 1967.

Aung, Maung Htin. 'George Orwell and Burma.' Ed. Miriam Gross. *The World of George Orwell*. London: Wiedenfeld and Nicolson, 1971. 19–30.

Bailey, Richard W. 'George Orwell and the English Language.' Ed. Ejner J. Jensen. *The Future of Nineteen Eighty-Four*. Ann Arbor: University of Michigan Press, c.1984. 23–46.

Baldry, H. C. *Ancient Utopias*. London: University of Southampton, 1956.

Ball, F. C. *One of the Damned: The Life and Times of Robert Tressell, Author of The Ragged Trousered Philanthropists*. 1973. London: Lawrence and Wishart, 1979.

Barr, Andrew. *Drink*. London: Bantam, 1995.

Barthes, Roland. *Mythologies*. Trans. and ed. Annette Lavers. London: Vintage, 2000.

Beadle, Gordon. 'George Orwell and Charles Dickens: Moral Critics of Society.' *Journal of Historical Studies* 2.4 (1969–70): 245–55.

Beauchamp, Gorman. 'From Bingo to Big Brother: Orwell on Power and Sadism.' Ed. Ejner J. Jensen. *The Future of Nineteen Eighty-Four*. Ann Arbor: University of Michigan Press, c.1984. 65–85.

Beauvoir, Simone de. *The Second Sex*. 1949. London: Vintage, 1997.

Beberich, Christine, 'A Revolutionary in Love with the 1900s: Orwell in Defence of "Old England".' Ed. Alberto Lázaro. *The Road from George Orwell: His Achievement and Legacy*. Bern: Peter Lang, 2001. 33–52.

Beddoe, Deidre. 'Hindrances and Help-Meets: Women in the Writings of George Orwell.' Ed. Christopher Norris. *Inside the Myth: Orwell: Views from the Left*. London: Lawrence and Wishart, 1984. 139–54.

Belloc, Hilaire. 'English Verse.' Ed. Hugh Kingsmill. *The English Genius*. London: Right Book Club, 1939. 17–32.

Berlin, Isaiah. *Against the Current: Essays in the History of Ideas*. 1979. London: Pimlico, 1997.

Bluemel, Kristin. *George Orwell and the Radical Eccentrics: Intermodernism in Literary London*. Basingstoke: Palgrave Macmillan, 2004.

Bolton, W. F. *The Language of 1984: Orwell's English and Ours*. Oxford: Blackwell, [1984?].

Bradbury, Macolm. *The Modern British Novel*. London: Secker & Warburg, 1993.

Bradshaw, David. Introduction. *The Hidden Huxley*. By Aldous Huxley. 1994. London: Faber, 1995.

Brogan, D. W. *The English People: Impressions and Observations*. 1943. London: Hamish Hamilton, 1947.

Brown, Alan. 'Examining Orwell: Political and Literary Values in Education.' Ed. Christopher Norris. *Inside the Myth: Orwell: Views from the Left*. London: Lawrence and Wishart, 1984. 39–61.

Buddicom, Jacinthia. 'The Young Eric.' Ed. Miriam Gross. *The World of George Orwell*. London: Wiedenfeld and Nicolson, 1971. 1–8.

Buitenhuis, Peter and Ira B. Nadal, eds. *George Orwell: A Reassessment*. Basingstoke: Macmillan, 1988.

Burleigh, Michael. *The Third Reich: A New History*. 2000. London: Pan Macmillan, 2001.

Burnham, James. *The Managerial Revolution, or What is Happening in the World Now*. 1941. Harmondsworth: Penguin, 1945.

Butler, Judith. *Gender Trouble: Feminism and the Subversion of Identity*. London: Routledge, 1990.

Campbell, Beatrix. 'Orwell – Paterfamilias or Big Brother?' Ed. Christopher Norris. *Inside the Myth: Orwell: Views from the Left*. London: Lawrence and Wishart, 1984. 126–38.

——. *Wigan Pier Revisited*. London: Virago, 1984.

Cannadine, David. *Class in Britain*. 1998. Harmondsworth: Penguin, 2000.

Carey, John, ed. *The Faber Book of Utopias*. London: Faber, 1999.

——. *The Intellectuals and the Masses: Pride and Prejudice among the Literary Intelligentsia, 1880–1939*. London: Faber, 1992.

——. *Original Copy*. London: Faber, 1987.

Carr, Raymond. 'Orwell and Spain.' Ed. Miriam Gross. *The World of George Orwell*. London: Wiedenfeld and Nicolson, 1971. 63–73.

Carroll, Lewis. *The Annotated Alice: The Definitive Edition*. Ed. Martin Gardner. Harmondsworth: Penguin, 2000.

Carter, Michael. *George Orwell and the Problem of Authentic Existence*. London: Croom Helm, 1985.

Chase, Mary Ellen. *In England Now*. London: Collins, 1937.

Clark, Jon, Margot Heinemann, David Margolies and Carole Snee, eds. *Culture and Crisis in Britain in the Thirties*. London: Lawrence and Wishart, 1979.

Cohen-Portheim, Paul. *England, the Unknown Isle*. Trans. Alan Harris. London: Duckworth, 1930.

Coleman, John. 'The Critic of Popular Culture.' Ed. Miriam Gross. *The World of George Orwell*. London: Wiedenfeld and Nicolson, 1971. 101–10.

Common, Jack. 'Jack Common's Recollections.' Ed. Audrey Coppard and Bernard Crick. *Orwell Remembered*. London: Ariel Books, 1984. 139–43.

Connelly, Mark. *The Diminished Self: Orwell and the Loss of Freedom*. Pittsburgh: Duquesne University Press, 1987.

Cooper, Lettice. 'Eileen Blair.' Ed. Audrey Coppard and Bernard Crick. *Orwell Remembered*. London: Ariel Books, 1984. 161–6.

Coppard, Audrey and Bernard Crick, eds. *Orwell Remembered*. London: Ariel Books, 1984.

Cottman, Stafford. 'In the Spanish Trenches.' Ed. Audrey Coppard and Bernard Crick. *Orwell Remembered*. London: Ariel Books, 1984. 148–55.

Crankshaw, Edward. 'Orwell and Communism.' Ed. Miriam Gross. *The World of George Orwell*. London: Wiedenfeld and Nicolson, 1971. 117–26.

Crick, Bernard. *George Orwell: A Life*. 1980. Harmondsworth: Penguin, 1992.

——. *In Defence of Politics*. 1962. Harmondsworth: Penguin, 1976.

——. Introduction. *Nineteen Eighty-Four*. By George Orwell. 1949. Oxford: Clarendon, 1984.

——. 'Nineteen Eighty-Four: Satire or Prophecy?' Ed. Ejner J. Jensen. *The Future of Nineteen Eighty-Four*. Ann Arbor: University of Michigan Press, c.1984. 7–21.

——. 'Orwell and English Socialism.' Ed. Peter Buitenhuis and Ira B. Nadal. *George Orwell: A Reassessment*. Basingstoke: Macmillan, 1988. 3–19.

——. *Political Thoughts and Polemics*. Edinburgh: Edinburgh University Press, 1990.

Croft, Andy. *Red Letter Days: British Fiction in the 1930s*. London: Lawrence and Wishart, 1990.

——. 'Worlds Without End Foisted Upon the Future – Some Antecedents of Nineteen Eighty-Four.' Ed. Christopher Norris. *Inside the Myth: Orwell: Views from the Left*. London: Lawrence and Wishart, 1984. 183–216.

Croucher, Richard. *We Refuse to Starve in Silence: A History of the National Unemployed Workers' Movement, 1920–46*. London: Lawrence and Wishart, 1987.

Crowther, M. A. 'The Tramp.' Ed. Roy Porter. *Myths of the English*. Cambridge: Polity, 1992. 91–113.

Cunningham, Valentine. *British Writers of the Thirties*. 1988. Oxford: Oxford University Press, 1993.

Dakin, Humphrey. 'The Brother-in-Law Strikes Back.' Ed. Audrey Coppard and Bernard Crick. *Orwell Remembered*. London: Ariel Books, 1984. 127–30.

Day, Gary. *Class*. London: Routledge, 2001.

Deutscher, Isaac. ' "1984" – The Mysticism of Cruelty.' Ed. Samuel Hynes. *Twentieth Century Interpretations of 1984*. Englewood Cliffs: Prentice Hall, 1971. 29–40.

Dollimore, Jonathan. *Sexual Dissidence: Augustine to Wilde, Freud to Foucault*. Oxford: Clarendon, 1991.

Dunn, Avril. 'My Brother, George Orwell.' Ed. Audrey Coppard and Bernard Crick. *Orwell Remembered*. London: Ariel Books, 1984. 25–32.

Dworkin, Andrea. *Right Wing Women: The Politics of Domesticated Females*. London: The Women's Press, 1983.

Eagleton, Terry. *Criticism and Ideology*. 1976. London: Verso, 1995.

——. 'Orwell and the Lower Middle-Class Novel.' Ed. Raymond Williams. *George Orwell: A Collection of Critical Essays*. Englewood Cliffs: Prentice Hall, 1974. 10–33.

Easthope, Antony. *Englishness and National Culture*. London: Routledge, 1999.

——. 'Fact and Fantasy in "Nineteen Eighty-Four".' Ed. Christopher Norris. *Inside the Myth: Orwell: Views from the Left*. London: Lawrence and Wishart, 1984. 263–85.

Edwards, Robert. 'With the ILP in Spain.' Ed. Audrey Coppard and Bernard Crick. *Orwell Remembered*. London: Ariel Books, 1984. 146–8.

Elliott, Robert C. *The Shape of Utopia: Studies in a Literary Genre*. Chicago: University of Chicago Press, 1970.

Ellmann, Maud, ed. *Psychoanalytic Literary Criticism*. London: Longman, 1994.

Empson, William. 'Orwell at the BBC.' Ed. Miriam Gross. *The World of George Orwell*. London: Wiedenfeld and Nicolson, 1971. 93–9.

Evans, Malcolm. 'Text, Theory, Criticism: Twenty Things You Never Knew About George Orwell.' Ed. Christopher Norris. *Inside the Myth: Orwell: Views from the Left*. London: Lawrence and Wishart, 1984. 12–37.

Fierz, Mabel. 'A Great Feeling for Nature.' Ed. Audrey Coppard and Bernard Crick. *Orwell Remembered*. London: Ariel Books, 1984. 94–8.

Forman, Charles. *Industrial Town: Self Portrait of St. Helens in the 1920s*. 1978. London: Granada, 1979.

Forster, E. M. *Two Cheers for Democracy*. London: Edward Arnold, [1951?].

Fowler, Roger. *The Language of Nineteen Eighty-Four*. Basingstoke: Macmillan, 1995.

Fulbrook, Mary. 'Myth-Making and National Identity: The Case of the G.D.R.' Ed. Geoffrey Hosking and George Schöpflin. *Myths and Nationhood*. New York: Routledge, 1997. 72–87.

Fyvel, T. R. *George Orwell: A Personal Memoir*. London: Weidenfeld and Nicolson, 1982.

——. 'The Years at *Tribune*.' Ed. Miriam Gross. *The World of George Orwell*. London: Wiedenfeld and Nicolson, 1971. 111–15.

Gasset, José Ortega y. *The Revolt of the Masses*. 1930. Trans. Anon. New York: Mentor, 1950.

Gellner, Ernest. *Nations and Nationalism*. Oxford: Blackwell, 1983.

Gerhardi, William. 'Climate and Character.' Ed. Hugh Kingsmill. *The English Genius*. London: Right Book Club, 1939. 57–80.

Gervais, David. 'Englands of the Mind.' *Cambridge Quarterly* 30.2 (2001): 151–68.

Green, Martin. *Children of the Sun: A Narrative of 'Decadence' in England after 1918*. 1976. London: Pimlico, 1992.

——. *A Mirror for Anglo-Saxons*. London: Longmans, 1961.

Gross, John. 'Imperial Attitudes.' Ed. Miriam Gross. *The World of George Orwell*. London: Wiedenfeld and Nicolson, 1971. 31–8.

Gross, Miriam, ed. *The World of George Orwell*. London: Wiedenfeld and Nicolson, 1971.

Grylls, David. *The Paradox of Gissing*. London: Allen & Unwin, 1986.

Gurney, Peter. ' "Intersex" and "Dirty Girls": Mass-Observation and Working Class Sexuality in England in the 1930s.' *Journal of the History of Sexuality* 8.2 (October 1997): 256–90.

——. ' "Measuring the Distance": D. H. Lawrence, Raymond Williams and the Quest for "Community".' Ed. Keith Laybourn. *Social Conditions, Status and Community*. Stroud: Alan Sutton, 1997. 160–83.

Habermas, Jürgen. *A Berlin Republic: Writings on Germany*. 1995. Cambridge: Polity, 1998.

——. *Moral Consciousness and Communicative Action*. 1983. Trans. Christian Lenhardt and Shierry Weber Nicholson. Cambridge: Polity, 1990.

Hall, Stuart. 'Conjuring Leviathan: Orwell on the State.' Ed. Christopher Norris. *Inside the Myth: Orwell: Views from the Left*. London: Lawrence and Wishart, 1984. 217–41.

Hamilton, Ian. 'Along the Road to Wigan Pier.' Ed. Miriam Gross. *The World of George Orwell*. London: Wiedenfeld and Nicolson, 1971. 53–61.

Hammond, J. R. *A George Orwell Companion: A Guide to the Novels, Documentaries and Essays*. 1982. Chippenham: Anthony Rowe, 1994.

Haynes, E. S. P. 'Law.' Ed. Hugh Kingsmill. *The English Genius*. London: Right Book Club, 1939. 81–97.

Heppenstall, Raymond. 'Raymond Heppenstall Remembers.' Ed. Audrey Coppard and Bernard Crick. *Orwell Remembered*. London: Ariel Books, 1984. 106–15.

Hitchens, Christopher. 'George Orwell and Raymond Williams.' *Critical Quarterly* 41.3(October 1999): 3–20.

——. *Orwell's Victory*. Harmondsworth: Penguin, 2002.

Hobsbawn, E. J. *Nations and Nationalism Since 1780: Programme, Myth, Reality*. Cambridge: University of Cambridge Press, 1990.

Hodgart, Matthew. 'From *Animal Farm* to *Nineteen Eighty-Four*.' Ed. Miriam Gross. *The World of George Orwell*. London: Wiedenfeld and Nicolson, 1971. 135–42.

Hoggart, Richard. *An English Temper: Essays on Education, Culture & Communications.* London: Chatto and Windus, 1982.

——. Introduction. *The Road to Wigan Pier.* By George Orwell. 1937. Harmondsworth: Penguin, 1989. v–xii.

——. 'Introduction to *The Road to Wigan Pier.*' Ed. Raymond Williams. *George Orwell: A Collection of Critical Essays.* Englewood Cliffs: Prentice Hall, 1974. 34–51.

——. *The Uses of Literary.* London: Chatto & Windus, 1957.

Hope, Francis. 'Schooldays'. Ed. Miriam Gross. *The World of George Orwell.* London: Wiedenfeld and Nicolson, 1971. 9–18.

Hosking, Geoffrey and George Schöpflin, eds. *Myths and Nationhood.* New York: Routledge, 1997.

Howard, Michael S. *Jonathan Cape, Publisher.* London: Jonathan Cape, 1971.

Howe, Irving. *Decline of the New.* London: Gollancz, 1971.

——. *Politics and the Novel.* New York: Horizon Press and Meridian Books, 1957.

Hutt, Allen. *The Post-War History of the British Working-Class.* London: Gollancz, 1937.

Hynes, Samuel. *The Auden Generation: Literature and Politics in England in the 1930s.* London: Bodley Head, 1976.

——, ed. *Twentieth Century Interpretations of 1984.* Englewood Cliffs: Prentice Hall, 1971.

Inge, W. R. 'Religion.' Ed. Hugh Kingsmill. *The English Genius.* London: Right Book Club, 1939. 1–16.

Ingle, Stephen. *George Orwell: A Political Life.* 1993. Manchester: Manchester University Press, 1994.

——. *Socialist Thought in Imaginative Literature.* London: Macmillan, 1979.

Irigaray, Luce. *The Irigaray Reader.* Ed. Margaret Whitford. 1991. Oxford: Blackwell, 1994.

Jacob, Alaric. 'Sharing Orwell's "Joys" – But Not His Fears.' Ed. Christopher Norris. *Inside the Myth: Orwell: Views from the Left.* London: Lawrence and Wishart, 1984. 62–84.

Jacobson, Dan. 'Orwell's Slumming.' Ed. Miriam Gross. *The World of George Orwell.* London: Wiedenfeld and Nicolson, 1971. 47–52.

Jameson, Fredric. *Postmodernism, or, the Cultural Logic of Late Capitalism.* London: Verso, 1991.

Jensen, Ejner J., ed. *The Future of Nineteen Eighty-Four.* Ann Arbor: University of Michigan Press, c.1984.

Jones, Bill and Chris Williams. *B. L. Coombes.* Cardiff: University of Wales Press, 1999.

Jones, D. A. N. 'Arguments Against Orwell.' Ed. Miriam Gross. *The World of George Orwell.* London: Wiedenfeld and Nicolson, 1971. 153–63.

Kaleb, George. 'The Road to *1984.*' Ed. Samuel Hynes. *Twentieth Century Interpretations of 1984.* Englewood Cliffs: Prentice Hall, 1971. 73–87.

Kaplan, E. Ann and Michael Sprinkler, eds. *The Althusserian Legacy.* London: Verso, 1993.

Keating, Peter. *The Working Class in Victorian Fiction.* London: Routledge & Kegan Paul, 1971.

Kegal, Charles. ' "Nineteen Eighty-Four": A Century of Ingsoc.' *Notes and Queries* 208 (April 1963): 151–2.

Kellas, James G. *The Politics of Nationalism and Ethnicity.* Basingstoke: Macmillan, 1991.

Kennan, J. 'With the Wigan Miners.' Ed. Audrey Coppard and Bernard Crick. *Orwell Remembered.* London: Ariel Books, 1984. 130–2.

Kingsmill, Hugh, ed. *The English Genius.* London: Right Book Club, 1939.

Klugman, James. 'The Crisis of the Thirties: A View from the Left.' Ed. Jon Clark et al. *Culture and Crisis in Britain in the Thirties.* London: Lawrence and Wishart, 1979. 13–36.

Knight, Patricia. 'Women and Abortion in Victorian and Edwardian England.' *History Workshop* 4 (1977): 57–68.

Laybourn, Keith. *Britain on the Breadline: A Social and Political History of Britain 1918–1939.* 1990. Stroud: Alan Sutton, 1998.

——. *A History of British Trade Unionism.* 1992. Stroud: Alan Sutton, 1997.

——, ed. *Social Conditions, Status and Community 1860-c. 1920.* Stroud: Alan Sutton, 1997.

Laybourn, Keith and Dylan Murphy. *Under the Red Flag: A History of Communism in Britain, c. 1849–1991.* Stroud: Alan Sutton, 1999.

Lázaro, Alberto, ed. *The Road from George Orwell: His Achievement and Legacy.* Bern: Peter Lang, 2001.

Lenin, V. I. *On Culture and Cultural Revolution.* 1966. Moscow: Progress Publishers, 1970.

Lewis, Peter. *George Orwell: The Road from 1984.* London: Heinemann/Quixote Press, 1981.

Light, Alison. *Forever England: Femininity, Literature and Conservatism Between the Wars.* London: Routledge, 1991.

Longhurst, Henry. 'A Sportsman Defends the Old Prep School.' Ed. Audrey Coppard and Bernard Crick. *Orwell Remembered.* London: Ariel Books, 1984. 35–6.

Lutman, Stephen. 'Orwell's Patriotism.' *Journal of Contemporary History* 2.2 (April 1967): 149–58.

Macherey, Pierre. *A Theory of Literary Production.* 1966. London: Routledge, 1986.

Maillaud, Pierre. *The English Way.* London: Oxford University Press, 1945.

Marx, Karl. *Capital: Volume One.* 1876. Trans. Ben Fowkes. Harmondsworth: Penguin, 1976.

——. *Marx: Early Political Writings.* Ed. and trans. Joseph O'Malley. Cambridge: Cambridge University Press, 1994.

——. *Marx: Later Political Writings.* Ed. and trans. Terrell Carver. Cambridge: Cambridge University Press, 1996.

Marx, Karl and Engels. *On Literature and Art.* Moscow: Progress Publishers, 1976.

——. *The Socialist Revolution.* 1978. Comp. F. Teplov and V. Davydov. Moscow: Progress Publishers, 1981.

McKenna, Brian. 'The British Communist Novel of the 1930s and 1940s: A "Party of Equals" (And Does That Matter?).' *Review of English Studies* 47 (August 1996): 369–85.

McKibbin, Ross. *Classes and Cultures: England 1918–1951.* 1998. Oxford: Oxford University Press, 2000.

McLaughlin, Joseph. *Writing the Urban Jungle: Reading Empire in London from Doyle to Eliot.* London and Charlottesville: University of Virginia Press, 2000.

Meyer, Alfred G. 'The Political Theory of Pessimism: George Orwell and Herbert Marcuse.' Ed. Ejner J. Jensen. *The Future of Nineteen Eighty-Four.* Ann Arbor: University of Michigan Press, c.1984. 121–35.

Meyer, Michael. 'Memories of George Orwell.' Ed. Miriam Gross. *The World of George Orwell.* London: Wiedenfeld and Nicolson, 1971. 127–33.

Meyers, Jeffrey, ed. *Orwell: Wintry Conscience of a Generation.* New York: W. W. Norton, 2000.

Meyers, Jeffrey and Valerie Meyers. *George Orwell: An Annotated Bibliography of Criticism.* New York: Garland, 1977.

Middleton, Drew. *The British.* London: Pan, 1957.

Miller, David. *On Nationality.* Oxford: Clarendon, 1995.

Miller, John, ed. *Voices Against Tyranny: Writings of the Spanish Civil War.* New York: Scribner, 1986.

Mitchell, Margaret. 'The Effects of Unemployment on the Social Condition of Women and Children in the 1930s.' *History Workshop* 19 (1985): 105–27.

Moènik, Rastko. 'Ideology and Fantasy.' E. Ann Kaplan and Michael Sprinkler. *The Althusserian Legacy.* London: Verso, 1993. 139–56.

Moi, Toril. *Sexual/Textual Politics.* 1985. London: Routledge, 1994.

Montefiore, Janet. *Men and Women Writers of the 1930s: The dangerous flood of history.* London: Routledge, 1996.

Morris, John. 'That Curiously Crucified Expression.' Ed. Audrey Coppard and Bernard Crick. *Orwell Remembered.* London: Ariel Books, 1984. 171–6.

Morton, A. L. 'The English Utopia.' Ed. Samuel Hynes. *Twentieth Century Interpretations of 1984.* Englewood Cliffs: Prentice Hall, 1971. 109–11.

Moya, Ana. 'George Orwell's Exploration of Discourses of Power in *Burmese Days.*' Ed. Alberto Lázaro. *The Road from George Orwell: His Achievement and Legacy.* Bern: Peter Lang, 2001. 93–104.

Muggeridge, Malcolm. 'A Knight of Woeful Countenance.' Ed. Miriam Gross. *The World of George Orwell.* London: Wiedenfeld and Nicolson, 1971. 165–75.

——. 'In Muggeridge's Diaries.' Ed. Audrey Coppard and Bernard Crick. *Orwell Remembered.* London: Ariel Books, 1984. 266–71.

——. *The Thirties: 1930–1940 in Great Britain.* London: Hamish Hamilton, 1940.

Mulvihill, Robert, ed. *Reflections on America, 1984: An Orwell Symposium.* Athens, Georgia: University of Georgia Press, 1986.

Murphy, Dervla. Introduction. *Down and Out in Paris and London.* By George Orwell. 1933. Harmondsworth: Penguin, 1989. v–xv.

New, Melvyn. 'Orwell and Antisemitism: Toward *1984.*' *Modern Fiction Studies* 21.1 (Spring 1975): 81–105.

Newsinger, John. *Orwell's Politics.* Basingstoke: Macmillan, 1999.

Nicholson, Tony. 'Masculine Status and Working-Class Culture in the Cleveland Ironstone Mining Communities, 1850–1881.' Ed. Keith Laybourn. *Social Conditions, Status and Community.* Stroud: Alan Sutton, 1997. 139–59.

Norris, Christopher, ed. *Inside the Myth: Orwell: Views from the Left.* London: Lawrence and Wishart, 1984.

——. 'Language, Truth and Ideology: Orwell and the Post-War Left.' Ed. Christopher Norris. *Inside the Myth: Orwell: Views from the Left.* London: Lawrence and Wishart, 1984. 242–62.

Overing, Joanna. 'The Role of Myth: An Anthropological Perspective, or: "The Reality of the Really Made-Up".' Ed. Geoffrey Hosking and George Schöpflin. *Myths and Nationhood.* New York: Routledge, 1997. 1–18.

Oxley, B. T. *George Orwell*. 1967. London: Evans Brothers, 1970.

Patai, Daphne. *The Orwell Mystique: A Study in Male Ideology*. Amherst: University of Massachusetts Press, 1984.

Pearce, Robert. 'Truth and Falsehood: George Orwell's Prep School Woes.' *Review of English Studies* 43 (1992): 367–86.

Pearson, Hesketh. 'Humour.' Ed. Hugh Kingsmill. *The English Genius*. London: Right Book Club, 1939. 33–55.

Pennington, Shelley and Belinda Westover. *A Hidden Workforce: Homeworkers in England, 1850–1985*. Basingstoke: Macmillan, 1989.

Porter, Roy, ed. *Myths of the English*. Cambridge: Polity, 1992.

Potts, Paul. *Dante Called You Beatrice*. London: Eyre and Spottiswoode, 1960.

——. 'Quixote on a Bicycle.' Ed. Audrey Coppard and Bernard Crick. *Orwell Remembered*. London: Ariel Books, 1984. 248–60.

Pritchett, V. S. '1984.' Ed. Samuel Hynes. *Twentieth Century Interpretations of 1984*. Englewood Cliffs: Prentice Hall, 1971. 20–4.

——. 'The New Statesman & Nation's Obituary.' Ed. Audrey Coppard and Bernard Crick. Ed. *Orwell Remembered*. London: Ariel Books, 1984. 275–7.

Pryce-Jones, David. 'Orwell's Reputation.' Ed. Miriam Gross. *The World of George Orwell*. London: Wiedenfeld and Nicolson, 1971. 143–52.

Rai, Alok. *Orwell and the Politics of Despair*. Cambridge: Cambridge University Press, 1988.

Rauschning, Hermann. *Hitler Speaks: A Series of Political Conversations with Hitler on his Real Aims*. London: Thornton Butterworth, 1939.

Rees, Richard. *George Orwell: Fugitive from the Camp of Victory*. London: Secker & Warburg, 1961.

Rothbard, Murray N. 'George Orwell and the Cold War: A Reconsideration.' Ed. Robert Mulvihill. *Reflections on America, 1984: An Orwell Symposium*. Athens, Georgia: University of George Press, 1986.

Runciman, Steven. 'A Contemporary in College.' Ed. Audrey Coppard and Bernard Crick. *Orwell Remembered*. London: Ariel Books, 1984. 51–4.

Russell, Elizabeth. 'Looking Backwards and Forwards from *Nineteen Eighty-Four*: Women Writing Men's Worlds.' Ed. Alberto Lázaro. *The Road from George Orwell: His Achievement and Legacy*. Bern: Peter Lang, 2001. 157–78.

Salkeld, Brenda. 'He Didn't Really Like Women.' Ed. Audrey Coppard and Bernard Crick. *Orwell Remembered*. London: Ariel Books, 1984. 67–8.

Sargent, Lyman Tower. *British and American Utopian Literature, 1516–1985: An Annotated, Chronological Bibliography*. New York: Garland, 1988.

Schöpflin, George. 'The Functions of Myth and a Taxonomy of Myths.' Ed. Geoffrey Hosking and George Schöpflin. *Myths and Nationhood*. New York: Routledge, 1997. 19–35.

Seshagiri, Urmila. 'Misogyny and Imperialism in George Orwell's *Burmese Days*.' Ed. Alberto Lázaro. *The Road from George Orwell: His Achievement and Legacy*. Bern: Peter Lang, 2001. 105–19.

Sheridan, Dorothy. *Wartime Women: A Mass-Observation Archive*. 1990. London: Phoenix, 2000.

Smith, Anthony D. 'The "Golden Age" and National Renewal.' Ed. Geoffrey Hosking and George Schöpflin. *Myths and Nationhood*. New York: Routledge, 1997. 36–59.

——. *National Identity*. London: Penguin, 1991.

Smith, Sydney. 'On a Street Corner in Wigan.' Ed. Audrey Coppard and Bernard Crick. *Orwell Remembered*. London: Ariel Books, 1984. 136–9.

Spender, Stephen. 'Introduction to *1984*.' Ed. Samuel Hynes. *Twentieth Century Interpretations of 1984*. Englewood Cliffs: Prentice Hall, 1971. 62–72.

——. 'Stephen Spender Recalls.' Ed. Audrey Coppard and Bernard Crick. *Orwell Remembered*. London: Ariel Books, 1984. 262–6.

Stanley, Liz. *Sex Surveyed 1949–1994: From Mass-Observations 'Little Kinsey' to the National Survey and the Hite Report*. London: Taylor & Francis, 1995.

Stevenson, Randall. *The British Novel Since the Thirties: An Introduction*. London: B. T. Batsford, 1986.

Strachey, John. 'The Strangled Cry.' Ed. Samuel Hynes. *Twentieth Century Interpretations of 1984*. Englewood Cliffs: Prentice Hall, 1971. 54–61.

Symons, Julian. *1984 and 1984: The Second George Orwell Memorial Lecture*. Edinburgh: Tragara, 1984.

——. *The Thirties: A Dream Revolved*. 1960. London: Faber, 1975.

——. 'Tribune's Obitury.' Ed. Audrey Coppard and Bernard Crick. *Orwell Remembered*. London: Ariel Books, 1984. 271–5.

Tentler, Leslie. '"I'm Not Literary Dear": George Orwell on Women and the Family.' Ed. Ejner J. Jensen. *The Future of Nineteen Eighty-Four*. Ann Arbor: University of Michigan Press, c.1984. 47–63.

Thurlow, Richard. *Fascism in Britain: From Oswald Mosley's Blackshirts to the National Front*. 1987. London: I. B. Tauris, 1998.

Trevor-Roper, H. R. *The Last Days of Hitler*. 1947. London: Pan, 1965.

——. 'The Mind of Adolf Hitler.' *Hitler's Table Talk: 1941–1944*. By Adolf Hitler. 1953. Trans. Norman Cameron and R. H. Stevens.. London: Phoenix, 2000. xi–xxxix.

Trilling, Lionel. 'George Orwell and the Politics of Truth.' Ed. Raymond Williams. *George Orwell: A Collection of Critical Essays*. Englewood Cliffs: Prentice Hall, 1974. 62–79.

——. 'Orwell on the Future.' Ed. Samuel Hynes. *Twentieth Century Interpretations of 1984*. Englewood Cliffs: Prentice Hall, 1971. 24–8.

Wagar, William W. 'George Orwell as Political Secretary of the Zeitgeist.' Ejner J. Jensen. Ed. *The Future of Nineteen Eighty-Four*. Ann Arbor: University of Michigan Press, c.1984. 177–99.

Wain, John. 'In the Thirties.' Ed. Miriam Gross. *The World of George Orwell*. London: Wiedenfeld and Nicolson, 1971. 75–90.

Warburg, F. *All Authors are Equal*. London: Secker & Warburg, 1973.

Weber, Max. *From Max Weber: Essays in Sociology*. Trans. and ed. H. H. Gerth and C. Wright Mills. 1946. Oxford: Oxford University Press, 1978.

Williams, Raymond. *The Country and the City*. 1973. St. Albans: Paladin, 1975.

——. *Culture and Society: Coleridge to Orwell*. 1958. London: Hogarth, 1993.

——, ed. *George Orwell: A Collection of Critical Essays*. Englewood Cliffs: Prentice Hall, 1974.

——. *Orwell*. London: Fontana, 1971.

——. *Politics and Letters: Interviews with New Left Review*. London: NLB, 1979.

Winnifrith, Tom and William V. Whitehead. *1984 and All's Well?* London: Macmillan, 1984.

Wolin, Sheldon. 'Counter-Enlightenment: Orwell's *Nineteen Eighty-Four*.' Ed. Robert Mulvihill. *Reflections on America, 1984: An Orwell Symposium*. Athens, Georgia: University of Georgia Press, 1986. 98–113.

Woodcock, George. *The Crystal Spirit: A Study of George Orwell*. London: Jonathan Cape, 1967.

——. 'From *Animal Farm* to *Nineteen Eighty-Four*.' Ed. Audrey Coppard and Bernard Crick. *Orwell Remembered*. London: Ariel Books, 1984. 199–210.

Woodruff, Douglas. 'Public Life.' Ed. Hugh Kingsmill. *The English Genius*. London: Right Book Club, 1939. 99–116.

Woodside, M. 'Courtship and Mating in an Urban Community.' *The Eugenics Review* (April 1946). 29–39.

Young, John Wesley. *Totalitarian Language: Orwell's Newspeak and Its Nazi and Communist Antecedents*. Charlottesville: University of Virginia Press, 1991.

Zeman, Z. A. B. *Nazi Propaganda*. 1964. Oxford: Oxford University Press, 1973.

Zwerdling, Alex. *Orwell and the Left*. New Haven: Yale University Press, 1974.

——. 'Orwell and the Techniques of Didactic Fantasy.' Ed. Samuel Hynes. *Twentieth Century Interpretations of 1984*. Englewood Cliffs: Prentice Hall, 1971. 88–101.

——. 'Orwell's Psychopolitics.' Ed. Ejner J. Jensen. *The Future of Nineteen Eighty-Four*. Ann Arbor: University of Michigan Press, c.1984. 87–110.

Index

County Council

Libraries, books and more . . .

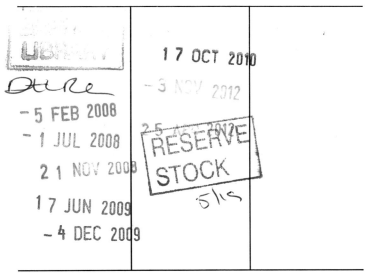

LIBRARY

17 OCT 2010

DuRe   - 3 NOV 2012

- 5 FEB 2008

- 1 JUL 2008

2 1 NOV 2008   RESERVE

17 JUN 2009   STOCK

- 4 DEC 2009   5/13

Please return/renew this item by the last due date.
Library items may also be renewed by phone or
via our website.

www.cumbria.gov.uk/libraries

Cumbria Libraries
CLIC
Interactive Catalogue

Ask for a CLIC password